The Biscuit Tin Murders

Menna van Praag

Copyright © 2024 by Menna van Praag

First published in Great Britain in 2024

The moral rights of the authors are hereby asserted in accordance with the Copyright, Designs and Patents Act 1988.

All characters and events in this publication,

other than those clearly in the public domain,

are fictitious and any resemblance to actual persons,

living or dead, is purely coincidental.

All rights reserved. No part of this publication may be reproduced, stored in a retrieval system, or transmitted, in any form or by any means without the prior written permission of the publisher, nor be otherwise circulated in any form of binding or cover other than that in which it is published and without a similar condition being imposed on the subsequent buyer.

ISBN 9798339269977

A CIP catalogue record for this book is available from the British Library.

No portion of this book may be reproduced in any form without written permission from the publisher or author, except as permitted by U.S. copyright law.

for Oscar
with all my love, Mama xxx

Contents

A Fatal Fall from King's College 6
A Body in the Graveyard 53
Death of a Businessman 100

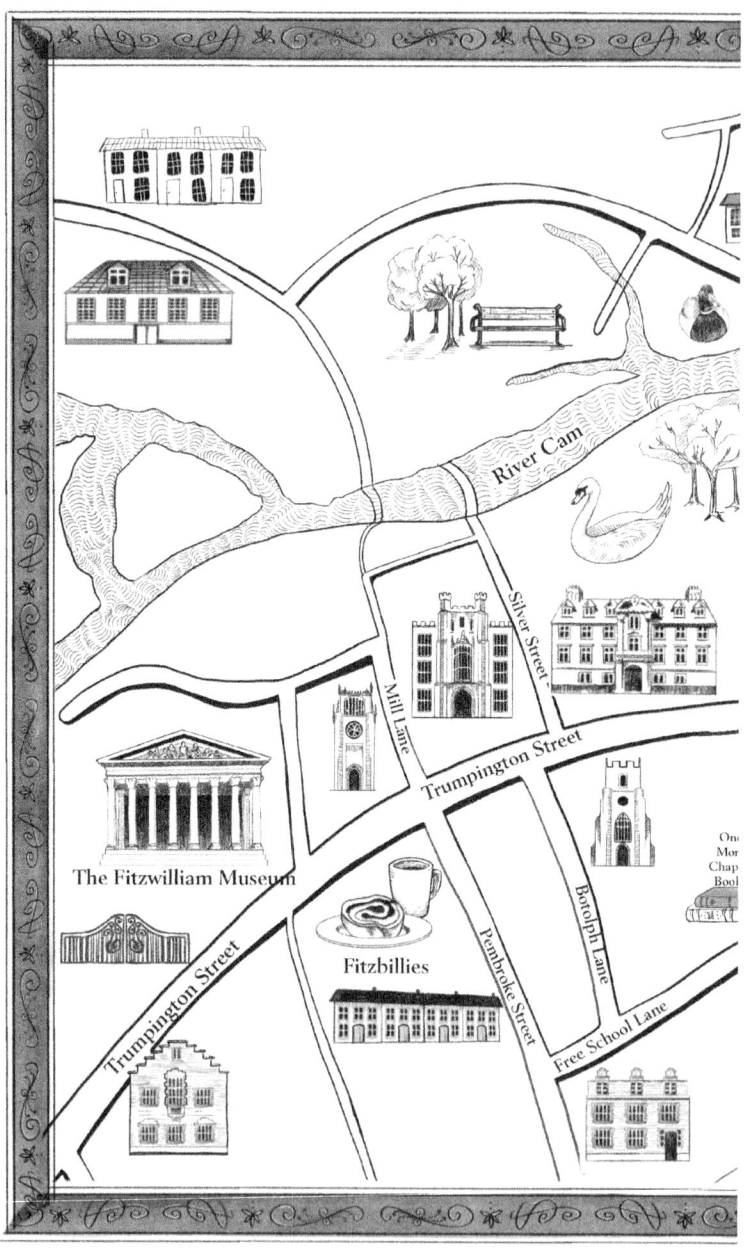

A Map of Olive Crisp's Cambridge by Naz Ekin Yilmaz

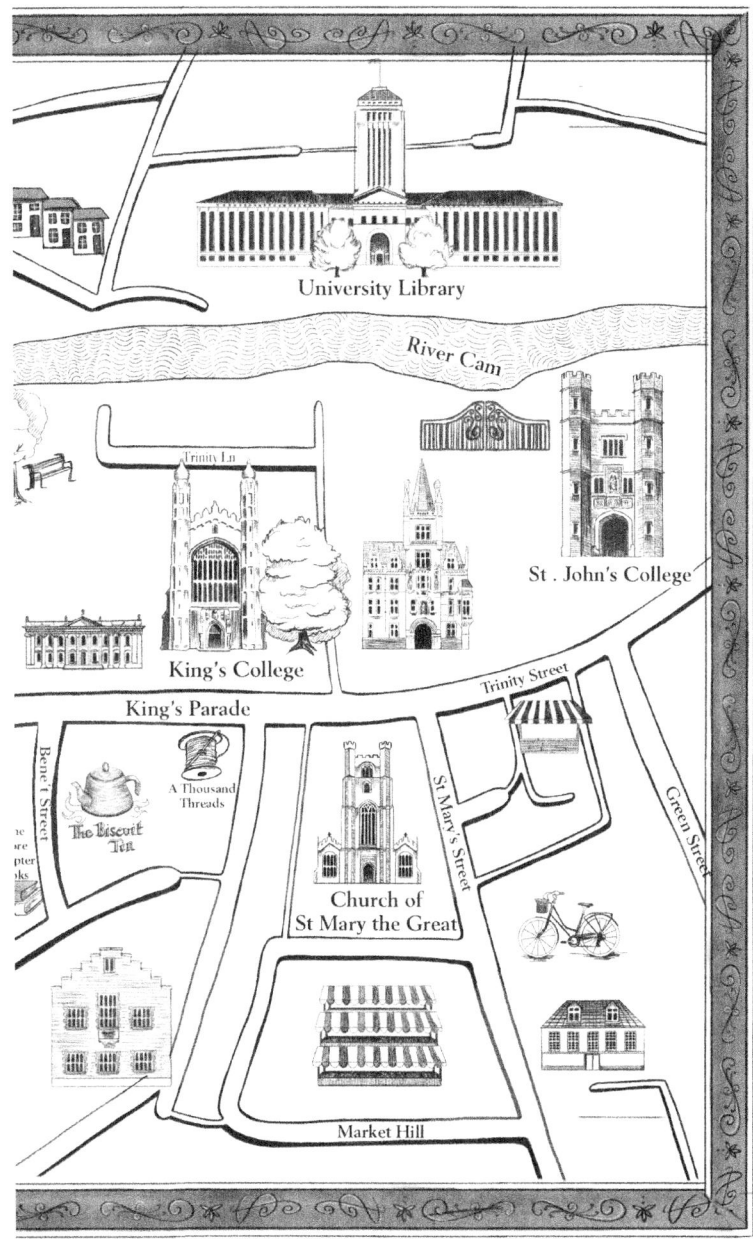

The Biscuit Tin Murders # 1

"A Fatal Fall From King's College"

Chapter One

Cambridge. 1st May, 1970.

IF THERE WAS ONE piece of advice Olive Crisp always followed, it was that "one should never attempt to solve a crime on an empty stomach". And so, since one never knew when a crime might present itself – and one could not afford, after all, to be caught unprepared – Olive remained diligent in ensuring that her stomach was never empty. But while Olive certainly enjoyed the amount of eating this lifestyle demanded, she lamented the scarcity of substantial crimes in the sleepy city of Cambridge. Mostly, she had to content herself with thefts of varying degrees of significance, along with the usual plethora of missing dogs, a few errant husbands and other assorted misdemeanours. Sadly, it'd been a slow year so far; the personal highpoint being in January with the capture of the culprit who'd been spiriting milk bottles from her neighbour Etta's doorstep[1]. In February she'd solved the mystery of the Valentine Meddler who, purporting to be the Mayor, had caused havoc sending racy cards to married women. In March she'd caught the Easter egg snatcher and in April had identified the disgruntled employee who'd been turning Clare College's laundry pink.

But it'd been six tedious months since a juicer crime had presented itself and, although she'd never admit it in company, Olive longed for a few more. It was unfortunate, of course, for the poor victim of the crime – especially if that crime was a murder – but it was still an undeniable fact that a good mystery made Olive's otherwise quite uneventful life rather more exciting. Solving mysteries gave her good reason to get up in the morning and provided an undeniable sense of purpose. Besides that, though she hardly admitted it to herself, let alone in company, Olive rather enjoyed seeing Detective Dixon, the officer in charge of overseeing serious crimes, and although falling in love was off-limits in her family there was no harm in looking. Was there? So, it sometimes seemed a shame that so many of her fellow residents proved so well-behaved, so law-abiding, so frustratingly *decent*.

Nevertheless, Olive lived in hope.

Meanwhile, she made sure to always have sustenance to hand, preferably of the sweet sort. A killer sweet tooth ran in the family and there was nothing to be done about it but follow its impulses and indulge. Fortunately, as the owner of a little café, that never proved to be a problem for, while The Biscuit Tin was small, it was always very well stocked. Tucked beside the famous Eagle pub on Bene't Street, away from the bustle of the market square and the book-laden academics scurrying between their colleges, the café still proved exceedingly popular, a perennial favourite among the locals and especially beloved for being the first coffee house ever established in England[2]. And, given that she had her own stomach to satisfy in addition to the steady stream of customers, Olive spent several hours every morning baking enough lemon chiffon cakes, lavender-sugar biscuits, blueberry scones, apple pies and Bakewell tarts to keep everyone happy. Indeed, the only thing she didn't bake was bread, since she could get every kind of loaf she could possibly want from the bread stall at the market. Olive made a daily pilgrimage to Derek's for her favourite raisin bread, which she exchanged for his favourite lavender-sugar biscuits, and thus they were both content.

The advice regarding crime solving and stomachs had been handed down to Olive, along with the café, by her mother, Myrtle, via the matriarchal lineage that dated back to Louise de Kéroualle, favoured mistress of Charles II, from whom all the Crisp women had also inherited their pretty faces and pleasingly plump physiques. Olive dutifully maintained her own voluptuous figure by the generous consumption of crumpets for breakfast, cake after lunch and pie after dinner – the flavours and fillings differing according to the time of year – and so the structure of her days were, during the duller months, shaped by stocking and consuming the contents of the café's counters and the many cups of tea that inevitably accompanied every treat.

Olive's favourites changed with the seasons, excepting the Bakewell tarts which remained a constant, as beloved by Olive as they had been by her greatest of great grandmothers who'd sampled one on her visit to the historic city in 1672, after which the King had bought his mistress The Biscuit Tin as a token of his devotion.

In her honour, the tarts had remained on the menu ever since.

This morning, Olive treated herself to a freshly toasted crumpet accompanied, of course, by lashings of butter and several spoonfuls of marmalade. A few crumpets served as reward for the pre-dawn starts to her days and the toppings rotated according to her moods. Today it was marmalade, tomorrow it might be honey or jam. If Olive needed to lift her energies or remedy a bout of melancholy, it'd be marmite.

But today was a happy day. The first of May, Olive's favourite month, and the soft morning breeze promised a sunny start to the time when wisteria and bluebells bloomed throughout the sleepy little city and which would hopefully mark a permanent turn from the chilly, drizzly British weather to warmer, drier days as spring slowly became summer. Had it been possible to pause the calendar, to replicate the lighter mornings and brighter evenings throughout the year, Olive would have done so in a heartbeat. Indeed, she sometimes wondered if there existed a place on Earth that boasted mellow weather all year round – not too hot, not too cold but as "just right" as the proverbial porridge enjoyed by Goldilocks. Unlikely, she thought. And, even if it did, Olive wouldn't really want to know since she could never leave the café.

'Don't worry, Mum.' Olive nibbled the warm crumpet thoughtfully, then took a long sip of milky tea. 'You know I'll never trust anyone but a Crisp with The Biscuit Tin.'

As she took another buttery bite, Olive tried not to think on the small matter of there currently being no other Crisps[3] lined up to take her place, when the time came. She tried not to worry about it too much, but she was already forty and the window of opportunity was closing with every passing year. Every matriarch had already given birth to their heir by their third decade and Olive could hear the collective whispers of her ancestors as they fretted over the future of their beloved café without a new little girl pottering about the shop floor or any sign of a man who'd provide the necessary means to produce one.

Crisp women never married and the men they chose to furnish them with their heirs never stayed around long enough to witness what they'd been party to, which was just the way the Crisp women wanted it. They might, regrettably, need the participation of a male to ensure the continuation of their line but because they didn't need his financial support they certainly weren't willing to give up their own property and rights by marrying, especially not the risk of losing their daughters. And they always had daughters. From Louise's offspring onwards, every Crisp woman for the past three centuries had given birth to a single girl who'd inherited The Biscuit Tin from her mother and then gone on, in turn, to do the same.

Olive took another sip of tea. Her own mother had rejected all but the most casual suitors for, even though the laws had changed a little in her favour, Myrtle argued that love weakened a woman's heart and caused her to do foolish things – "it's not only your money you can lose," she'd always say, "but yourself into the bargain." And so, ever since she knew what love was, Olive had been scared of it happening to her.

And so, while she occasionally took a suitor to bed she'd never allowed herself to develop feelings towards them that went beyond simple fondness. Fortunately, while they'd all been kind, attentive and even attractive men, they'd never proved a risk to her heart. Detective Dixon, on the other hand, already stirred slight dangerous feelings, though they'd never been on a date, let alone kissed.

Olive sighed.

In response, the beaded curtain that separated the entrance to her flat from the café, rustled as if blown by an amiable but concerned breeze.

'Stop fretting,' Olive insisted. 'I told you, I'm trying. And stop worrying, I promise I won't fall in love.'

In answer the bell above the door chimed: a gentle reminder that she mustn't lose her head – and certainly not her heart – over any man, no matter how lovely he might be.

This was how Olive's ancestors communicated; through nudges to the objects and affects of her immediate surroundings. A cynic might claim that these events were merely natural phenomena but Olive knew better. She'd lived in the building on Benet's Street all her life, taking her first steps in the living room upstairs, baking her first batch of lavender-sugar biscuits in the café's kitchen, and she knew every inch, every creak and crack, of the place like the back of her hand. Olive knew when a breeze was just a breeze, or a spilled bag of sugar just an accident, and she knew when it - along with the rattling of pictures on the walls (all sixteen ancestors were commemorated in oils or celluloid, their images clustered around the tiny café) or a jar falling off a shelf, or the bell above the door chiming in the absence of customers, or a shimmer at the edge of her gaze – was a sign from her family to remind Olive that, though she mustn't fall in love, she'd certainly never be alone.

Fortunately, she also had Biscuit, her Cavalier King Charles Spaniel, as reminder of that. And it was a job Biscuit took as seriously as Olive took eating; following her like a shadow and whimpering if she spent too long in places dogs weren't permitted to linger. If Olive hadn't finished baking by seven o'clock, Biscuit would whine and paw at the door until she coaxed her mistresses out. Not only were the Crisp women descended from Louise de Kéroualle but their spaniels were direct descendants of the first pet gifted to her by the King. Such regal pedigree furnished each spaniel with such airs and graces that they were very particular about the company they kept, socialising only with their own breed and permitting themselves to be petted only by a certain calibre of customer and, of course, only deigning to consume certain gourmet cuisines. It meant that Olive spent rather more time than she'd like at the stove sauteing chicken livers and frying fillet steak. Fortunately, Biscuit was also partial to Olive's baking, though Olive had to be especially careful when it came to keeping her away from chocolate.

Now, as Olive popped the last of the crumpet into her mouth and considered having a second, the bell above the door chimed. Biscuit, absorbed in gobbling her own helping of breakfast crumpets from a fine porcelain bowl at Olive's feet, paused to glance up as the door swung open – the café greeting one of its favourite customers – and ascertain whether or not this particular customer was deserving of her attention.

'Morning, Blythe.' Olive smiled. 'A little early for you, isn't it?'

Biscuit barked in greeting, then returned to her crumpets. She adored Blythe Loveday, Olive's neighbour and owner of the bookshop, One More Chapter Books, just not quite as much as she adored buttered crumpets.

'I opened for Mr Harrington,' Blythe explained. 'He wanted to study my recent purchase of Dickens' first editions. I said I'd pop out and pick up some coffee and cake to sweeten the negotiations. Do you have any of that divine blueberry and lemon buttercream left? Or did I eat it all yesterday?'

'You're in luck, I baked one last night and just finished icing it this morning.'

'Baking?' Blythe rolled her eyes. 'You shouldn't be baking at night, you should be out meeting nice marriageable men. How do you ever expect to catch a man if you never go fishing?'

'Oh, please.' Olive stepped carefully around Biscuit as she headed towards the counter. 'I have no intention of trying to catch a man and, as I've told you a million times, no intention of marrying one either. I might need an heir, but...'

'I know, I know' – Blythe held up her hand – 'Crisp women never marry, that's what you always say. But *I* say, that's only because none of them were ever lucky enough to meet the right man. When you fall in love, you'll rethink that independence stuff.'

Olive opened her mouth, then closed it again. Blythe was addicted to the glow of romance, the flowers and butterflies, she was always falling in love and not remotely scared of the consequences.

'Speaking of marriage,' Olive said. 'How long do you think it'll be before your Mr Harrington proposes?'

'Hush!' Blythe giggled. 'You might jinx it. Anyway, he's not *my* Mr Harrington, he's simply a dedicated bibliophile, like myself. He only visits the bookshop as a collector, he's not courting me.'

Olive swallowed a smile. Such was her friend's devotion to romance and all its affectations that she often acted as if she lived two hundred years ago in a Jane Austen novel, seeking eligible gentlemen in the 1770s instead of the slightly scruffier bachelors of the 1970s. And, although Olive generally prided herself on her far more pragmatic approach to such matters, she couldn't help but be touched by Blythe's hopeful naivety.

'Oh, no?' Olive slipped two porcelain plates from the stack beside the display cabinet then began to cut two very generous slices of blueberry and lemon cake. 'You really think he spends thousands of pounds on first editions because he's addicted to stories? No man needs *that* many books, B. And if he did, he'd go to London where he'd get a better selection and a better price. He comes to *your* bookshop because it has what none of those other places have...'

Blythe frowned. 'What's that?'

'Don't be daft.' Olive laughed. 'You, of course, you silly dolt. *You!*'

'Do you really think so?' Blythe blushed. 'It's just – he's never...'

'Some men need you to take the initiative,' Olive said, as she filled the kettle for tea. 'They're not all gung-ho Tarzan types, some are more...' she searched for an analogy her friend would appreciate. 'Like Mr Bingley.'

'Oh.' Blythe, who nurtured a life-long crush on Mr Darcy, looked a little crestfallen. It was no secret that her ideal man was one who'd knock aside obstacles to lift her into his arms and carry her into the sunset. 'Well, I suppose, perhaps you're right.'

'I am,' Olive said, pitching her voice above the whistle of the kettle. 'Trust me. Now, why don't you take the cake across the road and I'll follow with tea.'

'Would you?' Blythe smiled, glancing towards the door, clearly distracted by the thought of how she might induce Mr Harrington to make the first move. 'That's so–'

But whatever she'd been about to say was interrupted by the tinkle of the bell and the entrance of yet another early customer. Biscuit, annoyed by yet another interruption to her repast, didn't even glance up.

'Morning, Millie.' Blythe beamed. 'Lovely to see you. And, if it's breakfast you're after, I can highly recommend this cake.'

Millicent Burrows, owner of A Thousand Threads, the haberdashery on King's Parade, shook her head. 'Just tea for me,' she said. 'I'm too anxious to eat right now.'

'Anxious?' Olive, who'd been absently nibbling on stray sugared blueberries while the kettle boiled, looked up. 'Too anxious to *eat*?' This, in their circle of friends, was a phenomenon as rare and strange as sighting a UFO. 'Whatever's wrong?'

Shaking her head, Millicent pulled out a chair and sat at the table closest to the counter. Hands folded in her lap, she took several deep breaths.

'Well,' Blythe prompted, abandoning the plates of cake to sit beside her. 'What is it?'

But Millicent, never one to waste a dramatic moment, waited while Olive quickly filled the teapot and brought it, along with three cups, to the table. Nipping back for milk and sugar, she sat along with her two friends and waited for the beans to be spilled.

'Well?' She echoed Blythe. 'What's happened that you'll turn up your nose at a slice of my cake? It must be pretty awful. It's not your health is it? Please, tell me—'

'No, no.' Millicent shook her head again. 'Nothing like that.'

'Thank goodness,' Olive and Blythe spoke in unison, putting their hands over their hearts to punctuate their relief.

'You know what...' Millicent glanced at the display cabinet laden with fresh delights: peach flapjacks, iced buns, almond macaroons... 'Perhaps I *will* have something small. Just a morsel. How about a lavender-sugar biscuit?'

Olive smiled, relieved to see her friend returning. 'Certainly.' She stood and hurried back to the counter, picking up a plate and piling it high with newly baked biscuits. Glancing at a similar collection of warm crumpets beside the toaster, Olive suppressed the urge to prepare herself a second. For, much as her mouth watered for more melted butter, she knew her friend deserved her attention.

'Here you go.' Olive set the plate down, smiling as both Millicent and Blythe simultaneously reached out for one. Millicent's distress couldn't be *so* very bad after all, Olive thought with a smile. To compensate for the abandoned crumpet, Olive took a biscuit too. Closing her eyes while she chewed, silence fell and everything else was momentarily forgotten while they all savoured the happily delicious moment.

'So.' Blythe was the first to finish. 'You've held us in suspense long enough, now tell us everything.'

Still, Millicent hesitated, clearly enjoying the spotlight. To give her a nudge, Olive started pouring the tea.

'A little more milk, please,' Millicent said, helping herself to another biscuit.

'Enough teasing,' Blythe declared. 'Come on, out with it.'

'Alright, alright,' Millicent said, once more assuming the look of shocked distress she'd had when she'd entered the café. 'Don't rush me.' Lifting the cup to her lips to take a restorative sip of tea, she was about to take another when she noticed that Blythe was now holding her breath and had turned an unnatural shade of puce.

'Okay.' Millicent set down her cup in its saucer. 'The police have blocked off King's Parade. They're tight-lipped about what's going on, but—'

'The police?' Olive interrupted. 'Was Hugo–Detective Dixon there?'

'Hugo.' Millicent and Blythe crooned in unison. 'Hugoooo.'

'Stop it!' Olive did her very best not to blush. 'You sound like a couple of teenagers. I do *not* have a crush on Detective Dixon.'

'Don't you?' Blythe retorted. 'Well then you're the only woman in Cambridge who doesn't.'

'That's ridiculous,' Olive said. 'He's not *that* handsome.'

'Oh, yes he is,' Millicent sighed. 'Handsome and charming and clever and thoughtful and...'

'Okay, okay,' Olive interrupted. 'What's going on? And why are the police involved?' She could feel her heart starting to race in anticipation, here was a promise that life was about to get rather more exciting, and not simply because Hugo Dixon was involved.

'Fine,' Millicent huffed. 'So, the gorgeous detective wasn't letting anything slip, but the Dean's wife is a loyal customer, she knits her boys woollen jumpers at a furious rate and I always give her a good discount on wool. Not that she needs it really, given that her horrible husband is rich as Croesus, and rude as hell. I've never met such a hideous snob, but that's by the by. Anyway, she told me that last night one of their students was...' – even in the face of Blythe's frustration, still Millicent couldn't resist pausing again for an imaginary drumroll – 'murdered.'

Now Olive sat up. 'Murdered?'

She tried to frame her expression into one of studied concern. But secretly she could barely contain her excitement. Here, at last, was a crime she could get her teeth into. Especially now that her belly was pleasingly full of Earl Grey, buttered crumpets and lavender-sugar biscuits. Perhaps, Olive thought, this May would prove to be her favourite month in more ways than one.

'Well,' Olive said, keeping her voice calm. 'What happened?'

'Yes, go on.' Blythe took another biscuit. 'Tell us all the juicy details.'

'The students were climbing the college turrets again,' Millicent explained. 'You know, the ones calling themselves The Night Climbers, and one of them fell off.'

Olive's spirits sank. 'Wait, I thought you said it was murder. That sounds more like an accident.'

'Perhaps,' Millicent admitted. 'But Tabitha suggested there were whisperings of a love affair, and it's possible he might have been pushed by his rival. The Dean, naturally, is trying to keep everything hush-hush, avoiding a scandal and all that, but Tabby said she'd been hearing things...'

'Ah.' Olive brightened. 'Well, that sounds more promising. Which, of course, isn't to say that it's not a terrible tragedy.'

'No doubt,' Blythe agreed. 'An awful shame and all that. But really, you must have a death wish to do such a stupid thing, so I don't feel *so* very bad for him.'

'B!' Millicent chastised her. 'A young man is dead. Where's your compassion?'

'Oh, I feel terribly bad for his poor parents,' Blythe said. 'And him, of course. But really, it was only a matter of time before one of those Night Climbers fell to their deaths. Anyway' – she turned to Olive – 'why don't you get out your tarot cards? Then you can tell us whether it was an accident or murder...'

1. Dr Martin Harrison, the 45th Dean of Trinity College. The discovery had come as a surprise to all involved, including the dean himself who'd been unaware of his habit of sleep-stealing milk bottles as he wandered the Cambridge lanes in the pre-dawn hours.

2. This claim was, perhaps unsurprisingly, disputed by Oxford city council who attempted to wrestle the accolade from Cambridge city council's grasp with their own Grand Café, established (according to the diarist Samuel Pepys) in 1650. And who could argue with him? Deciding instead to ignore him, Cambridge City Council adorned *The Biscuit Tin* with its own blue plaque (alongside *The Eagle's* for hosting conversations between Crick and Watson that led to the discovery of DNA) and left it at that.

3. Without the financial necessity to marry, the de Kéroualle female line retained their independence (along with their surname) and it was only changed by the 10th granddaughter of Louise de Kéroualle at the outbreak of the Napoleonic Wars in 1803 and the accompanying surge of anti-French feeling in England. First "de Kéroualle" became "Krisp" then, thirty years and many misspellings later, "Crisp".

Chapter Two

MILLICENT AND BLYTHE WATCHED, breath held, as Olive set her tarot cards carefully on the table. They were silent now, all remnants of breakfast cleared away, as Olive solemnly shuffled the cards. Even Biscuit, sitting with her front paws on her mistress' feet, remained quiet. As she shuffled, Olive closed her eyes, focusing her mind on an image of a boy falling from a turret and her thoughts on one question: *was it an accident, or a murder?*

She shuffled and shuffled until, at last, she stopped. Slowly pulling three cards from the deck she placed them, face down, on the table.

Olive opened her eyes. Millicent and Blythe blinked back at her, till they turned their gaze in unison back to the cards. All three held their breath as Olive turned over the first card.

Death.

Blythe gasped.

'It doesn't mean death,' Olive said, quickly. 'Not literally anyway. Depending on its place in the spread it most often means a change, a new beginning, that sort of thing.'

Blythe looked unconvinced.

'Turn over the next one,' Millicent suggested.

Olive did so.

The Tower.

Now Millicent gasped. 'You can't say *that* card has any positive interpretations,' she said. 'The Tower is indisputably bad news, isn't it?'

Olive nodded. 'And it can hardly be a coincidence that he actually fell from a tower. I mean, that's too much... right?' As her friends nodded and Olive held her breath again, heart thudding in her chest, they all stared at the cards as she turned over the third one.

The Devil.
Now even Olive gasped. And she wasn't alone.
'I don't think there's any doubt about that now,' Blythe said. 'Do you?'
Slowly, Olive shook her head.

She'd been reading the tarot deck all her life and, as three-card readings went, it didn't come much more ominous. Except perhaps if she'd drawn the Five of Cups or Three of Swords instead of Death, but even then with a reading this unequivocal that'd only be splitting hairs. There was no question what the tarot was telling her. Whoever had tumbled from the rooftops of King's College, hadn't fallen. He'd been pushed.

Olive, Blythe and Millicent stared down at the cards a while longer without speaking, each lost in their own thoughts but each caught by the extra edge of sadness and shock that comes from discovering a death wasn't accidental but intentional. Even Olive, who welcomed a juicy mystery to spice up her otherwise humdrum life, felt that.

'You should talk to Detective Dixon,' Blythe was the first to break the silence. 'I'll bet he's still at the scene. Just take a moment to brighten your cheeks with a little blush; lipstick never hurts either, and perhaps a little mascara...' She tipped her head to one side to continue her appraisal. 'Also, with your pale skin those blonde brows are near invisible, you could–'

'Stop!' Olive covered her face with her hands. 'I'm *not* going on a date. This is a crime scene we're talking about. I hardly think Detective Dixon will be paying any attention to the way I look when he's got a murder on his hands.'

Blythe gave a derisive snort. 'Are you kidding? Men are *always* paying attention to the way a woman looks. They can't help it. It's in their DNA.'

'True,' Millicent agreed. 'Unless, of course, they've been married ten years and then they don't. At least, they stop noticing the way their *wife* looks, even when she's had a dramatically eye-catching and, I might add, very flattering, perm and dye which turned her from a brunette into a redhead...'

Millicent gulped down the rest of her words as tears filled her eyes. Olive and Blythe each reached across the table and squeezed her hands.

'Your husband was a fool, Millie,' Blythe said. 'A philandering scoundrel[1] who'll be rueing the day he ever let you go.'

'Oh, I don't know.' Millicent sniffed. 'I bet that secretary of his is still entertaining him well enough that he doesn't even spare me a second thought.'

Her friends fell silent a moment, both trying to think of something comforting to say, both studiously avoiding mentioning the fact that Olive had given Millicent a tarot reading the week before her wedding day which had strongly suggested she shouldn't walk down the aisle but run screaming in the opposite direction instead.

'That wretch didn't deserve you,' Olive said. 'You'll find someone who does.'

Millicent sighed. 'Twenty years ago I might've agreed with you, but no man wants a woman in her sixties. Not even men in their sixties. That's the sad truth of it.' She wiped her eyes and took a deep breath. 'Anyway, enough about all that. Why don't we pop along to my shop? That way, if you happen to bump into Detective Dixon…'

'Alright then.' Olive returned the three tarot cards[2] to the deck and packed them away in their silk-lined box. 'If it'll take your mind off that reprobate, I will.' That the mystery would provide a frisson of excitement and intrigue to her morning (in addition to seeing Hugo) Olive declined to mention.

Biscuit jumped up as soon as Olive stood, anticipating an adventure, and as soon as she'd put the cards away in their special hidden drawer in the antique dresser that covered most of the left wall, Olive lifted her coat from the hatstand beside the front door and slipped it on.

'Well,' she turned to her friends, still seated. 'Shall we go?'

Millicent stood but Blythe hesitated. 'Are you sure you don't want to take a minute to apply just a *little* makeup?'

'B,' Olive laughed. 'I'm not trying to seduce Detective Dixon. And, even if I was, I wouldn't do it by pretending to be someone I'm not. He can take me as I am or not at all.'

'Well said.' Millicent clapped. 'Well said.'

'Fine.' Blythe rolled her eyes. 'I was just trying to help.'

'I don't need your help,' Olive said. 'I told you, I'm perfectly happy as I am.'

'You say that now,' Blythe retorted. 'But in twenty years, when you're old and alone you won't be so…' She trailed off, suddenly aware of what she'd said. 'Sorry, Millie, I didn't mean…'

'Why is it that the young never think they'll be old?' Millicent said a little huffily as she pushed back her chair. 'And why do they think that the older generation are somehow a different species of human, without the same thoughts, feelings and desires as themselves?'

Blushing with shame, Blythe opened her mouth to protest, then closed it again.

'Thank you.' Millicent walked towards the front door. 'Because you didn't deny it, I'll forgive you.'

'Sorry,' Blythe muttered, as they both hurried after Olive, who'd already stepped out onto the street, followed by an excitable Biscuit, delighted by the unexpected morning walk. She trotted alongside the three friends as they turned along Bene't Street and headed for King's Parade.

Before they'd reached A Thousand Threads, Olive and Blythe saw what Millicent had meant. The shop stood almost directly across the street from King's College and half a dozen policemen were gathered in the cobbled courtyard outside the tall wooden gates, flanked by three police cars and a white van.

'Gosh,' Blythe gasped. 'You weren't wrong, Millie, it's like a film set.'

Olive gazed at the scene, her heart starting to race. At her ankles, Biscuit started to bark excitedly.

'Shush, Bics, shush.' Olive bent down to rub Biscuit's silky ears. 'There's a good girl.'

Across the road, Detective Dixon – a full head taller than his fellow officers and strikingly handsome even at a distance – glanced up. His gaze held on Olive. And when she looked up, she met his gaze and held it a moment too, then glanced away.

'Let's leave Olive to it, shall we?' Millicent gave Blythe a knowing look. 'Detective Dixon might get spooked if we all show up together.'

'Don't be a spoilsport,' Blythe protested. 'I want to meet the sexy detective too.'

'You're insatiable.' Millicent laughed. 'Anyway, I wouldn't waste your time, I don't think our detective has eyes for anyone else but our Olive. I–'

'Don't be ridiculous!' Olive interrupted. 'He's just a customer who happens to be a detective who I happen to have helped or, as he'd probably say, "interfered" with a few police cases. We've barely even had coffee together, let alone been on a date.'

'Oh, please,' Blythe said. 'He visits you at the drop of a hat. I see him in and out of the café all the time.' She held up her hands. 'Not that I've been watching, of course, I just happen–'

'–notice every single handsome man that passes your book shop,' Millicent finished.

'So?' Blythe shrugged. 'What's the harm in that?'

'Detective Dixon just has an appreciation for my Bakewell tarts,' Olive said. 'And no, before you say anything, B, that's *not* a euphemism.'

Blythe giggled. 'If you say so.'

Millicent pushed open the door to her shop. 'Come on, trouble-maker, we'll wait for Olive in here.'

'Fine, be a spoilsport.' Blythe sighed. 'But I'd better get back to the bookshop, Mr Harrington will be wondering where I am. I told him I was going out for tea and cake nearly an hour ago.'

'You'd better go then,' Millicent said. 'He might've made off with half your stock by now.'

'Hardly,' Blythe said, though she didn't sound entirely convinced. 'I'm sure I can trust him, a fellow bibliophile and all that...' She paused, glancing at her wristwatch. 'But still, I should probably, um, go.' And she'd hurried off along the street before either Millicent or Olive could say anything else.

Olive gave her friend a playful nudge. 'You're such a tease.'

'She shouldn't have called me "old",' Millicent said with a wink. 'Now, I think you'd better go too, before he's' - she nodded at the group of policemen - 'called back to the station for paperwork.'

'Meet me at the café for lunch?' Olive said. 'We can catch up then.'

Millicent nodded. 'What's on the menu?'

'Mushroom pie.' Olive started crossing the street. 'With tarragon and garlic.'

'Sounds delicious. Wouldn't miss it.'

'Great.' Olive patted her leg for Biscuit to follow and they both set off towards King's College at a brisk pace.

'Miss Crisp,' Detective Dixon said as she reached him. 'What a happy coincidence. I wondered how long it might be before you came sniffing about the crime scene.'

'What?' Olive assumed an air of innocence, inwardly cursing herself for not having the foresight to bring him an offering, a little apple-chestnut tart to sweeten her interrogation. 'I'm sure I don't know what you mean. I just happened to be visiting Millicent and saw all this hullabaloo across the street.' She gave a nonchalant shrug. 'And, well, you can't blame a girl for being curious, can you?'

Detective Dixon smiled, his large blue eyes bright with merriment. 'Just coincidence, eh? Like the time you stumbled upon the Histon Manor murder, or the Trinity College kidnapping, or…'

'You know I have a sixth sense about these things,' Olive whispered, surreptitiously guiding him away from the group of policemen, walking till they were out of earshot. 'I can't help it. And, anyway, if I rightly recall my assistance on those cases was rather invaluable in helping you catch the culprits, so…'

She gave him a winning smile and he returned it with a wry grin.

'Your *unauthorised* assistance,' Hugo amended. 'But yes, I can't deny it. You've been very helpful. To say nothing of those cherry tarts of yours providing rocket fuel for my weary brain just when I need it most.'

'Bakewell tarts,' Olive corrected. 'And you're welcome to one now, if you like. Fresh from the oven and on the house.'

Hugo raised a single eyebrow, pulling his hand through his thick black hair as he fought between the urge for a delicious pastry and the requirements of his job. Olive watched the fight on his face, before forcing herself to look away. Gazing at Hugo Dixon was like looking too long at the sun, it'd blind you and render you senseless to making sensible, rational decisions.

'Much as I'd love to take you up on the offer,' he broke the silence. 'I'm afraid I must remain at my post. Too many witnesses and wagging tongues' – he nodded towards his fellow officers, still gathered in a circle – 'to report on me shirking my duties. Even if...'

He stopped and Olive looked at him again. 'Even if, what?'

'I shouldn't say anything.' Hugo sighed. 'Not till it's public knowledge.'

Olive smiled. 'How about if I was to hurry back to the café and return with a chestnut-apple tart and cup of hot, sweet coffee? No milk, two sugars. Then might you tell me? In the strictest confidence, of course.'

'Oh, Miss Crisp, you drive a hard bargain.' The detective laughed. 'Alright then, you've got a deal but I'm afraid it's going to disappoint you.'

'Disappoint me?' Olive cocked her head to one side. 'How?'

'Well,' he said, still smiling. 'I suspect you wanted another mystery to solve, but I'm afraid you've not got one here. It was an accident.'

'An accident?' Olive echoed.

'Yes.' Hugo nodded. 'An accident.'

'But...' Olive shook her head, slightly dumbfounded. 'No, no it wasn't.'

Hugo frowned. 'Yes it *was*. And we've got six eye witnesses who've confirmed it. So unless you happened to be climbing the towers of King's College after midnight and saw him being pushed, then I'm afraid I can't just take your word for it.'

Olive opened her mouth, then closed it again.

'Sorry.' Detective Dixon gave her an apologetic smile. 'I know that wasn't what you wanted to hear, but...'

'But what if they're lying?' Olive protested. At her feet, Biscuit barked in agreement. 'You've only got their word for it too.'

'True enough,' he conceded. 'But their stories are all in accord and the specific details are consistent with how the body fell, along with the lack of suspicious markings or injuries to suggest anything other than an accidental death.' He paused. 'Besides, the Dean vouches for their general good conduct and, in the absence of any evidence to the contrary, and since we won't be recommending an autopsy, that will be the coroner's verdict.'

Biscuit barked again and Olive shook her head. 'But, but...'

'Dixon!'

The detective turned back to his officers.

'The Dean called the boy's parents,' the officer said. 'Says they'll be here in four hours. Coming all the way from up north, Middle Earth or some such. Will you be able to meet them today?'

'Middle Earth?' Hugo's frown deepened. 'Do you mean *Middlesborough*?'

The officer shrugged. 'If you say so, sir.'

'Sorry.' Hugo turned back to Olive, lightly touching her shoulder. 'Much as I'd love to take you up on that offer, I'm afraid I'd better get back to the station and start on the mountain of paperwork that awaits me.'

Olive nodded, frustrated that his touch gave her goosebumps in spite of herself. This was only about the mystery, she told herself, not the man investigating it.

'Of course,' Olive said. 'Duty calls.'

As Hugo hurried off, she followed his departure down the street, grateful that neither her mother nor her assorted ancestors were there to watch her watching him go.

---

1. It was an unspoken agreement between them that the name of Midge's despicable ex-husband would never be spoken aloud. They refused to afford him that basic respect (since he'd shown Midge no respect at all) and instead used a variety of insults and expletives whenever reference to him was unavoidable.

2. The tarot cards, like the café, had also been owned by Louise de Kéroualle and passed carefully down the generations in the same mother-of-pearl casket engraved with her initials and now rather priceless. Each daughter had learnt the craft of the cards at her mother's knee long before she discovered the secrets of the café kitchen. It was how the Crisp women learned their letters, along with the knowledge that they, like their ancestors, had the gift of "sixth sight".

Chapter Three

'Are you sure?'

Olive nodded. 'That's what he said.'

'Perhaps he was lying. Perhaps he just didn't want to tell you. Perhaps the police are keeping it a secret for now because they don't want it leaking to the press.'

Having waited until five o'clock, when each of their respective shops closed, the friends reconvened at the café to decide what was to be done. They now sat around the table at the window, with Biscuit at Olive's feet, and a pot of tea, three mushroom and tarragon pies and a small selection of cakes and biscuits leftover from the day's sales.

'Perhaps.' Olive smiled. 'But you think I can't tell when a man lies?'

'I wish *I* could.' Millicent sighed. 'Then I might've saved myself years of heartbreak.'

'It's much harder when you're in love.' Blythe rested her hand on Millicent's wrist. 'And almost impossible when they're handsome and seductive into the bargain.' She gave a sad smile and shrugged. 'It's the fatal trifecta.'

'True.' Olive agreed. 'Not that I've ever experienced it myself.'

'Really?' Blythe raised an eyebrow. 'Well, if you're not in love with Mr Charming Detective yet, then just give it time. A man like that is hard to come by.'

'Anyway,' Olive changed the subject. 'That's not the point right now. The point is that the police are convinced that this boy's death is an accident when we know it wasn't. And yet–'

'And yet, you can't exactly tell Mr Charming that your evidence is based on a tarot reading,' Millicent finished. 'Since I'm guessing such claims won't hold up in court and would probably even have you laughed out of the station.'

'Yes,' Olive said. 'I can't tell Hu—Detective Dixon about the cards, he'd think I'm crazy. I mean, in the past, whenever I've got involved in his cases, I've just told him I had hunches, women's instinct, then found actual concrete evidence to back it up. If he had any idea I was basing it all on some kind of mystic intuition, he'd never take me seriously again.'

Millicent and Blythe sighed simultaneously, as if to say: "men."

'What if you gave him a reading?' Blythe suggested. 'That might change his mind, or at least give him pause for thought. Remember how sceptical Mrs Wilder was before you gave her that reading on her daughter-in-law and it revealed she was having an affair with her boss? The cards are never wrong, after all.'

'True,' Olive considered. 'But something tells me Detective Dixon isn't going to open up his professional or personal life to a tarot reading, so I don't see how I can convince him of anything.'

Millicent sipped her tea. 'So, what are you going to do?'

'I don't know yet,' Olive mused as she took a thoughtful bite of her pie. 'But I think the first thing to do is speak to the porters at King's College. They know everything that goes on: the literal and metaphorical gatekeepers, the holders of all gossip.'

'Yes.' Millicent set down her cup. 'But I wouldn't be very optimistic about getting anything out of them, they're a tight-lipped lot and exceedingly loyal to their colleges. If anything untoward is going on, you'll never hear it from them.'

'Perhaps...' Olive smiled. 'But I've got my ways of making men talk.'

'I'll bet you do.' Blythe laughed. 'Let me guess, it involves that pretty green summer dress of yours that's the exact colour of your eyes and happens to perfectly highlight two of your other assets as well.'

'That won't be necessary.' Olive winked. 'The Head Porter is a regular customer, coming in for elevenses every morning for a cup of Earl Grey and an almond croissant. I daresay he's as loyal to The Biscuit Tin as to King's College; I don't think he'd risk losing access to his favourite treats...'

'Oh, Olive Crisp!' Blythe grinned. 'Aren't you the wily one?'

'Well.' Olive popped a coconut macaron into her mouth. 'Until women are granted access to the real channels of power and influence, we'll just have to make best use of whatever alternative routes present themselves now, won't we?'

'Amen.' Millicent grinned. 'Amen to that.'

Chapter Four

THE FOLLOWING MORNING, OLIVE packed up a box of warm almond croissants, along with a flask of Earl Grey tea and set off, with Biscuit at her heels, towards King's Parade. The grand building of King's College, stretching along (almost) the entirety of one side of the road, only making way for the Senate House[1] at the far end and although a bastion to social exclusivity it was nevertheless an edifice of undeniably breathtaking beauty: with intricate stone carvings across an expansive facade, stained glass windows of dazzling, detailed loveliness and impossibly delicate stone pinnacles and turrets that stretched high into the sky. Olive could (almost) understand why someone of a daring disposition might want to climb the towers to sit on the rooftops among all that splendour.

'Be on your best behaviour now Biscuit,' Olive instructed the spaniel. 'You know Mr Bennett isn't keen on yapping.'

Biscuit gave a disgruntled yap in response.

'I know, I know,' Olive tutted. 'At your last encounter he admonished you quite severely. Unnecessarily so. Which is why I'm warning you now; the Porter's Lodge is his territory after all, so we have to respect his rules. Besides, we need to be at our most charming today since I'm very much hoping to extract some information from our Mr Bennett today.'

Biscuit yapped again, softer this time. Inquisitive.

'I don't know,' Olive admitted. 'That's the thing. And I'm not even sure if he knows anything. But if there *is* anything to know, anything to prove my position, then Mr Bennett will know it.'

Olive slowed as they reached the front gate of King's College. One of the junior porters, fully kitted out in suit, tie and bowler hat, stood beside the large wooden doors of intricately carved oak, casually barring the way.

'Good morning, Miss.'

'Good morning,' Olive said, assuming her most authorial, yet friendly, tone. 'I'm here to see Mr Bennett.'

The junior porter frowned, officiously adjusting his tie. 'Is he expecting you?'

'Well, no,' Olive admitted. 'But I'm quite sure he'll be happy to see me.'

The young man's eyes narrowed. 'You're not one of them journos, are you? We've had a bunch of them sniffing about since the...' He bowed his head. 'Terrible incident here yesterday. And the boss has told me to tell anyone like that to sling their hook. So–'

'Oh, no,' Olive exclaimed, as if the mere idea was horrifying. 'No, no. I'm the owner of *The Biscuit Tin*. I'm bringing' – she opened the Tupperware lid just enough to reveal a tantalising glimpse of the contents – 'a box of his favourite breakfast pastries. I was passing this way anyway, so then he doesn't have to leave his post to come to the café.'

The junior porter, who'd clearly been relishing the opportunity to banish Olive from the scene, quickly reconsidered at the sight of the head porter's beloved croissants. A number of emotions passed in quick succession across his pale face: annoyance, concern, irritation, frustration and, finally, resignation. Who was he to stand between his boss and his breakfast? And what would be the consequences if he did? The junior porter gave a slight shudder at the thought.

'Alright.' Unfolding his arms, he took a few steps to heave open the door. 'But you can't bring *that* in with you.' He directed a disgusted nod at Biscuit, who glowered up at him. 'Mr Bennett can't abide dogs.'

'Would you rather I left her out here with you?' Olive smiled her most innocent, gracious smile while Biscuit affected her most aggressive snarl. 'It's so kind of you to offer to watch her. I didn't–'

'No, no,' the junior porter shook his head so rapidly his bowler hat nearly fell off. 'I can't be doing that. Against college rules. You'll have to take her in and if Mr Bennett chucks you out again, then don't say I didn't warn you.'

'I won't.' Olive gave him a parting, triumphant smile, before stepping through the open doors and into King's College. 'Come on Biscuit, let's go.'

Olive took a sharp left turn towards the Porter's Lodge, as Biscuit bounded in after her, and the ancient wooden door slammed shut behind her.

Just as she was walking in, another man, dressed to the nines in a silk suit, tie – diamond tie-pin glinting in the sunlight – and scholars' robes, was marching out.

'Oh, for goodness sake,' he snapped. 'Would you get out of my way?'

'Sorry–'

'Forever faffing and dilly-dallying,' he muttered, pushing past her towards the door. 'And you expect us to give you the honour of admittance – we've got enough of the bloody working classes as it is, a plague, that's what...'

The heavy wooden door banged behind him, swallowing the rest of his rant. Olive watched him go, wide-eyed as Mr Bennett stepped out of the Porter's Lodge.

'Well, Miss Crisp.' Mr Bennett's face lit up at the sight of her.

'Mr Bennett,' Olive smiled. She nodded back at door. 'Who was that delightful gentleman?'

'Ah,' the Head Porter nodded. 'That would be our new Dean. He joined us in January, formerly headmaster at Eton. He can be a little... brusque.'

'That's putting it mildly,' Olive said.

'So,' Mr Bennett said. 'Whatever brings you to our humble dwelling?'

'Hardly humble.' Olive nodded towards the chapel, a spectacular creation in stained glass and stone. 'You've got arguably the best view in Cambridge from where you stand.'

'Well.' Mr Bennett's smile widened into one of indulgent pride, as if he'd hewn the stone from the rocks himself five hundred years ago and chiselled each statue and carving. 'It's not too shabby, I suppose. Now, am I wrong in imagining that I can detect the scent of your delectable almond croissants in my vicinity?'

'You are not wrong.' Olive snapped open the Tupperware to display her offering in all its glory. '*Six* of my delectable almond croissants, to be exact.'

'Oh!' Mr Bennett brought his hands to his mouth, as if the plastic tub contained gold bullion instead of laminated pastry. 'My goodness, Miss Crisp, whoever has ordered such a banquet? I can only imagine–'

'You.' Olive grinned. 'They're all for you.'

'Me?' The Head Porter dropped his hands in astonishment and pressed one to his chest. 'Please tell me you're not teasing. I don't think my poor heart could take it.'

'I'm not teasing.' Olive handed over the box. 'I brought you a flask of your favourite tea too – steeped for three and a half minutes, a dash of milk and a soupcon of sugar – to accompany them.'

'Oh, Miss Crisp!' He took the Tupperware and, pressing it to his chest, took a long, appreciative sniff of the sweet, warm contents. 'Whatever have I done to deserve this? Mrs Bennett doesn't spoil me this well even on my birthday.'

'Take a bite,' Olive suggested. 'They're at their best when they're fresh.'

Not needing to be told twice, Mr Bennett took a bite, then another and, a moment later, had polished off two of the six. Olive fished the flask of tea from her bag, glancing down at Biscuit who stood to perfectly silent attention at her feet. Not a peep. Olive gave the dog a grateful wink.

'Here you go.' She handed him the flask. 'Keep hold of it.'

Mr Bennett took the flask with a nod and a smile. 'So, whatever can I do to repay such generosity?' He asked, removing a monogrammed handkerchief from his pocket and dabbing his lips. 'Surely this is not a service you provide to all your devoted customers, or you'd be rushed off your feet running errands all over the city!'

'Well...' Olive ventured. 'Now that you mention it, I was hoping to pick your brains about a small matter.'

Mr Bennett gave her a knowing smile. 'Let me guess. This wouldn't have anything to do with yesterday's terrible tragedy on the college grounds now would it?'

'As a matter of fact,' Olive said, returning his smile with a wry smile of her own. 'That's exactly what I wanted to ask you about.'

She held her breath, fully expecting to be dismissed. Kindly, but quickly.

'Go ahead then,' he said. 'Ask away.'

'Really?' Olive exhaled. 'You're sure? I promise I won't whisper a word of whatever you tell me to a living soul. That's to say,' she thought of her two best friends and knew it was hopeless to expect herself to keep a secret from either of them for more than a minute. 'I mean, no members of the public or press, only–'

Mr Bennett held up his hand. 'Do not worry, Miss Crisp. I have full confidence in your discretion and no doubt of your wisdom in assessing the discretion of others. I will tell you what I know. Now, what do you wish to ask?'

As they talked, clutches of students, in small groups and alone, hurried past as they left or entered the college, weaving round Olive and Mr Bennett as if they were two inanimate obstacles blocking the path. Only one paused to acknowledge them: a tall skinny young man wearing a tight flowered shirt and bell-bottom cords the colour of mustard.

'Morning George,' he said. 'Fine start to the day, isn't it?'

'It certainly is, Mr Simpson.' The Head Porter doffed his hat. 'And I trust that you'll enjoy the rest of it now.'

'Not when I'm spending the duration in the engineering department,' Mr Simpson returned with a resigned grin. 'But I'll try.'

'How many of them know you by name?' Olive asked, as Mr Simpson darted away.

'Oh, not many.' Mr Bennett shrugged, as if it didn't matter. 'But these young men have a lot on their minds; the future leaders of our country. They can't be expected to keep hold of every inconsequential fact.'

Olive said nothing, though it saddened her to hear him speak of himself like this. He was just as important as the boys he presided over – organising a great many unseen administrative and organisational aspects of their college lives – be they future Prime Ministers or not.

'Well.' She touched his arm gently. 'You're a man of consequence to *me*. And a great many others too, of that I'm quite certain.'

Mr Bennett gave her a grateful smile. 'I've been manning this post, with diligence and deference, the best part of forty years,' he said. 'After doing my duty and serving my country. And I daresay not a handful of fifty thousand boys in all that time would recognise me in the street.' He gave a little sigh. 'It might be nice to be acknowledged now and then. Anyway,' he shook his head. 'What was it you wanted to ask?'

Olive made a mental note to bring almond croissants to Mr Bennett every Friday morning from now on. 'I wondered if there was anything you could tell me about the boy who fell,' she said. 'Was there anything to suggest...' She dropped her voice, as another gaggle of noisy young men barrelled past them. 'That it might *not* have been an accident?'

'I've been asking myself the same thing,' Mr Bennett admitted. 'I know he wasn't too popular; one of the grammar school boys who are increasingly common of late. Hardly ever saw the likes of them when I started. A jolly good thing, equality and all that, though there are those who disagree, who'd have them banished given half the chance, claiming they've not got the manners and ways of the Eton and Winchester boys, if you catch my drift.'

Olive nodded. She knew what he meant well enough, encountering their type on a daily basis in the café: loud voices and even louder opinions. And, as for their "manners"... Well, she didn't think much of those either. The tutors were usually far better behaved, excepting the odd obnoxious one. But for the Dean of King's, well, he was as bad as his snottier students, often worse, treating Olive like his personal servant.

'What was his name?' She asked.

'The boy? Jack Witstable. Second Year Classics student. Shy, sensitive type. But even then he always said his greetings whenever he passed the lodge.' Mr Bennett gave a sad smile. 'I appreciated that. I must say, I didn't have him pegged for a ladies man. Even thought he might've sailed in the other direction, if you catch my drift.'

Olive frowned a moment before understanding dawned. 'What makes you say that?'

Mr Bennett shrugged. 'Experience. One gets a sense of these things. But I'll admit I may have been wrong on that count since he used to entertain a lovely young lady here from time to time. He was such a nice boy, and he seemed so friendless that I'd even let him sneak her up to his room after hours sometimes.' He dropped his voice, looking slightly stricken. 'I do hope that doesn't make you think less of me, or offend your sense of propriety. It's certainly not something I'd permit in any other student. It was just...'

'Just, what?' Olive prompted.

'He always seemed so sad,' Mr Bennett explained. 'As if he was carrying the weight of the world on his shoulders. And then, a few weeks ago the young lady stopped visiting and Jack became even more melancholic than usual. He never said as much, of course, but I'm guessing she broke his heart, poor chap.'

Olive considered this. 'I don't suppose you know her name?'

The Head Porter shook his head. 'I'm afraid not, Miss Crisp.'

Olive looked crestfallen.

'But…'

She glanced up, suddenly hopeful. Biscuit's ears twitched.

'She often wore a Newnham scarf,' he said.

'Really?' Olive brightened.

'Yes.' He nodded and smiled, clearly pleased to be able to offer this nugget of good news. 'And though it's hard to judge, I'm quite certain she was a second or third year. Freshers have a look about them, a cloak of anxious anticipation they wear like their Matriculation robes. Most don't divest themselves of that till the end of Easter term, and we only began it last week, so…'

'Alright,' Olive said. 'And how many new students joined the college last year?'

'One hundred and twenty.'

'A hundred and twenty,' Olive echoed, weighing up the possibilities presented by this new information. While she did so, Mr Bennett munched thoughtfully on his third almond croissant. And then, just as she seemed struck by a plot of inspiration, Olive's delight crumpled.

'What is it, Miss Crisp?' He asked. 'Whatever's wrong?'

'I just realised the flaw in my thinking,' Olive replied.

'What thinking?'

'When you mentioned the girl and then him being heartbroken, naturally I thought that she must have left him for one of the other boys – the Night Climbers – and then… But if that was the case then surely it'd make more sense for Jack to have pushed *him* off the rooftop, not the other way around. Don't you think?'

'Yes,' Mr Bennett agreed, dabbing the crumbs from his mouth. 'That's true.'

'So then, why would another boy have cause to push Jack?'

Mr Bennett gave a slight shrug. 'Perhaps the young lady has nothing to do with it,' he suggested. 'Perhaps it was another reason entirely. These boys can be awfully competitive and Jack was smarter than most. Perhaps they were jealous of that.'

'Perhaps…' Olive considered. 'But exam results are hardly a motive for murder. Love, in my experience, is far more common.'

Mr Bennett smiled. 'In your experience, Miss Crisp? I didn't realise, if you'll forgive the liberty, that you had a great deal of experience when it came to murder.'

'Well...' Olive blushed. 'Not especially, not *personally*. Nor love either, come to that. But I've worked, well, consulted with the police on a few cases and I do recall Hu–Detective Dixon saying that love and money were the two main motives for murder.'

'That makes sense, I suppose,' Mr Bennett agreed. 'In which case it might be worth trying to track down this young Newnham student anyway and seeing what light she might be able to shed on it all.'

'Yes.' Olive nodded. 'I was just thinking exactly the same thing.'

---

1. An impressive building of white stone pillars from which the university students graduated in a cryptic ceremony of Latin speeches and strange finger-holding rituals, ceremonies from which women were still forbidden to participate in by a good many of the 31 colleges, King's included.

Chapter Five

'And how exactly do you intend to interrogate the entire first year cohort of Newnham College?' Millicent absently flicked through a copy of *The Mysterious Death at Styles*. 'You can't exactly hold an assembly in the hall. What will you do, bribe them all with batches of almond croissants?'

The friends had decamped to One More Chapter Books to help Blythe package special deliveries which she'd then cycle around Cambridge delivering by hand. Olive and Millicent usually accompanied her on these trips, especially when the weather was pleasant and, in the height of summer, Olive brought leftovers from the café along so they could picnic on Grantchester Meadows or Jesus Green or Midsummer Common, depending on which part of town they ended up.

This evening though, they weren't getting much work done.

'I don't know,' Olive admitted as she slipped another copy of the same novel – it was Blythe's book club choice of the month – into an envelope and sealed it shut. 'It certainly won't be easy. And I don't know the porters at Newnham, so it'll be a lot harder gaining entry. By the way, I've brought a batch of lavender-sugar biscuits so we give them a treat along with the book.'

'Thank you.' Blythe smiled. 'You're a marvel. Though, at this rate…' She gazed at the stacks of books scattered all around them. 'I'm not sure those biscuits won't be stale by the time we're done.'

'I'm sorry.' Olive picked up another envelope, determined to double her efforts. 'I'm a little distracted. It's just, I'm so sure this boy, Jack, was murdered but if we don't find some evidence soon then the police will put him and the case to rest without justice being done.' She sighed. 'And it sounded like he was such a nice boy too, not like a lot of these entitled public school students who'll hold court in the café giving their friends – and anyone within a fifty foot radius – their invaluable opinions on the state of the nation.'

'While protesting against the entry of women to their colleges because, of course, our teeny tiny brains are too emotional to deal with anything more than raising babies and tidying homes.' Millicent snapped her book shut with a little more force than necessary. 'When I was a girl their fathers were arguing against giving us the vote, wearing black armbands when women were finally admitted to lectures, yet they're still excluded from every college excepting Newnham and Girton[1]... And they say this is the age of women's lib and look how far we've come.' She snorted. 'What do they take us for?'

'Twits,' Blythe said. 'With baby brains, literal and figurative, just as you said.'

'True enough,' Olive agreed. 'But what *am* I going to do?'

Dropping another envelope onto the pile, she reached out to rub the soft fur between Biscuit's eyebrows, as she often did when seeking inspiration. The spaniel was always close at hand, never leaving Olive's side unless her mistress entered a place that prohibited dogs. Biscuit even joined the book deliveries, sitting in Olive's bike basket with her tongue lolling out and the wind blowing back her silky ears, yapping with delight at the adventure.

'Just turn up at the college,' Millicent suggested. 'You can make up some excuse to get past the porters easily enough, then start asking around the students and see if you can find the boy's girlfriend. The whole town is abuzz with the accident, it won't be hard to strike up conversations on the subject without arousing suspicions.'

'I guess so.' Olive nodded, still stroking Biscuit's head. 'It's certainly worth a shot.'

'So, um, how was Mr Bennett?' Millicent asked, innocently. 'Is he well again?'

'Again?' Olive frowned. 'What do you mean? He seemed perfectly fine to me.'

Millicent gave a slight shrug. 'He had a nasty cold last week, so I just–'

'Oh my goodness,' Blythe exclaimed. 'You're sweet on him, aren't you? You do know he's a married man.'

'Of course I do,' Millicent said. 'And I am *not* sweet on him. Don't be ridiculous.'

'If I know anything about anything,' Blythe said. 'It's love. And you most certainly *are*.'

'Stop teasing her,' Olive laughed. 'And I don't blame you if you are, Millie. Mr Bennett is a lovely man. Kind, thoughtful and handsome too. What's not to like?'

'Yes,' Millicent agreed. 'He's perfectly nice but I'm *not* in love with him. We, um, courted a long time ago that's all. Before he met Elsie, before I met the cad. In another life.'

'Hold on!' Blythe sat up, momentarily abandoning the books. 'You never told us any of this before. Come now, I need all the gossip. Details. Spill.'

Millicent laughed, but her smile was wistful. 'There's nothing to tell. We were together a while, then we weren't. That's all. No bad feelings, no broken hearts. Just friends.'

Blythe and Olive exchanged a look.

'Likely story,' Blythe said, raising an eyebrow. 'I think you're holding out on us, Millie. I think it was a tempestuous love affair, complete with smashed hearts and years of silent longing and-'

'Don't be ridiculous,' Millicent cut her off. 'You should write romance novels with that overactive imagination of yours. Really.'

Olive smiled. 'So, who wants to come with me?'

'Come with you where?' Her friends asked in unison.

'Newnham College,' Olive said. 'As soon as we've delivered these books and biscuits, of course.'

'Tonight?' Blythe frowned. 'Won't it be a little late? Shouldn't we wait till tomorrow?'

'We can't afford to wait,' Olive said. 'Or the police will close the case and then it'll be impossible to get them to reopen it. Not without any physical evidence, which we'll never get. Uncovering the truth through confession or incrimination is the best we can hope for and for that, we need to act fast.'

'Alright,' Blythe said. 'Tonight it is. In which case, we'd better crack on with stuffing these envelopes.'

---

1. Darwin College (founded in 1964) was the first college established for both men and women. Churchill College (founded in 1958) was the first all-male college to admit women in 1972. King's College (founded in 1441) and Clare College (founded in) quickly followed suit. But it took 15 years for the other all-male colleges to follow their lead.

Chapter Six

Olive, Blythe and Millicent parked their bikes against the dark red brick of Newnham College's walls. The leafy green road flanked with chestnut trees was one of Olive's favourites and she often took Biscuit walking behind the backs of the colleges and following the winding path of the River Cam.

'So, what's the plan?' Olive said, scooping Biscuit out of her bicycle basket. 'How are we getting in?'

'I thought you were the maker of plans in this scenario,' Blythe said. 'You're the one so intent on solving this mystery, after all. We're just along for moral support.'

'I've thought of something,' Millicent said, hitching her cloth bag into her arms. 'You just leave this to me.'

'Fantastic.' Olive breathed a sigh of relief. 'Fine by me. Lead the way.'

Olive and Blythe followed Millicent, scurrying behind as she strode towards the college, through the open gate and into the Porter's Lodge.

'Good evening,' Millicent declared in strident tones as she entered. 'I've brought a delivery for the Principal. She placed a sewing order this afternoon.'

Two porters sat behind the desk, both nursing cups of tea. One nodded. Neither got up. Which was fortunate, since it meant they couldn't see Biscuit silently circling Olive's ankles.

'Very well, just leave it here,' he said. 'We'll be sure she gets it.'

Millicent shook her head. 'I promised to deliver it personally. She needs me to explain the specifics of the cross stitch, catch stitch, blanket stitch and slip stitch. She also -'

'Alright, alright.' The porter raised his hand. 'Go on then. The Principal's lodgings are through the second quad, past the fountain and at the end of the rose garden.'

'Thank you.' Millicent smiled. 'I shall return within an hour or so, depending on how many stitches she wants to -'

'As you wish,' the porter interrupted. 'I know once you ladies get talking there's not much that stops you.'

Millicent's smile tightened but she said nothing, only gave a perfunctory nod and started to walk on. Blythe, Olive and Biscuit hurried after her.

'Hold on.' Now the porter stood. 'And where do you think you two are going?'

They stopped. Olive turned, fixing a winning smile to her face. 'We're the assistants,' she said quickly. 'We hold the threads.'

The porter frowned then, clearly not wanting to display his ignorance, waved his hand to dismiss them. 'Fine, fine,' he said. 'Carry on.'

'"We hold the threads"?' Blythe giggled, as soon as they were out of earshot. 'Where did you get that from?'

'Shush!' Olive nudged her. 'It was the best I could come up with under pressure.'

'Hurry up, you two,' Millicent hissed. 'Before they realise we're talking nonsense.'

Still giggling, Olive and Blythe scampered on.

Halfway across the first quad, they were stopped by the sounds of chatter and laughter drifting out of an open window and across the lawn. A long row of illuminated windows ran along the nearest wall and, in the midst of them, a door.

'Let's go and see what's going on,' Olive suggested. 'If those are students, they sound like the chatty sort.'

'They sound like the drunk sort,' Blythe said.

'Even better.' Olive smiled. 'Come on Biscuit, best paw forward.'

Following the cobbled path towards a door, Olive took the lead and paused only briefly at the door to read the small wooden sign drilled into the wall: *The Iris Bar*.

'We're in luck,' she whispered. 'It's the bar. And they are definitely drunk.'

Pushing open the door, Olive slid into the room, immediately followed by Millicent and Blythe and Biscuit. They hung back together in the corner, gazing out at the small room crowded with clutches of leather chairs around short tables and flanked by a bar at one end, considering their best approach.

'I know you!' A young woman a few metres away, sat forward in her chair and raised aloft the glass of red wine she was holding. 'You're the cake lady!'

In response, the last words echoed through the room: "Cake lady, cake lady, cake lady!" As the rest of the group – about a dozen students in total – joined the chorus.

The first young woman stood and walked towards Olive, who shrank back against the wall, casting desperate glances at her friends who shrugged helplessly.

'Cake lady.' The young woman, sporting a tweed skirt and matching jacket, along with a tight bun of bright blonde hair, reached out her hand. 'Arabella Fitzgerald. Welcome to our den of iniquity.'

This evoked ripples of giggles through the small crowd.

'Thank you, Miss Fitzgerald.' Olive shook the student's hand. 'Olive Crisp. And this' – she nodded nervously at her friends in turn – 'is Millicent Burrows and Blythe Loveday.' Anxious not to be left out, Biscuit gave a sharp bark. 'Sorry. Along with Biscuit too. It's a pleasure to be here.'

'And why *are* you all here? If that's not an impolite inquiry.'

'Not at all,' Olive said, stalling for time. 'It's a perfectly polite, and indeed entirely understandable, inquiry. So...'

The young woman, who'd stopped listening to the answer, cocked her head to one side. 'Do you have any cake?'

'I'm sorry?'

'Do you have any cake with you? Is that why you're here? To bring us cake?'

A hearty cheer went up.

'Well, um, I...' Olive opened her bag. Unfortunately, the leftover batch of lavender biscuits had already been distributed to Blythe's book group. But, fortunately, Olive also never went anywhere without a stash of treats secreted about her person. Just in case. One never knew, after all, when one might be on the edge of having an empty stomach. It was a risk she was not willing to take.

'Macarons!' Olive exclaimed, triumphantly, as she pulled a small box from her bag, followed by another. 'I have macarons!'

She heard both Millicent and Blythe breathe audible sighs of relief.

The student closed one eye. 'What flavour?'

Olive opened one box. 'Chocolate,' she pronounced. 'And vanilla.'

'Chocolate!' The student broadcast to her fellows. 'She's got chocolate!'

Another cheer erupted and Olive hastily handed over the boxes before the crowd turned wild. The gaggle of delighted, squealing, slightly drunk girls crowded around Arabella to grab at the treats. When the boxes were empty, Arabella turned back to Olive.

'I don't suppose..?'

'Sorry,' Olive said quickly. 'That's all I have. You've cleaned me out.'

'Oh.' Arabella sighed. 'What a shame.' She glanced back at the bar, the shelves of wines and spirits. 'Well, I suppose we still have plenty of tipple.'

'Indeed.' Olive nodded, rather wishing she had a glass in hand to better cope with the unravelling situation. 'So, I was wondering... I'm sure you heard about the dreadful accident at King's...'

'Oh, yes, of course!' Arabella put her palm to her lips, suddenly stricken. 'Terrible, terrible thing. We all knew Jack here, lovely, lovely boy.'

'You did?' Olive asked, suddenly alert. Beside her, she felt Millicent and Blythe stiffen. Even Biscuit pricked up her ears.

'Absolutely, he was a regular visitor to the bar,' she said. 'Came over most weekends. Much preferred our college to his, unsurprisingly.' Arabella laughed again, a light, kind laugh. 'I think sometimes he wished he was a girl so he might have joined us at Newnham instead of King's.'

Olive frowned. 'Why was he so unhappy there?'

Arabella mirrored Olive's frown. 'Why wouldn't he be? A sensitive chap like Jack could never be happy in a place like that, so full of bullies and bores. It's like the Houses of Parliament. A riotous brawl. Have you ever had dinner in Hall?'

Olive shook her head.

'Well, I have, sorry to say. Father's the MP for South Herts. Anyway, it's a frightful place, full of men shouting at each other like they're still in the school playground. It's a wonder they get around to running the country at all, really.' She sighed. 'They're a bunch of bullish savages, the King's chaps, just like most of the all-male colleges.'

'And did they bully Jack?' Blythe asked, stepping forward slightly.

Olive swallowed a smile, remembering how Blythe, despite her protestations, never liked to be left out of anything for too long.

In response, Arabella laughed again. But this time it was tinged with bitterness.

'Did they bully Jack?' She echoed, as if this was by far the most idiotic question ever asked of a person. 'Of course they bloody did. Well, the public school chaps anyway, they picked on anyone who wasn't one of them. And they hated the fact there were so many more coming in – blamed Harold Wilson, Labour government trying to make everything equal. Anyway...' She shrugged as she trailed off.

'So why was Jack climbing with them?' Blythe asked. 'Why would he go with boys who'd been so mean to him?'

By now the rest of the girls had drifted off back to their chairs and wine glasses. But Olive noticed that one girl who sat far across the room continued to fix her gaze on them, as if she wanted to join the conversation but didn't have the courage. Her long brown hair was pulled into plaits and her rapidly blinking eyes framed by tiny, round glasses; she held the perpetually anxious look of a mouse hiding from a cat.

'I'm not sure,' Arabella admitted. 'Perhaps he was trying to fit in. Perhaps they dared him. Jack was a nice boy but still a boy; I doubt he could resist a dare.'

'Do you think it's possible his fall wasn't an accident?' Olive asked. 'Do you think one of them could have pushed him?'

If the measure of Arabella's incredulity at the stupidity of Blythe's question had been high, now it went off the scale.

'Are you – is that a serious question?' She gaped at Olive, for the first time letting the mask of her good breeding slip. 'Of *course* he was pushed. What do you think? That it was an accident?' She said this final word with such venomous disbelief that Biscuit emitted a short, nervous bark.

'No,' Olive said quickly. 'No, I don't. But that's what the police think. And that's why I'm here.'

At the mention of the police, Arabella rolled her eyes.

'Imbeciles. The constabulary have all the insight and imagination of a fish. They're just like politicians; they believe only what's put in front of them and they're infinitely corruptible.'

Olive raised an eyebrow. Here, she thought, was someone with daddy issues. Making a non-committal noise in response, she hesitated to agree, feeling fairly certain that Detective Dixon wasn't a simpleton and dearly hoped he wasn't corrupt. Still, Arabella was proving very helpful and loquacious and the last thing Olive wanted to do was shut her down.

'So,' Blythe stepped in. 'If you're sure it wasn't an accident, why don't you go to the police?'

Arabella snorted. 'And what good would that do? You think they'll listen to *my* word, which is pure speculation, against the word of six eye witnesses?'

'Even when those eye witnesses might have been in cahoots?' Millicent interjected. 'Don't you think they will–'

'Even when those eye witnesses absolutely *were* in cahoots,' Arabella clarified. 'Have you heard of the Loki and Pan Society?'

'No.' Olive shook her head, her pulse starting to race. 'What's that?'

'One of their clubs, like The Bullingdon Club in Oxford, the source of many a scandal and–'

'Oh!' Blythe's eyes widened. 'Weren't they in the papers a few years ago, accused of assaulting those poor waitresses?'

'Yes,' Arabella said. 'Except, of course, it never went to court and they were never charged.'

'Why not?' Millicent asked.

Arabella rolled her eyes. 'Aren't you listening? Don't you realise who the fathers of these men are? Politicians, barristers, judges... Who's in the business of prosecuting their own sons?'

Olive glanced again at the girl sitting across the room and, sure enough, she was still gazing at them. But, as soon as Olive caught her gaze, the girl looked away.

'These are leaders of the Empire,' Arabella went on. 'And, believe me, they'll have done even worse in their own day and got away with it. Rich men get away with everything. Did you not know that?'

Millicent dropped her eyes to the floor, embarrassed.

'So, tell me more about this club,' Olive persisted. 'Was Jack a member?'

'No!' Arabella exclaimed. 'Of course not. Only entitled arseholes belong to clubs like those, and Jack was quite the opposite.'

'Right.' Olive nodded. 'Of course, I just…'

'They have a motto,' Arabella said. '"Malum Vita". Do you know what that means?'

Olive shook her head. 'No.'

'It's Latin,' Arabella said. 'It means "mischief is life" or "life is mischief". One or the other, I can't quite recall. I'm not a Classics scholar. Anyway, it meant that they loved going about causing mischief. Taking cats off the street and putting them in students' rooms, that sort of thing. Once they even stole a farmer's sheep and released it into the grounds of St John's. How on earth they got it past the porters, I've no idea. But you see why climbing up college rooftops would appeal.'

'Yes,' Olive said. 'I see.' She took a deep breath. 'Look, I hope you don't mind me asking but how do you know all this? Did Jack tell you? Are you – were you – his girlfriend?'

'His girlfriend?' Arabella exclaimed. 'No, of course not. I…' Suddenly, she looked embarrassed. 'I was seeing – only for a few weeks, during which time he quickly revealed himself for the absolute reprobate he was – the club's leader, Rupert Middleton. He loved to brag about their escapades at the drop of a hat. Oh, they once stole a policeman's hat – helmet, along with a whole smoked salmon and a whole sack full of cats and locked them in the college library[1]. Apparently they were copying a scene from a book or something equally ridiculous, I don't know… Anyway, it was the sort of stupid, pointless nonsense Rupert loved to get up to. Elected members all wear diamond cufflinks, or some such, the gems stolen from a necklace belonging to the first wife of Henry VIII by the founding member. Bunch of bloody idiots.'

'And you think that poor Jack got involved in their antics,' Blythe said. 'And then they used that as an opportunity to kill him? But why? What do you think their motive might have been?'

'That I don't know,' Arabella admitted. 'I know they didn't like what he represented; the infiltration of the lower orders, the "pollution" of their precious elitist institution, the purity of which they were desperately fighting against being diluted by the watered-down blood of the working classes. King's used to be populated entirely by Etonians in the old days and Rupert would've loved to continue excluding anyone but those just like him if he could've, but times change and–'

'And you think that'd be cause enough for him to kill?' Olive interrupted. 'Truly?'

Arabella gave a slight shrug. 'Perhaps. Look, I'm not saying Rupert planned it all in advance like some dastardly murder plot, but I've also no doubt that events could've unfolded while they were up there, things said in the heat of the moment – diatribes about the plague of the working classes, or whatever – so one of them shoved him...'

'And do you think any of them would speak to me?' Olive asked. 'Do you think there's any chance that one of the six, who didn't do anything wrong, might tell the truth?'

'Talk to *you*?' Arabella gave another snort of laughter. 'You think one of Rupert's fellow club members is going to rat on him? Really? No offence, but that's the most foolish, naïve notion I've ever heard.'

Olive sighed. She didn't much like this arrogant, opinionated young woman yet she could only imagine, if the girls were this bad, what the boys would be like. And how they would treat her. And this girl was at least trying to be helpful, the boys would be hostile from the start.

'Do you know Jack's girlfriend?' Olive tried another tack. 'Perhaps she could tell us something that might help, even if she doesn't–'

'Girlfriend?' Arabella's incredulity reached, if that were possible, new heights. 'Jack didn't have a girlfriend. He was a homosexual.'

Olive blinked. Biscuit barked.

'Oh.' Olive blinked again. 'Are you quite sure?'

'Am I *sure*?' Arabella echoed. 'You think I can't tell when a man's attracted to women or not?'

Olive glanced across the room again at the silent, staring girl. She was getting rather fed up with Arabella and was increasingly tempted to leave her and try approaching the other young woman instead. *Just because he wasn't attracted to you*, Olive thought, *doesn't mean he wasn't attracted to women at all.*

'I know what you mean,' Blythe was saying, when Olive came out of her reverie. 'I'm glad you mentioned it, honestly, since it hadn't properly occurred to me. There's a particular man who comes into the shop and, no matter how friendly I am, he simply never looks at me *that* way. And I was starting to wonder if I'd said something...'

'Excuse me a moment,' Olive addressed Arabella, before glancing down at her dog. 'Wait here, Biscuit, I won't be long.'

Leaving her friends chatting with their slightly obnoxious informant, Olive hurried across the room towards the reclusive student - slow enough that the girl wouldn't get spooked but quick enough that she wouldn't have a chance to escape. The girl started to stand by the time Olive reached the halfway point, but Olive caught her just before she could scuttle away.

'Please,' Olive huffed, a little out of breath. 'I-I only wanted to ask you one question.'

The girl shook her head, the long plaits swinging against her shoulders.

'Please,' Olive repeated. 'You might know something that could help me - the police catch whoever killed Jack. You want that, don't you?'

The girl only stared at her, saying nothing.

'I'm sorry,' Olive tried again. 'I might be wrong but I thought… you're, you were Jack's girl–his friend, weren't you?'

Olive waited for her to speak, but the girl shook her head again.

'I'm not,' she said, at last. 'I'm not who you think I am. And the boy who was killed, I didn't know him.'

Olive frowned. 'Are you sure?'

It clearly wasn't in the girl's nature to make an arrogant retort, so she merely shook her head for a third time.

'I didn't know him,' she said again. 'So I'm sorry, but I can't help you.'

She turned to walk away but, just before she did so she met Olive's gaze.

Olive didn't need her cards to know that the girl was lying.

---

1. Their antics were inspired by P.G. Wodehouse's short story, *Sir Roderick Comes to Lunch*, featuring the antics of the twins Claude and Eustace and Lord Rainsby, all applying to be members of The Seekers Club; to be elected one must steal something. That's what the twin and Rainsby decided to pinch. Published *The Strand* magazine in 1922 and well worth a read.

Chapter Seven

'So, whatever Rupert's motive – since he sounds like the ringleader – it wasn't love,' Blythe said. 'Or lust. Or whatever it is young men mostly feel towards young women nowadays.'

'The same as whatever older men feel,' Millicent sniffed. 'They're no different. Same deceptive species.'

'Oh, Millie,' Olive said sympathetically. 'I might not be the best advocate for love, but we've really got to find you a nice man so you can stop hating the whole lot of them. A lovely, kind, loyal one. That's what we need.'

'Good luck,' Millicent retorted. 'You're more likely to find a unicorn or a flying pig.'

'Don't be ridiculous,' Blythe chastised. 'There are good men everywhere. What about ... Churchill? He was never unfaithful to his wife. Or Paul Newman. And *he's* the handsomest man in the world, he could have any woman he wants. But he doesn't.'

'How do you know?' Millicent said. 'He might be knee deep in women and he's just never been caught. You only *want* to believe he's faithful and truthful because you're a hopeless romantic.'

'And you're a hopeless cynic,' Blythe said. 'That doesn't mean you're right.'

'How about you both stop bickering,' Olive said. 'And focus on the matter at hand.'

Instead of cycling back into town, the friends had decided to push their bikes down the path that ran alongside the road behind Clare College, King's and Trinity, affording them sweeping views across the fields and the river and the backs of the university buildings that stood proud and majestic against the bright blue skies.

'Which is what, exactly?' Millicent asked. 'I'm afraid I'm losing track.'

'How on earth we're going to prove that one of those boys pushed Jack to his death if we've got no physical evidence, no honest witnesses and no one who'll give us any information that might enable us to persuade the police to treat his death as suspicious.'

'Perhaps you could use alternative powers of persuasion on the investigating detective,' Blythe suggested with a wink. 'I'll bet you could get him to change his mind.'

'Stop teasing,' Olive said. 'It's not helping.' She glanced back at the spaniel who had scampered off the path and now had her nose in a rabbit hole. 'Bics, leave that alone!'

Obediently, Biscuit returned to her mistress and began trotting alongside her again.

'Any more of that and you'll be back in my basket,' Olive said softly. 'I'm *not* giving you a bath when we get home.'

'You could interrogate the witnesses,' Millicent suggested. 'One of them might let something slip.'

'Nice idea,' Olive said. 'But I'm afraid that's wishful thinking. Those boys will be fiercely loyal to each other and I've got nothing to offer to break those bonds except a lifetime supply of lavender biscuits and, somehow, I don't think that'll quite cut it. And anyway they're probably all rich enough to buy my café and everything in it, so–'

'What about…?' Blythe winked. 'You *are* a woman, after all.'

Olive's burst of laughter was so sudden and sharp that it startled Biscuit, who started yapping. 'Now, of all the absurdly ridiculous things you've ever said, *that* is far and away the most patently, certifiably crazy.'

'I wasn't suggesting you *do* anything,' Blythe protested. 'Only that you flutter your eyelashes and play dumb, they'll eat that right up. And then, when their defences are down–'

'B,' Olive interrupted her friend. 'I'm old enough to be their *mother*. That's all they'll see when they look at me. So, no, I'm…'

As they turned the corner onto Silver Street, Olive trailed off. For, walking towards them was Detective Dixon. Spotting Olive, he smiled and waved.

'Well,' Blythe whispered. 'King's College boys might be immune to your feminine charms, but here's someone who most definitely isn't.'

'Shush!' Olive hissed as the detective approached. 'He'll hear you!'

'Why don't we leave them be?' Millicent mounted her bike. 'I'm quite sure Olive will do much better without our moral support on this occasion, don't you?'

'Thank you, Millie.' Olive gave her friend a grateful smile. 'Breakfast tomorrow?'

Millicent nodded. 'See you at the café.' She glanced at Blythe as she pushed off from the curb. 'Come with me, you mischief maker – you know, you'd be a perfect candidate for their Pan and Loki Club. I've never known anyone more mischievous.'

'What about Mr Bennett?' Blythe interrupted, following behind Millicent on her bicycle. 'I'm quite certain *he's* been faithful to his wife. He's no Paul Newman, but still you can't deny that he's one of the good ones.'

'Yes.' Olive snatched the end of her friend's reply, her voice rather wistful, on the wind. 'In his case, I do you're right.'

'Well, fancy bumping into you here.' Detective Dixon grinned as he reached her. 'I swung by the café earlier today but you'd closed early.'

'Only fifteen minutes,' Olive said, a little defensively. 'I had, um, things to do. Deliveries to make.' Although, it had occurred to her that, in the absence of a daughter, she really ought to hire a girl to help her in the café if she was going to spend so much time solving mysteries.

'Ah, yes.' He nodded. 'Deliveries.'

'That's right,' Olive iterated, starting to feel like she was in a police cell under interrogation. 'I make personal deliveries from time to time. This evening it was for Blythe's book club.' She was about to go on but remembered Hugo himself once telling her that liars often betrayed themselves by giving too many details, so she shut up.

'Blythe's book club, eh?'

Olive fiddled with the fraying leather on the left handlebar of her bike. 'There's no harm in that, is there?'

'No, of course not,' Hugo pinned her with his amused gaze. 'So long as you weren't doing anything else like, I don't know, pursuing lines of inquiry... Investigating a crime which wasn't a crime.'

'So you say,' Olive blurted out, then instantly regretted it.

'Yes, I *do* say,' he said, still smiling. 'Because I've interviewed all the witnesses and spoken with the Dean and examined the scene and because twenty years of murder investigations tells me that this was an accident. And what, pray tell, gives you the idea that it wasn't?'

Olive opened her mouth. *My tarot cards*, she wanted to say. *Oh, and the claims of a slightly obnoxious Newnham student.* Then she closed it again.

'Instinct,' she said instead. 'I think one of them pushed him. Everyone knows he wasn't well liked and those Night Climber boys – who were all Etonians and members of some society called the Loki and Pan Club or something and went about wearing stolen diamonds – didn't want him at King's, so–'

'And how do you know all this?' Hugo's smile dropped.

'Well, I, um...' Olive shrugged. 'It's common knowledge apparently. My customers have been chatting about it all day; it's the latest scandal and everyone loves to gossip, don't they? And, of course, I can't help overhearing.'

'Of course.' He raised an eyebrow. 'And you wouldn't be, um, contributing to this chatter, would you? Or soliciting opinions from interested parties?'

'No,' Olive said, a little too quickly. 'No, of course not.'

The flicker of amusement returned to the detective's eyes and he pinned her with his gaze. Olive tried to look away, but she couldn't. For a second she imagined him reaching out to take hold of her shoulders and pull her into a tight embrace; her fingers drifted up to her lips as she felt the touch of his kiss and a shiver ran through her.

'Miss Crisp? Miss Crisp? Are you quite alright?'

'What?' Olive returned abruptly to reality and instantly started to blush as she realised what he'd witnessed her thinking. *Thank goodness he wasn't able to see those thoughts.*

'Yes, yes, I'm fine,' she said. 'I was only thinking about, about...'

He looked at her quizzically, waiting.

Just then, Biscuit came to the rescue and started barking. Relieved, Olive glanced down at her dog.

'Oh, yes, of course,' she said. 'I need to pick up treats on my way home. We've run out and Biscuit can get quite disobedient without her treats.'

Biscuit wined at this, offended at having her character maligned, even for such a good cause as protecting her mistress' dignity.

'I know,' Olive glanced down at Biscuit, offering silent apologies. 'Don't worry, I won't forget.'

'But, I believe all the shops are shut now, aren't they?' Hugo frowned. 'So I don't think you can...'

'Oh, it's not from a shop,' Olive interrupted, as the idea occurred to her. 'I pick them up from my neighbour. She, um, makes them by hand. Special dog treats with, um, biscuits and bacon bits.'

The detective's frown deepened. 'Couldn't you just make those yourself?'

Olive gave a nervous laugh. 'Yes, of course I *could*. And I do. But Biscuit prefers these so I let her have them every now and then, on special occasions.'

'And today is a special occasion?'

Olive wiped her brow. 'I'm starting to feel like I'm under interrogation. Has there been a crime involving cake?'

Hugo laughed. 'Oh no, nothing like that. But if there is, don't worry you'll be my first suspect.'

'That's good to know.' Olive smiled. 'I'm glad I'll be top of your list.'

What are you doing? She told herself. *Stop flirting with the police officer!*

'But, of course,' Hugo said. 'I respect you far too much to put you anywhere else.'

Feeling suddenly flustered and not trusting what she might say next, and realising that the longer she stayed to chat the more likely it was she'd make a fool of herself, Olive bent down to scoop up Biscuit and place her in the bicycle basket. She was about to set off when she realised that amid all this flirtation, she'd forgotten to ask the most important question of all.

'Have you closed the case yet?'

'What – oh, the one you seem so convinced is murder,' Hugo said. 'The boy who tragically fell from the roof of King's College.'

'Or was pushed,' Olive added. 'Yes, that one.'

'No.' Hugo shook his head. 'No, not yet. The coroner is ruling on Friday, but I can tell you now, without any other evidence to the contrary, he will certainly conclude that it was accidental.'

Olive sighed.

Three days. She had three days to prove otherwise.

Which meant she had to act fast. Fortunately, what the detective had just said had given Olive a flash of inspiration, one she needed to act on straightaway.

'Alright,' she said, mounting her bicycle. 'Well, it was lovely bumping into you like this, but I'd better be off. It's late and I need my beauty sleep. I'm not getting any younger!'

She gave him what she hoped was a wryly self-deprecating smile, but his gaze remained serious.

'You certainly don't,' Hugo muttered. 'You're dangerously beautiful enough already.'

He spoke so softly, his lips barely moving, his mouth barely open, that Olive couldn't be at all certain whether or not she'd imagined his words altogether.

'Don't be in such a rush to get to bed,' he said, much louder. 'That you forget those dog treats.'

'Oh, yes, of course.' Olive chastised herself for having already forgotten her initial excuse. 'D-don't worry, Biscuit won't let me forget her. So, on that note, I'd, um, I'd better go. Have a good evening. See you soon.'

Hugo raised his hand. 'See you soon,' he echoed.

Olive didn't look back until she'd cycled to the end of Silver Street. And, when she did, she saw that Detective Dixon was still gazing after her. She was seized by a sudden impulse to turn and cycle back to him, to ask if he'd really just said what she thought he'd said, but instead Olive turned, reluctantly, onto King's Parade and he disappeared from view.

Olive kept cycling, past the turning onto Bene't Street, past King's College, until she reached the end of the road, then she took a left past the Senate House and headed back towards Newnham College. She only hoped that when she arrived she'd be able to find Arabella again and persuade her to carry out this rather maverick and somewhat dangerous idea.

◈

Chapter Eight

'So, you want me to seduce my old boyfriend? Someone I despise with every fibre of my being, in the hopes of getting him to slip up and tell me something that might incriminate him. Is that right?'

'Well...' Olive hesitated. She'd managed to slip past the porters when they'd disappeared to make cups of tea and mercifully found Arabella still in the bar. 'Not "seduce" exactly, so much as charm.'

'Charm?' Arabella grimaced, as if the notion revolted her. 'How exactly do you want me to "charm" him?'

'I don't know...' Olive gave a slight shrug, feeling increasingly uncomfortable at what she was asking this young woman to do. Rupert was clearly a cad and might very well be a killer; she didn't like Arabella but she didn't want to put her in danger. 'What do you think? Might you consider meeting with him? I could come with you. I mean, I could be waiting outside his room, or some such, ready to burst in as soon as you called me.'

Arabella laughed. 'That all sounds delightfully dramatic but entirely unnecessary. I've got nothing to fear from Rupert Middleton. He might be a stain on the handkerchief of humanity, but he's a total pussycat too. He'd never lift a finger against me.'

Olive frowned. 'But... You said you thought he was the most likely one to have pushed Jack from the roof. How can you say-?'

'Yes,' Arabella agreed. 'But that's very different. Giving someone a sharp shove and letting gravity do the rest - and with your gang right behind you as backup - what does that take? But hurting me, when we're alone together...' She shook her head. 'He never would.'

'You're sure?'

'Absolutely.'

'Then,' Olive ventured. 'Does that mean you'll do it?'

Arabella sighed. 'What's the point? Even if he confesses everything to me – which he won't – it'd just be my word against his. And he dumped me, so I'm biased. My word will mean less than nothing to the police. You understand that, don't you?'

Olive's spirits fell. Reluctant to admit that she hadn't considered this, she hesitated. 'Yes, of course I do. But what if... what if...?'

Arabella frowned. 'What if what?'

And then inspiration struck. 'My friend Blythe has a cinecamera. Her mother used it to take film reels of her sister's wedding. We could use that to record his confession. And then it wouldn't matter if they believed you or not, because it would be his own word against himself.'

Arabella nodded. 'Yes, it's a fine idea. But it's based on the notion that he'll say anything to incriminate himself, which he won't. Anyway, he knows I despise him, why would he talk to me?'

'Flatter him,' Olive suggested. 'From what you said it sounds like he thinks pretty highly of himself, and that sort of person is usually very responsive to fawning. I'm sure you can manipulate him into meeting with you easily enough. And, as for getting him to confess, I find that alcohol usually does the trick.'

'He does like a drink or five,' Arabella admitted. 'That part of it certainly wouldn't be hard. But I can't bear the idea of fawning. It'll be humiliating.'

'Only at first,' Olive said. 'But then, if it works, you'll be the one responsible for putting him in prison for the rest of his life, or a good portion of it. So surely it'll be worth it.'

Arabella shrugged. 'That's only *if* it works. If it doesn't, then it's just humiliating.'

'I suppose so,' Olive admitted. 'And I'm sorry about that. But isn't it worth the risk?'

Olive looked at Arabella, desperately hoping that this appeal – offering her the chance to fulfil her civic duty or the opportunity for revenge – would win her over. Yet Arabella's face remained inscrutable as she considered the options and Olive couldn't tell which way she would go.

Chapter Nine

'TELL ME AGAIN WHY you need my mother's cinecamera?' Blythe asked.

'Because I'm setting a trap,' Olive explained. 'And if Rupert walks into it I need proof.'

'So you're going to film him?'

'Yes, exactly.'

Blythe frowned. 'But I don't understand. Surely he won't confess if you're filming him.'

Olive rolled her eyes. 'Of course not, but he won't *know* I'm filming him, will he? Because I'll be in hiding.'

'In hiding?' Blythe's frown deepened. 'In hiding where?'

'I'm not certain yet,' Olive said. 'We haven't decided on the best location – somewhere private so he feels comfortable talking and, um, incriminating himself without being overheard. Probably in his room.'

'His room!' Blythe exclaimed. 'And how on earth do you plan on breaking into his room and hiding without getting seen or caught?'

'I don't know,' Olive admitted. 'I haven't thought out the finer details yet.'

'The finer details?!' Blythe shrieked, startling Biscuit, who sat between them on the bookshop floor, waiting for someone to suggest a walk. So far, with all the endless chatter, she'd been disappointed.

'Olive, I love you,' Blythe said. 'I'd walk into a burning building after you, you know that. But this is crazy. It'll never work. And you'll probably end up going to prison for spying or something like that.'

Olive felt a flash of panic. *Was that possible? Surely not. Perhaps she should try to find out.* In an attempt to conceal her nerves, she smiled weakly. 'Don't be silly, B. I don't think that's a thing. I mean, I don't work for the government. I'm just an amateur, not a real detective, so they can't put me in front of a tribunal or fire me or anything like that.'

Blythe narrowed her eyes with suspicion. 'You don't even know what a tribunal is, do you?'

'No,' Olive admitted. 'Not really. But, whatever it is, I won't be subjected to it. Anyway, *I'm* not a criminal, I'm trying to catch a criminal. That's a good thing, I won't be punished for doing a good thing and I'm certainly not doing anything illegal - he's the one who killed a boy, not me.'

'Exactly!' Blythe exclaimed, causing poor Biscuit to startle again. 'Can you hear yourself? This person you want to spy on probably killed someone. Doesn't that worry you? Aren't you at all concerned that he might try to kill *you*.'

'Oh, no.' Olive shook her head. 'No, no. Arabella assured me that he wasn't the type to do something like that single-handedly. Or with a weapon – not that he has a weapon, so far as I know – but anyway, it's very different to shoot a person, or stab them, versus simply giving them a quick shove off a roof.'

Blythe stared at her friend, wide-eyed with incredulity. 'Olive, my dear, are you listening to yourself? You have no idea what kind of killer he is, or what kind of killer he might become. Perhaps he's got the taste for it now and he'll expand into other avenues – the first time of anything is the hardest after all. He might become a serial killer!'

Olive stared back at Blythe, her heart thudding. 'Don't be silly. That's not going to happen, that's utterly ludicrous...' She trailed off, worrying she was protesting too much.

'Is it?' Blythe raised an eyebrow. 'How can you be so sure?'

Chapter Ten

Am I crazy? Olive wondered as she slipped a second batch of madeleines into the oven. *Is Blythe right? Am I being stupidly naïve?* It was certainly possible, of course, but even then Olive couldn't see any way around it. Yes, attempting to record the confession of a killer wasn't perhaps the wisest way to spend one's time but what other choice did she have? In the absence of any physical evidence and in the face of no police support, her options were limited. And anyway, she'd be in the room with Arabella too. If Rupert went rogue, they could surely overpower him together. So long as he didn't have a gun.

Olive swallowed nervously as she began arranging the Bakewell tarts on decorative cake stands. She'd made a selection of different jams: apple, elderflower and apricot. She planned on adding fig jam and pear jam (in addition to the traditional blackberry and raspberry) to the menu soon too, when the fruits came into season in late summer. Olive paused to bend down over the plate and inhale the scent of sugar which she always found to be exceedingly calming. Deciding she needed an extra dose of sweetness for breakfast this morning, Olive picked an apricot tart and set it on the plate beside her crumpets. Then, upon consideration, she added an elderflower tart for good measure.

Today was the day of the sting operation, or The Crazy Suicidal Spying Plan as Blythe was calling it (in a bid to scare Olive off doing it) and she needed all the fortification she could get.

Arabella had arranged to meet Rupert in his rooms that evening and, since no female visitors were allowed after nine o'clock, he would sneak her in through the back gate behind the chapel. It turned out, just as Olive had thought, that such was Rupert's giant ego he hadn't even questioned why his ex-girlfriend wanted to see him again. No doubt, he imagined that she'd be trying to win him back and, at the very least, he'd get one more chance to take her to bed again.

However, while this plan was all well and good, it didn't account for how Olive would smuggle herself into Rupert's room in advance of nine o'clock to hide in his wardrobe, or under his bed, or behind his sofa – whatever place presented itself as most auspicious and least painful – since she couldn't very well ask him to sneak *her* in via the back gate. She wondered also how she would get into his room in the first place, since no doubt it'd be kept locked, and, if she managed to surmount this hurdle, how she would know when he'd be out so she wouldn't get caught creeping in.

After giving all these questions a good deal of thought, and entertaining a fair amount of ridiculous notions and impossible scenarios, Olive had finally settled upon the undeniable fact that she would have to ask Mr Bennett for help.

It was the only way.

༄

'He'll never do it,' Blythe said. 'Not in a million years.'

The three friends sat in the café eating leftovers for supper. Olive had flipped the "closed" sign on the door before confessing what she planned to do. She'd not told them until the last minute, knowing what their objections would be, but now she realised she had to. Just in case something went horribly wrong. *If* Rupert did end up killing her, she at least wanted her friends to be able to see justice done. It was too awful to imagine him getting away with *two* murders.

'He might,' Olive said, taking a thoughtful bite of a vanilla cream puff. 'If I ask very nicely. And promise him free almond croissants and pots of Earl Grey tea every morning for the rest of his life.'

Millicent laughed. 'Well, yes, that might swing the deal. But are you sure? He could lose his job over something like that.'

'No, I don't think so.' Licking cream from her fingers, Olive shook her head, unable to even contemplate such a thing. 'He's been Head Porter for nearly forty years, they'd never fire him.'

'What?' Blythe's eyes widened and she looked at Olive as if she was a certifiable idiot. 'Of course they would! How naive are you? If he was caught slipping you into a student's private room – to *spy* on him, no less – it'd be a violation of privacy, of civil rights, of…whatever. Plenty of things that could probably not only get him fired but also sent to prison or, at the very least, land him with a criminal record and render him unemployable. And no man in his sixties is going to risk his pension like that, no matter how delicious your almond croissants are.'

Millicent nodded, sadly. 'Blythe's right. Do you think the College would care about a mere porter, no matter how loyal and dedicated, if one of their students – the son of an alumni, no doubt, and probably a significant donor – kicked up a stink against him?'

'But he wouldn't be able to kick up a stink, would he,' Olive said. 'Not if he was imprisoned for murder. They wouldn't care about the word of a murderer, even if we had broken into his room and hidden there. They'd just be relieved he'd been caught. And then they'd want to disassociate themselves from him as quickly as possible. Don't you think? King's College won't want anyone to know they harboured a killer.'

'Well,' Millicent considered. 'Yes, I'm quite sure you're right about that at least. They wouldn't touch him with a bargepole if he confessed to murder. But don't forget, you don't actually know for certain that he *is* a murderer. After all' – she dropped to a whisper, not wanting to voice her dissent too loudly – 'we can't be absolutely sure that it wasn't in fact an accident.'

'What?' Olive dropped the remainder of the cream puff to her plate. 'What are you saying? The cards are never wrong, you know that!'

'Well...' Millicent ventured. 'I know, I know they've never been wrong before. But you're risking an awful lot on them being right this time. And what if they're not? What if you get into that boy's bedroom, putting George's job on the line and, quite possibly, your own safety – to say nothing of your reputation – at risk, only to discover that you, that they, were wrong?'

'That's ridiculous,' Olive snapped. 'Come on B, back me up here. You know the cards are never wrong.'

Blythe, who'd been devouring a slice of lemon cheesecake, paused a moment to look up. 'I agree with you, and I *do* believe that the poor boy was killed, but I don't necessarily think that means it's worth putting everything in jeopardy in order to prove it. What will it achieve, at the end of the day? It can't bring him back. It can't-'

'Can't bring him back?' Olive echoed. 'Can you hear yourself? I know it can't bring him back, but you can't let someone – an absolute cad and a frightful snob, by all accounts – get away with something like that. With *murder*. Can you?'

For a few moments, neither Blythe nor Millicent spoke. Then, at last, they both glanced up from their plates to exchange a silent but meaningful look. And, as so often happens with very old friends, an understanding passed between them which they mutually, but again silently, agreed that Blythe would speak their thoughts aloud.

'We think you're being cavalier and reckless,' she said. 'And we wish you'd just drop this whole regrettable business and let life return to normal. Men like Rupert Middleton, rich, powerful, influential men, have been getting away with murder, and worse, for centuries and, sadly, will continue to do so unless there's a revolution and society is forever changed. And as we all know, that's exceedingly unlikely and, probably, impossible. As Lord Acton said, "power tends to corrupt, and absolute power corrupts absolutely." So...'

'But,' Olive protested. 'But that doesn't mean we can–'

Blythe set down her fork and held up her hand. '*But*, even though we think this, you are our dearest and most beloved friend and we will always support you in everything you do–'

'No matter how crazy it might be,' Millicent finished.

Frowning, Olive looked from one to the other. Then she laughed. 'I don't know whether to be offended or touched,' she said. 'But, in the interests of friendship and justice, I'm going to go with the latter.'

'Wise decision,' Millicent said. 'Now, if you're really set on this path then I propose I come with you to talk to Geor–Mr Bennett and see if I can't persuade him to help. While Blythe stays behind to dog sit. I presume you're not planning on taking Biscuit with you?'

At the mention of her name, Biscuit, who'd been laying under the table strategically catching crumbs, looked up and barked. Olive, meanwhile, exhaled a breath she didn't realise she'd been holding.

'Thank you,' she said. 'That would be wonderful.' She reached out across the table to take her friends' hands. Tears filled her eyes. 'I'm so grateful for you both. Really and truly, you're the two most glorious blessings in my life.'

Biscuit barked again, this time in protest.

'Oh, yes.' Olive smiled. 'And you too! My silly pup. How could I ever forget you?'

'Alright then.' Millicent squeezed Olive's hand, then stood. 'Let's go. The students will be having dinner now, so it's the perfect time to sneak into a bedroom without being caught.'

Olive nodded. 'Thank you,' she said again. 'Thank you.'

'Of course,' Millicent said.

'Anytime,' Blythe said, her mouth once more full of cheesecake. 'And next time I want to break the law or do something foolishly dangerous, I don't want to hear any objection from you, alright?'

Olive giggled. 'Alright.'

'Now, you remember how to use the camera?'

Olive nodded.

'And you promise not to get hurt?'

Olive nodded again. 'I promise.'

'And you promise not to get caught?'

'I promise.'

The three of them held hands once more, then parted.

'Okay,' Olive said, trying to keep her voice steady. 'Let's go.'

Chapter Eleven

'He'll do it.' Millicent said, returning to Olive after having spent almost fifteen minutes in whispered conversation with Mr Bennett in the Porter's Lodge.

'Really?' Olive was wide-eyed. 'Are you sure? Is he sure? I don't want to–'

'He's sure,' Millicent said. 'But don't ask twice.'

For a moment, Olive forgot about the very dangerous thing she was about to do and just gazed at her friend. 'He must have really loved you.'

'Shush!' Millicent glanced back into the lodge. 'He might hear you.'

'Sorry.'

'We were very close once,' Millicent muttered. 'But that was a long time ago.'

'Oh?' Olive raised an eyebrow. 'It seems like–'

'Now is not the time,' Millicent said, shaking her head. 'Focus. George said they'll be coming out of Hall in twenty minutes, so you don't have long.'

'Yes.' Olive nodded. 'Yes, of course.'

Just as she spoke, Mr Bennett stepped out of the lodge with a heavy ring of keys in hand. He looked at Olive, his face a placid mask. 'Ready?'

It wasn't a question, for he started walking away towards the quad before Olive could answer. With one final grateful look to Millicent, she hurried after him. Keeping a few metres behind the Head Porter, Olive fixed her gaze on her shoes. Now that she was actually embarking on this escapade, her heart had started thudding so hard and her pulse racing so fast that she felt she might be about to faint. They needed to reach Rupert's room without being seen by a tutor or any other member of staff.

Mr Bennett picked up his pace. Olive followed suit.

A few minutes later, they reached the second quad and entered staircase XVI. Olive noticed a list of eight names painted in black on white as soon as they entered the stairwell. The fifth name was "Middleton". Without pause, the Head Porter mounted the stairs and, moments later alighting from the second flight he stopped and walked towards a door which bore another sign proclaiming it to be the room of the very same Middleton.

Without hesitation, Mr Bennett withdrew his keys and slid one into the lock. Olive held her breath. A second later, he pushed the door open. Olive lingered behind him and he turned to her, cocking his head towards the room.

'Thank you,' Olive mumbled. 'Thank you so–'

'I wasn't here,' Mr Bennett muttered in response. 'I wasn't here and I didn't see you.'

'Yes,' Olive said. 'Of course.'

And then, clutching her bag to her chest, and wishing her friends and Biscuit were beside her, Olive stepped into the room of Mr Rupert Middleton.

As she entered and quietly clicked the door shut behind her, Olive soon realised it wasn't one room, as she'd imagined, but a whole suite of rooms containing a bedroom, living room, bathroom and even a small balcony overlooking the quad. All in all, it was probably larger than her own flat. With a sigh, Olive quickly pulled herself together and sought out a place to hide. Somewhere she couldn't possibly be seen and somewhere from which she could make an easy escape, once Rupert fell asleep or left again.

Olive had suggested to Arabella that she try to take Rupert out once she'd extracted the confession, to enable Olive to leave more easily. But they both knew that his movements would be impossible to predict and it was equally likely that Arabella might have to make her own swift exit – should things take a turn for the worse – without him. With this in mind, Olive decided against hiding under the bed. A decision that was assisted by the strong probability that she couldn't anyway fit underneath it.

A cursory glance around the rooms ruled out most places that didn't offer a decent view of the sofa, which was where she'd instructed Arabella to sit. In the end, there was no better option than the wardrobe which, frustratingly, was already bulging with Rupert's crowded collection of suits, trousers and dozens of identical shirts. *How many white shirts does one man need?* Olive wondered as she squeezed in between a long black leather coat and a pair of yellow corduroy flares. She'd only been standing a few minutes when she felt a tickle in her nose and sneezed.

Sniffing loudly and rubbing her nose, Olive prayed that the dust wouldn't irritate her again. If she betrayed her position before Rupert had a chance to say anything, it'd all be for nothing and worse. Questions would be asked about how she'd managed to slip past the Porter's Lodge and break into the room and Olive was far from certain whether or not she could convince the authorities that she'd climbed up the drainpipe and entered through the balcony. Fortunately, he'd left the catch to the balcony window unlocked. Unfortunately, Olive was not in possession of a physique that was suggestive of serious (or even amateur) athletic ability. This was a shame. Still, if it came down to interrogation, she'd sooner rot in prison than implicate dear Mr Bennett.

After she'd set up the camera ready to record at a moment's notice – checking the batteries, clicking in the film, switching on the button inside and outside – Olive amused herself while she waited by inventing new recipes to try at the café: pear and blue cheese quiches, courgette, French bean and salmon pie, mushroom and red onion tarts…

Then she had to stop because the thoughts were making her stomach rumble – though she wasn't remotely hungry – and her mouth water. Olive worried, without reason, that a watering mouth might trigger an itchy nose. Still, it paid to be on the safe side so she changed her thoughts to focus on Biscuit and Blythe and what they might be getting up to now. But that soon made her worry that something might go wrong and she might never see them again. So Olive switched the track of her thoughts yet again to think on something truly mundane and benign: speculation over Prime Minister Edward Heath – successor to the hated egalitarian Harold Wilson – and his lack of a wife and whether or not he'd ever obtain one.

It was in this moment of nonsense that the door opened and Rupert and Arabella entered. At least, Olive assumed it must be them since she could only hear voices but not see anyone. Opening the wardrobe door a crack, she peered out into the living room to see Arabella walking towards the sofa and sitting. When Rupert followed and sat down beside her, Olive breathed an inaudible sigh of relief.

'What are you doing all the way over there?' Rupert patted a spot on the sofa beside him. 'Come here.'

Even from her hiding place across the room, Olive could see the revulsion on Arabella's face at the proposition. Rupert, used to being adored and admired all his life, fortunately remained oblivious.

Olive watched Arabella inch slowly closer to Rupert and held her breath. Even though she wasn't very keen on Arabella, Olive still felt terribly guilty to be putting the girl through this ordeal, and she prayed it wouldn't get out of hand. If it did, if Rupert tried to take advantage of the situation, Olive was primed to tumble out of the wardrobe and leap into the fray. She only hoped it wouldn't come to that. Admittedly, given Rupert's proprietorial personality, he'd probably try something on but, hopefully, it wouldn't be anything Arabella couldn't handle alone.

We have to do this, Olive reminded herself. *It's necessary. There's no other way.*

'What do you have to drink?' Arabella asked, as Rupert lifted a finger to trace the line of her face. 'Any cognac?'

'Oh, yes. Of course. What was I thinking?' Rupert stood. 'How rude of me not to offer you any libation. It's the sight of you in my bedroom, you quite took all the thoughts out of my head.'

Now Arabella smiled. 'We're not in your bedroom, Rup. Not yet.'

Olive's eyes widened. It was like witnessing the instant transformation of a caterpillar into a butterfly: the slightly nervous, disgusted girl had been suddenly replaced by a savvy, confident, seductive young woman. Olive had to give it to Arabella, she could certainly act.

'Not yet,' Rupert repeated, as he crossed the room to a small tray of bottles and glasses set atop a bookshelf. 'I like the sound of that. It's promising.'

'Don't bring me any of the cheap shit you keep for guests,' Arabella called after him. 'I'm not one of your Girton girls. I won't drink anything under ten years old.'

'Naturally.' Rupert slid aside a line of books and pulled out a bottle that'd been hidden behind them. 'I'd forgotten your penchant for the finer things.' Taking two glasses, he poured an inch of cognac into each.

'Don't be stingy,' Arabella said. 'Try to serve me fewer than two shots and I'll send you right back.'

'My, my, we are being demanding tonight, aren't we?' Rupert laughed. 'Alright, you can have mine.' He tipped the contents of one glass into the other. 'I'm already drunk on cheap Hall wine anyway. The Dean saves the best for High Table and gives the rest of us the dregs. Well, he'll have to give me the good stuff when my father visits next week, or he can kiss goodbye to the funding for that new library he's so desperate to build.'

Uncorking a nondescript bottle of red, Rupert liberally filled a new glass and brought both back to the sofa.

'Here you go, princess.' He handed Arabella the double-cognac. 'Bottoms up.'

And, with that, Rupert put his own glass to his lips and downed the entire contents in three gulps. From the wardrobe, Olive gawped at him. Arabella hadn't been wrong, it was clear that he certainly enjoyed a drink.

'Piss poor,' Rupert spat. 'For a hundred quid a bottle I'd expect better than this. Tastes like turps.'

Olive clasped her hands over her mouth to conceal the gasp that rose in her throat. *A hundred pounds?* It was more than she made in a week. She watched him saunter back to his wine collection and take up another bottle – or it might have been the same one, she couldn't tell since his back blocked her view – which he swigged without bothering to pour it first.

'Still...' Rupert wiped his mouth on his sleeve. 'It all does the same job in the end, doesn't it? I'm not fussy.'

'Really?' Arabella said playfully. 'And yet you dine on oysters and caviar and dress in silk and cashmere. If I'm a princess, then you're a prince.'

'Then perhaps we should get married,' Rupert said, as he headed back towards the sofa, stumbling on a rug before he reached it but managing to right himself before falling. 'I'd have proposed to you, you know, if you hadn't broken my heart.'

'Your *heart*?' Arabella snorted. 'You have only one fully functioning organ in your body, Rup, and it's certainly not your heart.'

'Oh, no?' Rupert giggled as he sat beside her again. 'Are you quite sure about that?' He took her free hand and brought it to his chest. 'You see? Can't you feel it? It beats only for you.'

'Only for me?' Arabella smiled. 'Gosh, I am flattered. And how many other women have you fed that line?' She leaned closer to him, so only an inch of air remained between them. 'But you forget that I gained the highest marks in History Mods last year, beating even you. Isn't that right?' She kissed his cheek, then drew back and took a sip of her cognac. 'I'm not a naïve little Fresher anymore.'

In the wardrobe, Olive gripped hold of the camera, wondering if she should start recording yet. Blythe had warned her that she could only film in short bursts – something to do with the focus or the zoom, Olive wasn't entirely certain – so she had to time it well. She wasn't sure what sort of game Arabella was playing – it didn't seem like a good idea to tease him like this if they wanted to extract a confession – but she had to trust that the girl knew what she was doing. Anyway, what other choice did she have?

Olive uncapped the camera lens, focused the viewfinder and set the focus distance before, tentatively, pressing the trigger. Instantly, the air was pierced by a sharp whirring noise that caused Rupert to spring away from Arabella as if he'd just been bitten. Olive instantly took her finger off the trigger, but it was too late.

'What's that?' He said, looking wildly around the room. 'What the hell is that noise?'

'What noise?' Arabella asked, all innocence. 'I didn't hear anything.'

'Then you're deaf, because I definitely heard something.'

'It was probably outside.'

Rupert stood. 'It didn't sound like it was outside. It sounded like it was inside.'

In the wardrobe, Olive held her breath.

'Don't be silly, Rups.' Arabella reached for him. 'You're drunk. Sit down.'

Rupert hesitated. 'I might be a little tipsy but I'm not high.'

'Are you sure?'

'Of course I'm sure.' He lingered by her side like a tiger stalking prey, ready to pounce into the room at any moment. 'I'm not hallucinating. I've not taken anything since last weekend at Tristan's house party.'

'Well, what does it matter?' Arabella persisted. 'Stop focusing on imaginary noises and start focusing on the very real woman sitting on your sofa.'

Still, Rupert hesitated, glancing all around the room. When his gaze lingered on the wardrobe, Olive thought she might faint. But, mercifully, the presence of Arabella pulled his gaze back to the sofa.

'How could I be so remiss?' Rupert took a wobbly step towards her. 'What does it matter if the building collapses atop of us, so long as we're together in each other's arms?'

Very quietly, Olive exhaled the breath she'd been holding but her pulse continued to race so fast that she had to lower the camera and lean against the back of the wardrobe to steady herself.

'Speaking of arms, I was wondering...' Arabella paused to take a long sip of cognac.

'Yes?' Rupert asked, clearly impatient to stop talking and start canoodling. 'What were you wondering?'

'I was wondering,' Arabella repeated. 'Whether or not you can still dance...'

At this, Rupert let out a guffaw of laughter. 'Can I *still* dance? What sort of question is that? Of course I can! If anything, I'm better than before. And...' He folded his arms, but still swayed a little, as if in slight danger of toppling over at any moment. 'I'm quite sure I can still sweep you off your feet.'

'Oh, really?' Arabella fixed him with her inquisitive, seductive gaze. 'Prove it.'

'What?' He frowned. 'Now?'

Olive mirrored Rupert's frown, wondering what on earth Arabella was planning with this introduction of dancing into the interrogation scene. What did she hope to achieve?

'Yes.' Arabella nodded. 'Now. And, if you can recall my favourite song, then you'll graduate tonight with a distinction.'

For a split-second Rupert looked blank and slightly panicked. Then, all at once, he laughed. 'You thought I'd forgotten?'

'No.' Arabella smiled slowly. 'I have every faith in you, Rupert Middleton.'

'Good,' he said, as he sashayed over to the corner of the room where Olive now noticed a small cabinet with a record player sitting on top. Kneeling down at the cabinet, Rupert made a show of scrolling through all the records stacked in rows until, plucking one out, he stood again.

'Let's see if your faith is justified, shall we?' Rupert said as he slipped the record from its cover and, careful only to touch the sides, placed it onto the turntable. The needle squeaked as it met the plastic and slid into the groove.

For a moment, the silence in the room was palpable as three collective breaths were held, waiting for the music to begin. And then, the familiar notes heralded the voice of Paul McCartney as he began to sing the opening lines of *Hey Jude*.

Arabella clapped. 'Yes!' Setting her glass down on the floor, she danced over to join him. 'But turn it down a little,' she said, as she slipped into his arms. 'I still want to be able to hear myself think.'

And then, at last, Olive understood. The music was to cover the noise of the Super 8 camera whirring away in the background. Although, it wouldn't work unless they were considerably closer to the wardrobe. Close enough for Olive to be able to pick up their conversation.

'Come on,' Arabella said, as he turned the music down. 'Show me those moves.'

'Oh, I'll show you my moves,' Rupert said, picking her up and swinging her around till she squealed with delight. 'I'll show you all the moves I've got.'

Olive watched in awe as Arabella subtly and expertly manoeuvred Rupert towards the wardrobe, while all the time letting him feel as if he was the one leading her. It helped, of course, that he was three sheets to the wind, but still Olive could see that here was a woman who would always get what she wanted in life, while enabling those she manipulated to believe they'd initiated the idea. Olive once more focused the camera and switched it on. This time the whirring was swallowed by the song and, though it still sounded awfully loud in Olive's ears, Rupert noticed nothing amiss. He allowed Arabella to pull him into a slow dance while she whispered in his ear. Olive couldn't hear what she was saying but, judging by Rupert's widening grin, she could guess.

'So, I heard a rumour.' Arabella raised her voice.

'Oh, yes?' Rupert held his grin. 'That I'm a fantastic lover?'

'Well, of course,' she conceded. 'Though I already know *that* first hand.'

'Right, right.' Rupert laughed. 'Of course you do, you lucky girl.'

He must be pretty drunk, Olive thought, if he'd forgotten that they'd already slept together.

In that moment, Rupert seized the opportunity to give Arabella's bottom a quick squeeze. In response she turned her head away and Olive captured her grimace on camera.

Then, the recording stopped. Inwardly, Olive cursed. She would have to wait and, if she only had a window of a few minutes to capture a recording, try to time it right.

'No, this was another rumour,' Arabella said, speaking carefully so that she could certainly be heard. 'That *you* were the one who pushed that frightful upstart off the roof.'

For a second, Rupert froze.

Quickly, Arabella placed her hand on his lapel. 'I was hoping *someone* would,' she said, smoothly. 'Nasty little cuckoo didn't belong here – I know you agree – so when I heard, I must confess, I thought it was probably you.'

Quickly, Olive pressed the trigger on the camera again so it whirred into action. She focused the lens, zooming in for a close-up on Rupert's face.

'Really?' His tone changed. 'You'd like that, would you?'

'Oh, yes,' Arabella said, as if she couldn't imagine anything more sensual. 'Very much.'

'Well...'

In that moment, Olive's nose began to itch again.

Not now, not now, not now!

She scrunched up her nose and prayed.

'Well, in that case I wish I could say I pushed him.' Rupert sighed. 'But regrettably I didn't, so I can't.'

Then, he promptly bent over and vomited on his shoes.

'Oh!' Arabella recoiled. 'Rup, that's disgusting!'

'Sorry,' he moaned, wiping his hand across his mouth. 'Sorry, I think I had a touch too much to drink.'

'I'll say,' Arabella snapped, no longer able to conceal her disgust. 'And if you think I'm cleaning up that mess, you've got another thing coming.'

Stepping quickly away from the mess, Arabella sought refuge on the sofa and Rupert stumbled after her to sit, now at a respectful distance, at the other end. As they continued to bicker, Olive stared at them through the camera lens and the grainy picture it provided, in disbelief. Then she let the camera drop to her side.

No, it couldn't be. She'd been so certain. So utterly certain that it'd been a murder and that Rupert had been the one who'd done it. She couldn't have been wrong. Worse still, the cards couldn't have been wrong. It simply wasn't possible.

Olive, feeling utterly bereft, stared hopelessly out at the room. Overwhelmed with disappointment, defeated at the final hurdle, she didn't know what to do. It had all been for nothing. Putting Mr Bennett's job at risk, putting Arabella's safety at risk, and her own. It'd all been ultimately pointless.

Rupert was now slumped over the arm of the sofa, moaning loudly while Arabella reached her own arm across the divide to gingerly patted his back with the tips of her fingers while casting surreptitious and meaningful glances towards the wardrobe. *Yes*, Olive wanted to say, *I want to get out of this damn wardrobe too.* All at once it felt like the wooden walls were closing in and she felt a scream rise in her chest. She desperately wanted to run home, curl up on her bed with Biscuit, and a plate of chocolate biscuits, and cry.

How could the cards have been wrong?!

When the endless instrumental ending of *Hey Jude* finally started to fade Olive could hear Rupert's piggy snores rising from the sofa and she breathed a long sigh of relief.

'It's alright,' Arabella called out. 'You can come out now. He sleeps like a log when he's drunk. A marching band could strike up outside and it wouldn't wake him.'

Hesitating only a moment, Olive nudged open the wardrobe door and stepped out into the room. Arabella, having abandoned Rupert on the sofa, crossed the carpet to meet her.

'I'm sorry,' Arabella said. 'I really thought he'd done it too.'

'You shouldn't be apologising to me.' Olive shook her head. 'I should be apologising to you. I dragged you into this. I put you at risk. I was just so convinced I knew the truth that I let it blind me to everything else.'

Arabella patted Olive's arm. 'Don't worry,' she said, offering a sympathetic smile. 'We're all wrong sometimes.' She winked. 'Even me.'

'You're very kind.' Olive gave her a grateful smile, no longer finding Arabella remotely obnoxious. 'And thanks so much for trying.'

Together they snuck out of Rupert's room and, under cover of night, slipped out of King's College without being seen by anyone except Mr Bennett who, while his eyebrows twitched at the unexpected sight of Arabella, pretended to notice nothing.

It wasn't until she was crossing King's Parade, heading back towards The Biscuit Tin, that Olive realised what she'd been too distracted and distressed to realise earlier.

This realisation stopped her in the middle of the road.

It was the way Rupert had said "I". With a particular emphasis, a certain inflection, that didn't simply imply that he hadn't pushed Jack because it'd been an accident, but that *he* hadn't pushed Jack because someone else *had*. The more Olive thought about it, the more convinced she was. And, just to be sure, she fished the camera out of her bag and played back the recording, right there in the street. Yes, it was clear. Rupert's tone clearly suggested that there was another culprit, another boy who'd pushed poor Jack to his death. It was unfortunate, of course, that he hadn't provided a name but still Olive dearly hoped this was enough evidence to go to the police and at least get them to postpone the inquest and interview the boys again. And since the coroner was ruling tomorrow, she couldn't afford to wait.

Olive glanced at her watch: 11.23pm.

The station would be closed and, unfortunately, she couldn't call 999 because, desperate as she was to get hold of Detective Dixon and show him the recording, it still didn't constitute an emergency. Which meant that she'd have to turn up at the station first thing in the morning.

Olive sighed. She wouldn't be sleeping tonight.

Chapter Twelve

'But that's what it *must* mean,' Olive insisted. 'Don't you see?'

She'd turned up on the doorstep of the Cambridgeshire Police Station at sunrise with Biscuit in tow. She'd had to walk because, frustratingly, her bike had somehow acquired a puncture, and was out of breath and irritable when she arrived. Olive did not like walking; fortunately Biscuit did most of her own running about whenever they went to the park. Failing that, Millicent, who loved walking so much she even took holidays to climb mountains, would take her.

Olive had then had to wait nearly an hour before a junior officer had arrived to open up. She'd persuaded him to call Detective Dixon into work early – first having tried reason and, when that failed, resorting to hysterics – and was now, after having shown him the video, trying to persuade *him* of the voracity of her claims.

'I'm not disagreeing with you Olive,' Hugo said, lowering his voice every time Olive raised hers which, though he intended it to calm her, only served to make her even more irritated. 'I see that it certainly suggests that someone else pushed him. However, I also know that suggestions and implications and the like – especially in the absence of more substantial evidence – don't tend to hold up in court.'

'But,' Olive protested. 'Can't you at least–'

'And,' Hugo continued, 'given that you obtained this video by sneaking into a private residence and hiding in a wardrobe – something I'm still very upset about, by the way, given that you put yourself, to say nothing of that girl, in an unpredictable amount of danger – it was thus acquired not only without the subject's knowledge but also while you were effectively breaking and entering, any barrister worth his salt will probably be able to suppress it and stop us from using it in prosecution so–'

'No!' Olive marched up and down the room. 'That's ridiculous! It doesn't matter *how* it was obtained, it only matters *that* it was obtained. I mean, I know you've got all those laws and rules to follow, but once you get evidence like this, surely all that is irrelevant.'

'Oh, Miss Crisp.' Detective Dixon said, sounding truly regretful and, perhaps surprisingly given his position, not in the least patronising. 'If only it worked like that. If only the legal system was concerned only with Truth and Justice, as it purports to be. However, in our pursuit of these things we must follow certain protocols and obey certain rules and, if we do not, then it doesn't matter if we're absolutely in the right, we might still lose our case. Thus, given that this video isn't a direct confession but one person merely implying that another person *might* have...'

'Might?' Olive echoed. 'Might?! Look, can't you just show it to a judge. It's on video, for goodness sake! No one can dispute it. Surely, if you showed a judge he'd agree that, if nothing else, it at least gives you grounds to open the investigation as a murder case.'

The detective gave a regretful shake of his head. 'We wouldn't be showing it to a judge unless we went to court,' he explained. 'And we can't go to court unless we have a defendant who we've charged with murder. So, you see–'

'So, then charge someone with murder!' Olive heard herself shrieking but was unable to stop. She simply couldn't believe that, after all she'd gone through, after all Arabella and Mr Bennett had gone through, it still wasn't enough. 'One of them did it. So why don't you charge them all? And then lock them up in your cells until one of them confesses?'

Detective Dixon gave Olive what he hoped was a soothing smile. 'I'm afraid that's not really how it works. We can't just go around charging people with murder willy nilly, we have to have some basis, otherwise their solicitor will simply refute the charge and, essentially, get it overturned. Otherwise we'd be violating people's civil rights and that's not–'

Unfortunately, Olive found the smile, coupled with his words, more condescending than soothing, which only served to incense her further. 'So, what are you saying? You're still going to recommend that the coroner rule Jack's death as an accident, even though you now know that it's not?'

'Why don't you sit down?' Hugo suggested, nodding at the chair. 'I could get you a cup of tea.'

'I don't want a cup of tea!' Olive shrieked again. 'I want you to take me seriously!'

As soon as he'd arrived on the scene, Detective Dixon, keen to contain and calm the hysterical state in which he'd found her, had ushered Olive into an interrogation room and tried to persuade her to sit down and take deep breaths. She had refused to do either. He'd also, for the past hour, proffered numerous cups of tea. All of which had been rejected.

'I *am* taking you seriously,' Hugo insisted. 'I believe you. I agree with you. His inflection certainly suggests that *someone* did push Mr Whitstable. But we don't have a name, nor anything concrete to go on. So, I'm afraid it's not really enough to sway the case. I'm a police officer; there are certain protocols I have to follow.'

'Protocols?!' Olive's tones reached dangerous levels of stridency, the pitch of her shriek now threatening the safety of the double-sided mirror on the wall. 'Protocols?! We now know that the poor boy was killed, on purpose, and you're harping on about protocols?!'

An unfortunate side-effect of Olive's fury was that her face puffed up like a frog and took on a purplish hue, a look which proved rather comical for whoever she was arguing with and thus served to undermine the strength of her argument. Olive herself was well aware of this but, no matter how she'd tried to combat it she could not.

Hugo, finding this look not only comical but exceedingly endearing, did his very best to swallow a smile and remain serious. 'I understand,' he said. 'Truly, I do. And given this new evidence that you've brought me I can, on that basis, at the very least bring Mr Middleton in for further questioning. The coroner's case isn't till after lunch, so we've still got time before his ruling to present more evidence. How does that sound?'

Olive folded her arms. 'I suppose that would be a start. But of course he'll just lie to you. I mean, that was the whole point of Arabella, and getting him drunk... He wouldn't have confessed otherwise. He's a heartless snob, but he's not an idiot.'

'Yes,' Hugo said. 'But the fact that he was drunk at the time is just another reason the defence could use to make the video, and everything he said on it, inadmissible in court. You see, we have to–'

'But people tell the truth when they're drunk,' Olive interrupted. 'Everyone knows that. "In vino veritas" and all that. So surely that stands in our favour?'

'I'm afraid not, Miss Crisp. If a subject was not "of sound mind" when he said something then–'

'What?!' Olive threw up her hands. 'This is ridiculous! You can interrogate him all you want, but he won't tell *you* what he told Arabella. He didn't the first time you questioned him, so why would he now?'

'Yes,' Hugo conceded. 'I appreciate that it's unlikely he'll just give up the name of whoever did this, but you need to trust me. I've been doing this a long time, I'm no idiot either. I have my ways, my techniques to encourage people to let their guard down and tell me the truth...'

'Your techniques?' Olive repeated. For a moment she was distracted by the word, no longer thinking about crimes and interrogations, but about how Hugo talked to *her*. 'I'm not sure...'

'Oh, no.' Hugo felt a blush rising to his own cheeks. 'Don't worry! I don't, I'm not... I don't go around using my "techniques" in everyday life, only with suspects. I'm perfectly normal with other people.'

Olive breathed a sigh of relief. 'Well, good. I don't want you using any of your special tricks to get me to tell the truth.'

At this, a look of curiosity slipped onto his face and he pushed back his chair and stood. 'Why not?' Hugo asked, as he stepped towards her. 'Why wouldn't you want to tell me the truth?'

With a nervous laugh, Olive stepped back. 'No reason. It's just... We all have thoughts...' She felt herself start to sweat, as if she was suddenly the one being interrogated. 'Thoughts that we want to keep private.'

Slowly, Hugo smiled. It was a knowing, secret smile. And, all at once, Olive believed that he *could* see into her mind and knew exactly what she was thinking. Her pulse started to race and her heart to thud in her chest and she glanced around for something to hold onto to steady herself. But the only thing within reach was Hugo.

He continued smiling and now that they were only inches apart again, Olive was again struck by the notion that he might be about to kiss her. She held her breath.

And then, there was a knock at the door.

Hugo leapt back from Olive as if he'd just been burned and she did the same.

The door opened and a junior officer, the very one Olive had become hysterical with that morning, poked his head into the room. At the sight of Olive he flinched slightly and averted his eyes to focus on Hugo.

'I'm terribly sorry to bother you, Detective,' he said. 'But you're needed at the front desk. Urgent phone call. Judge Abernathy. I'm afraid he's refusing to wait.'

'Yes, yes, of course.' Hugo nodded. 'I'll be right there.'

'Thank you.' The junior officer extracted himself from the room and the door closed again behind him. Hugo turned back to Olive.

'Sorry, I've got to go.'

'Yes, of course.'

'I'll visit Mr Middleton this morning, first thing.'

'But you won't show him the video, will you? I mean, if it's not in court, by the sounds of what you say, right now I think it'd only make things worse.'

'Don't worry,' Hugo said. 'I'll be discreet. And hopefully none of that will be necessary. Just leave me to work my magic.'

Olive gave him a wry smile. 'Your techniques.'

'Indeed.' He returned it. 'My *techniques*.'

Chapter Thirteen

Olive stood behind the café counter staring at the clock. Biscuit, who lay under the table closest to the counter, also kept glancing up at the clock clearly wondering what her mistress was so preoccupied by. Her ancestors assisted by keeping out the more obnoxious customers – including several groups of strident Etonians and the Dean of King's College himself, who rattled the jammed door so vigorously that he nearly broke the handle before giving up and seeking substandard treats elsewhere. Olive served the other customers without engaging as enthusiastically as she usually did and, whenever the café was empty, she reached for something to nibble on. It didn't really matter what: Bakewell tarts, almond pastries, vanilla cream puffs, lemon chiffon cakes and lavender-sugar biscuits... She simply needed the distraction of delicious food to take the edge off the dreadful tension of waiting.

At eleven o'clock, the bell above the door chimed, the door swung open – helped by the gentle tug of a ghostly hand – and Blythe bustled in. Olive didn't need to check the clock, though she still did so, for her friend appeared at the same time every morning without fail for a "little morsel" of something sweet to enjoy with a cup of tea for her elevenses. "Like Winnie the Pooh", she always said if ever one of her own customers – objecting to being momentarily abandoned – queried her routine.

'What'll it be today, B?' Olive, who'd been leaning on the counter contemplating her own next "little morsel", straightened. 'I can recommend the apple flapjacks; they've come out particularly well today. If I do say so myself.' She rubbed her eyes. 'I knew I wouldn't sleep last night, so I just stayed up baking.'

'Two of those then please,' Blythe said. 'And a cup of your finest.'

Olive nodded and, after slipping four slices of apple flapjacks onto a plate, turned to flick on the kettle for a pot of tea.

'Did he say he'd come to the café with any news?' Blythe asked as she bit into one of the flapjacks. She was never able to wait for the tea to brew or even the kettle to boil. 'Gosh, you're right, these are utterly delicious.'

'I don't know,' Olive admitted. 'He didn't say. I'm guessing he'll probably call, but he might pop by. It'll depend how busy he is, or if he had any luck getting anything out of him...'

Blythe nodded thoughtfully. She'd been waiting in the café last night, along with Millicent, anxious for news and worried that something might have gone wrong. When Olive had finally arrived – safe and sound – and told them everything they'd both been incredibly relieved. And now, delighted that the cards and Olive's instincts had been vindicated, they were as eager as she was to see that justice was done.

The kettle whistled and Olive set about filling the tea pot with Earl Grey leaves and bringing it, along with cups and saucers, to the table where Biscuit was keeping guard. Blythe followed, bringing the plate of apple flapjacks – now only three remaining – and setting them down before pulling out a chair.

'Do you still think there's time?' She asked, taking her second tart as Olive poured the tea.

Olive frowned. 'Time for what?'

Blythe shrugged, as if the answer was self-evident. 'To meet a man, to settle down and have children...'

'I don't know,' Olive admitted. 'I hope so. I mean, I'm sure you'll get married, if only you'll find someone worthy of you. But I'm starting to think I might never have a baby. Forty-one is no spring chicken, after all.'

'Don't be silly.' Blythe patted Olive's hand. 'My grandmother had her last baby at forty-eight. And that was back in the last century! You've still got plenty of time.'

'Her last?' Olive took a sip of tea. 'I've not even had my first. And perhaps I just can't. Not every woman can.'

Blythe shook her head. 'I don't believe it.' She swallowed the final bite of her custard tart and whetted her finger to pick up the remaining crumbs of pastry. 'But, are you still so certain you don't want a husband to go with that baby?'

Olive hesitated.

She always told her friends everything, they all did. Every secret thought, every embarrassing event, every joy, every sorrow. And yet. She hadn't told them what had been going on between her and Hugo. There had always been a mild frisson between them, ever since he'd transferred to the Cambridge constabulary from Ely last year, which was why Millicent and Blythe loved to tease her about it. But lately, unless she was imagining it, this frisson had escalated to a flirtation which intensified every time they met. And, even if she was imagining *that*, still she couldn't deny her own feelings for him which were certainly intensifying daily.

'No.' She shook her head. 'Not a husband, never.'

Blythe raised an eyebrow, but Olive was, at least, certain on this point.

'The Crisp women have done very well without husbands for three hundred years,' she said. 'And, unless and until the laws change to give us greater authority and control over our bodies, children and property, then I hope no Crisp woman ever will.'

'You're so cynical,' Blythe said. 'You sound like Millicent. We're not in our grandmother's times anymore, you know.'

'Oh, no?' Olive raised an eyebrow. 'And given that women's work, raising a family and tending a house, is unpaid is she not left homeless and abandoned when divorced?'[1]

Blythe sighed, unable to deny it.

'And were you not refused a drink at *The Mitre* last month because you were unaccompanied by a male companion?'[2]

Blythe scowled.

'And can a woman still be sacked for falling pregnant?'[3]

Blythe grunted.

Olive folded her arms. 'I rest my case.'

Blythe's reply was lost on them both because, in that moment, the bell above the door chimed and a girl stepped inside. As she approached the counter, Olive stood, brushing her hands on her apron and checking for crumbs, then hurried over to serve her. She was standing behind the counter just as the girl reached it.

'Good morning,' Olive said. 'What would you...?'

She trailed off, gazing at the girl who blinked rapidly back at her. And all at once she understood that this customer hadn't come to the café for cakes.

'You've come to tell me your secret?'

The girl nodded.

'Are you sure you're ready?' Olive glanced at the clock: almost eleven thirty. She still had an hour or so before the inquest. She prayed the girl would say yes.

After a brief hesitation, the girl nodded again.

'Good.' Olive tried not to sound too relieved. 'Then let's sit down.'

1. This was improved somewhat by the Matrimonial Proceedings & Property Act passed on May 29th, 1970. But married women in the UK still had a long way to go...

2. Astonishingly, it wasn't made illegal for a woman to be refused a drink on these grounds until 1982.

3. This only became illegal in 1975. It was also common practice to terminate a woman's employment upon marriage. Alas, in reality there was usually a significant gap between the law and common practice.

Chapter Fourteen

'I'm Grace,' the girl said timidly. 'Jack was my best friend.' She paused, taking a deep breath before she carried on. 'We… we spent every day together, we told each other everything… We weren't in love, not like that. Jack didn't…' She trailed off before picking up her thread again. 'But we loved each other deeply.'

'I understand.' Olive nodded. 'I have two friends I love like family. We always meet for breakfast, and often dinner too. And I tell them everything.' As she spoke, Olive thought guiltily of what she hadn't told them about her growing feelings for Hugo. 'Well, anyway, please go on.'

'So…' Grace stared at her hands, fiddling with the embroidered edge of the tablecloth.

Blythe had politely made herself scarce as soon as she'd recognised the girl and even Biscuit had retreated to sit beneath a corner table in the café and keep an eye on the door, ready to jump up in case a customer dared to enter.

'When I was… hurt,' Grace found her voice again. 'Jack was the first person – the only person – I told.'

'Yes,' Olive said, softly. 'I see.'

And she did see. For, although Grace hadn't yet told her everything, or indeed much of anything, Olive knew what she was going to say. Perhaps it was because she'd just been talking about that very topic with Blythe, or perhaps she really had inherited a soupçon of the psychic gene rumoured to run through her matriarchal lineage, but either way Olive was quite certain what had happened to poor Grace.

She waited for Grace to find the courage to go on but the girl fiddled with her glasses, adjusting them, pushing them back on her nose, then tugging on her plaits. Olive noticed that the girl's nails were bitten down and bleeding and she deeply suspected that, if she looked, she'd find self-inflicted scars somewhere on her skin. Olive reached for Grace's hand, but the girl pulled away.

'Would you like a hot drink?' Olive asked. 'Or something to eat?'

The girl, thin as a whippet, looked as if she hadn't eaten in days. Weeks. Not, probably, since the dreadful event had occurred.

'No, thank you,' she mumbled, shaking her head.

Olive watched the girl's plaits swing back and forth and felt her heart contract. Grace must be eighteen or nineteen, she thought, but she didn't look a day over twelve. Either way, she could easily have been Olive's daughter and that fact made Olive want to cry – even more than she already did.

'I'm sorry,' Olive mumbled, blinking away tears. 'I'm so sorry for what happened to you.'

Now, at last, Grace looked up to meet Olive's gaze and Olive saw that the girl's eyes were also brimming with tears.

'I-it was my fault,' she stuttered. 'I went to his r-room. After hours, after I'd seen Jack…' She took a deep breath. 'And…'

'You don't have to explain,' Olive whispered. 'Don't say anything if you don't want to. Just tell me his name. And I'll do the rest.'

But Grace wasn't listening. She had, it seemed, returned to the past and was now lost in her memories and unreachable.

'H-he told me afterwards that I'd led him on,' she whispered. 'That I was asking for it. An innocent girl, he said, d-doesn't go to a boy's room at night.' A single tear slid down her cheek, quickly followed by another. 'But I-I *was* innocent, I was…'

'You still are.' Quietly pushing her chair back, Olive stood and stepped gently over to Grace. She hoped she wouldn't startle the girl, but she simply couldn't sit and watch someone in so much pain without reaching out to hold her. 'It wasn't your fault,' Olive said softly, slipping her arm tenderly over Grace's shoulder. 'It was never your fault.'

At Olive's touch, as if she'd pressed an invisible button, Grace burst into tears. She sobbed and sobbed, while Olive held her and prayed that no one would come into the shop till Grace had calmed. But she knew she needed to cry, for the trauma of the violence and the grief of the loss. The poor dear girl had suffered immeasurably in the past few weeks and Olive wanted nothing more now than to share the burden of that trauma in the hopes that it might help lift Grace's pain just a little.

Once or twice, the bell above the door chimed, but whoever opened the door quickly closed it again as soon as Biscuit sprang up and yapped them away. Mercifully, Grace seemed oblivious to either the intrusion or the noise. Olive, mindful of the ticking clock, kept glancing at the wall. Desperate to call Hugo and tell him everything before it was too late. It was half past eleven. She held

Grace's shoulders, eyes fixed on the big hand of the clock as it slowly made its way towards the highest point.

At three minutes before midday Grace's sobs slowed, till they ceased and she finally fell silent. Then she spoke, her voice a whisper.

'Buckingham.' The words were low but clear. 'His name is Charles Buckingham.'

Chapter Fifteen

Olive didn't wait for Detective Dixon to come to her, she went to him. After Grace had spoken those two words, she had wiped her eyes, stood and turned to walk out of the café. Olive did not call after her, there was no need. She knew where to find her when the time came for testimonies and all that, and first she needed to find Hugo. He'd said that the inquest would be held after lunch and it was now just gone twelve thirty so, hopefully, there was still time.

First, Olive called the station. But the officer on duty, the very same Constable Cooper she'd encountered that morning, had fobbed her off, saying that the detective was engaged in important business and couldn't be disturbed. No doubt interrogating Rupert Middleton, Olive thought, with whom he was probably making very little progress.

Which meant there was only one thing for it. She would have to go in person. She would have to run.

'Wait here for me, Biscuit,' she instructed her spaniel. 'I'm afraid they won't allow dogs at the station. Urgent crime-solving business. I won't be long; the ghosts will keep you company.'

Biscuit barked her assent, Olive blew her a kiss, flipped over the "closed" sign, locked the door and started to run.

Now, Olive was not a runner. She wasn't a jogger either, nor even much of a walker.[1] Occasionally, she hurried to the post-box in order to catch the postman but even that minimal exertion always left her panting and sweating in a most unladylike manner. Thus, as a general rule, she gave exercise of all kinds a wide berth.

Now, however, Olive ran.

She ran down Bene't street, past the Guildhall, pausing at the corner to gulp air before plunging on again. Stumbling along the next street, stopping several times to lean against the brick walls of the Corn Exchange to stop from passing out, then pushing on till she reached Downing Street and almost crawled across to the other side of the street to collapse on the low wall flanking the Sedgwick Museum. When, at last, Olive reached Parker's Piece she dropped to her knees on the grass and cried, while desperately trying to slow her breathing, suppressing the urge to vomit.

Olive tackled the final two hundred metres like a person rounding out the last mile of a hundred mile marathon: wheezing, spluttering, stumbling and dribbling till at last she reached the doors of the Cambridge Police Station, flung herself against them and then, gaining entry into the hallowed ground, collapsed, face-planting onto the carpet.

The officer standing behind the front desk – Constable Cooper – removed his helmet and set it down carefully beside his cup of tea before hurrying to her aid.

'Madame? Are you alright? What's wrong? Please...'

With great effort of will, Olive rolled over then pulled herself onto her elbows to squint up into the face of Constable Cooper, who she'd scared with her hysterical demands to see Detective Dixon. Upon recognising her in turn, Constable Cooper flinched violently and quickly scuttled back to his original position behind the front desk looking decidedly shaken.

'I'm calling you an ambulance,' he declared, already dialling. 'You *must* leave. You, you need help.'

Olive shook her head wildly, trying to protest, but she couldn't catch her breath.

'Yes?' Ignoring her, Constable Cooper spoke into the phone. 'Ambulance please. Yes. 39 Parkside, CB1 1JG. I'm calling from the Police Station. We have a woman here who's collapsed. No, I don't know. Yes. She came off the street.' He lowered his voice, cupping his hand over the mouthpiece. 'She seems to be on drugs and drunk, probably a vagrant. I'm not certain. But yes, straightaway please.'

'Stop!' Olive finally found her breath. 'I-I'm not drunk, I j-just ran all the w-way across town.' Gripping onto the edge of the front desk, legs shaking, she slowly pulled herself up. 'I-I need to see D-Detective Dixon, it's an e-emergency.'

Constable Cooper shook his head. 'No, no. You cannot see him. As I already told you over the phone, he's engaged in a very important matter and cannot be disturbed. His instructions were most insistent.' Realising that the emergency operator was still on the line, Constable Cooper muttered inaudibly into the phone and set it back, a little briskly, into its cradle.

'Sorry,' Olive said, regaining control of her legs again and marching towards the door separating the entrance room from the main building. 'But I must.'

'No,' Constable Cooper hurried in front to block her way. Reaching the door first he folded his meaty arms across the considerable bulk of his chest and stood immoveable. 'I will not allow it.'

'Let me in!' Olive cried, a little embarrassed to be making such a scene again. But if she had to play the hysterical woman card again, she would. 'Let me in!'

'No!' Constable Cooper, deciding in his desperation to match like with like, shrieked back. 'No! I will not!'

'Let me in!'

'No!'

Several minutes of further back-and-forth shrieking ensued before, at last, another police officer burst in from behind the doors to break up the melee.

'What on earth is going on here?' He demanded. 'I have never... Constable, why in all Christendom are you behaving in such a hysterical manner? I expect such behaviour from the public' – he cast a derisive eye over Olive – 'but not an officer of the law. Explain yourself.'

Looking sheepish, Constable Cooper dropped his gaze to the floor. 'Sorry, Sir. She was insisting on seeing Detective Dixon, Sir. I was attempting to enforce protocol.'

Protocol. That word again. Olive bristled.

'I must see Detective Dixon immediately,' she said, forcing herself to remain calm. 'It's a matter of absolute urgency and the utmost importance. Any delay could result in a...' – she scrambled in her brain for the correct term – 'serious miscarriage of justice.'

But this officer, clearly used to dealing with the deranged and demented, remained unruffled. 'I'm afraid that is out of the question, Mrs...'

'*Miss*,' Olive corrected. 'Miss Crisp. I'm the owner of The Biscuit Tin and an, um, good friend of Detective Dixon's and when I tell him that–'

'Miss Crisp?' the officer's tone shifted instantly. 'Well, of course. Why didn't you say so? We are all great fans of your café, none more so than Detective Dixon. And I know he'll want to see you as soon as he's done.' He nodded sharply at Constable Cooper. 'Go to the staffroom and make Miss Crisp a cup of tea. And bring the best biscuits, not the garibaldis, the fancy ones we save for the Superintendent.'

With a single nod, Constable Cooper scampered off, tail between his legs.

'Now, I'm sure this has all been a misunderstanding, Miss Crisp,' the senior officer said as he ushered her towards the chair behind the desk. 'Why don't you take a seat and I'll–'

Not waiting to hear the end of his sentence, Olive seized her opportunity to make a dash for it and, slipping out of his guiding hand, plunged towards the doors and nose-dived through into the other side. Not pausing a moment to see if she was being followed, Olive hurtled along the corridor calling "Detective Dixon!"

She hadn't reached halfway down when a door opened and he stepped out.

'Miss Crisp!' He exclaimed, as Olive careened into him. 'Whatever are you doing here?'

'Sorry, I'm sorry.' Olive gathered herself and patted him down, checking for wounds. 'Are you–? You're fine, right? I didn't see you there...'

'Nor I you, Miss Crisp.' He closed the door behind him. 'Tell me, why exactly are you here?'

'I have information,' Olive said, dropping her voice to a whisper. 'A breakthrough. I–'

'Wait!' The senior officer burst through the doors after Olive, just as Constable Cooper emerged from the staff room to see what all the hullabaloo was about. 'I'm sorry, Sir.' He said, now addressing his superior officer. 'I tried to stop her but she - she wouldn't be stopped. I - would you like me to put her in a cell? I can–'

'No, no.' Detective Dixon dismissed both men with a wave of his hand. 'I can take it from here. Return to your posts.'

Nodding, they both retreated, relieved to be dismissed, to be freed from the unfolding drama.

'Apologies.' He returned to Olive. 'Now, what were you saying?'

'I think,' Olive began. 'That's to say, I know who pushed Jack from the roof.'

Detective Dixon frowned and Olive tried not to focus too hard on his face, the laughter lines around his intense blue eyes, the twitch of his full lips, the cut of his jaw...

'You were right,' he said. 'Mr Middleton is sticking to his story. He claims that Mr Witstable fell and he assures me that the other five members of the Night Climbers will maintain the very same. I employed all of my techniques but I'm afraid he remained immune to my charms.' He sighed. 'I'm thinking it might be time to show him the video; that's what I was just coming to call you about. I know it'll have significant repercussions but given that it may also force him to change his testimony, I believe it could be worth it.'

Olive regarded Hugo quizzically. 'For someone who was quite convinced this morning that Rupert was innocent and Jack's death accidental, you've certainly changed your tune.'

'Yes.' Hugo nodded. 'Because the first time I questioned him I was, foolishly, assuming his innocence and so had my radar – my internal lie detector – turned off. This time it was fully switched on and when that's the case, I know when someone's lying to me. And Mr Middleton is definitely lying to me.'

Olive narrowed her eyes, momentarily forgetting her own news. 'But why? Why did you assume that he was innocent? I thought the police were always primed for guilt and crime.'

'Yes, I suppose we should be,' Hugo admitted. 'Yet, sadly, we're also only human and often flawed, susceptible sometimes to being persuaded by an convincing authority into-'

'What authority?' Olive interrupted. 'Who–?'

But she in turn was interrupted by the door to the interrogation room opening and the infuriated face of Rupert Middleton poking out into the hallway.

'What the hell's going on?' He snapped. 'I know my rights. You can't hold me here without charge. I've said all I'm going to say and now, unless you want me to call my father's solicitor, I'm leaving.'

'Wait.'

It was not Detective Dixon who spoke but, to her own surprise, Olive.

'What?' Rupert scowled. 'Who the hell are you?'

'Watch it,' Hugo warned. 'That is not how you address a lady.'

But Rupert's scowl only deepened. 'And she's no lady. Nor a police officer, so I don't have to listen to anything she says.' He pushed past Olive. 'And you've got no cause to keep me here, Detective. So I'm going.'

'Wait!' Olive called, as she watched him marching away. 'I know what Charles did!'

Rupert stopped.

'That's right,' Olive said. 'I know what he did to Grace and I know that she told Jack and I know that Jack was going to tell the police, to tell everyone, and that's why Charles pushed him.'

For a moment, Rupert simply stood with his back to them, still facing the exit. Olive held her breath, waiting, hoping that she'd got it right, that she'd said what was needed, that she'd aimed the bullet and hit the bull's eye.

'You know nothing of the sort.' Rupert turned slowly to face them. 'You don't know what the hell you're talking about.'

'Is this true?' Hugo muttered to her. 'Are you quite certain?'

'Yes.' Olive nodded. 'Grace came to see me. She told me everything.'

'She did not.' Rupert spat the words. 'And if she did, she's a lying little bitch.'

'And why?' Olive asked. 'Why would she lie?'

Rupert shrugged. 'How should I know? For attention. For revenge. I expect she loved him and he broke her heart. He does that a lot. But why do I care?'

'You should care.' Detective Dixon stepped forward. 'You should care because now both your necks are on the line.'

Olive glanced from Hugo to Rupert and back. She wasn't entirely certain what was unfolding now, but she knew enough, trusted Hugo enough, not to interrupt.

'Oh yes?' Rupert said loftily. 'And how's that?'

'Because you might not believe Miss Crisp, but I do. And when I interrogate this Charles fellow, my guess is that he'll deny it – just like you – but he'll also have no way of knowing that you didn't turn on him, that you didn't break the pact and betray his secret and confess to what he did.'

'Don't be ridiculous,' Rupert snapped. 'Why would he think that?'

'Because that's what I'll tell him.'

Hugo stepped forward and Rupert stepped back.

'And I'll tell him you're lying.'

Hugo shook his head. 'But you won't be able to, Mr Middleton, because I'll have you both in separate interrogation rooms and I'll keep you there until one of you turns on the other. Do you trust him not to do that?' He stepped forward once more. 'Do you think your dear friend, your comrade in arms, would stay loyal to you with his own life on the line?' Hugo put his finger to his lips, as if considering. 'If you're both threatened with prosecution, which one of you will betray the other first, I wonder...?'

'That's absurd.' Rupert tried to step back again but he was now pressed against the wall. 'Why would *I* do it? What's my motive? Charles was the one who screwed that fag's girlfriend – I didn't go anywhere near her.'

'Ah.' Detective Dixon raised an eyebrow. 'So you *did* know.'

Rupert shrugged. 'So what if I did? You still can't prove she wasn't gagging for it. You've got nothing to–'

'Oh no, you're quite wrong there,' Hugo persisted. 'I've got everything I need. Enough to put you back in that room and keep you there till I can round up this nasty little friend of yours and tell him what you just told me.'

Rupert lifted his chin. 'I'll deny it. It's your word against mine. And my father–'

'True enough,' Hugo cut him off. 'But what about your word against your friend's? If this Charles fellow insists that *you* did it, what defence will you have? And I'm guessing that *his* father is pretty hot stuff too. Right?'

Rupert opened his mouth but said nothing.

'So...' Detective Dixon leaned forward, pushing his face towards Rupert's, till there was only a whisper of air between them. 'What do you say? Given that you didn't do it and he did, don't you think it'd be best to make a statement against him, before I give him the chance to do the same against you?'

'You can't do that,' Rupert protested. 'You're not allowed. That's illegal. It's – you wouldn't.'

'Oh, no?' Detective Dixon dropped his voice to a whisper. 'Watch me.'

1. Cycling was Olive's preferred mode of transport, affording as it did a modicum of effort and dignity of person. But, unfortunately, she'd had a flat tire for several days now and hadn't, being too distracted by current events, yet taken it to be fixed. She'd never learned to drive, both because the notion made her nervous and because she couldn't afford to run a car. Besides, Cambridge was virtually a village and Olive could get wherever she wished to go by bicycle.

Chapter Sixteen

'Would you have done it?' Olive asked. 'Really?'

Hugo gave her a wry smile. 'Of course not,' he said. 'That'd be immoral, and I like to think I'd never stoop that low. But he didn't know that, did he?'

Olive grinned back. 'Nice technique.'

'I told you so.' Hugo winked. 'I have my ways.'

'Yes,' Olive said. 'You certainly do.'

'And you,' – he doffed an invisible cap to her in deference – 'have rather impressive techniques of your own.'

'Why thank you.'

'In fact, if you wanted a career in law enforcement, I'd hire you in a heartbeat.'

'Is that why you're letting me come along now? You're preparing me for a role as a female police officer?' Olive asked. 'I can't say as I've seen one of those before.'

'They aren't common,' Hugo admitted. 'But they're becoming more so. The Police Force is an archaic and ancient institution and, like all archaic and ancient institutions, is still set very much in the past. Rather like this institution here,' – he nodded up at King's College – 'although I believe they even admitted their first female fellow two years ago. So progress is being made.'

'Oh, yes.' Olive laughed. 'Such great progress.'

'Slow to be sure,' Hugo said. 'But better than nothing is the best that can be said about it, I suppose.'

'Yes,' Olive agreed. 'I suppose so.'

They crossed King's Parade and, when they reached the college, the Junior Porter opened the gate without being asked. Detective Dixon stepped inside first, followed closely by Olive.

'I've dispatched Constables Smith and Cooper to bring Mr Buckingham into the station,' he said as they entered the Porter's Lodge. 'I've got someone else I need to visit first.'

'Good afternoon, Miss Crisp.' Mr Bennett came out of the lodge to greet her. 'To what do we owe the pleasure of your visit?'

'I brought you these.' Olive proffered a box. 'Four of the freshest and most delicious almond croissants. And I'll be bringing you the very same every day till you retire.'

Mr Bennett beamed. 'A true kindness.' He put his hand to his chest. 'What can I say but thank you?'

Olive smiled. 'One good turn and all that. And thank *you*.'

'I'm sure I don't know what you're thanking me for, Miss Crisp,' he said. 'Or what I've done to deserve it. But I'd be an unmitigated fool to say no to such an offer.'

Olive nodded, honouring their silent pact that last night had never happened. She could hardly believe it had only been the night before that she'd been hiding in Rupert's wardrobe. So much had happened since.

'Would you wait here for me?' Detective Dixon asked. 'I need to pay a quick visit to the Dean before I return to the station and charge Mr Buckingham. I won't be long.'

'Of course,' Olive said. 'I'll wait with Mr Bennett. I have a few questions about his youth and a certain Miss Millicent Burrows that he can politely decline to answer.'

'Alright then,' Hugo said, sounding slightly perplexed. 'I'll be back soon.'

Olive smiled again, slipping her arm through Mr Bennett's. 'Take your time.' She patted his arm. 'I've been meaning to ask if I might call you George?'

'If you keep bringing me these pastries,' he said with a wink. 'You can call me anything you wish.'

∽

Detective Dixon entered the Dean's offices without knocking. He'd strode nearly halfway across the room – a sumptuous suite of Persian rugs and mahogany antiques upholstered in leather – before the Dean looked up from the papers spread across his vast oak desk.

'Excuse me!' The Dean stood. 'Just who are you and what do you think you're doing barging in like this?'

'You don't recognise me?' Hugo smiled. 'I'd have thought that lying to an officer of the law might have had more of an impact on your conscience. But then perhaps it's something you've done so often that you don't even register it anymore.'

The Dean folded his arms. He wore a tweed suit, scholar's robes and the silver sheen to his tie intentionally brought out the silver in his thick hair. The whole ostentatious effect perfectly brought together by the diamond flashing in his gold tie-pin. 'I'm sure I don't know what you're talking about and, since you've not been invited, I'll kindly ask you to leave.'

But the detective shook his head. 'You knew, didn't you?'

The Dean frowned. 'Knew what?'

'That one of those boys pushed Jack Witstable off the roof.' Detective Dixon sized up the Dean. 'You probably knew which one and you might even have known why, but then I don't suppose the motive bothered you too much, did it? Only the cover-up.' He sighed. 'I should have realised at the time. Their stories were all too straight, too neat. But it wasn't until I heard about the Loki and Pan Society and their penchant for stealing diamonds, then saw Mr Middleton wearing the very same tie-pin to dinner that you're wearing now.'

Without thinking, the Dean's hand went to his throat. 'That's hardly evidence,' he said quickly. 'Merely coincidence.'

'Perhaps,' the detective conceded. 'But I'm betting that every one of those boys owns one too and then I think "mere coincidence" will be a little harder to claim, don't you?'

'Get out.' The Dean's tone was bitter, his mouth a thin line. 'Get out now.'

'When I interviewed you first, you'd seduced me with all this' – Hugo swept his hand to encompass the room, the building, the college – 'your authority, your dignity, your distinction. And I let it fool me into thinking that with it came morality, virtue, decency... But you only behave like true gentlemen with each other, don't you? Shaking hands and patting backs while standing on the heads of those like poor Jack Witstable.'

'What rot,' the Dean said. 'What ridiculous nonsense. How dare you come in here spouting these wild accusations which have absolutely no basis in fact and–'

'The boy is going to confess,' the detective said. 'I've got evidence that will crack apart their conspiracy of silence and lies. And when he does, I'll make damn sure that he implicates you into the bargain. And I don't think the other parents and governors will be too understanding about it, not once–'

'Understanding?' The Dean spat out the word, for the first time looking ruffled, his poise shaken. 'Understanding? Who do you think instigates these matters, who do you think insists and expects me to deal with these unfortunate situations? You think these alumni make massive donations out of the goodness of their hearts? It comes with strings. Money always comes with strings. And I... I am merely the puppet.'

Hugo held the man's gaze for a moment, impressed, despite himself, by the eloquence of the defence. Then he smiled. 'Nice try. And while that might work with the governors, I'm afraid it won't stand up in court.'

Chapter Seventeen

OLIVE WAS STILL STANDING with George, formerly known as Mr Bennett, when she saw Charles Buckingham for the first time. He had his head down, so she could hardly see his handsome, arrogant face, and his arms behind his back and he walked between the two police officers escorting him along the path. Olive wanted to say something, something significant and meaningful, something that would make him regret what he'd done to Grace, to Jack. But she couldn't think of anything. She had no words for such cruelty. The Head Porter, so used to greeting every student as they came and went, opened his mouth – the "Sir" hovering on his lips – then closed it again.

And so, Mr Buckingham walked out of King's College for the final time, without acknowledgement. Ignored, disregarded, demeaned. Just as he had done to those he'd hurt so dreadfully. And that, for now, was something.

The rest was to come.

Chapter Eighteen

'I STILL WISH YOU hadn't put yourself at such risk,' Hugo said. 'Hiding in his wardrobe! What were you thinking? What if he *had* been the killer? He might have killed you too!'

Olive laughed. 'Yes, it was a little rash, I'll admit.'

'A little?'

She smiled. 'I promise I'll be more careful next time.'

Hugo raised an eyebrow. 'Next time?'

Olive laughed again. 'Why do you keep repeating everything I say?'

'Because,' Hugo clarified. 'I'm incredulous.'

They were walking along King's Parade towards The Biscuit Tin. They were walking rather more slowly than was warranted by the fact that the detective was needed back at the station to question a murder suspect and the café owner was needed back at the café to serve a queue of waiting customers. Still, they dawdled like two school sweethearts reluctant to leave each other's company.

'Well, if you're planning on helping me – unofficially – solve more crimes,' Hugo said. 'Then you might want to hire someone to help you in the café, otherwise you'll have plenty of disappointed customers on your hands.'

'Yes,' Olive agreed. 'I've been thinking about that too and I've got the perfect person in mind. I just need to ask.'

'Oh, yes?'

Olive smiled. 'You'll just have to wait and see. Do you fancy popping over now? I've got coffee and Bakewell tarts…'

Hugo hesitated and Olive wondered, as he did so, whether or not the café would welcome him or not. Would her ancestors sense that her heart was in jeopardy and shut him out? Olive thought of her mother and grimaced.

'Actually, I should probably get along,' Olive said quickly, as they reached the corner that turned onto Bene't Street. 'People to feed and all that...'

Hugo nodded, though he looked disappointed. 'Yes, I should go too,' he conceded. 'People to interrogate and all that...'

Olive nodded.

Hugo nodded again.

'Well, then...'

'Well, then...'

Hugo looked at Olive.

Olive glanced down at the pavement.

'Perhaps...' Hugo began. 'Perhaps I'll be passing by tomorrow and I could pop in for a cup of tea and a slice of something sweet.'

'I'd like that.' Olive gave him a slow smile, crossing her fingers that he'd have no trouble opening the door. 'I'll be there.'

Chapter Nineteen

When Olive arrived at the café, Millicent and Blythe were waiting outside. Upon seeing her, they exploded with delighted relief. Still locked inside the shop, Biscuit started barking wildly, wanting to join the fray. Olive's friends pulled her into a great big hug.

'You're here!' Millicent exclaimed. 'Thank goodness for that.'

'Oh, Olive!' Blythe cried. 'Where on earth have you been? We were just about to call the police.'

Olive laughed. 'Well then you would've found me, because that's where I've been.'

'You have?'

'What happened?'

Fumbling for her keys, Olive opened the door to let Biscuit bound out.

'Good girl,' she said. 'Well done for waiting for me so well – I think you deserve a buttermilk blueberry scone, don't you?'

Biscuit yapped with approval, dancing around everyone's legs as they tumbled into the café. Olive flipped over the "open" sign while her friends sat at their favourite table by the window and Millicent lifted the spaniel into her lap, stroking her ears.

'Sit,' Blythe ordered. 'Sit and tell us everything.'

'Yes,' Millicent said. 'But first scones and tea for all, *then* tell us everything.'

'Excellent idea,' Olive agreed as she sank into the third chair. 'And I give you full permission to go behind the counter and do the honours. Because I ran from here to the police station and am utterly exhausted.'

'Ran?!' Millicent and Blythe exclaimed in unison. '*You* ran?!'

Olive let out a long sigh. 'I had no choice. My bike had a puncture. But never again. Never again.'

'Alright, this I have to hear.' Millicent passed Biscuit over to Olive then stood and walked behind the counter to begin preparing a pot of tea and a plate of pastries.

'Okay then.' Olive sat back. 'When we're all sitting comfortably, I'll begin.'

Hours later, when her friends had left, regrettably, to return to their own shops, and Olive had cleaned everything up and flipped the "closed" sign on the café door, she sat down with Biscuit at her feet and the tarot cards in her lap. Now that the cards had helped her solve the mystery of Jack Witstable's death, she wanted them to solve another mystery, one inside her own mind. And about her own life.

'Am I falling in love with Hugo Dixon?' She asked as she shuffled the cards. 'Will I ever be in a relationship? Will I ever have a child?'

Olive shuffled and shuffled, asking the questions over and over again. Until, at last, she stopped and slowly laid out the top three cards on the table.

The Lovers. The Sun. The Three of Cups.

Olive smiled and let out a breath she didn't realise she'd been holding. It was, by any measure, an auspicious reading: love, hope, new beginnings, fertility, friendship, celebration... Which must mean that the handsome detective would be bringing all of those things into her life.

For the cards were always right.

Weren't they...?

THE END

Bakewell Tart Recipe

If Olive Crisp didn't own The Biscuit Tin, I'm certain she would spend a great deal of time in Fitzbillies and the Bakewell tart would be one of her favourite treats. It's certainly one of mine and I've spent, and continue to spend, a great deal of time in Fitzbillies myself. I've written several of my novels there, fuelled by their delicious pastries and cakes. The cafe (and some of its staff) has also featured in The Witches of Cambridge and Night of Demons & Saints. If you're ever in Cambridge, England, I highly recommend a visit! Along with a trip to Jack's Gelato, which serves the most delectable ice cream I've ever tasted.

❦

Fitzbillies Bakewell Tart

This recipe can be found in the Fitzbillies recipe book (pgs 142 & 146) by Alison Wright & Tim Hayward. It contains a great many other delicious recipes too.

1 batch of sweet pastry
6 medium eggs
250g caster sugar
250g ground almonds
250g unsalted butter, melted. Plus extra for greasing
100g raspberry jam
125g fresh raspberries
30g flaked almonds
plain flour, for dusting

Make a batch of sweet pasty (see below). Chill in the fridge for an hour or more.

Preheat the oven to 185oc (165oc fan) and grease and flour a loos-bottomed 28cm tart tin.

Beat together the eggs and sugar in a bowl until pale and fluffy. Add the ground almonds and melted butter and mix until combined.

Remove the pastry from the fridge. If it's been there a long time, e.g. overnight, get it out half an hour before so that it comes to room temperature. Lightly flour a surface and roll out the pastry until it's a few inches wider than the tin. Ensure it doesn't stick by moving it around gently as you work and keeping the surface well floured.

Roll the pastry over the rolling pin and then place it over the tart tin. Gently press into the sides, then trim the top edge all the way around with a sharp knife. Prick the base with a fork. Blind bake for 15-20 minutes until lightly golden – you don't want to overtake the edges, but nor do want a soggy bottom.

Spread the raspberry jam onto the base of the tart and sprinkle the whole raspberries over it. Pour the almond mixture over the jam and raspberries, then sprinkle with the flaked almonds.

Put the tart in the oven (on a baking sheet in case of any overflowing or spills) and bake for 40 minutes until the mixture rises and is golden. Serve warm or cold, with clotted cream.

Sweet Pastry Recipe
　85g unsalted butter
　85g baking margarine
　60g caster sugar
　1 medium egg, beaten
　255g plain flour, plus extra for dusting
　¼ tsp salt

Mix together the butter, margarine and caster sugar in a bowl, but do not cream. Mix in the egg.

Add the flour and salt and mix until combined. If it doesn't come together after a minute, add a little water (a teaspoon at a time) until it comes together.

Form into a ball, wrap in cling film and chill for an hour before use.

The Biscuit Tin Murders # 2

"A Body in the Graveyard"

Chapter One

Cambridge. 1st October, 1970

'EARLY *AGAIN*? THAT'S THE fourth day in a row. Grace, you're a marvel!' Olive declared as the young woman bustled into the café, scarf wrapped tight and duffle coat buttoned to the neck against the autumn winds. At her entry, Biscuit, Olive's spaniel, barked delightedly and encircled both pairs of feet with tail wagging so vigorously it might be in danger of injury.

'Why wouldn't I be?' Grace bent down to stroke the dog before beginning to unwrap her scarf and unbutton her coat. 'This is my favourite place in the world – better even than Newnham College Library. I'd sleep here if I could.'

'I've only got the one bedroom upstairs, I'm afraid.' Olive laughed. 'Otherwise you'd be most welcome. Then you could help with the morning's baking.'

'Oh, I'd love to. Please,' Grace begged as she fumbled with her buttons. 'May I?'

'You might want to take your gloves off first,' Olive suggested gently. 'It'd make that task a little easier.'

'Oh yes, of course, silly me.' Grace pulled off her mittens with her teeth, holding them in her mouth to shrug off her oversized coat and hang it, along with her scarf on the hat stand beside the front door.

'Another month working here and I might just be able to fatten you up enough to see you through winter,' Olive said as she eyed Grace's still-skinny frame. 'Buttered crumpets for breakfast every day ought to do it, plus three types of cake for tea.'

Grace giggled. 'I'll eat all your profits.'

'Oh, don't you worry about that,' Olive said. 'You're worth twice your weight in gold, let alone cake.'

When she'd hired Grace to help out in The Biscuit Tin, it'd been as a favour to support her after the trauma she'd suffered that spring. Yet the girl had proved not only invaluable, hardworking and adored by the customers, but had become a good friend into the bargain. Olive was pleased to see that Grace, in turn, had thrived in her role, becoming a little rounder and a little happier with each passing day.

'I'm taking Biscuit out for a walk,' Olive said. 'Are you all right to watch the café while I'm gone?' Grace nodded eagerly. 'Excellent. So, there's a batch of blackberry tarts in the oven that need to come out in ten minutes, along with two trays of apple crumble cakes and a few dozen almond pastries cooled and ready to put out on the counter...'

'Leave it with me,' Grace said, already heading towards the counter. 'I'll have everything ready before we open.'

'I've said it before, no doubt I'll say it again...' Olive lifted Biscuit's lead from the hat stand and clipped it on. 'But you are a bloody marvel, my dear. And we are very lucky to have you.'

'Likewise.' Grace turned to give Olive a shy smile. 'A hundred times over.'

∽

For their morning walks, Olive let Biscuit take them wherever she wished to go, turning down streets and alleyways at random, while Olive let her thoughts wander along with her feet. She liked not having to be responsible, for once, not worrying about what she needed to control or which direction to take. She had enough of that pressure at the café, though less so now that she had Grace to share the burden a little. For her part, Biscuit was thrilled by the new state of things. It meant that she was no longer rushed along, tugged away from every intriguing lamppost and wall in her mistress's haste to get back to work but instead allowed to sniff away at whatever she wished to her heart's content. *Happy Days.*

Today, Biscuit ambled along King's Parade, following a scent trail she recognised as one of her favourite park companions: a rather attractive golden labrador of mature years who'd been unfortunate enough to have bestowed upon him the slightly humiliating moniker of Lord Tuffington. Sometimes, Biscuit didn't know what humans were thinking and considered herself lucky to have such a sensible mistress.

Following the scent past St Catharine's College, pausing to pick up the enticing whiff of fried bacon drifting out of their kitchen window, Biscuit trotted along to cross Silver Street. Spotting the stone walls of Little St. Mary's Church and, alongside that, the entrance to a tiny and very pretty graveyard – one of Olive's favourite's – she hurried past Pembroke College and towards the cemetery's iron gate so they might enjoy its twisting cobbled paths, overhanging trees and ivy-blanketed stones.

'Oh, how lovely,' Olive said, shaking herself free of her thoughts as Biscuit came to a halt at the gate. 'You've brought us here. One of my favourite places.'

Biscuit barked twice, as if to say "of course" and "you're welcome", while Olive lifted the catch and opened the gate. Since no-one was likely to be frequenting the graveyard, with the possible exception of the vicar, who was anyway very fond of Biscuit, Olive slipped the lead from the spaniel's neck to let her roam free. And, while Biscuit scampered off, Olive strolled more sedately through the gardens of the tiny graveyard, glancing at the names and dates on the stones, imagining the life stories that might accompany them.

It'd lately occurred to Olive that she might start writing stories of her own, tales about the crimes she'd been solving recently. People enjoyed such stories, she thought, if the efforts of Ms Christie were anything to go by. Blythe had recently lent Olive copies of several Poirot novels and she'd enjoyed them immensely. The detective himself was too much of a snob for Olive's tastes but she liked to think that he'd approve of her café if he were ever to frequent it. She'd bake him Belgium custard buns and he'd feel just at home. How she'd manage to find the time to actually write these stories, of course, was another matter. Although, now she had Grace to help out it might be possible. Perhaps she ought to teach the girl some of her secret family recipes. And, though Olive worried that her ancestors might not approve of such a move, it wouldn't hurt to ask.

Olive's thoughts continued to meander in such absent and curious directions while she walked, enjoying the soft early morning sunlight through the leaves dappling the path as she went. Olive was just wondering what type of cake Miss Marple might favour when she heard Biscuit's frantic barking around the corner. Olive knew well the wide variety of Biscuit's barks and could easily decode them: food, walk, play, affection... The spaniel's needs were few and simple, predictable too, given that Olive could usually set her watch by when she wanted to be walked, fed and cuddled.

But this bark was different. It was one Olive rarely heard. It meant danger.

Chapter Two

Olive never ran, not if she could possibly help it, but she ran now. Picking up her long, flowered skirt, she ran as fast as she could – which was, admittedly, not very fast – more of a frantic shuffle than a sprint, in the direction of Biscuit's increasingly agitated yelps. Darting past the headstones but still sticking to the paths (it'd be unconscionable, she felt, to actually step across the graves, no matter the circumstances) till she finally rounded the corner of the church that led to the little garden and benches along the south side.

'Biscuit!' Olive called, suddenly panicking that perhaps her dog was being dog-napped. 'Bics, I-I'm coming, Bics!'

When the first thing Olive saw was her beloved spaniel alive and well, alone and unmolested by kidnappers, she exhaled a deep sigh of relief and, blinking back tears, felt a little silly for having worked herself up into such a state.

'Oh, B-Bics,' she gasped, leaning against a bench to catch her breath while Biscuit had her muzzle and front paws pressed inside the shrubbery, her tail wagging ferociously. 'Th-there you are. Th-thank goodness for that.'

It wasn't until she'd fully recovered her equilibrium, released her life-grip on the bench and started walking over to where Biscuit stood, still barking, that she realised she'd been wrong about one thing. For, while her dog was, certainly, alive and well and untouched by kidnappers, she was not alone. Very far from it, in fact. For, protruding between her paws was a pair of feet.

'Oh!' Olive exclaimed as soon as she registered the sight. 'Oh!'

It was probably an unfortunate chap without a home or bed for the night, she thought, such as she sometimes saw sleeping in the doorways of shops and would bring offerings of hot coffee and leftover cakes. On very cold evenings Olive would even invite them, those she knew well, to sleep on blankets on the café floor. Although, she realised as she approached, that the shoes did not suggest a man of little means, but one quite well-monied, so it was more likely to be a student who'd been revelling into the wee small hours and then, mistaking the church for his college, given up looking and passed out among the bushes. It *might* even be the vicar, for his body was entirely concealed within the shrubbery and it was no secret that he frequently enjoyed rather more than his fair share of communion wine, and could often be found sleeping off the effects on the wide variety of church benches happily fit for the purpose. Indeed, Olive now found herself wondering, as she stepped closer, if it was certainly possible that he'd acquired the plethora of benches for that very reason.

Whoever it was, Olive thought, as she now peered down at the feet – large and clad in highly polished brogues – they must be very drunk indeed to be sleeping through the racket that Biscuit was still making.

'Hush,' Olive patted the spaniel's head. 'Hush, girl. It's all right. I'm here.'

Tentatively, Olive bent down and wiggled the left foot.

'Hey, there,' she said. 'Sorry to wake you. I'm just checking that you're all right.'

Because there was, of course, the possibility that the drunkard was injured and in need of medical attention. There was even the possibility – which Olive was right now not allowing herself to entertain – that he was past the need for a medic and only in need of a mortician.

'Hello,' Olive said, a little louder. 'Hello? Are you all right?'

Wiggling the foot more vigorously still, Olive felt her heart start to race – as if she was running again – and her breath catch in her throat. There was, alas, only one thing for it, she would have to abandon the man's feet and seek out his head.

Wishing she wasn't alone with only a small dog for company – where was Detective Dixon when you wanted him? – Olive held her breath and plunged bravely, with Biscuit at her side, into the shrubbery. It took her only a moment to locate the man's head given that it was, mercifully, still attached to his body. That was, however, the only good thing to be said about the matter. Because it was unfortunately clear, after even a cursory glance, that the man was quite dead. Indeed, given the purplish hue of his lips and the clammy pallor of his skin, it was likely that he'd been dead for quite a while. Certainly hours, possibly even days. Although, on second thoughts, if it'd been *that* long it wouldn't only be Biscuit who could smell him.

'Oh, dear,' Olive mumbled as she stepped back. 'Oh dear, oh dear.' She glanced down at Biscuit, who looked back up at her mistress with a perpetually curious and ever-trusting doggy gaze. 'Whatever shall we do now?'

Given that the overgrown shrubbery obscured everything but his face, it was impossible to tell yet, unless one was especially brave – which Olive was not – or particularly discourteous, whether or not his death was due to natural or unnatural causes. Either way it was best, she concluded, to call the police. That this might mean "bumping into" Detective Dixon (or Hugo, as he now insisted she call him, given the number of times he'd frequented The Biscuit Tin for coffee and cake) was simply a bonus.

༄

'Well, well, fancy seeing you here,' Hugo said, as he opened the door to his police car and stepped onto the pavement. 'Of all the people who might accidentally stumble upon a dead body, why am I not at all surprised it was you?'

'You say that as if I go around looking for them.' Olive folded her arms, attempting to look affronted but finding it difficult in the face of the detective's playful smile and friendly blue eyes.

'Don't you?' He retorted. 'Given the regularity with which you "stumble" upon crimes, I'd be surprised if you didn't.'

'I do nothing of the sort,' Olive huffed, though it was hard to deny that she did seem to get herself entangled in an unusually high number of murders (after the fact) whether by accident or design. 'I was merely out walking Bics. And she was the first to find him, not me.'

Hugo flashed Olive another smile. 'Did you train her? Like we do on the force.'

'Certainly not,' Olive said, while also thinking that this wasn't a half-bad idea. A crime-sniffing dog would ensure that life remained rather exciting no matter what.

'Right then, why don't you take me to the body?' he said. 'Lead the way.'

'I wasn't sure you'd come to this,' Olive said as she led Biscuit back towards the little church and its graveyard. 'Given that we don't yet know whether it's a murder or not. It might just be a heart attack or something like that.' She tried not to sound too disappointed at the suggestion.

'Yes,' Hugo agreed. 'Constable Cooper was keen to come, but given that it was you who called it in I thought I'd come along and say hello.'

Given that he was walking slightly behind her, Hugo missed Olive's happy grin in response to this statement. She opened the gate and held it so he could follow her through.

'It's just around the corner,' Olive explained. 'On the south side of the church. Biscuit found him in the bushes. I-I thought it best not to touch the body, just in case.' This was a plausible explanation, she thought, and preferable to cowardice. For, while Olive relished the potential for solving the mysteries afforded by such events, she was particularly squeamish when it came to details of those deaths. As for blood, she definitely didn't want to see any blood! If not for that small point, Olive would've thought she'd missed her calling as a police officer.

'Very wise,' Hugo commended her. 'It's always best not to touch anything; you never know what might be a clue – if it's a murder that is.'

Touched by this compliment, Olive hid her smile.

'There.' She pointed to the pair of shod feet protruding from the overgrown shrubbery. 'That's where he is.'

Getting close enough to get a look – albeit infuriatingly veiled – at what was going on, but far back enough to give the detective his space, Olive watched as he tried to ascertain whether or not the body had reached its state by fair means or foul. Bending down for a closer inspection, Hugo was silent for several minutes until, finally, he stood and stepped away.

'Well.' The detective folded his arms. 'I can now unequivocally conclude that this was definitely a murder.'

'What makes you say that?' Olive asked, feeling her heart start to race again.

'A few factors,' Hugo offered. 'The drag marks around the body suggest he's been moved after he died, the defence marks on his hands indicate he was probably defending himself from attack, the multiple rips to his shirt imply likewise... Oh, and there's a bloody great knife sticking out of his chest.'

Chapter Three

A BLOODIED KNIFE. A *murder*.

This confirmation sparked in Olive a thrill of excitement, quickly followed by a pang of guilt. One must, after all, pause to feel sympathy for the poor unfortunate man who'd been thus assailed. To calm herself, and assume a suitable air of concern, Olive lifted Biscuit into her arms and affected a contrite look as she lowered her head and rested her chin between Biscuit's ears.

'So, um, what'll you do now?' Olive asked. 'Find out who he was? His, um …' She nodded in the direction of the man whose torso remained obscured by the shrubbery. 'Wallet perhaps?'

Hugo shook his head. 'No, as I said, touching anything now risks disturbing vital evidence. I'll call it into the station and get a team down to detail the scene before removing the body. Forensics will search his person before the autopsy. If we're lucky, he'll be in possession of identification – even a monogrammed handkerchief will help – if not, then we'll wait to see if anyone reports a man missing who matches his description. Failing that, we'll search the database, put out alerts and even posters…'

As the detective continued iterating the long and increasingly arduous steps in the identification process, Olive swallowed a sigh. Impatient by nature, she hated waiting for anything – her birthday, Christmas, the baking of a cake – and right now she longed to simply leap into the bushes and rifle through the man's pockets. If only she hadn't been thwarted by both police procedure and her own squeamishness.

'Sounds like it might take an awfully long time,' Olive suggested. 'And meanwhile the murderer could escape, jump on a bus to London and never be seen again.'

'Unlikely,' Hugo said, as he began walking away from the body and back in the direction of the street and the waiting police car. 'Most people are killed by someone they know, usually quite well, and it won't be easy for anyone with ties to their community to simply up and leave everything they have behind. Also, they didn't even think to remove the murder weapon, so I doubt we're dealing with a criminal mastermind here. They'll probably just lay low and pray we don't find them.'

'And we will pray that we do,' Olive said, casting a longing glance back towards the bushes as they rounded the corner of the little church and left the garden behind.

'Well, I don't know about that,' Hugo said. 'I don't find that particular method of catching criminals to be as effective as actual police work. But yes, metaphorically speaking, I suppose so. You don't recognise the victim, I assume? He wasn't one of your many loyal fans?'

Olive laughed. 'Customers, you mean? They're not fans of *mine,* they're fans of my baking and the café.'

'So you say.' Hugo smiled. 'So you say.'

They reached the gate and he held it open. 'After you.'

'Thank you.' Olive was still carrying Biscuit, who never passed up an opportunity to be conveyed from place to place like a Roman emperor. 'But, to answer your question, no, sadly I don't recognise him. I know most of my loyal customers by name but I don't think he's ever visited The Biscuit Tin.'

'Then, not to speak ill of the dead,' Hugo said. 'But he clearly had very poor taste.'

Olive laughed. 'Perhaps he just didn't like sugar. More of a savoury man. Anyway, judging by the twig-like ankles, it looks like he didn't really eat much of anything at all.'

'True enough,' Hugo agreed. 'True enough.'

Olive eyed him. 'What?'

'What do you mean, what?' Hugo reached the police car and, pulling a bunch of keys from his pocket, opened the door.

'You've got that distracted look,' Olive said. 'When you've stopped properly listening to what I'm saying because you're too busy thinking.'

'Oh, really?' Hugo smiled. 'I didn't realise I was quite so obvious. Nor that you were quite so observant.'

Olive sniffed. 'I bet I'm just as observant as most of your officers, twice as observant as some. That Constable Cooper, for instance, is a bit of a–'

'Half-wit,' Hugo finished. 'Yes, I know. But his father plays golf with the Chief of Police, so there's not much to be done about that.'

Olive set Biscuit down on the pavement. 'So, um, what will you do after you've called it in?'

'Wait for them to arrive.' Hugo shrugged. 'Not much else to do except ensure that no other members of the public accidentally wander into a crime scene. And' – he gave Olive a knowing look – 'ensure that one particularly curious one doesn't decide to nip back and search the victim for his identification papers.'

'Oh!' Olive's exclamation of outrage was so sharp that Biscuit pricked up her ears and looked up in case her mistress was in distress. 'That's outrageous. I can't believe you'd suspect me of doing something so…'

'Indecent?' Hugo offered. 'Immoral? Unconscionable? No, what was I thinking? A fine upstanding citizen like yourself would never dream of expressly contravening police procedure now, would you?'

'No,' Olive huffed, annoyed at proving so transparent herself. 'I certainly would not.' She took a deep breath to regroup. 'I was merely asking because it's early and, since you've probably not had breakfast yet, I was going to offer to bring you a cup of coffee and one of those Bakewell tarts you love. That's all. But if you're not interested, then…' She feigned walking away. 'Come on, Bics, let's go back to the café where we're appreciated.'

'Hold on!' Hugo declared. 'Hold on! Let's not be so hasty.' He reached out towards her but, just before he touched her arm, dropped his hand. Olive felt a stab of disappointment. 'Bakewell tarts, you say?'

'Yes.' Olive shrugged. 'But perhaps I should save those for my "fans", don't you think? It'd be a shame to let them down.'

'Nonsense,' Hugo said. 'No one's a bigger fan than me.'

'Oh?' Olive smiled.

'Of your café, of course.' He averted his gaze. 'And your… baking.'

'Right.' Olive nodded, delighted to have once more regained the upper hand. 'Yes, of course.'

'So…' Hugo hesitated.

'So.' Olive winked at him. 'Then I'll prove what an upstanding citizen I am by doing my civic duty and bringing our dedicated city detective his breakfast.'

Chapter Four

'A body?' Grace echoed. 'You found a *body*?'

'Well, technically speaking, it was Biscuit who found him,' Olive said. 'He was hidden in a bush, most of him anyway.'

'Gosh.' Grace looked horrified. 'Gosh. You must be feeling dreadful, you poor thing, you must be in frightful shock. Sit down, I'll put the kettle on.'

Olive, who was not feeling remotely in shock nor dreadful – the only thing she felt was excited – nevertheless realised that these were emotions she *should* be feeling and so allowed herself to be ushered into the nearest chair and furnished with a plate of lavender biscuits while Grace prepared a pot of tea. At least an appetite was one thing Olive didn't have to feign since she always felt like eating biscuits.

'It *was* rather a shock.' Olive began in on the biscuits, devouring the first in three short bites. 'I mean, it's not the sort of thing one expects to see on one's morning walk. Not that I saw any bodily evidence of the crime – no blood or anything like that.'

'Thank goodness,' Grace murmured, as she set cups upon the table. 'That's the sort of thing, once seen, it's hard to ever forget.'

The young woman shuddered and Olive gave her a sympathetic smile, reaching out to give Grace's hand a gentle squeeze. For, although her time spent in the comforts of The Biscuit Tin, absorbing the warmth of the ovens, the softness of the cakes, the sympathies of Olive and her ancestors (the latter stubbornly secretive with their recipes but generous with their affections), was gradually easing Grace's pain, still the trauma of the girl's terrible ordeal lingered beneath the surface, arising at moments both expected and unexpected.

'I know, my dear,' Olive said softly. 'I know. Now, why don't you sit a while, take a break, and I'll fetch the tea.'

Grace shook her head but Olive stood anyway, guiding the girl into her own chair then scurrying off in the direction of the whistling kettle before another word could be said about it. While Olive decanted hot water into the teapot to steep the leaves before pouring the tea, she glanced over at her new employee who was now tentatively nibbling on a biscuit as a squirrel might nibble on a nut. Olive smiled to herself, hearing a satisfied rustle of the beaded curtain behind her in response. Her ancestors were pleased she'd brought Grace in to find refuge and regeneration in the café; taking her under their collective ephemeral wings as soon as she'd arrived. For her part, Grace hadn't yet been told of the collective of ghosts, currently numbering sixteen since the death of Olive's mother a few years before, that had peaceably inhabited the small building for several centuries now. For their part, Olive's deceased relatives remained uncharacteristically well-behaved and discrete and would continue, so it seemed, until their descendant decided to have "the talk" with her employee. Olive was well versed in the particulars of this talk, having given it to both her best friends, Millie and Blythe, who spent a considerable portion of their lives in the café, but the only other people who knew about the ghosts were the ghosts themselves.

'I'm glad you approve,' Olive whispered. 'She's a sweetheart, isn't she?'

The curtain rustled in response and, though she never caught sight of her relatives' spirits so never knew which one, or many, she was conversing with it didn't matter. The only exception being her mother, whose impact on Olive's surroundings tended to be made with a heavier hand – as opinionated in death as she had been in life – and thus their many disagreements (mainly concerning Olive's current childless state) continued in a partially muted, but no less vociferous or lively way, given that one party had passed over to the other side.

'I must say,' Olive continued in hushed tones, so as not to disturb Grace who was still nibbling the same biscuit. 'Though I hired her for her sake as much as mine, I think I'm going to miss her dreadfully when she finishes her Masters next summer and moves back to London.'

The set of six regency tea cups[1] jostled and clinked on the shelf. Olive looked up.

'July, I believe,' she whispered. 'So, happily, we've still got a while yet.'

Biscuit, who'd been waiting patiently for her mistress to emerge out from behind the counter, abandoned her post, trotting over to Grace's table and nuzzling at her legs till the young woman glanced down and, with an affectionate smile, started scratching behind the spaniel's ears, slipping the dog the rest of her biscuit in the process.

'But perhaps we can persuade her to stay a few months longer,' Olive said, before carrying the teapot over to the table.

'You're talking to yourself again,' Grace said, as Olive set down the teapot.

'Oh, yes.' Olive blushed. 'So I am.'

Fortunately, before Grace could ask any awkward questions, the bell above the door tinkled and Millie bustled inside, rubbing her arms as protection against the chill.

'What a fool I was to come without my coat,' she said, teeth chattering. 'Thought I wouldn't need it to pop round the corner.'

'Yes, it's chilly in the mornings lately,' Olive said. 'Autumn has truly set in. But you've come at the perfect time to join us for tea and biscuits.'

Millie, owner of A Thousand Threads, the haberdashers on King's Parade, grinned and quickly took the seat beside Grace before the offer could be withdrawn.

'You've also arrived at the perfect time to hear all about the dead body Bics and I found on our walk round Little St Mary's Church this-'

'Hold on,' Millie interrupted, brow suddenly furrowed. 'What did you just say? *Dead* body?'

'Yes, I-'

'And yet you drop it into the conversation as if you're mentioning a new flavour of cake.' Millie tutted. 'Oh, Olive. What is it with you? You're simply a magnet for death and disaster!' She sighed. 'At least we should be grateful that, touch wood' - she knocked on the table - 'it always seems to be other peoples' deaths and disasters, never your own.'

'For which I am very grateful,' Olive said, trying not to betray her excitement too fully. 'The only frustrating thing is that we now have to wait till the police identify the body to find out who he was and what happened.'

'You know...' Millie regarded her friend curiously as she lifted the pot and began to pour the tea. 'Sometimes I wonder about you and your peculiar blood lust... If you didn't make such delectable cakes, I'd think you missed your calling as a police detective.'

'Don't be ridiculous.' Olive laughed. 'I do not have a *peculiar* interest in these things, just the *normal* amount of inquisitiveness that any normal person has. Anyway, have you ever heard of a female police detective?'

'You sound wistful,' Millie said. 'And full of longing.'

Olive reached for the sugar bowl and dropped two lumps into her tea, then stirred in a splash of milk. 'I do not.'

'Do so.'

'Do not.'

'Do so.'

'Do *not*.'

Grace watched the verbal sparring match as one might watch two great players on centre court at Wimbledon, her head snapping back and forth from one competitor to the other.

'Well,' Millie huffed. 'Just because there's never been a female officer doesn't mean there never will be. Who's to say that you couldn't be the first?'

At this, the photograph of Olive's mother, Myrtle, fell from its spot on the wall – nestled among the pictures of every past owner of The Biscuit Tin[2] – and crashed to the floor.

'Oh!' Grace jumped.

'Oops,' Millie laughed. 'I don't think your mother approves of that idea.'

'Don't be silly.' Olive gave Millie a sharp look, reminding her that her employee didn't yet know of her busybody ancestors and so secrets must still be kept. 'It's just a loose nail, I've been meaning to fix it.' Hurrying over to the photograph, which depicted Myrtle Crisp in her apron standing behind the café counter surrounded by dozens of her award-winning cakes and bakes, grinning broadly. 'Let's keep you in the kitchen, shall we? Till I can sort that out.'

The photograph trembled in Olive's hands as she shoved it onto a shelf above the kettle laden with cookbooks.

'Now, stop it,' Olive muttered under her breath. 'You *know* you've got nothing to worry about; I'm a forty-year-old woman, I've got as much chance of becoming a police detective as I have of becoming Prime Minister. So stop causing mischief.'

Hurrying back to the table to sink into her chair and take a long sip of Earl Grey, Olive proffered the plate of biscuits to Grace. 'They're delicious dunked in tea.'

'Or just scoffed up without accompaniment,' Millie said, biting into a biscuit to prove her point. 'Oh, I almost forgot why I came.' Popping the rest of it into her mouth, she delved into the hand-quilted bag at her feet and withdrew a small knitted garment: a tartan pattern jumper with elaborate cable detail and tiny sleeves.

'What's that?' Olive asked as Grace glanced from the garment to Olive and back again, her gaze lingering momentarily on Olive's belly. 'Do you know something I don't? Because I can assure you that, much to my mother's dismay, I am not yet with child.'

Millie laughed. 'Don't be daft. It's not for a *baby*, it's for a dog.'

Olive frowned. 'A dog?' She also realised that she'd just spoken of Myrtle as if she was still alive which might raise some questions from Grace though, fortunately, the girl seemed not to have noticed.

Biscuit barked, emerging from under the table as Millie nodded. 'I had the idea during the summer, but there was no need till the mornings got chilly enough.' She addressed Biscuit. 'What do you think? Fancy trying on your new winter coat?'

Biscuit cocked her head to scrutinise the garment, raised her eyebrows as if to question the need for such a thing given the beautiful and luxurious fur coat

Nature had already so generously bestowed upon her, and finally gave a single bark of approval. *Let's see what the mongrels think of this when I hit the park.*

Olive smiled. 'Well, there you go. I wasn't at all sure, given that she's a fussy little princess[3], but that looks like a vote of approval to me.'

'Excellent.' Millie grinned as she slipped the jumper over Biscuit's head and carefully slid her legs into the sleeves. 'There you go! Doesn't she look a picture?'

'She certainly does,' Olive said, swallowing a smile.

'Very noble,' Grace agreed.

Biscuit, delighting in the attention, sauntered up and down the small shop wagging her tail and showing off all her best angles as if she were parading through the winners' enclosure at Crufts.

'If other dog owners admire it in the park,' Millie said, 'be sure to send them my way; I'll make them to order. Right, now that's done, tell us everything about this dead body you just happened to stumble over while the rest of us were minding our own business and keeping out of trouble.'

∞

---

1. These, Olive's mother always insisted, housed the spirit of their ancestor, Charlotte Krisp, who'd acquired such a grand reputation for her strawberry tarts that she'd been invited to bake them for the Prince Regent and his family in St James's Palace. Becoming a confidant of his wife, Caroline of Brunswick, Charlotte had been awarded a peerage in 1816 and had bought the gold-plated porcelain cups to commemorate the occasion. They'd remained on display - untouched - ever since.

2. Numbering all of Olive's direct female descents back to Louise de Kerouille. Most of these, given that the first photograph was only taken in 1826 and the camera not widely used till a decade or so later, were oil paintings or drawings, depending on the wealth of the sitter.

3. While, of course, dogs cannot technically be princesses (though why not, given that human princesses are no different from human bus drivers), Tilly did possess royal blood in so far as being a direct descendant of the Cavalier spaniels owned by King Charles II and, as such, certainly gave herself regal airs and graces as much as the monarch himself had done. She was, in short, a snob.

Chapter Five

OLIVE SPENT THE NEXT few days in anxious anticipation waiting for Detective Dixon to call. After she'd plied him with coffee and pastries the morning of the discovery, he'd promised to let her know as soon as he made any progress with identifying the body. But, so far, she'd heard nothing.

So distracted was Olive during this vexatious waiting period that she kept making mistakes, giving customers coffee instead of tea and biscuits instead of cake. Most, with their affable British manners, took whatever they'd been given without complaint, not wishing to embarrass their host and anyway thought themselves fortunate to be patrons of a place that offered such a wealth of delights in comparison to every other British culinary establishment of the 1970s yet to discover the point of flavour in food. So, if one was given a delicious lemon cream bun instead of a delicious lemon meringue pie, then one simply nodded, smiled and said "thank you", considered oneself lucky and left it at that.

Thus it was Grace (suffering most from her boss's anxious distraction) rather than the customers, who greeted the final arrival of Detective Dixon with (almost) as much enthusiasm as did Olive herself.

'Hugo!'

Abandoning the counter, which she'd been absent-mindedly, and unnecessarily, polishing for the fifth time that hour, Olive hurried across the café with as much haste as dignity would allow, though the accompanying squeals of excitement anyway ensured that no dignity remained.

Hugo smiled as she reached him. 'Much as I'd like to think that this enthusiasm is personal,' he said. 'I'm guessing it has less to do with me and rather more to do with the information I possess.'

'Well...' Olive gave him an embarrassed grin. 'Naturally, I'm always pleased to see you, of course. But-'

'But, you'd send me packing if I didn't tell you what I know,' Hugo finished. 'Am I right?'

'Well...' Olive said again, this time having the decency to blush. 'I wouldn't throw you out. At least, not till I gave you a cup of tea first.'

'Coffee,' Hugo reminded her. 'I don't drink tea.'

'Oh yes, right.' Olive tapped herself lightly on the head. 'I knew that. No milk, two sugars.'

Hugo's smile widened. 'Three sugars. The mysterious identity of this man really is driving you to distraction, isn't it?'

Olive exhaled. 'Utterly and completely. Completely and utterly. Now, just put me out of my misery would you? Please.'

Hugo laughed. 'I will, though I confess I'm enjoying teasing you enormously.'

'Fine.' Olive folded her arms. 'Though you should know that I've been known to ban persistent teasers from the café for life. So, if I were you-'

'Dr Gerald John Hopkins of number eleven Arthur Street,' Hugo interrupted so fast that his words were barely comprehensible. 'Though keep that last bit to yourself, I wasn't supposed to divulge that. And don't' – he eyed her suspiciously – 'go around making your own investigations, causing trouble and possibly putting yourself in danger into the bargain. Leave that to the police. Understood?'

He paused, waiting for Olive to respond.

'Yes?'

Olive nodded, placing her hand over her heart. 'I promise.'

The other hand, with fingers crossed, she hid behind her back.

'You'd be wasting your time anyway,' Hugo assured her. 'We've already interviewed every neighbour along the street and, so it seems, Dr Hopkins was an upstanding citizen and university tutor who wished harm to no one and, in turn, to whom no one wished any harm.'

Olive opened her mouth.

'And, before you object,' Hugo said. 'No, none of them were lying. It might surprise you to learn that, as a police officer, I'm trained to know when people are lying. It's an essential part of the job description.'

Olive gave him a wry smile. 'Yes, Officer, I know you are. But that doesn't mean...'

'No.' Hugo shook his head. 'Do *not* go and make enquiries yourself. I do not permit it, I refuse it, I forbid it. I-'

Chapter Six

HALF AN HOUR LATER, Olive stood on tip-toes outside number 11 Arthur Street peering in through the window into a small front room containing only a small sofa, single free-standing bookshelf and a chair set in front of the fireplace. [1]The mid-afternoon sun shone in through the back windows, illuminating the emptiness. After Hugo had left, and she'd promised dutifully not to go anywhere near the deceased's home address, Olive had waited a full five minutes before betraying her promise and leaving the café, along with Biscuit, in Grace's capable hands, before stuffing a bag full of baked goods, mounting her bike and cycling across town.

She'd half-expected to be met with a police guard but, clearly deciding it best not to draw attention to a place which, anyway, was not a murder scene, there was no-one and nothing barring her way. Of course, the police would have already been through Dr Hopkins' home and its contents with a fine-toothed comb, but that didn't mean that they hadn't missed anything. And Olive knew that, along with missing potentially vital clues, the police were also in danger of missing potentially vital witnesses simply due to the fact that many people – guilty or not – had a tendency to become tongue-tied when the time came to converse with Her Majesty's constabulary. Most, indeed, possessed as much enthusiasm to chat with the members of the police force as they did with doctors or tax inspectors, wishing for a life where the time for such conversations never came.

Café owners bearing biscuits, on the other hand, were likely to be afforded a rather warmer and more edifying reception. She might even, if she were very fortunate, be able to gain access to the house in question.

Stepping away from the window, since it seemed nothing was to be gleaned from staring at it any longer, Olive glanced up and down the little street trying to decide which house to pick on first. Numbers 9 or 13 would make most sense, being the closest neighbours and, given that 13 was (considered by most to be) an unlucky number, Olive plumped for number nine.

She knocked once, then twice. And, just as she was about to give up and try number thirteen instead, Olive's patience was rewarded by the door being opened.

'Yes?' A woman of advancing years, with a fluff of white hair held in place by a kerchief, and her ample bosom similarly enclosed by a paisley housedress and apron, regarded Olive with a look of curious suspicion. 'I'm not buying anything.'

Olive smiled. 'I'm not selling anything.'

'Well, good.' The woman folded her arms. 'Because I've got everything I want, all that I need, and more besides.'

Olive nodded. 'I understand. My own flat's so full of clutter that I swear it's restocked by elves at night. No matter what I clear away, still more piles up in its absence. But no, what I'd like is just a few minutes of your time to ask you a few questions, to get your opinion on a recent matter.' She offered the woman her most charming and endearing smile as she reached into her bag and brought out a small box of lavender biscuits. 'If you can spare ten minutes for a cup of tea, I can offer accompaniments. I'm the owner of The Biscuit Tin,' Olive added; reassurance in the form of her credentials as a local business owner and not a wandering criminal or confidence trickster.

The woman, unaccustomed to having her opinion sought and, resigned to a society that valued women little and older women even less, smiled; clearly delighted to encounter someone who bucked that trend.

'In that case,' she said, 'please come in.'

※

'I want to ask you about your neighbour.' Olive, having exhausted the obligatory British small talk about the weather – a shame about the chillier mornings but still admittedly quite mild for the time of year[2] – finally came to the point. 'The one who was killed.'

'Ah.' Mrs Irene Barnes, for that's who she was, nodded. 'A sad sorry business that. The police was round here, checking his house, asking his neighbours questions...' She made the sign of the cross across her bosom. 'A young man too, not yet forty I'd say. Always a sad business when they die young. Just like our boys in the war.'

'Yes,' Olive agreed. 'Very sad.' She waited a moment, marking this sadness with a moment of silence, then offered Mrs Barnes the box of biscuits that sat open, but as yet untouched, beside the teapot. 'Please, have a biscuit. It's important to keep up your strength at times like these.'

Her host hesitated, perhaps considering that it might be unseemly to eat biscuits while discussing social tragedies, then reached for one. To keep her company, Olive took one too.

'So...' Olive was tentative, careful, wary of pushing her potential source of information into silence. It'd happened before, although Olive was usually very good at reading people and knowing their limits. She took a sip of her tea. It was too milky and Mrs Barnes had added far too much sugar – even for Olive who liked sweet tea – but she swallowed anyway. Olive was nothing if not polite. Manners, her mother had always taught her, cost nothing, and were worth everything. 'Did you... Did you know your neighbour well?'

Mrs Barnes nibbled thoughtfully on her lavender biscuit. 'Not really,' she conceded, sounding a little regretful. Though whether this was because she would've liked to know him better or because it meant she had little gossip to offer, Olive couldn't tell. 'But then,' Mrs Barnes continued. 'Nor did anyone, so far as I knew. Except his students, I suppose. Kept himself to himself. One of those types, you know. Secretive. Furtive. Not an engaged member of the community, despite being a professor. You'd think-'

'Professor?'

Mrs Barnes nodded. 'At one of the colleges. I'm not sure which one... Pembroke, I think.'

'Pembroke?' Olive set down her teacup. The college was directly across the road from where his body had been discovered and she wondered if that was relevant. 'What did he teach?'

'He taught - now, let me think - it was one of them subjects that don't count for much, all about myths and ancient languages nobody speaks any more, that sort of thing. I–'

'Classics?' Olive offered.

'That's it.' Mrs Barnes nodded. 'Waste of time, if you ask me. But he seemed to take it serious enough. So did his students, by all accounts, given that those were the only visitors he ever seemed to get.'

'Really?' Olive frowned. 'I wonder why he didn't live in college, being a bachelor, I mean. It would've been a nice life at Pembroke, having his laundry done, his rooms tended, availing himself of breakfast, lunch and dinner in Hall. I hear Pembroke's chef is particularly excellent. Makes Pembroke's fellows the envy of all those at the other colleges by all accounts.'

Mrs Barnes gave a slight shrug, then reached for her own cup to take a dainty sip. 'I wouldn't know,' she said. 'I've never had the opportunity – the likes of me aren't invited to college dinners.'

'Me neither,' Olive added quickly, lest her companion might think she had airs. 'I only hear my customers complaining sometimes, that's all. So, his students often visited him at home?'

'Now and then. They were the only ones that did, anyway. He wasn't a man with many friends, as I said. Nor did he much get involved with the community.' She shook her head, tutting. 'You'd think a man of such social standing would be more…' She paused, searching for the word. 'Generous to those around him.' She took another sip of tea and sighed. 'Whatever happened to the privileged taking care of the less fortunate? Back before the war, they did. But look at us now. Sometimes I'm glad my Harold isn't around to see the state of things anymore. It would've broke his heart so it would.'

Olive gave Mrs Barnes a sympathetic smile. She'd seen a photograph above the fireplace of a thin man with a pinched face who she'd assumed to be Mr Barnes, but she didn't want to enquire and risk derailing the conversation too significantly. She knew from experience with her customers that women were wont to get rather distracted when it came to discussions of their families, widows especially. And while she might have had the time to indulge such trips down memory lane, Olive certainly didn't have the patience. She took a deep breath, hoping that she'd already established enough of a rapport with Mrs Barnes to ask the next question.

'Did you…' Olive ventured, taking another sip of the over-sweet tea for good measure. 'Did you ever… find yourself in the position where you, perhaps, by chance overheard anything to suggest why Dr Hopkins…?' she trailed off, not wanting to invoke the spectre of murderers into the conversation nor, worst still, imply that Mrs Barnes herself might have associated with such unseemly things.

'Overheard?' Mrs Barnes echoed, feathers clearly ruffled. 'Miss Crisp, if you're insinuating that I go around' – she shuddered – '*eavesdropping* on my neighbours then I–'

'Oh, no,' Olive exclaimed, instantly assuming an incredulous expression. 'No, no, no, nothing of the sort. I only wondered if, while you were hanging out your washing, say, you might have heard anything – an argument perhaps – that could shed some light on what happened to poor Dr Hopkins.' Olive picked up the biscuit box again and offered it to her host. 'Please, have another.'

Mrs Barnes narrowed her eyes and gave a haughty sniff. 'Well.' She feigned reluctance but took one anyway, as if she were doing Olive a favour in eating it. 'I've certainly never *intentionally* heard anything, but it's impossible not to, you know. What with thin walls and these small houses pressed up against each other like this.'

'Oh, yes.' Olive nodded. 'Of course, it must be awfully frustrating when one just wants a little peace and quiet.'

'Yes,' Mrs Barnes agreed. 'It most certainly is.'

Olive watched as a series of expressions passed over Mrs Barnes' face as she chewed: the desire to maintain her dignity fighting with the desire to share a juicy bit of gossip. Olive crossed her fingers and hoped that Mrs Barnes' baser nature would win out.

'Well...' Mrs Barnes leaned forward, her bosom settling on the table top dangerously close to her teacup. 'You didn't hear this from me, but I think Dr Hopkins was engaged in an extra-marital affair with Mrs Greene – from number thirteen.'

'Oh?' Olive's eyes widened. 'Are you certain?'

'I saw them several times sneaking into his potting shed,' Mrs Barnes confirmed, an undeniably gleeful twinkle in her eye. 'And I once heard a lover's tiff – couldn't make out all the words exactly, but I saw her slap him, a smarting blow across the cheek such as one only sees from a woman scorned, if you catch my drift.'

'Yes,' Olive nodded, desperately trying not to sound *too* excited by this thrilling revelation. 'And did you, um, tell the police about this?'

'Oh no.' Mrs Barnes shook her head. 'I didn't want them thinking poorly of our street. This is a fine neighbourhood, not some sort of' – she dropped her voice – 'den of iniquity, riddled with illicit liaisons and the like. Not,' she added hastily, 'that I ever had any personal experience of such things. My Harold was as honest and loyal as the day's long.' Her eyes filled with tears. 'They just don't make men like that anymore.'

'He sounds like a fine husband.' Olive reached across the table to pat the woman's hand. 'Very fine indeed.'

'Oh yes,' Mrs Barnes sniffed, dabbing her eyes with her apron. 'That he was. Let me tell you about the time...'

And so, she embarked on what would be the first of several anecdotes about the many wonders of her marvellous husband and Olive listened, no longer minding about a little time wasting now that she had a delicious new clue under her belt.

1. The furniture, as found in many working class living rooms during the 1970s, was upholstered in dark brown corduroy and the bookshelf fashioned of mahogany. And, spread across the bare wooden floorboards, a woollen rug sporting a sickly pattern of orange and yellow flowers swirling together in a way that suggested the creator might have been hallucinating at the time of designing it.

2. This conversation concluded, as do almost all British conversations about the weather, with the agreement that, while it could be better it could also be worse. "Mustn't grumble" being such the order of the day that it might as well be the national motto, along with "keep calm and carry on."

Chapter Seven

'So, do you think she killed him?' Blythe asked.

She'd just arrived at the café after shutting down her bookshop for the day and was now sitting with Olive and Millie at their favourite table by the window, half a dozen pastries and other assorted delectables on plates between them.

'I don't know,' Olive admitted. 'I've not met her yet, so I don't know if she's capable of such a thing. It wouldn't be an easy thing for a woman to kill a man, especially not face-to-face.'

'Maybe the husband did it,' Millie suggested. 'After he found out about their affair. I certainly wanted to kill the little tart who stole away my own philandering cad. I might've too, if the opportunity had presented itself.'

'Well, I'm glad you didn't,' Blythe said. 'They weren't worth it, neither prison nor a guilty conscience. And they'll get what's coming to them one day, you mark my words. What goes around comes around, that's what my mother always said. And she was never wrong.'

'Agreed,' Olive said, as she slipped a sausage roll under the table onto Biscuit's plate. The spaniel gave it a delicate sniff to ascertain its worthiness, then gobbled it up in two delicate bites. She was still annoyed with Olive for having abandoned her earlier and not taking her on the fun investigating adventure and had been giving her the silent treatment ever since. She was, however, still deigning to eat Olive's delectable treats.

Just then, a clatter of pans could be heard in the kitchen, as if someone was banging on their bottoms with a wooden spoon. Startled, Blythe and Millie both jumped.

'I thought Grace had gone,' Millie said.

'She has.' Olive scowled in the direction of the kitchen. 'That's just my dead relatives expressing their disdain for my life choices.'

'Oh,' Blythe said. 'Nothing new there then. What's up now?'

Olive shrugged. 'Just the usual "get a man and get pregnant" nonsense. Anyway, to get back to–'

'Well, they've got a point,' Blythe interrupted. 'You'll be forty-one in a few months and the clock is ticking. You need to jump on that dishy detective while you've still got the chance.'

'She doesn't have to if she doesn't want to,' Millie objected. 'Not everyone's as obsessed about fulfilling the traditional feminine roles as you. Goodness, to hear you speak, anyone would think the sixties sexual revolution didn't happen at all. I'm not a wife or a mother and I'm perfectly happy about it. You should read *The Feminine Mystique*.'[1]

'And you should read *Pride and Prejudice*,' Blythe retorted. 'It might give you some tips.'

'Stop it you two,' Olive said. 'The state of my love life, or lack thereof, is not the topic at hand. I'm planning on visiting this Mrs Greene tomorrow to see if I can get her to talk.'

'I don't think she'll confess to murder,' Millie said. 'You're a good talker, admittedly, so people usually end up telling you things they wish they hadn't. But telling a stranger you've got a foot fetish is one thing, offering yourself up for a life sentence is quite another.'

'Of course, I don't expect her to tell me she did it.' Olive scooped a dollop of cream onto a blueberry scone. 'But if I can get her talking then I might get a notion of whether or not she's guilty. It's often about what people *don't* say as much as what they do.'

Blythe frowned. 'Perhaps it might be wiser just to tell Detective Dixon what you learned and let him take it from here. I mean, if she *did* kill her lover then who's to say that she won't kill you too?'

'Don't be ridiculous,' Olive retorted, taking such a big bite of her scone that she gave herself a cream moustache. 'What reason would she have to kill me? I wasn't sleeping with her.'

'I know,' Blythe said, picking at the edges of an almond croissant. 'And I know you find all these investigations fun, but it's the job of the police to actually catch these killers, not yours. Now that you've made this major breakthrough, you could just stay here and bake and let them do the dirty work.'

Olive licked the cream from her top lip and grinned. 'I could,' she said. 'But what would the fun be in that?'

After her friends had left, Olive retired to her bedroom to mull over the day's events. Biscuit jumped onto the bed, circling her side till she found a comfortable position then contented herself with licking pastry crumbs from her paws. Meanwhile, Olive extracted her tarot cards from the pocket in her skirt where she'd secreted them downstairs and sat at her dressing table to shuffle them. As she did so, her thoughts drifted to Detective Dixon and she wondered if Blythe was right. It would be nice to have someone to cuddle with at night - someone a bit bigger than Biscuit - and though she'd admittedly rather like to indulge in a little more than that with him too, given half the chance, she couldn't say the same for the natural consequences of where that "little more" might lead. For, despite her family history and the insistence of her ancestors, and her romantic friend, Olive simply didn't feel the tick of her biological clock. She never had and, perhaps, she never would. Which was most troublesome, given that she needed a daughter so she could pass on The Biscuit Tin when the time came.

'Just like every other Crisp for the last three hundred years,' Olive said aloud, addressing her spaniel. 'Right, old girl?'

Biscuit glanced up, but she was still giving her mistress the silent treatment so only raised her silky eyebrows then returned to licking her paws.

'You know, you hold a grudge awfully long for a dog,' Olive said. 'If I wanted a pet to give me the cold shoulder, I'd have got a cat. You're supposed to be unwaveringly loyal and friendly, didn't you know that?'

Still intent on her mission to hoover up every last crumb, Biscuit didn't dignify the question with a bark.

'Fine,' Olive huffed. 'I don't need you right now anyway, I've got more important things to do and mysteries to solve.'

She stopped shuffling and slowly laid out three cards face down on the table. Ritual complete, she didn't hesitate before turning over the first.

The Lovers.

Olive gazed down at the image: a man and woman locked in an embrace as they danced under a tree. 'Well,' she said. 'It looks like *someone* was having an affair. Either that or Mrs Greene had an exceptionally happy marriage. Let's see if the next one gives us a better idea.'

The next card was the Three of Swords.

'Not a happy marriage then,' Olive said, running her finger over the picture of a heart pierced by three swords. 'Poor things.' Though it was pointing towards criminal activity – unhappiness and infidelity were breeding grounds for such things, not happiness and contentment. Still, it was a shame.

Turning over the third card, Olive held her breath. It was reversed; never usually a good sign; especially when that card was Justice. Olive had always liked the image of justice: a queen astride a stallion, brandishing a sword in one hand and a set of scales in the other. Strength was another of her favourites: a woman standing beside a lion, the lion's paw resting on her shoulder. As a girl at her mother's knee, Olive wanted to be as powerful as these women.

'Injustice then,' Olive said now. 'Unfairness. Dishonesty. Along with heartbreak and deceit...' She paused, swirling the words around in her mind like milk in a cup of tea. They were all quite damning, especially linked together, telling a story with a very unhappy ending. But it was the third card that was the most damning of all. Since there weren't many injustices greater than murder.

---

1. Written by Betty Friedan in 1963 and selling over a million copies, this was one of the cornerstones of the feminist movement. It dared to challenge the tenets of the patriarchy - that "fulfilment as a woman had only one definition for American women after 1949 - the housewife-mother" and suggest that women might find greater happiness if they stepped out of the home and out into the wider world.

Chapter Eight

THIS TIME, OLIVE BROUGHT Biscuit. Not simply because the spaniel had been giving her the cold shoulder ever since being left yesterday though that, admittedly, was the main reason. But also because some people – dog people – opened up to humans, strangers, when accompanied by a friendly canine. And, having taken a quick peek into Mrs Greene's front room, the sight of a golden labrador snoozing on the sofa suggested that this possible murder suspect might be one such person.

'Now, I need you to be on your best behaviour, all right?' Olive instructed Biscuit as they reached the doorstep of number thirteen Arthur Street. 'No barking and no begging for food. Okay? Remember, we're on an investigation.'

Biscuit gazed up at Olive with large, soft brown eyes and blinked. Her way of saying: *of course I'll behave and, by the way, butter wouldn't melt in my mouth.*

Olive smiled, bending down to give her spaniel an affectionate scratch behind her silky ears. 'Yes, I know, you're the very soul of decorum and discretion, aren't you? How could I ever doubt it?' she straightened again and, after taking a deep breath, knocked on the door. 'Alright,' Olive muttered. 'Here goes nothing.'

A minute passed, then another and Olive was just about to knock again when the door flew open and the woman behind it stepped forward, then back again, now regarding Olive with a look of confusion, as if she'd been expecting someone else. *Her lover,* Olive thought, before realising that was wrong since Mrs Greene certainly knew that Dr Hopkins was already dead. Especially so, given that she was, right now, the most likely suspect for having killed him.

'Mrs Greene?' Olive asked. The woman seemed to be about Olive's age but with the dark circles under her red, swollen eyes – she'd clearly been crying – and the weariness of her expression, now looked to be at least a decade older.

'Yes.' The woman frowned, blinking into the bright morning sunshine as she sized up Olive with evident suspicion. 'What can I do for you?'

'Well, I'm...' Olive wracked her brains, inwardly cursing herself for not having thought up a plausible lie that might help her gain access to the woman's home. This time she didn't want to mention the murder, for fear of spooking the one who might actually have committed it.

'Oh yes,' Mrs Greene said. 'I know who you are.'

'You do?' Olive was momentarily startled; it wasn't often someone - especially someone (potentially) involved in a murder - knew more about her than she did about them. But Mrs Greene was smiling now, so at least that boded well.

'From the café,' the woman continued. 'The – what's it called? Sorry, my memory's awful; the perils of having four kids, you've got no room for your own thoughts anymore.' She smiled again, though it was laced with exhaustion and it made Olive shudder at the notion of being responsible for so many. She could barely juggle the demands of her own life, let alone the lives of four others.

'Four?' Olive echoed. 'That's ... a lot.'

'You're telling me.' The woman laughed, the strain on her face suddenly lifting. 'But try telling that to my husband. He'd happily have four more if I let him. I tell him that if he'd birth them and raise them, then he can have as many as he likes.'

'Fair enough,' Olive smiled, feeling a sudden rush of sympathy for this woman and wishing there was something she could do to help. *She seems lovely now,* Olive reminded herself, *but there's a fair chance she might be a cheater and a murderer too.* Although, at this moment, Olive wouldn't have judged her for the cheating: the woman clearly deserved a break. And who was Olive to judge her for that? She thought of the tarot card and thought it sad that so many people were so quick to judge others when they had no idea what it was like to live their lives. 'I'm sorry I don't remember you,' she added. 'I have so many customers, but I don't usually forget a regular.'

'Don't worry, I'm not offended.' She brushed a strand of grey hair from her face and gave a self-deprecating smile. 'I'm not someone people tend to remember. Anyway, it's my eldest, Charlie, who's the regular. He's a devotee of your lemon chiffon cake.'

Olive felt another pang of sympathy, wanting to give the woman a hug. Sadly, however, when one was British one could not hug virtual strangers. Olive knew couples married for decades who wouldn't even do such things in public. 'And what's your favourite?' she said instead, making a silent promise to bring a box of whatever it was later that day and leave it on her doorstep, murderer or not.

'*My* favourite?' the woman gave a small smile. 'Gosh, I hardly know. I, um, I had a bite of Charlie's cake once, it was delicious.'

Olive realised her mistake; of course, she'd never bought anything for herself, only her boys. 'Well, next time he's stopping by for a slice,' she said. 'He'll have one – on the house – for you too.'

The woman blushed, all at once looking a decade younger, momentarily light and carefree. As she might have done before life – and her husband – piled so much onto her shoulders. 'That's very kind of you,' she spoke softly. 'Though what I've done to deserve it, I can't say. Oh look,' – her hand flew to her mouth – 'where are my manners? Here you are offering me slices of cake and here I am leaving you out on the doorstep. Please, come in. I don't know – you've not said why you're here, but if you've time for a cup of tea, you'd be most welcome. Your dog too.'

'That'd be lovely,' Olive said. 'Thank you so much.'

Chapter Nine

'Gosh, where on earth did I put the sugar?' Mrs Greene flew about her kitchen with an air of mild panic, as if Olive was timing the preparation of tea and would deduct points for every second she was late. 'I swear, I'd forget my head if it weren't attached to my shoulders.'

'Please, don't worry,' Olive said from the table. 'I'm in no rush. And no need for any biscuits, I've brought my own. Ginger snaps.'

'Really?' Mrs Greene said, sounding as relieved and delighted as if Olive had just said she'd won The Pools.[1] 'You have?'

'They're not so delicious as the lemon chiffon cake your Charlie loves,' Olive admitted. 'But they're rather tasty with a cup of tea.'

'I'm sure they're delicious,' Mrs Greene said, at last locating the sugar bowl in a cupboard. 'And far better than the packet of custard creams or week-old fruit cake I've got in the pantry.'

'Don't worry,' Olive reassured her. 'I'm sure you've got quite enough on your plate to worry about baking every day. And anyway, there's nothing wrong with a custard cream.'

'True enough in a pinch,' she said, setting the sugar bowl on the table to join the tea pot, milk jug, two cups and plate of ginger snaps. 'But anyway, I'm all right. Charlie's at the university now, Trinity College' – she said this with no small amount of pride – 'and the middle two are at school, so that helps. The youngest is upstairs having his mid-morning nap, which gives me an hour to get on with things. Anyway' – she poured the tea – 'I'm so silly, here I am yapping away and I've never even asked you your name nor why you're here.' She looked suddenly mortified. 'Oh, it's not Charlie is it? He wasn't rude to you? He didn't try to' – she dropped her voice – 'steal anything? It's just, we've not – my husband hasn't been–'

'No, no,' Olive interrupted, putting the poor woman out of her misery. 'Nothing like that, nothing at all. I don't know your Charlie by name, but I'm sure he's never been anything but perfectly well behaved. No, I...' She trailed off, delaying the inevitable by reaching under the table to scratch Biscuit behind the ears. What would she say? She no longer wanted to lie to this woman for, not only was Olive now quite convinced that Mrs Greene couldn't possibly be a murderer but she also didn't feel right lying to someone so clearly kind, good-hearted and trusting. It'd be quite wrong. Olive took a deep breath and sat up straight again.

'Well,' she began. 'I should first say, I'm Miss Crisp, but please call me Olive. And the thing is... I'm, um, something of an amateur sleuth. Just to amuse myself when I'm at a loose end and, well–'

'Dr Hopkins,' Mrs Greene provided. 'You want to question me about his death.'

'No, no,' Olive said, studying the woman's face for traces of grief – or even guilt – at the mention of his name. But she couldn't discern anything. 'Not *question* you exactly. I'm not a detective, I'm only curious. I spoke with your neighbour yesterday, Mrs Barnes, and she–'

'Probably told you all sorts of nonsense no doubt,' said Mrs Greene. 'She's a silly gossip, ears always twitching, along with her curtains. Why, between the police and you, I bet she had a field day. What did she say about me? That I'm stealing milk bottles or running a gambling den? Just because we've stopped going to church, she thinks us second only to the Devil, I'm sure.'

'No, no.' Olive shook her head. 'She didn't say anything of the sort. She was only speculating on who might have murdered Dr Hopkins, but no mention was made of you or your family, I can assure you.' She took a ginger snap, hurriedly munching on it to cover the lie. She felt a little guilty but considered that, of the two evils, sowing discord among neighbours was surely the greater sin. The mention of church had made her suddenly self-conscious of wrongdoing. 'But, why do you no longer attend church, Mrs Greene? If you don't mind my asking. And please, don't worry about offending me; I'm not much of a church-goer myself.'

Mrs Greene stared down at her teacup as if searching for the answer in its shallow depths. She reached for a biscuit, toying with it, before taking a small bite. 'It's Charlie, he's... Since he started at Trinity - the first in our family to go to university,' she added, proudly. 'Anyway, last year he started getting involved with all sorts of intellectuals and now he comes home spouting all sorts of progressive ideas... Anyway, he thinks the vicar a conservative and traditionalist, so...'

'Don't worry, I understand,' Olive said quickly, feeling her host's embarrassment and anxious to change the subject. She nodded at the photograph on the mantelpiece, in almost precisely the same position as Mrs Barnes' picture of her husband, except that this photo depicted the family of Mrs Greene and her four boys, the baby in her arms and each sporting a mop of curly red hair. 'Those are some very handsome boys,' she said with a smile. 'I'm sure they'll all grow up to be heartbreakers.'

Mrs Greene smiled, the indulgent proud smile of a mother accepting a compliment on behalf of her offspring. 'Thank you,' she said. 'And yes, I fear Charlie's broken a few hearts already, though he's quite discrete about his girlfriends. We can't get a peep out of him, he's ever the gentleman.' She paused to munch on the rest of the biscuit. 'These really are delicious. You must love what you do.'

Olive blinked, a little taken aback by the statement and unsure how to answer it. 'Yes,' she said, tentatively. Under the table, her spaniel, sensing that she needed a nudge, nuzzled her ankle. 'Yes, I do. Very much. Although, as I said, it can get a little... repetitive. Which is why–'

'You like being a detective too.' Mrs Greene's smile took on a sad, resigned edge. 'And yes, I know repetitive only too well, it's the story of my life.'

'I'm sorry,' Olive said. 'I understand. It's the story of most women's lives. Though I know I'm luckier than most. I wish I could help–'

As if on cue, the wail of a baby pierced the air. With a weary sigh, Mrs Greene pushed back her chair.

'Duty calls,' she said. 'And I wish I could help you too, that I could offer you any clue that might help you solve Dr Hopkins' murder, but I'm afraid I hardly knew him. He was the type who kept himself to himself, went to work and came home again. He only ever really socialised with his students. I'm sorry.'

Mrs Greene was halfway across the kitchen when the wail ceased and a blissful silence descended again.

'That's what Mrs Barnes said,' Olive said thoughtfully, relieved that the conversation wasn't over just yet and thinking of what else the neighbourhood gossip had said about Mrs Greene and Dr Hopkins and the potting shed. But there was no point in bringing that up right now, not when her host had already claimed that she hadn't known him well. And anyway, perhaps Mrs Barnes had simply made it up for a good story to tell. Gossips had a tendency to be a little liberal with the truth, after all. Olive would have to try another approach.

'Please,' Olive said. 'Have another biscuit. And I'll stop interrogating you. I'm sure it's the last thing you want while the baby's sleeping. Peace and quiet, that's all I'd want in your position, a little peace and quiet.'

'You're very kind,' Mrs Greene gave her a small smile, all at once looking utterly exhausted again. 'But I'm sorry I couldn't be more helpful, really I am.'

Olive reached across the table to pat her hand. 'Don't you worry about that,' she said. 'Please. I don't mind, I don't mind at all.'

Partly, of course, Olive was being polite. But not purely. For the visit hadn't been a complete waste of time. She hadn't expected Mrs Greene to confess to an affair, even less so to murder, after all. But now Olive believed she'd learnt three things: that Mrs Greene wasn't a philanderer, or a murderess, but she was a liar. She knew something about the death of Mr Hopkins, something she was keeping a secret from Olive and the police. And now Olive just had to find out exactly what.

∞

---

1. A form of betting involving predicting the results of football matches, especially popular among housewives. My grandma Rene played every week and whenever she won we were treated to fish and chips. She was also the best baker in the family and made the most delicious black treacle flapjacks I've ever tasted.

Chapter Ten

Olive had left number thirteen Arthur Avenue without discovering Mrs Greene's secret. The baby had woken again a few minutes after his mother had claimed to know nothing about the murder and his affronted wailing had put paid to any further conversation. Olive had left soon after that, leaving the box of ginger snaps behind for Mrs Greene to enjoy when she next got the chance. Never, Olive thought, had a woman been more deserving of biscuits.

'Perhaps she knows who did it and she's protecting them,' Olive mused as she crossed Midsummer Common, her spaniel – no longer giving her the cold shoulder – trotting alongside. 'What do you think?'

Biscuit barked.

'Yes,' Olive said. 'I agree, if we can discover *why* Dr Hopkins was killed then we'll be a good deal closer towards discovering who killed him.'

Biscuit barked again.

'You're feeling peckish?' Olive asked. 'Me too.' Recalling again her mother's advice: "never try to solve a crime on an empty stomach", Olive delved into her bag in search of a snack. A moment later, she retrieved a rhubarb and custard tart. 'You see,' she said. 'That's why I never go anywhere without bringing food. For times like these.'

Breaking the tart in two, Olive offered half to Biscuit – who gratefully wolfed it down in a single gulp – while taking the other for herself.

'Quite delicious,' she said with her mouthful. 'If I do say so myself.'

After lingering a while outside Pembroke College, before popping across the street into Fitzbillies to pick up one of their famous Chelsea buns[1], Olive was crossing Trumpington Street when a police car pulled up alongside her.

'Why, hello, Miss Crisp.' Detective Dixon slowed to a stop, sticking his head out of the window. 'Fancy seeing you here.'

Uh-oh. Olive turned to see the detective regarding her with a knowing smile. *Caught.*

'Hello, Detective,' Olive said with all the nonchalance she could muster. 'What an unexpected pleasure.'

'A pleasure, certainly.' Hugo Dixon got out of the car. 'But not unexpected, at least not for me given that I've spent the past half hour looking for you.'

'Oh, yes?' Olive glanced down at Biscuit, wishing her dog could offer her an alibi. 'Well, we've been in the café, doing a little research. Always worth keeping tabs on the competition. Plus, their Chelsea buns are astonishing: rich and syrupy and–'

'I'm sure they are,' Hugo said. 'But for an amateur sleuth you certainly are a dreadful liar.'

'Liar?' Olive echoed. 'Me?'

'Yes,' the detective smiled, his blue eyes glittering with amusement. 'You.'

Biscuit barked.

'She doesn't like it when you call me that,' Olive said, tugging at the thick scarf wrapped around her neck against the morning chill.

'And I don't like it when you do exactly what you told me you wouldn't do,' Hugo retorted. 'And start interviewing the victim's neighbours.'

'Who told you that?' Olive folded her arms.

'You did, just now.'

'I did not.'

'You forget,' Hugo smiled again, 'that it's my job to know when people are lying. And you, my dear Miss Crisp, are also one of the most predictably defiant, headstrong characters I've ever met. So, as soon as I told you not to do it, I knew it'd be the first thing you'd do.'

Olive frowned, unsure whether she was more annoyed at being accused of lying or of being predictable. Of course, the most annoying thing of all was that he was right.

'Then why didn't you stop me?' Olive said. 'If you knew what I'd do.'

'Stop you?' Detective Dixon raised an eyebrow. 'And has anyone ever been able to stop *you* from doing something once you've set your mind to it?'

Olive swallowed a smile. 'Not usually.'

Hugo threw up his arms. 'I rest my case.'

'So? What are you going to do now?' Olive asked. 'Arrest me?'

The detective seemed to consider this. 'Well, I certainly *could* charge you with interfering with a police investigation, perverting the course of justice... That's well within my purview.'

Olive giggled. 'Your *purview*? That's a fancy word.'

'You know,' Hugo said. 'Most people would take the threat of arrest, along with the officer making it, a little more seriously.'

'You're not going to arrest me, Detective,' Olive said. 'If you did, who would make your favourite Bakewell tarts?'

Hugo nodded at the Fitzbillies bag in Olive's hand. 'Maybe I'll switch to Chelsea buns instead.'

'You wouldn't!' Olive feigned horror. 'Anyway, as usual, my "interfering in the investigation" has yielded results. I've got information that I bet none of your proper police interviews managed to unearth.'

'Oh, yes?' Hugo fixed her with his gaze, suddenly serious. 'And what might that information be?'

Olive hesitated, reluctant to relinquish her lead.

'Um, did I not mention the police cells?' Hugo reminded her. 'They're particularly cold and damp this time of year. And' – he nodded down at Biscuit – 'I'm afraid dogs aren't allowed.'

Biscuit barked in protest.

'Sorry, buddy.' Hugo shrugged. 'But rules is rules.'

'Alright then.' Olive sighed. 'Fine. Let's go to the café and I'll tell you everything I know.'

---

1. Established in 1920, Fitzbillies has been selling its scrumptious Chelsea buns for over a century and now has two more branches in Cambridge, on Bridge Street and King's Parade. See the first book in the series, *The Biscuit Tin Murders* #1, for its delicious Bakewell Tart recipe.

Chapter Eleven

'ARE YOU QUITE SURE that's everything?' Hugo peered at Olive over the top of his coffee cup. 'There's nothing you're not telling me?'

'You tell me.' Olive gave him a rueful smile. 'You're the one who always knows when I'm lying. Apparently.'

'You're a wee rascal,' Hugo grinned at her. 'Did anyone ever tell you that?'

'Plenty,' Olive said. 'But not usually police officers. My mother, plenty of times, every teacher I ever had, a few of my customers. But officers of the law, not so much.'

'Why am I not surprised?' Hugo set down his coffee cup, his smile widening.

The café was empty now, Grace having gone home for the day and the "closed" sign flipped over on the door. Hugo leaned over the table towards Olive so there was only an inch or so between them. His fingertips brushed hers and Olive felt her heart start to race. She was vaguely aware of the clattering of cutlery from the kitchen drawers – the sound of her dead relatives' delight – as he leaned towards her, his lips now so close to hers that she could feel the warmth of his breath. 'What is it about you, Olive Crisp? You're so…'

'So?' she echoed softly. 'What?'

Hugo gave the slightest shake of his head, as if he couldn't fathom it himself. 'I don't know, but I can't seem to…'

'What?' Olive asked again. 'What?'

This was it, she thought, after months of flirtation, at last he was about to kiss her.

'I, I…' Hugo whispered the words. 'I…'

Just then, the bell above the door tinkled and Millie hurried in, obscuring the remainder of Hugo's intentions.

Instantly, Olive pulled back and Hugo did the same.

'Oh, Olive,' Millie cried, hardly seeming to notice the slightly compromising position her friend had just been in. 'Olive, have you heard?'

Before Millie could say anything else, Olive was on her feet and ushering Millie to the closest seat. 'What's wrong, Mill?' Biscuit was at Millie's feet before she'd even sat down. 'What's wrong?'

But Millie could only shake her head, tears sliding down her cheeks.

'Hugo,' Olive turned to him. 'Go behind the counter, make a cup of tea. Milky, plenty of sugar. She needs it sweet.'

Not needing to be told twice, Hugo stood and hurried to the back of the café to avail himself of a kettle and all the necessary paraphernalia to boil up a medicinal brew. Olive took Millie's hand, waiting till her friend was ready to talk.

It wasn't until she'd taken several sips of hot tea that Millie wiped her eyes and took a few deep, restorative breaths.

'It's George,' she said at last. 'His w-w...'

'George?' Olive echoed, her stomach twisting. 'Mr Bennett?'

Millie nodded. George, the head porter of King's College was an old flame of Millie's and beloved regular of Olive's, who'd also helped her solve the mysterious murder of Jack Witstable only three months earlier[1]. Now that she thought of it, he hadn't been in for his usual breakfast of almond croissants and Earl Grey for almost a week now.

'Is he all right?' Olive pressed. 'Please, tell me he's okay?'

'H-his wife, Elsie, died on Sunday,' Millie managed at last. 'T-the Bursar's wife just told me. She came in wanting special wool for her husband's scarf and – she thought I already knew, but ... isn't it awful?'

'So awful,' Olive echoed. 'Poor George. He must be devastated.'

Millie nodded. 'She'd been sick a long time, by all accounts, though of course they hadn't told anyone. The funeral's tomorrow. I didn't know her well, but I'll shut the shop and go. I'm sure George will be touched by a large congregation. Will you come?'

'Of course,' Olive said. 'Of course I will.'

Hugo, who'd been standing a respectful distance from the table so as not to eavesdrop – although, given the snug size of the café such secrecy was virtually impossible – now stepped forward to whisper in Olive's ear.

'Do you want me to stay? Or would you rather I go and leave you two alone? I think your friend might prefer a little privacy.'

Olive nodded, thinking briefly of how close his lips had been to hers. 'Thank you, yes. I'll see you soon.'

With a single nod and quick squeeze of Olive's shoulder, Hugo left. Rather regretfully, she watched him go, then returned to her friend.

'Poor George,' Millie lamented. 'Poor, poor George.'

You really love him, don't you? Olive wanted to say, but it was neither the time nor the place. So instead she held her friend's hand until Millie was finally ready to let go.

'You're staying here tonight,' Olive said. 'And I won't hear any objection. I'm going to take care of you, whether you like it or not.'

Millie frowned. 'But–'

'What did I just say?'

Millie's frown softened into a weak smile. 'Thank you, my dearest, thank you.'

---

1. For this case, see the first in the series of *The Biscuit Tin Murders: A Fatal Fall from King's College.*

Chapter Twelve

OLIVE LAY ON THE sofa, staring up at the ceiling. Biscuit lay beside her, head resting on the soft pillow of Olive's belly. Worries pinballed through Olive's mind and she wished she could contain them, gather them up like ingredients and bake them into a cake. But her worries would not be contained.

She'd given Millie the bed, of course, though she'd had to insist several times before her friend would accept it. She'd also insisted that Millie drink her special hot chocolate spiked with whiskey, along with a few pinches of special herbs that promised to induce a deep, restful sleep. Unfortunately, Olive hadn't had enough of those secret herbs to add to her own hot chocolate so now she was wide awake, unable to stop worrying.

Mainly, Olive worried about her friend, but she also worried about Mrs Greene and herself. She couldn't help herself from returning, again and again, to the moment just before Millie had stumbled into the café. Had Hugo really been about to kiss her? And, if so, what did it mean? How did she feel about him? Not love – she wouldn't allow that – but an undeniable attraction and one that, left unchecked, might very well veer into dangerous territory. She had promised her mother she would never fall in love, that she would find a man to furnish her with a child but would never risk the possibility of a broken heart. In which case, she'd have to stay well clear of Hugo Dixon.

'The state of poor Millie is reason enough to avoid love like the plague,' Olive told Biscuit, who pricked up her ears at the sound of her mistress's voice. 'I mean, look at her. She's been in love with George Bennett for years, unable to act on it, and she still loves him so much that now she's broken hearted, not for herself, but for him.' Olive sighed. 'Her love is so pure, so true, that she cannot stand to see him suffering; she'd rather he be happy with his wife for the rest of his life than have him endure any suffering that might give her a chance of happiness. Isn't that admirable? Admirable but miserable.'

Biscuit whined in agreement and nuzzled Olive's belly.

'I know,' Olive said. 'My mother was right. Love is something to stay away from.'

At around two o'clock in the morning, Olive gave up trying to sleep and, leaving Biscuit snoring on the sofa, shuffled off to the kitchen to bake. Baking was the one thing that soothed Olive above all else, especially when she wasn't under any pressure to stock the café with dozens of pastries and cakes. Tomorrow – rather, today – she'd decided to close The Biscuit Tin as a mark of respect for Mr Bennett's loss and she knew that many of the other businesses on and around King's College were doing the same. Certainly, Millie's haberdashery, A Thousand Threads, would be shut, along with Blythe's bookshop and Derek's bread stall. Half the town, it seemed, would be attending the funeral.

'A lemon curd cake,' Olive decided, as she opened the pantry doors to survey the ingredients on offer: shelves heavy with a variety of flours, sugars, fruits, spices, nuts and chocolates... 'That's Millie's favourite. I doubt she'll be much in the mood for eating today, but I'm sure she'll appreciate the gesture.'

As she worked, sieving the flour and sugar, adding the baking powder and ground almonds, Olive chatted to herself - and her ancestors, since they, although unable to contribute to the conversation, were invariably eavesdropping – about her investigations into Mr Hopkins' death. Studiously avoiding the topic of love, since she didn't want the inevitable clanging of pots and pans (as her ancestors "voiced" their opinions) to wake Millie, Olive focused instead on her theories on the latest murder to fall under her (unauthorised) "purview".

'I really don't think it was Mrs Greene,' Olive said as she squeezed the lemons and stirred the juice into the saucepan with more butter and sugar. 'Well, I could be wrong. I know she was lying to me about something, after all, so she might have been lying about that too. But she just didn't seem like the type. If she *did* kill him, then she's a better actress than that Jane Fonda, because I couldn't see through her at all. She might have been having an affair with him, of course, but then that doesn't make her a killer, does it?'

A single spoon clinked against a porcelain cup, but the rest of Olive's relatives maintained a bored silence. Her mother, Olive knew, wouldn't dignify such speculations with a response, since she very much disapproved of her daughter's hobby. When alive, Myrtle Crisp had tolerated Olive's yen for solving crimes, so long as it didn't distract from or interfere with her running the café, but witnessing Olive's increasing delight in and desire to solve such crimes had made her far less tolerant in death.

'But the cards were quite clear about a tragic love affair,' Olive continued. 'So that *must* have been a part of it. Perhaps Dr Hopkins was involved with another of his neighbours, or one of his colleagues. Even a student! Though I sincerely hope not. That would be most untoward.'

The spoon sounded out its agreement.

Cracking the eggs into a bowl[1], Olive continued to ruminate.

'I should go to Pembroke College,' she muttered. 'Of course. Take a batch of my best bakes and find a few of his students. If Dr Hopkins' neighbours didn't know him well enough then I'll bet they will. Sounds like he was very popular, after all. And I've not yet met a student who didn't delight in sharing their opinions, usually at high volume.'

Olive shook her head, knowing that with the start of term the noise levels in the small café would soon reach painful heights with the gaggles of students squawking like geese in mating season, and the posher they were the louder they spoke. In contrast, the summer was a haven of peace and quiet, the days only punctuated by clutches of friendly holiday makers venturing in for a taste of her infamous Bakewell tarts and blueberry buttermilk scones.

While Olive whisked the eggs, she formulated her plan to visit Pembroke the following day, after the dust of poor Mrs Bennett's funeral had settled. The start of term was always a good time for sneaking into the colleges since, with the fresh influx of freshers, the porters hadn't yet ascertained who was to be let in and who to be kept out. Of course, Olive thought, she couldn't be mistaken for a new student anymore, but she could certainly pass as the mother of one.

As she stirred the mixture of lemon, sugar and butter in with the eggs, Olive found her mind returning again to the near-kiss with Hugo - but had it been that? Or had she merely imagined it? As she closed her eyes and thought of his lips touching hers, she heard the echo of her mother's voice, the constant refrain she knew so well she could say it by rote: *Never fall in love, Olive. Keep yourself safe, then you will never know the pain of a broken heart.* What about a child? Olive had asked, the first time Myrtle had made this declaration. Can't they break your heart? But her mother had shaken her head. *If you raise your children with kindness and treat them with love, they will always love you back. But shower a man with love and it's no guarantee he'll love you back. The greatest heartbreak a child can inflict is only if they die before you do.*

'Then I've at least spared you that,' Olive mumbled. 'But I wonder, if I went against your wishes, if I fell in love or left the café, would your heart be broken then?'

It was a ridiculous thought, of course, Olive thought as she returned to the sponge mix to add dashes of ginger, cinnamon and nutmeg, since she didn't even *want* to leave the café. She adored it, everything about it, the café was her happy place, the one place on earth where she felt safest and most content. The only thing she didn't love – and it was a small thing, in comparison to all the rest – was that she hadn't made a choice, not really, either to work in the café in the first place or to stay. Everything had been decided for her, a journey already mapped out, a future already planned, a life in which Olive had followed a path she'd been told to take, without taking any diversions along the way. And, although it was a lovely path, a beautifully scenic route, still it might have been nice to discover it for herself.

Once she'd slipped the cake tins into the oven, Olive turned her attention to making a batch of almond croissants; Mr Bennett's favourite. It was unlikely he'd eat them, of course and, even if he did, he wouldn't taste them. But that didn't mean that Olive would make them with any less love than if she'd known he would savour every morsel. And she only hoped that the simple offering of the pastries would provide a tiny balm to his broken heart.

'I suppose you're right about that at least, Ma,' she mumbled as she pulled a tray out of the cupboard. She glanced at the clock: 3.33am. If she worked quickly she'd still have enough time for the dough to prove and the croissants to bake before the funeral at midday. 'Love is a painful business, even a happy marriage will end in heartbreak for someone.'

---

1. Three whole eggs plus one yolk. See the end of the book for an excellent lemon curd recipe. As of Sep, 2024, the *most* delicious homemade lemon curd can be sampled at The Savoy with their delectable afternoon tea. The price is astronomical but worth every bite. (I was lucky enough to be taken by a dear friend, so I had a free tea and delightful company too - between us we ate *a lot* of lemon curd, along with every other delicious treat.)

Chapter Thirteen

As soon as Olive, Millie and Blythe reached the graveyard, the drizzle which had been falling since early morning shifted to a heavy downpour by mid-morning which, while unsurprising for British weather, especially in autumn, pleased Olive as a fitting atmosphere for a funeral. It was only right, after all, that the sky should seem to be as sad as the mourners, sympathetically reflecting their tears. And a great many tears there were. As Olive predicted, hundreds of townsfolk had come in support of Mr Bennett. Even if they hadn't known his wife very well – for the couple had lived several miles away in the village of Girton[1] – they nevertheless admired and respected him.

The memorial service had taken place in King's College Chapel, and the eulogies given by friends and family had brought Olive to tears. George himself had stood up to speak but then, too overcome with emotion, had been forced to sit again. Mr Bennett's eldest son had read the tribute to his mother in his father's stead. And all the while Olive fixed her gaze on the head porter and decided that, lovely though Hugo was, she would never, ever allow herself to fall in love.

When the service finally came to an end, when every word had been spoken or left unspoken, the large congregation filed out and walked in a snaking line across town until they were quite bedraggled, their clothes as wet as their cheeks.

The cemetery stood a little out of the centre, on Huntingdon Road[2], the place where most college members, along with their families, were buried, unless they arranged otherwise. The coffin had been borne ahead of the congregation and though he might have been driven too, Mr Bennett had decided to walk with everyone else. The procession of mourners, containing as it did so many robed fellows, reminded Olive of the graduation ceremonies that frequently brought Cambridge to a standstill when the students and staff shuffled slowly along Trumpington Street to reach the Senate House.

Olive tried to focus on the moment: while she wrapped her arm around Millie's waist; while she protected the box of almond croissants in her bag from the rain: while the vicar shared his words of condolence. "I am the resurrection and the life. Whoever believes in me, though he die, yet shall he live…" And what, Olive wondered, for those who don't believe? Was it fair that they weren't given the same deal? Faith, after all, was rather like love; you couldn't force yourself to feel it. She tried not to think of Hugo – who wasn't present – nor Dr Hopkins who, she presumed, would be joining Mrs Bennett in this very graveyard soon enough and where, along with Mr Bennett when his time came, they would all pass an eternity together.

Yet, despite her best efforts, Olive found her attention wandering back to the mystery of Dr Hopkins' murder. It was, after all, quite difficult not to think about death in a place of death, where everywhere she looked her gaze snagged on a gravestone, when all she could hear was the vicar's voice droning on about mortality, and the sniffles of grieving mourners.

Olive cast her eye around the graveyard, wondering again where the victim would be buried, wondering who would be mourning at his graveside and wondering if it might be a good idea to join that service too. Probably. Although, it would be bad form to try and interview people at a funeral. Still, perhaps she could be subtle. It would, Olive reasoned, at least be interesting to see who turned up. And yet, it would also mean waiting. She'd learnt from Millie that Mr Bennett had followed his wife's wishes in organising a fast funeral - typical of her generation she hadn't wanted a fuss to be made over her, though it'd been made anyway - but then her death had been by natural causes with no need of an autopsy nor anything else to delay matters. Who knew when Dr Hopkins' funeral would be, especially given that it didn't seem he had anyone to organise it for him.

~

It wasn't until soil had been scattered over the coffin - "ashes to ashes, dust to dust" - that she'd offered her own heartfelt condolences to George. She received, much to her surprise, a heartfelt hug in exchange for the almond croissants. As the mourners began to disperse, Olive left Millie in Blythe's care in order to wander through the graveyard. She'd told them she just wanted to take a little air though, in truth, she was seeking clues. It was possible - even probable – that the murderer of Dr Hopkins was among the congregation.

Olive glanced at peoples' faces as she passed them by, though exactly what she was looking for she wasn't entirely sure. She'd had enough experience to know that it wasn't possible to spot a murderer on sight, indeed it was the good who felt (and showed) guilt far more easily than the bad. Sometime during the burial the rain had eased, so now water was no longer dripping from Olive's nose, but her shoes still squeaked along the path. She'd reached the entrance to the little church and was contemplating going inside when she nearly bumped into the vicar coming out.

'Oh, I'm so sorry,' Olive said, quickly stepping back. 'I didn't see you there.'

'No harm done,' the vicar – a short, stout, amiable fellow – said. 'Would you like to go in? There are no more services today, but of course our doors are always open.'

'Thank you.' Olive hesitated. 'I – might I ask you about something else?'

The vicar smiled. 'You may ask anything you wish, my dear, though I cannot promise that I'll be able to answer it.'

'Well…' Olive considered how best to phrase it. 'You've heard, I'm sure, the most unfortunate news of the um, unnatural death of poor Dr Hopkins.' For reasons of propriety she avoided using the word "murder" for it seeming, along with saying "sex" or engaging in any kind of swearing, to be sacrilegious. Even if Olive wasn't a believer herself, good manners were always sacrosanct.

'Yes, indeed,' the vicar said. 'Dreadful news. He wasn't a parishioner of mine, though I frequently dine with the Master of Pembroke and he told me the sad news only yesterday. I do hope the police catch the fellow who committed the crime soon, it's never nice to know that there might be a murderer walking among us.'

Olive nodded, noting that she'd been wrong to worry about using such vernacular. She vaguely recalled then that the Bible itself was full to bursting with all kinds of gruesome killings and thus stood to reason that the clergy must be well versed with the darker sides to life.

'Yes, absolutely,' Olive agreed. 'And I'm quite sure they will.' She did not add that the police were far more likely to apprehend the killer with her help, since it was unlikely anyway that the vicar would take her seriously and she presumed he would not appreciate such a display of hubristic pride. 'I'm guessing that he'll be buried here, poor Dr Hopkins, is that right?'

'Yes.' The vicar nodded. 'I took the liberty of marking out the spot myself yesterday. It's around the back, beside the poplar tree. He didn't have any family, so we set him between two other bachelors. I'm sure he'll be most comfortable there, it's a place that gets a good deal of sunshine in the late afternoon.'

'Sounds lovely,' Olive agreed, though she couldn't understand why the sunlight mattered, given that Dr Hopkins wouldn't be able to enjoy it from six feet underground. 'Might you show me the spot?'

'Of course,' the vicar said. 'Were you close with the deceased?'

'Um, no, not really,' Olive said, suddenly aware that she was verging on lying to a member of the clergy. 'We were, um, neighbours. Sort of. That's to say...'

'Well, it'll be good to know he'll have a few visitors,' the vicar said, as he started to lead Olive towards the spot. 'I always find it an awful shame to see the newly buried without anyone to see them. Being alone in death isn't nearly so sad as being alone in life, naturally, but it's a sorrow all the same.'

Again, Olive couldn't quite see the logic of this – at least not so far as the deceased themselves were concerned – but she didn't question it as she followed the vicar through an avenue of trees towards the back of the graveyard. And there, resting on the earth between two ancient gravestones clad in lichen and ivy, was a marker for a new grave.

'Oh,' the vicar said, as he approached. 'That wasn't there a few hours ago.'

At first, her view partially blocked by the vicar's back, Olive didn't see what he was referring to. And then he shifted and she saw it: a single red rose placed against the marker, its petals glistening with raindrops.

---

1. Girton College, the first female college, established in 1869 by Emily Davies and Barbara Bodichon. It wasn't granted full college status till 1948, when women were officially recognised as members of Cambridge University. It would be many decades more till they were allowed to join the other all-male colleges. The final college to admit women was Magdalene in 1988.

2. The Ascension Parish Burial Ground is a beautiful cemetery and, should you ever have the chance, you must visit. Many members of the university are indeed buried there, along with other imminent personages, including the family that founded Heffers bookshop and several members of Charles Darwin's enormous brood.

Chapter Fourteen

'It means that Dr Hopkins definitely had a lover,' Olive said. 'It wasn't just Mrs Barnes gossiping. Of course, that doesn't mean that it was Mrs Greene, but it was certainly *someone*. The tarot cards were right, his murder was a crime of passion.'

'It certainly seems that way,' Blythe agreed. 'But I don't know how you're going to find out who. I mean, how many women are in this city? Fifty thousand? She could be a neighbour, member of staff, even a student…'

'I know.' Olive sighed. 'Though I really hope it wasn't a student.'

They sipped their tea thoughtfully. Blythe had taken Millie home after the funeral to have a much-needed nap after the emotions of the day and then returned to The Biscuit Tin for some much-needed tea and cake.

'This lemon curd cake is utterly delicious.' Blythe scooped a finger through the filling and licked it with great relish. 'I could eat the whole thing.'

'I'm flattered.' Olive smiled. 'But I'm afraid you'll have to share it with me.' She took a large fork full of cake and curd. 'I need to go to Pembroke College. I was planning to go after the funeral anyway. No need to wait, after all. Not when the café is closed and we don't have anything else to do today.'

Blythe laughed. 'You must be the most impatient person in the world.'

'Nonsense,' Olive sniffed. 'There are plenty of people far more impatient than me. Every three-year-old I've ever met, for example. The number of snatch and runs I've dealt with in my time, they can't even wait to be served before they've got their sticky little fingers on the biscuits-'

'Right,' Blythe giggled. 'So, you're the most impatient non-toddler, and curious to boot. I'd bet even the three-year-olds are more obedient than you.'

'Obedient?' Olive frowned. 'What's that supposed to–'

'The lovely detective' – Blythe raised an eyebrow – 'telling you to stay out of the murder and you instantly popping off to interview the neighbours on the sly...'

'Oh, yes.' Olive blushed. 'That. I'd forgotten I told you what he'd said about that.'

'Then you're even more distracted than usual.' Blythe poured herself more tea. 'If you've forgotten that you always tell me everything.'

At this, Olive couldn't help but smile. Her friend noticed immediately.

'What?' she sat forward, nearly spilling the tea. 'What is it? What haven't you told me?'

Olive's smile widened.

'What?' Blythe demanded. 'Tell me, right now!'

'Why?' Olive took another, deliberately slow, bite of cake. 'When it's so much fun teasing you...'

'You tell me right now, Olive Crisp,' Blythe said. 'Or I'll, I'll...'

'You'll what?'

'I won't tell *you* about the new man *I* just met.'

Olive laughed. 'B, you meet a new man every Tuesday, and most other days too. I don't think I'll miss the odd update; I can hardly keep track as it is.'

'That's a wild exaggeration,' Blythe said sniffily. 'And anyway, I really think this one might be *the* one.'

'Oh, B.,' Olive said. 'You *always* think that the latest one is the one.'

'That's not true.'

'It is.'

'It is not.'

'It is. Three months ago it was Mr Harrington. Then Mr Moulde. Then Mr Dupont. And last week it was Mr Graves.'

'Yes,' Blythe sniffed. 'Well, I can't help it if men are fickle.'

Olive opened her mouth, about to contradict Blythe again, but changed her mind. 'Hugo nearly kissed me,' she said instead.

It was, as Olive anticipated, a surefire way of ending the argument.

'He *what*?' Blythe gawped at her friend. She might have been speechless, except that Blythe Loveday was never speechless. Not even in moments of great shock. 'When? How? Where? Tell me everything!'

'It only happened yesterday,' Olive said. 'In the café, just before–'

'*Yesterday?*' Blythe shrieked. 'And I'm only just finding out about this now? Oli, how could you? You're my *best* friend. I thought I was yours too.'

'Don't be ridiculous, of course you are.' Olive rolled her eyes. 'Millie too. I'd die for you both, you know that. And–'

'And yet you've been keeping secrets from me,' Blythe huffed.

'Secrets?' Olive echoed, incredulous. 'It was only yesterday! And, it was interrupted by something far more important, so–'

'More important?' Blythe interrupted. 'What could be more important than you nearly being kissed by Detective Dixon?'

Olive laughed. 'Er, a million things: world peace, equal rights, political corruption – Mr Bennett's wife.'

'Oh, please,' Blythe said. 'That goes without saying, of course, but' – she dropped her voice – 'don't you think that perhaps the unfortunate demise of poor Mrs Bennett is a, well...' She trailed off, trying to find a delicate way of putting a very indelicate thought. 'Well, I mean, given that Millie has been in love with him all her life n'all...?'

Olive set down her fork. 'You're saying that her death is a *good* thing?'

'No, no.' Blythe shook her head. 'Of course not. Only that it, potentially, um, has an upside.'

Olive stared at her friend. 'An *upside*?' She echoed. 'B, that's ruthless, even for you.'

Blythe shrugged, unrepentant. 'When it comes to love, you've got to seize every opportunity whenever you can. Otherwise there's a very good risk that some other woman will end up married to *your* husband. Just look at poor Millie.'

'That sounds absolutely ridiculous,' Olive said. 'And yet I suppose I have to concede that your thinking has some sort of weird logic.'

'Too right,' Blythe said. 'Now, stop stalling and tell me everything. And I mean *everything*.'

After telling Blythe *everything* in exhaustive detail, enduring her endless questions, multiple speculations and frequent squeals, Olive escaped as soon as she could. Packing a few boxes of lavender biscuits and several dozen custard tarts, she hefted her bag over her shoulder and set off for Pembroke College. She'd left a reluctant and annoyed Biscuit with Blythe in her bookshop, given that it'd be harder to go incognito with a dog in tow, and prepared herself to deftly interrogate Dr Hopkins' former students.

The sun had already dipped behind the turrets of King's College, but it wasn't yet dark as Olive hurried across the road towards Trumpington Street and towards the college. It was only once she'd snuck past the porters sipping tea in the lodge that the challenge of actually identifying these students, and in the dwindling light, had occurred to Olive and she spent a few minutes walking in aimless circles around the first quad while wracking her brains for inspiration. Eventually - three minutes was a lifetime to Olive - she gave up and decided that she'd simply have to plunge forward and pick students at random and ask where to find Classics students. She only hoped that Mrs Barnes had correctly identified Dr Hopkins' subject.

'Excuse me,' Olive accosted the first student that passed: a young man in a brown corduroy suit. She noticed now that all the students were male: yet another college that didn't admit women. Olive swallowed a sigh while the student regarded her with a bored gaze.

'Yes?'

'I just wondered...' Suddenly remembering her bribes, Olive opened her bag and pulled out the custard tarts. 'Do you fancy a custard tart?'

The student eyed her with suspicion.

'I'm the owner of The Biscuit Tin, a café on Bene't Street,' she added. 'I'm giving out free samples to spread the word.'

At mention of the word "free", the student's suspicion and frown both evaporated. He reached for one so fast that Olive almost dropped the box.

'In that case, don't mind if I do.'

'So,' Olive said as he chewed. 'I don't suppose you're a classicist are you?'

He shook his head. 'God no, I'm a mathematician.'

'Do you know any Classics students?'

'Fraid not, lady, I don't waste my time with feckless wastrels.'

And with that, he sauntered off. A little taken aback, Olive watched him go. Still, she knew that when one fell off the horse it was essential to jump straight back on it, and so she grabbed the next young man within grabbing distance. This one wore bell-bottom jeans and a flowered shirt, which gave Olive more hope.

'Excuse me,' she said, this time not opening the box of custard tarts. She'd save them, she thought, for people who gave helpful answers. 'Are you, or do you know any, Classics students?'

'Fraid not,' he replied in friendly tones. 'Not personally anyway, but there's a bunch of them discussing Plato or Socrates or some such in the bar right now. I can't recommend you join them though, they'll send you right to sleep. Tedious bloody subject if ever there was one.'

'Thank you.' Olive smiled, ignoring the bulk of this statement but delighted by the pertinent facts. 'Here, have a custard tart.'

She gave him one and he, slightly bemused, took it.

'Far out,' he exclaimed, immediately taking a bite. 'That's damn good.'

Olive's smile widened. 'If you want more, come to The Biscuit Tin café on Bene't Street, we're open nine till five, six days a week. Now, if you could point me in the direction of the bar, I'd most appreciate it.'

Chapter Fifteen

It didn't take Olive long to find the Pembroke College watering hole, given the steady stream of students trickling towards and away from it. As the only female, she received the odd curious look, but most young men were too involved in their own profoundly intellectual thoughts and earnest conversations to give her a first glance, let alone a second.

A few judicious questions led Olive to the group of Classics students in the corner of the bar gathered in a circle around an open fire. She stood back to observe them for a few minutes, getting a feel of their personalities – fortunately seeming to be a fairly merry, if slightly manic, band – before stepping forward.

'Good evening.' Olive held the box of tarts out in front of her. 'I've brought you gentlemen some treats. It sounds like you're having some serious discussions over here.' Setting the box down on the table between the assorted glasses of beers and bourbons, she waited for one of them to question the offering and her presence in their college, but they were all too busy devouring the custard tarts, quickly diving in for seconds and fighting among themselves for scraps.

'Smith, you're a savage, anyone'd think your mother didn't feed you.'

'She doesn't, we've got staff for that sort of thing.'

'You have not, anyway I hear the food at Harrow is frightful.'

'Not as bad as Gordonstoun[1],' another chipped in. 'Gruel and water all the way.'

This produced a chorus of laughter. Olive hesitated momentarily, feeling grateful that this hyperactive bunch didn't frequent the café, then coughed. These chaps, she could see, would respond best to a little exertion of authority. Clearly all public school-educated, they wouldn't respect anything less. What was needed here was the firm hand of matron.

'A little quiet please!' Olive demanded.

Instantly, silence fell and they turned – as one – to face Olive who, folding her arms across her chest, assumed her best Mary Poppins impression.

'That's better,' she said. 'Now, I understand that you're all Classics scholars, taught by Dr Hopkins. Is that correct?'

Olive felt the sudden shift in the group's demeanour, an invisible ripple of anxiety that instantly flattened their exuberance, as if Olive had opened the oven too soon on a soufflé. Some boys looked at the floor, others to their glasses of beer, others to the ceiling. Whatever else was going on, the mention of their deceased tutor had clearly hit a nerve.

'Not all of us.' The Gordonstoun survivor was the first to speak. 'He specialised in Aristotle's Poetics. We didn't all elect to take on that topic.'

'Did you?' Olive asked.

Her question produced another ripple as they all focused their attention on their Gordonstoun spokesman.

'I did. Why do you ask?'

'I'm his sister,' Olive said, having already prepared her backstory prior to arrival. 'We were close but I didn't know much about his life in college. I'm preparing his eulogy and want to be sure I represent him fully. All his interests, all his passions, his friends...' She prayed, even as she said this, that they didn't ask her any questions she wouldn't be able to answer. Especially nothing that would require even a rudimentary knowledge of any of those things. All she knew about Dr Hopkins was his address.

'Well, we can't tell you much,' the boy said. 'Tutors don't tend to divulge the personal details of their lives to their students. Not unless they've had a drink or two.'

This produced a ripple of laughter, serving to lighten the mood.

'Fair enough,' Olive conceded. 'But I know a fair few students visited his house, which suggests a certain degree of friendship, wouldn't you say?'

As she spoke, Olive retrieved a box of lavender biscuits from her bag and set them atop the other box now empty save for a few crumbs from the custard tarts. 'These were Gerald's favourite. And I'm sure he would've wanted me to share them with his favourite students.'

This time, the boys all hesitated before leaning in to grab one, until the Gordonstoun boy, clearly their leader, did so. Five seconds later, the biscuits had gone the way of the tarts and only crumbs remained. Even these were quickly hoovered up by a chubby young man in a t-shirt that declared "Make Love Not War" who then took the opportunity to gobble up the flakes of pastry from the box underneath. Olive smiled to herself. *A boy after my own heart.*

'I presume you also want to know who killed him,' the leader said. 'I know I would.'

Olive paused, unsure how to best react to such an unexpected and direct question. He was trying to rattle her, she knew, trying to catch her in a lie. Thus hesitation was fatal. But how would a sister react? A normal, everyday type of sister, not one who was also a secret detective on the side.

'The police are working on that,' Olive said innocently. 'And I trust them to do their jobs. I just wanted to know–'

'We can help the police with that,' he interrupted. 'If you want to pass on a message.'

'Josh!' Another boy blurted out. 'What–?'

'Don't worry,' Josh held up his hand, reassuring them all that he had this under control. 'Leave this with me.'

Olive leaned forward, on tenterhooks. If only Detective Dixon could see her now, on the verge of making another breakthrough in the case. Perhaps she should advise him to bribe potential suspects with baked goods, it might do wonders for their arrest-rate. On second thoughts, she'd rather keep that edge for herself. In the business of catching criminals, after all, it always paid to have an ace or two up one's sleeve.

'So,' Josh continued. 'You should probably know that Dr Hopkins was engaged in a romantic relationship with a Girton student, a feisty little redhead. I saw her at his house several times and I know she didn't study Classics.' He paused, seemingly to recall further details. 'Rosie, I think, Rosie Andrews. I knew there was something between them, we all did, but of course no one spoke about it.'

Several of the other boys nodded, murmuring in agreement.

'What are you saying?' Olive asked. 'Are you suggesting' – she dropped her voice – 'that *she* killed him?'

Josh gave a slight shrug. 'I couldn't say that for certain. But crimes of passion are common enough, aren't they? And a knife through the heart, that sounds like a crime of passion to me.'

༺༻

---

1. A co-educational independent/public (US: private) school for boarding and day pupils situated in Moray, Scotland. It is named after the 150-acre (60-hectare) estate owned by Sir Robert Gordon in the 17th century. King Charles was educated there and, allegedly, had a miserable time.

Chapter Sixteen

Olive walked slowly back through the grounds of Pembroke College, watching her step in the dark, contemplating what she'd just learnt. It was certainly an intriguing revelation and one that needed investigation, yet she still had a niggling feeling that the Gordonstoun boy and his fellows hadn't been telling her everything. It'd all been too easy, they'd volunteered this dramatic secret without so much as a skirmish, and Olive felt in her bones that Rosie Andrews wasn't the whole story. So, she decided it'd be best not to tell Hugo anything just yet. He'd only be annoyed that she was continuing to investigate the case on her own, and she'd have to endure a tedious lecture on the importance of "keeping out of police business" and "not doing things that might be dangerous." Olive had heard these lectures so often she could virtually recite them by heart and they didn't improve with repetition. Anyway, she reasoned, why get the police involved if it might all just come to nothing? No, it was for the best, she decided by the time she'd reached the Porter's Lodge, that she would continue to investigate the matter on her own and, once she'd gathered some more pertinent and convincing evidence, then she'd share her findings with Detective Dixon.

Hopefully, Olive thought, as she munched on one of the biscuits she'd kept back, if she brought him some game-changing clues – perhaps even caught the murderer – then she might be spared a lecture.

Keen to avoid a confrontation herself, Olive hurried past the Porter's Lodge, head down and intent on getting out onto the street as swiftly as she could. Until something brought her to a halt so fast she nearly fell to the ground.

A student was walking out of the light of the Porters' Lodge holding a clutch of correspondence, presumably having just picked it up from his pigeon hole, and Olive – to her great surprise – knew him. Not personally, of course, nor professionally, but because she'd seen his photograph on Mrs Greene's mantlepiece.

It was unmistakably him. Not many, if any, other students in town were sporting such an unruly mop of bright red curls. Yes, it was Charlie all right, walking out of the Porters' Lodge of Pembroke College, carrying his letters and wearing a tie in the college colours, no less. This meant that, contrary to what his mother had claimed, Charlie Greene was undeniably a student here. He wasn't visiting, he was studying at the very same college where Dr Hopkins had taught. Which begged the question: why had his mother lied and said that he went to Trinity instead? Lying about an infidelity made sense; no one wanted anyone to know they were philandering, especially not with a murder victim. That Olive understood. But why lie about which college your son attended? Unless, of course, you were trying to protect him. Which meant, she realised, that Charlie Greene must have been involved in the murder of Gerald John Hopkins.

Chapter Seventeen

'THAT WAS A LOT for one night,' Millie said.

'I know.' Olive sat beside her friend behind the counter in A Thousand Threads, just round the corner from The Biscuit Tin. 'I thought you might like a bit of distraction with your breakfast.'

Millie smiled. 'You're very sweet.' She nodded at the pastry in a paper bag on the counter. 'And this apple turnover is delicious.'

'It should've been a lemon curd cake,' Olive confessed. 'I made you one the night you stayed at mine but I'm afraid Blythe and I accidentally ate it all after the funeral.'

Millie gave her a sad smile. 'Accidentally? How does one – never mind, silly question, I've accidentally eaten enough treats in my time. Never an entire cake though.'

'In my defence, I was sharing it with Blythe. So I didn't eat it *all* myself.'

'Well, even if you did, you'll get no judgement from me.' Millie took another bite of her pastry. 'How did you know that, lemon cake aside, three of these was exactly what I needed?'

Olive squeezed Millie's knee. 'I know you didn't eat yesterday. And I guessed you wouldn't have the energy or inclination to make yourself anything this morning... Speaking of which, are you sure you're ready to come back to work? I could ask Grace if she'd step in for you.'

Millie shook her head. 'If I'm not here I'll only be moping around miserably at home. Like you said, distraction at this point is definitely better than silence.'

'I'm so sorry,' Olive said. 'I hate to see you so unhappy.' She paused, lowering her voice as if about to reveal a secret. 'You must love him an awful lot to be feeling this way.

Millie sighed, a long deep exhale. 'It's not only that,' she said. 'It's… a lot of things. I suppose, to see George so… broken. I wish that he'd loved me that way. Or, even, that someone else had. That I'd known a great love like that in my lifetime. You know?'

Olive nodded, though she didn't. Not really. 'But you still can,' she said. 'I mean, you're only in your sixties. It's not over yet. Far from it.'

'I'm sixty-seven, which is nearly seventy. The odds are rapidly diminishing.'

'Nonsense,' Olive said. 'Anyway, have you considered that…' She hesitated, experimenting with how to best phrase what she was thinking. 'After a suitable mourning period has passed, perhaps you might rekindle…'

'Oh, no!' Millie exclaimed. 'Absolutely not. He won't want anyone anymore and he certainly doesn't want *me*.'

'How can you be so sure?' Olive suggested gently. 'I mean, he wanted you once. So–'

'No, stop it,' Millie interrupted. 'I don't want to talk about it. It's all too miserable. You can only stay if you tell me more about your murder investigation. That's all I want to think about right now.'

Olive took the last bite of her own apple turnover and chewed slowly. 'Okay,' she agreed. 'But there's nothing more to tell. After I close the café today I'm cycling up to Girton College to see if I can find this Rosie Alders–Andrews and persuade her to tell me her version of events.'

Millie set her apple turnover on the counter. 'Sounds like you don't think she *was* having an affair with the victim.'

'I don't know… I mean, a student seduced by a professor, that's something I hoped wasn't true. Which doesn't mean it wasn't. Still, I do think, judging by the person who told me and the way he did, that it wasn't the whole story.'

'Will you tell the police?'

'No, not yet.'

Millie raised an eyebrow. 'Surely this is something they should know. Then they can interview Miss Andrews and probably discover more than you could alone. You know I love you, Olive, but I think sometimes you forget you're not actually a detective.'

'Don't be silly,' Olive said, a little defensively. Beside her, Biscuit – ever aware of slights made against her mistress, no matter how small – barked. 'Of course I know that. I just think… I don't want to tell Hu–Detective Dixon, in case it's nothing and then he'll be annoyed that I've been wasting police time. And anyway, the fact that I'm *not* a police officer might work in my favour. It has before. People will often let something slip to little old me that they'd never say under official questioning. Especially if they've done something wrong.'

She did not add that she wanted to be the one to question this new suspect because she was the one who'd found out about her. She should be the one, it was only fair.

'Why don't you come with me tonight?' Olive suggested. 'If it's distraction you're after, doing a little detective work is as good as it gets.'

Chapter Eighteen

OLIVE AND MILLIE CYCLED the two or so miles from Bene't Street to Girton College, fuelled by a tray of buttermilk scones and a batch of fresh lemon curd. They'd invited Blythe along on the trip too but she, having been invited on a lunch date by her new beau, declined. The two friends fell into sync alongside each other as they glided along Huntingdon Road having just endured the huffing and puffing of making it up Castle Hill, discarding their scarves into their bicycle baskets in the process.

'After coming all this way I do hope she'll actually be there,' Millie said. 'She might have left to go to a party, or the library or something. Much as I'm enjoying the excursion, it'd still be a shame not to find her there.'

'Don't worry,' Olive said. 'This time I'm prepared; I know she'll be there. Popping over to Pembroke or Newnham or King's is one thing, but I'm not cycling all the way out of town without checking first.'

'How exactly do you know?' Millie threw her friend a suspicious glance. 'What have you been up to?'

Olive gave an innocent shrug. 'I called the college and asked. The porter was very helpful.'

'Oh?'

'Yes.' Olive smiled. 'Turns out he's one of my regulars; always picks up a slice of Bakewell tart whenever he's in town. I promised him one on the house next time he stops by.'

'Oli,' Millie laughed. 'You're incorrigible. No wonder people will talk to you when they won't talk to the police, you just bribe them with delicious freebies.'

'Not a bad strategy, eh?' Olive grinned. 'The police have their methods and I have mine. And, I daresay, mine are a lot more fun.'

'No doubt,' Millie agreed. 'But, even though we know she's there, how will we find her? We don't know what she looks like and it's a bit suspicious to go about asking everyone where she might be. Plus, it'll take forever.'

'Did anyone ever tell you that you worry too much? I know what she looks like.'

'Wait, what? How on earth do you know that?'

'Well...' Olive's smile widened. 'I might have told the porter that I was bringing a surprise birthday cake commissioned by her parents and they'd asked me to deliver it to her, so that's why I needed to know where she'll be and when, so I can give it to her.'

'A birthday cake?' Millie echoed. 'But it's not her birthday, is it?'

'No, of course not. But happily the porter just took my word for that.'

'And so there's no cake?'

Olive laughed. 'Of course there's no cake. But the porter won't know that either now, will he. I did bring her some fairy cakes and fig rolls. Hopefully that'll put her in a chattier mood.'

'You know, I'm glad you use your cunning for good,' Millie said. 'Because you could be a master criminal if you applied your deception and manipulation to evil ends.'

'Really?' Olive asked. 'A master criminal. Do you think so?'

Seemingly buoyed by the statement, she sped up. Biscuit, who was sitting in the bicycle basket, yelped with delight.

'Wait!' Millie called after her. 'And that wasn't a compliment!'

∽

Olive and Millie positioned themselves on a bench outside the dining hall to wait for "the feisty redhead" Rosie Andrews. Biscuit sat between them, also on lookout.

'I don't like this,' Millie said. 'It feels like we're stalking her. Or setting up an entrapment, or something.'

'That's because we *are* stalking her,' Olive said. 'We're on a stakeout. Isn't it fun?'

Millie narrowed her eyes in Olive's direction. 'You know, sometimes you say things that make me think I don't know you at all.'

'Don't be silly,' Olive laughed. 'Of course you know me. We tell each other everything. I just happen to enjoy solving mysteries too. It's my hobby. You love knitting scarves and playing whist and I love-'

'Hunting down murderers,' Millie finished off. 'It's hardly in the same league.'

'It's a little different, I grant you,' Olive admitted. 'But–wait, there she is!'

Millie glanced in the direction Olive was looking to see a group of three young women emerging in a gaggle from the door to the dining hall.

'Which one?' Millie hissed.

'The brunette,' Olive hissed back. 'With the yellow jumper.'

They watched as the girls walked on and then each split from the group to go their separate ways. Instantly, Olive stood.

'Come on, let's go.'

Biscuit jumped off the bench to follow her mistress. Millie took a moment longer to get off the mark, but soon caught up.

'Rosie, wait!' Olive called after her. 'Please, I need to ask you a question.'

The girl turned just as Olive reached her, so they almost collided.

'Sorry.'

'Sorry.'

'No,' Olive said. 'My fault entirely.'

'Can I help you?' The girl, Rosie, folded her arms.

'Perhaps,' Olive said. 'I hope so. I needed to ask you a few questions.'

'About what?'

'Well…' Olive had her hand on her bag, ready to remove the treats she'd brought but by the look of suspicion in the girl's eye she didn't think that she would be as easy to win over as the boys. 'I'm sure you've heard about the murder…'

'Of course,' Rosie said. 'Why?'

Olive tilted her head to one side, trying to look as unthreatening as possible. 'Because I was speaking to some of his students recently and, well, I'm his sister–'

'You're not his sister,' Rosie interrupted. 'He doesn't have a sister.'

For a second Olive was thrown, then she realised something. 'How do you know that?'

'What?' the girl glowered at her, angry to have been caught out so easily and by her own admission. 'I don't – I don't have to listen to this.' She started to walk away. Biscuit darted after her, yapping. Rosie stopped. Millie hung back.

'Wait,' Olive said. 'Please, I'm not with the police. I just want to ask you a few questions.' It was time to seize the moment, she knew, lay all the cards on the table and hope that Rosie's instinct for self-preservation kicked in. 'One of the students –Josh – he claimed that you were having an affair with Dr Hopkins and–'

'What?'

Rosie's shriek was so explosive that it even startled Olive. Biscuit ran back, away from this scary, unpredictable force and to the comfort and safety of her mistress.

'Yes, well, of course I didn't believe him,' Olive hurriedly assured her, in hopes of pre-empting any further exclamations. 'But I thought it only fair to ask you myself, given that it throws suspicion on–'

'Who *are* you?' the girl interrupted, looking ready to throttle Olive, despite the witnesses present.

'A private detective,' Olive said, thinking that near enough to the truth to be only a minor lie. 'I consult with the police, but I don't–'

'I wasn't having an affair with Gerald,' Rosie interrupted again. 'That's the most ridiculous thing I've ever heard. Josh only said that because he was trying to throw the scent off himself. Plus, he and I slept together a few times and then I broke it off. He's still sore about it, not 'cause he loved me or anything, just his stupid pride was hurt. I suppose this is a good revenge.'

'Throw the scent off himself?' Olive frowned, thinking of foxes and hounds. 'What do you mean?'

'That's for him to confess,' Rosie said. 'I'm not dobbing him in. But as far as I'm concerned, I can prove I wasn't sleeping with Dr Hopkins and so had no reason to kill him. We weren't having an illicit affair, and I wasn't a woman scorned.'

Olive thought of Mrs Greene. Had it been her after all? Had she been the one, just as Mrs Barnes had suggested? It was a surprise, since Olive had been so convinced of her innocence in that regard but then perhaps she'd been fooled, perhaps her sympathy for Mrs Greene's plight had blinded her to the truth.

'How?' Olive asked. 'How can you prove it?'

'Because' – Rosie folded her arms again, defiant – 'because he'd never sleep with me or with any other woman. Dr Hopkins was a homosexual.'

Olive stared at the girl, still trying to catch up. 'He was?'

'Yes,' Rosie said. 'And a wonderful man into the bargain. His home was a safe haven for those of us who shared his... way of life. He created a community where we were always welcome and could be ourselves without fear of judgement or violence.'

Olive nodded slowly as the pieces of the puzzle shifted about in her mind, disconnecting and reconnecting, assumptions and beliefs reforming with this new information.

'I'm sorry,' she said softly. 'I'm sorry that you needed a place to hide and that you lost that haven.'

'Thank you,' Rosie said. 'He is a great loss to us all, though poor Horace feels it more than anyone.'

Olive frowned. 'Horace?'

'His lover,' Rosie explained. 'The love of his life. His neighbour. Horace Greene.'

Chapter Nineteen

'Well, that was unexpected,' Olive said for perhaps the fiftieth time. 'I still can't quite believe it.'

Despite the long trek, she and Millie were walking back into the town centre, the shock having rendered it too dangerous to cycle. Biscuit, deciding she'd had enough exercise for the day, was hitching a lift again in Olive's basket.

'It never even occurred to me,' she said again. 'I feel so stupid. *That's* why Mrs Greene was so sad, that's why she was keeping secrets. Not because *she* was having an affair with Dr Hopkins but because her husband was.'

'Don't be so hard on yourself,' Millie said. 'It's only been legal for a few years and most people are still pretty judgemental about all that. The world is rife with injustice, so it's not surprising if most homosexual men – and women – are still hiding their relationships, don't you think?'

Justice, Olive thought, *of course*.

'I did a tarot reading,' she told Millie. 'A few days ago, on Dr Hopkins. And I got The Lovers, The Three of Swords and Justice, reversed. I thought it was just an affair, but it was so much more.'

'Then do you think that Mr Greene was the one who killed him?' Millie suggested. Perhaps to cover it up after his wife found out.'

'I don't know,' Olive mused. 'I mean, why try to cover it up *after* she's found out? The cat's already out of the bag, you can't shove it back in again. Well, you could if it was an actual cat, of course, but not a metaphorical cat... So it makes more sense that it was Mrs Greene herself, though I find it hard to believe. She seemed so thoughtful and kind, but also timid and nervous, not the sort you'd imagine could stab a man through the heart.'

'Oh, I don't know about that,' Millie said. 'I'd consider myself a good person, a loyal friend, soft and kind... But when I found out my bastard husband had been cheating on me, I felt so betrayed, so hurt, so full of rage that I think I could've stabbed him if I had the chance.'

Olive raised an eyebrow. 'Really?'

Millie blushed. 'Are you shocked?'

'No, I mean, yes, a little,' Olive admitted. 'But, funnily enough, it pleases me to hear you say it. I think it's much better than the other response – wanting to kill yourself. And women too often go down that route, since we're always taught to be good and sweet and kind, even when people don't treat us that way. They tell us that anger is bad and dangerous, but in fact I think it's a good thing, a protective force that shows us when we're not being treated as well as we should be.'

Millie smiled. 'Yes, I suppose you're right. I hadn't thought about it like that before.'

'I'm still glad you didn't stab the asshole though,' Olive hastened to add. 'Rage is one thing, prison another.' She smiled. 'It's a long trek to bring lemon curd cakes and apple turnovers out to Her Majesty's Prison in Peterborough.'

'You'd still bring me cakes?' Millie asked. 'I'm touched.'

Olive laughed. 'Of course I would. No question. Since I can guarantee they wouldn't be feeding you properly. I very much doubt they serve afternoon tea in prison.'

'Yes.' Millie smiled. 'I think you're right about that.'

'Okay, how about this,' Olive suggested. 'Maybe Mr Greene killed Dr Hopkins after they had a fight or something. Perhaps Dr Hopkins rejected him, or threatened to make the affair public... I mean, that might matter more than just his wife knowing. It's one thing to damage your marriage and another to damage your entire reputation. Wives tend to be more forgiving than strangers, after all.'

'Especially wives with four kids to raise,' Millie added. 'And no income of their own. Women dependent on their husbands can't really afford the luxury of anger, can they? In that way, I suppose I was lucky.'

'True enough.' Olive nodded. 'It's why Crisp women don't marry, exactly so they can maintain their independence. [1]We worked hard for ours and I wouldn't give my café to any man.'

'Not even Detective Dixon?' Millie winked.

Olive shook her head. 'Not even him.'

'I don't blame you,' Millie said. 'All men *seem* nice enough while they're courting you. It's only once they've pinned you down that you see the truth.'

'Sadly so,' Olive agreed as she gazed at a passing car, suddenly distracted. 'You know, their son might be involved too. I'm not sure how, but Mrs Greene was trying to keep him out of it all when she lied to me about which college he went to. So maybe the whole family is in on it, maybe Mr Greene was the one who killed Dr Hopkins but his wife and son know his secret...'

Millie slowed down, pulling her bike to a stop. 'Look Oli, I know you love doing all this detective stuff unencumbered by rules and regulations and all that. But I think now that you've uncovered this particular clue you really *have* to tell the police.'

Olive stopped walking too, stared up at the sky and sighed.

'Yes,' she agreed, at last. 'Yes, I think you're probably right.'

---

1. Until the Sex Discrimination Act passed in 1975, women couldn't get a mortgage without a man, nor open a bank account of their own. 100 years earlier, until the passing of The Married Women's Property Act, everything a woman owned automatically became her husband's upon marriage. In the US, women won the right to open their own bank account in the 1960s but most banks refused to allow them to do so without their husband's signature. Not until the Equal Credit Opportunity Act of 1974 was it made illegal for banks to prohibit a woman from opening a bank account without a man.

Chapter Twenty

IN OLIVE'S DEFENCE, SHE *had* been full of good intentions. She'd fully *intended* to go to the police station, as soon as she'd said goodbye to Millie and dropped Biscuit back at the café and picking up several slices of lemon chiffon cake (and eating several apple flapjacks for a quick late lunch) she'd headed off in that direction. And yet, somehow, along the way she'd become diverted. Exactly how it happened, she couldn't possibly have said, but fifteen minutes later Olive found herself not on Parkside Street at the police station but on Arthur Street standing outside number thirteen.

And, she reasoned, since she was already there, she might as well knock. She'd just have a quick chat with Mr Greene and then, she promised herself, then she'd definitely go to the police. But the temptation to interview him herself was simply too great to resist.

When her knock went unanswered, Olive knocked again.

It was Mrs Greene who answered, a fat baby balanced on her hip. 'Oh,' she said. 'It's you.'

Olive nodded. 'Do you have a minute?' She glanced at the baby who, although quiet, was red-faced from crying. 'I-I brought you some lemon chiffon cake, like I promised.'

'Really? But...' Mrs Greene trailed off. 'I never expected you to bring cake to the house. How kind.' She stepped back so Olive could enter. 'Please, come in.'

'Thank you,' Olive said, feeling a twist of guilt. How would Mrs Greene feel when she discovered Olive wasn't being altruistic but had ulterior motives? Trying to suppress her rising shame, and not entirely succeeding, Olive followed Mrs Greene along the hallway and into the kitchen.

'I'm so touched you came,' Mrs Greene said. 'I can't believe you'd do something like this for someone like me; a virtual stranger. You went to all this bother. Now, you must stay for a cup of tea.'

'Oh, it wasn't any bother, Mrs Greene,' Olive said, feeling increasingly like an utterly despicable human being. 'I was doing deliveries in your area anyway, so–'

'Please, call me Hannah.' The baby squirmed on her hip. 'Now, sit while I make the tea.'

With this tentative offering of friendship on first name terms, Olive felt her guilt swell to precipitous levels.

'Would you like me to hold the baby?' she suggested, feeling a desperate need to do something, *anything*, to be helpful and supportive, just to take the edge off her otherwise shameful behaviour.

'Would you?' Hannah handed over the red-faced baby with such a trusting ease that Olive felt another stab of shame to her heart.

She might be a murderer, Olive reminded herself, as she balanced the baby awkwardly on her lap. *Or covering for one. You're the good one here - you haven't killed anyone - you're only doing your civic duty.*

Yet, as hard as she tried to reason with herself, she remained unconvinced. A lie was a lie and a betrayal a betrayal no matter how you tried to frame it. Anyway, she'd always thought that crimes of passion were far more forgivable (so long as the perpetrator was an undeniably decent person who'd been pushed to the edge) than those that were coldly calculated and planned. Who could say for certain what they'd do if confronted with something similar, after all. *We do not know our shadow selves until we truly suffer, after all.* Millie being a case in point. Although, thankfully, she hadn't actually stabbed her scumbag husband.

'I said, do you take milk and sugar? I'm afraid I can't recall, head all over the shop.'

Olive looked up to see Hannah talking, it took a moment to realise that she'd clearly said the same sentence a few times already.

'Sorry,' Olive said, wondering as she spoke if there might be any more delicate way to handle the situation in a way that would spare her new friend any unnecessary pain. 'I didn't – I was just lost in thought. Splash of milk and two sugars please.'

The baby, sensing Olive's discomfort and deciding he didn't like being separated from his mother, started to wail. In a desperate attempt to soothe him, but not having the first notion of how to go about it – what was it they always said about a woman's motherly instinct? – Olive started jiggling her knee and emitting shushing noises.

'So sorry,' Hannah said. 'He's a fussy little minx. The other boys were good as gold – till they started to walk anyway, then they wreaked enough havoc to rival an army, but Sammy won't be put down for a moment.' She ran her fingers through her hair and Olive noticed again how utterly exhausted, how haggard she looked.

'Don't worry,' Olive said, feeling another pang of sympathy and guilt. 'I've got him.' She stood, increasing the rapidity of her jiggling and the volume of her shushing.

Unfortunately, this only made it worse.

'Here, give him over.' Mrs Greene reached for her baby and Olive, secretly relieved, relinquished him into her arms.

'You sit,' Olive said. 'I'll sort out the tea and cake.'

'Bless you.' Hannah sat and the wailing receded. 'You're a godsend.'

'Um, I...' Olive hid her guilty expression behind the cupboard door as she searched for cups and saucers. 'Where are the rest of your boys, then? I was worried I might interrupt dinner, but I don't see them.'

'Believe me, you'd hear them before you saw them,' she said, with a sad smile. 'But no, they've all been fed hours ago and now they're playing in the alley round the back. Thank goodness, or we'd barely be able to hear ourselves think right now, let alone have a chat.'

Olive offered her a sympathetic smile in return as she set a single slice of cake on the table. 'And your husband? Is he–'

'Oh, he's in his garden shed. As usual,' Hannah said. 'I think he'd move in there if he could, just to avoid all the chaos.'

She clearly tried to sound light, as if she didn't mind, but Olive could hear the hurt in her voice. Setting the teapot, cups and saucers on the table, she nodded at the plate she'd just placed in front of Hannah.

'That slice is for you now,' she said, now torn between wanting to stay and comfort Mrs Greene and wanting to seek out Mr Greene. 'And the other four slices are for you too. I've hidden them in the bread tin and I forbid you from giving them away or sharing them with anyone else. Okay?'

Hannah laughed. 'If you insist, I think I can manage that. Though I'll need to find a better hiding place - the oven - the boys are always stealing slices of bread, but none of them could even locate the oven, let alone open the door.'

'Alright then,' Olive said. 'The oven it is.'

∞

After she'd bid Mrs Greene goodbye, reiterating her orders regarding the cake, Olive wheeled her bike around to the alleyway that ran behind the gardens of Arthur Street. It was highly likely, she'd assumed, that the back gate to number thirteen would be left unlocked for the boys to cut through after they'd finished their games. And thus it'd be possible for Olive to sneak into the garden and find Mr Greene in his shed without alerting his wife to the fact. She'd suffered –

was still suffering – enough that she could do without another interrogation or confrontation, Olive thought. Now it was time to talk to the most likely suspect. Perhaps, she thought, she could get him to confess and keep his wife out of it altogether. As much as possible, anyway.

Olive sighed as she leaned her bike against the back wall. She'd made a big mistake getting so personally involved with Hannah Greene; her sympathies had already compromised her investigation and now, instead of feeling excited – thrilled to be closing in, on the verge of catching a killer and finally solving the mystery – now she only felt regret. She didn't *want* him to have done it. Because then she'd *have* to tell the police and that would ruin everything, especially Hannah's life. And the poor woman had already suffered enough.

For a moment, Olive contemplated turning around and walking away. But she'd come this far and though she felt horrible, still her curiosity was too great to let her leave now. So, she pushed on the Greenes' garden gate and, sure enough, it creaked open.

Their garden, like every garden on the little terraced street, was small and narrow, flanked on either side by high wooden fences that kept the neighbours from seeing anything but not from hearing everything. Olive tip-toed along the stone path – praying that Hannah wasn't standing in the kitchen or, if she was, wasn't looking out of the window that had a direct view onto the garden – until she reached a tiny wooden shed.

She knocked and waited.

A moment later, the door opened and a man, tall and thin with the same shock of bright red hair possessed by all his offspring, peered out. Clearly expecting the knocker to be one of those children, or his wife, at the sight of Olive he flinched.

'Hello?'

'Hello, Mr Greene.' She reached out her hand and lowered her voice, just in case Mrs Barnes might be eavesdropping. 'I'm Olive Crisp, a friend of your wife.'

'My wife's inside. I don't know why you'd be looking for her in here.'

'I'm not looking for her,' Olive whispered. 'I'm looking for you.'

'Me?' he frowned. 'Why on earth would you be looking for me?'

He could've been furious, would have been well within his rights to be, Olive thought, but he wasn't. He only seemed curious and, despite her best intentions, Olive found herself warming to him almost as much as she'd warmed to his wife. Despite the fact that he'd broken that woman's heart. Although she couldn't entirely blame him for that. Homosexuality had only been legalised a few years ago, so it wasn't as if Mr Greene had had the freedom to follow his true desires. He'd had to live a covert, clandestine life, forced to keep secrets and lie to everyone he knew.

'I just wanted to ask you a few questions,' Olive muttered. 'Although, perhaps it'd be better if we stepped inside?'

He frowned, but still stepped back to allow her in. It wasn't until the door closed behind her that Olive realised it probably wasn't terribly wise to be concealed inside a tiny shed with a possible murderer. A shed that was, into the bargain, very well-stocked with potential murder weapons. Olive glanced around the walls to see hammers and files and saws and pliers and spades and hoes and nails and ropes... She gulped.

'So,' Mr Greene prompted. 'What do you want to ask me?'

Olive swallowed again. It was certainly a very bad idea to accuse a man of murder when he was within reaching distance of all these sharp objects and yet, now that she'd come this far, Olive found that she couldn't stop. Making sure she was closest to the door and had her own hand within grabbing distance of a hefty screwdriver, Olive took a deep breath.

'Well,' she began. 'I... it has come to my attention that you, um, knew your neighbour Dr Hopkins in such a way... that you were very, um, close friends, that's to say...'

Mr Greene, who was staring – incredulous – at Olive while she rambled, took them both by surprise when he suddenly burst into tears.

'Oh!' Olive exclaimed, abandoning her proximity to the screwdriver to throw her arms around the potential murderer. 'I'm so sorry, I didn't mean to, I wasn't... Oh dear, are you all right?'

But Mr Greene was too busy crying to affirm whether or not he was all right, leading Olive to (rightly) conclude that he was not. When he pressed his face into her shoulder she patted his back, summoning more of the reassuring shushing she'd tried earlier on his baby boy, this time to greater effect. A few minutes later, Mr Greene lifted his head up, wiped his eyes and took several deep, restorative breaths.

'I-I-I'm sorry, I s-shouldn't have - you're a s-stranger and I...' Appearing on the brink of tears again, he trailed off, much to Olive's relief.

'Please, don't apologise,' she said, anxious to stem the tide. 'Don't worry, it's my fault entirely. I come into your shed, asking you about' – she stopped herself, thinking it best not to mention his name again lest it induce a resurgence of tears – 'anyway, please, don't give it another thought.' She opened her bag and produced a handkerchief. 'Take this, it's yours.'

'You're so kind,' Mr Greene sniffed. 'So thoughtful.' He emitted a hearty blow into the fabric, then wiped his nose. 'And I don't even know your name, or why you're here. Were you a friend of G...'

'No, no, that's not,' – Olive waved away the proffered handkerchief – 'please, keep it, really. I just wanted to see if you... how you were feeling and...'

Her words producing a fresh flood of weeping, Olive shut her mouth and decided not to ask any more questions.

∽

Chapter Twenty-One

'WHY ARE YOU TELLING me this now?'

Olive frowned, trying to look more contrite than she felt. 'Because I knew I shouldn't keep it to myself,' she said. 'I felt bad and-'

'No,' Hugo interrupted. 'I meant, why the hell are you *only* telling me this now? Why didn't you tell me before? The moment you found it all out!'

Olive studied the desk. It had a plastic coating with fake wood underneath; the plastic was broken all along the edge, presumably chipped away by the nervous fingers of the numerous suspects who'd sat exactly where Olive was sitting now.

After the encounter with Mr Greene, and having finally extracted herself from his shed and parting with three more handkerchiefs, Olive had finally fulfilled her intentions of going to the police station to confess all to Detective Dixon and, when she'd arrived – past nine o'clock at night – he'd suggested that they go to an interrogation room for a little privacy. A suggestion Olive, who now felt like a suspect herself, was now heartily regretting having agreed to.

'I know,' she said. 'I know I should have and I meant to, really I did. I just... I thought if I could find out first what was true and what wasn't then I wouldn't be wasting police time with a lot of nonsense, so I decided–'

'Oh, please,' Hugo interrupted. 'You don't really expect me to believe that do you?'

'Of course I do!' Olive protested. 'I'm telling the truth, I...' She stopped suddenly and sighed. 'Alright, all right. I'm sorry, I'll admit it, I was just enjoying it all too much. Feeling like a detective, being in charge of my own case...' She pulled her gaze up from the table to look him in the eye. 'And I knew, of course, that the moment I told you – you'd take over everything and I, wouldn't have anything to do anymore.'

Suddenly, Hugo softened. 'Oh, Olive,' he said. 'Whatever will I do with you?'

Olive shrugged, sheepish.

Hugo sighed. 'Are you quite sure that Mr Greene didn't do it? Because it really sounds like we should bring him in for questioning. His son too.'

'No, no.' Olive shook her head, once more recalling the weeping. 'Look, I might be a meddler and a mischief maker and whatever else you want to call me, but if there's one thing I know it's people. I can promise you, that family is innocent.'

Hugo raised an eyebrow. 'You're certain?'

'I'm certain,' Olive said, ninety-nine percent sure that she was. 'And, I know there's no reason you should say "yes" to this and every reason you'll probably say "no", but I've got a hunch about the Greene boy and I think, if you just give me a chance to chat to him, that I might actually make a breakthrough. What do you think?'

Hugo sighed again; a long, exhausted sigh. 'I think you're crazy. And audacious. And you've got some nerve asking me that after everything else you've just told me.'

'Oh.' Olive, who'd just been holding her breath while he spoke, now exhaled and deflated with disappointment. 'Well, I just thought–'

'And yet you, alone, have made far more progress in the past three days than the entire police force have, with all the resources at our disposal. So...'

Olive sat forward, once more on tenterhooks.

'Twelve hours,' Hugo said. 'You've got twelve hours. Plus one more for luck. That's thirteen, till ten o'clock tomorrow morning. That's it. And then I'll go to Pembroke and find Charlie and bring him, along with the whole family, in for questioning.'

Chapter Twenty-Two

OLIVE'S ELATION AS SHE cycled back to the café in the pleasantly chill air of the dark evening was only dampened by one thing: the nearly-kiss. He hadn't mentioned it, she hadn't mentioned it; it was as if it'd never happened. So much so that Olive was starting to think she'd imagined the entire thing. This thought left her disappointed and this, in turn, made her doubly disappointed since it demonstrated that her mother was right: romance was a dangerous thing to dabble in.

In order to distract herself, Olive spent several hours baking before bed and, after a few restless hours, gave up trying to sleep and baked half a dozen lemon chiffon cakes, several batches of custard tarts, lavender biscuits and chocolate flapjacks before Grace arrived early to open the café.

'Thank goodness you're here,' Olive said upon her arrival. 'Could you set everything up while I pop back upstairs for a quick nap? I've hardly slept.'

'Of course,' Grace said, in her usual unflappable way. 'Take as long as you like.'

'Bless you.' Olive reached for Grace's hand and gave it a grateful squeeze. 'Help yourself to anything you want for breakfast, of course. Now, I'm off before I collapse right here on the floor.'

A few hours later, leaving the café in Grace's charge, Olive set off with Biscuit at her heels and a slice of cake in hand, for Pembroke College. It was early morning, just past eight o'clock, and she didn't know how long she'd have to wait for Charlie Greene to arrive but hoped, based on his mother's reports of his conscientiousness, that it wouldn't be too long. And, since she could hardly set up camp on the street outside to wait for him, nor really risk planting herself on a bench inside college grounds, it meant that she would have to walk up and down the street while keeping a beady eye on the entrance.

'Sometimes it pays to have a dog, eh?' Olive smiled down at Biscuit, who barked as they took their fifteenth turn at the corner of Trumpington Street. Biscuit barked again and Olive glanced up into the window of Fitzbillies. 'I know, you want a Chelsea bun, don't you?' Biscuit whined and Olive felt a pang in her stomach. She'd been in such a rush to get out and ambush Charlie – time was of the essence after all, she only had four hours of Hugo's deadline remaining – that she'd forgotten to have breakfast.

That was a first.

'I don't know,' Olive said, glancing back at the college doors before gazing once more at the tray of glistening currant buns in the window. 'What if he comes while we're inside? Hugo'll be here with the police at ten o'clock. That's when our thirteen hour deadline is up.'

She hesitated, torn between her mind and her stomach. It didn't take much more than a minute before Olive's stomach won the fight.

'Alright,' she said. 'I'll just pop in and buy a couple. Quick as a flash, all right? You wait here and keep watch. Bark if you see anyone going in those doors.' Olive pointed across the road and Biscuit yapped, though Olive wasn't certain whether it was in agreement or excitement at the anticipation of something delicious coming her way.

Olive darted into Fitzbillies and smiled at the girl behind the counter.

'Alison, so lovely to see you! I need two Chelsea buns for breakfast please, in a box. Thank you so much.'

'Lovely to see you again, Oli.' The girl grinned, looking genuinely pleased. 'And an honour, given that you've got a dozen delicious cakes on your own counters...'

'I know' – Olive glanced out of the window to see Biscuit still waiting patiently on the pavement, eyes focused intently on the college doors – 'but I don't make these buns. Now, if you'd give me your recipe, I'd be able to stop bothering you...'

'Nice try.' Alison laughed. 'Anyway, food is like foot rubs, don't you think? It always tastes better when someone else does it for you.'

'True enough,' Olive conceded. 'We should do a daily swap–'

Just then, Biscuit started barking so loudly that Olive, suddenly faltered, spun round and darted back onto the street, leaving a bemused Alison gazing after her.

'I'll pay in a moment!' She called back over her shoulder, before looking for Biscuit. 'What is it? Who is it?' In her haste to see, Olive stumbled over the spaniel and nearly flew into the road. Righting herself, she saw that the entrant to the college, whoever he was, did not sport a mop of bright red curls and she sank back, deflated.

'Nearly, Bics,' she patted Biscuit's head. 'Well done. You're an excellent lookout.' She glanced at her watch. 'It's okay; we've still got plenty of time.'

Time which, Olive knew, she would not easily endure without something sweet in her stomach. Turning back towards Fitzbillies, patting her bag to be sure the cake slices were undamaged, Olive looked up again only to be whacked by the door opening into her face. Sent flying again, she tripped backwards over Biscuit and, a second later, landed firmly on the pavement, bottom first.

'Oh, no!' She heard a male voice above her. 'I'm so sorry! I didn't see you there!'

Rubbing her head, Olive groaned. Fortunately, she seemed to have avoided serious injury - no blood or broken bones - but her bottom ached and her pride was dented.

'I'm fine,' she said, taking the hand that was offered to help her up. 'I'm fine, I–'

And then Olive stopped, because now she was looking into the face of Charlie Greene.

'Oli! Are you okay?' Alison had rushed out of the shop and was alongside Olive now, taking her other hand. 'Come and sit down, you need to sit.'

'No, no,' Olive protested. 'Please, I'm…' Then, all at once realising that she stood a far better chance of her target sticking around if she *wasn't* fine, Olive feigned a slight swoon. 'Oh, dear,' she mumbled, as the grips of her two anxious assistants immediately tightened. 'Oh, dear. Yes, p-perhaps you're right, Ali, perhaps I'd better sit down.'

Olive allowed Alison and Charlie, followed closely by Biscuit, to spirit her into the café and into a chair at a table beside the window.

'You stay with her,' Alison told Charlie. 'Make sure she's not concussed. I'm off to get buns and coffee. She needs caffeine and sugar.'

'I'm so sorry,' Charlie said, for perhaps the hundredth time. 'I'm so sorry I didn't see you there, I was distracted, I was thinking of - I don't know how I didn't see you. I'm so sorry, I…'

'Don't worry.' Olive patted his arm. 'Don't worry, it wasn't your fault. I should've been looking where I was going too.'

'That's awfully generous of you,' Charlie said. 'But it was entirely my fault.'

Olive affected a shrug, then remembered to rub her head. Achieving the perfect balance of being injured just enough to need attention but not enough for hospitalisation wasn't so simple.

'Well, I *am* feeling a little dizzy,' Olive admitted. 'So perhaps if you could keep talking to me, at least until I feel steady on my feet again…'

'Yes, yes.' Charlie sat forward. 'Of course. What do you want me to talk about?'

'Well…' Olive, still unable to believe her good fortune – never had a knock to the head been so fortuitous – pretended to consider it. 'You're a student, yes?' She indicated the college scarf knotted round his neck. 'Why don't you tell me about your studies?'

'Are you sure?' Charlie asked. 'It's Classics; you might find it a little boring…'

'Nonsense,' Olive said, noting how proud he sounded in spite of his disclaimer. 'Tell me everything.'

'Alright then, if you think it'll help.' He bit his lip, deciding where best to start. 'This term we're studying *The Odyssey*. I've got my first tutorial on Monday, so I'm getting a head start on the term's reading list. I've just finished the translation by-'

'*The Odyssey*,' Olive repeated, thoughtfully. 'Isn't that by Homer?'

'Yes.' Charlie looked surprised. 'Do you know it?'

'A little,' Olive said, enjoying his surprise. It was always fun to thwart expectations, especially the underestimations most young men made about middle aged women. 'How does it go? "*Of the cunning hero, The wanderer, blown off course time and again After he plundered Troy's sacred heights…* Something like that?"'

Charlie stared at her open-mouthed and, at the sight of him, Olive couldn't help - though it didn't fit with her injured demeanour - but laugh. In truth, she only knew the lines because she'd heard them recited by various self-important Classics students over the years, but he didn't need to know that.

'Yes,' Charlie said. 'That's word perfect. The Lattimore translation, right?'

'Right.' Olive nodded, having not the first idea what that meant. 'I-I enjoyed it very much. Especially the, er, Ali!'

Fortunately, in that moment the arrival of Alison bearing a tray of coffee and Chelsea buns, saved Olive from any awkward interrogation as to the particulars of Lattimore's translation.

'Here you go,' she said, setting the plate and cup down in front of Olive. 'Drink up and eat up. I've got to get back behind the counter, but you stay here. You're not leaving till not a crumb remains, all right? Cook's orders.'

'Alright.' Olive smiled. 'I think I can manage that. Especially when I have this young man to entertain me with Homer.'

'Good, good.' Alison patted Charlie's shoulder. 'Well, you take excellent care of our Olive and you' – she turned to Olive – 'shout for me if you need anything. More buns, coffee, buns – it's all on the house. Promise?'

'Promise,' Olive echoed. 'And you're too kind.'

'Not at all,' Alison said. 'We've got to keep you on your feet, the citizens of Cambridge need The Biscuit Tin, we can't cater for everyone, can we?'

Laughing as she hurried off, Olive found Charlie regarding her with a newly curious look.

'You own The Tin?' he said. 'I love that place. The lemon cake, it's out of this world.'

'Oh, you do?' Olive smiled. 'Well, then you'll be delighted to know that I just happen to have a slice or two on me.' She reached into her bag at her feet, being diligently guarded by Biscuit, and extracted the box of cake. 'I was saving it for my breakfast, but since I have these now' – she nodded at the plate of Chelsea buns – 'why don't you take it instead.'

'Really?' Charlie took the box as if she'd just given him the keys to Buckingham Palace. 'Are you sure?'

Olive gave a nonchalant shrug, secretly rather delighted to have made him so happy. This is what she loved about the students who didn't come from privileged backgrounds, who hadn't grown up in castles or been educated at Harrow; they were so easily impressed. 'Of course, just to show I don't hold a grudge.'

'I think you're my fairy godmother,' Charlie said, opening the box.

Olive felt a twinge of guilt and, with some effort (aided by a bite of Chelsea bun), suppressed it. *Hopefully, you're here to demonstrate his innocence,* she told herself. *To pre-empt an unnecessary police interrogation. Just imagine the humiliation if all his fellow students witnessed that...*

'So,' Olive said, before her worries spiralled out of control. She slipped a pinch of sweet bun to Biscuit under the table. 'Have you studied Aristotle yet?'

'Last year,' Charlie said, mouth full of cake. 'Though, if I'm honest, I'm already preferring Homer. I think–'

'Ah,' Olive said, trying not to sound too excited. 'Then you must have had tutorials with Dr Hopkins.'

At this seemingly innocuous statement, Charlie flinched so violently that he nearly choked on his cake.

'Oh, I'm sorry,' Olive said innocently, while Charlie struggled to regain his composure. 'Did you know him well?'

'N-no,' Charlie protested. 'Not at all. At least, only so far as he taught me. No more than that.'

Olive took another bite of the bun, slowly drawing the moment out. 'But you lived next door to him too, didn't you? So you must have known-'

'What?' Charlie stared at her, incredulous. 'How did *you* know that?'

'I-I'm one of your mother's friends,' Olive explained. 'She told me.'

Charlie narrowed his gaze, the cake forgotten in its box on his lap. 'I've never seen you before.'

'Well, you have,' Olive bluffed. 'After all, I must've served you several times at the café, you just don't recall. Do you generally notice your mother's friends?'

Charlie sat with this, unable to contradict it. Still, he continued to regard her with suspicion. 'Why are you asking me these questions? Was this a set-up? I don't understand. Who *are* you?'

He was less adept at putting on a front than his fellow students, Olive noted, less able to maintain a front. Whatever Charlie Greene would end up doing for a career – so long as he didn't end up in prison – he wouldn't be a politician.

'I'm just trying to find out what happened to Dr Hopkins,' Olive said. 'I spoke with your father last night and–'

Suddenly, Charlie looked scared. 'I thought you owned a café? But you don't, do you?' He threw the cake onto the table, startling Biscuit beneath it. 'Are you trying to poison me? Or drug me.' He clutched his throat, starting to cough and quickly unwrapped his scarf, dropping it to the floor. 'Are you a spy? Did you lace that cake with truth serum?'

'What?' Olive gazed at him in shock. 'No, of course not! I'd never do such a thing. I don't want to hurt you, I just want to know–'

But Charlie, who'd stopped coughing but was looking more terrified with every passing minute, wasn't listening. 'You're with the police then, aren't you? And you think Dad was involved in Gerry's murder.'

'Why would you say that?'

Startled, Charlie dropped his face into his hands. *The Greene men*, Olive thought, *are a surprisingly emotional bunch.* It made a refreshing change from the usual stoics of the typical Englishman and Olive quickly found herself becoming as drawn to Charlie as she had been to his father. She'd make a dreadful policewoman, she realised then, simply because she lacked the capacity to be objective and impartial.

'Oh, no.' Charlie dropped his face into his hands. 'No, no, no...'

'What?' Olive was surprised, not least by the efficacy of her interrogation techniques. 'What is it?' she watched as he slumped over the table, dangerously close to squashing the cake and spilling the coffee. Hurriedly, Olive removed them to safety. 'Please, don't–'

Charlie peered up at her from between his fingers. 'This is about their affair, isn't it? That's why you're here.'

Olive nodded, thinking of what Mrs Barnes had said about seeing Hannah Greene in the shed with Gerald Hopkins. But, of course, she'd been confronting him. So, they had all known. 'Yes,' she said thoughtfully. 'I wasn't absolutely certain that you knew, but I guessed that you probably did.'

'Yes,' Charlie admitted. 'Of course I did. And I know what else you're thinking but you're wrong. I didn't kill him. On my honour, I didn't.'

Chapter Twenty-Three

OLIVE GAZED AT CHARLIE. She felt a sudden and unusual maternal urge to comfort him and, though she feared it would significantly undermine her authority in the circumstances, she reached out to pat his head, just stopping short of therapeutically scratching behind his ears as she did when soothing Biscuit.

'I didn't do it,' Charlie said again as he finally pulled his face up from the table and sat up. 'I promise I didn't.'

'I know,' Olive said, almost certain he was telling the truth. For the Greene men, in addition to being rather theatrical, seemed to lack the killer instinct. Although, she could be wrong. She had been before, though it was rare. 'Don't worry, I know.'

'Of course I was upset,' Charlie sniffed. 'Of course I was. Who wants to discover their father having an affair and, not only that, but realise their parents' marriage was based on a lie? And I was angry, at them both, yes. Still, not enough to do something like that, especially knowing how it would've devastated my dad. That would've been too cruel. I didn't agree with his choices, but only 'cause of Ma. Otherwise, I would've understood. I didn't judge him for who he was, for how he felt.'

'That's very ... I'm happy to hear it,' Olive said. 'For a young man, you're very mature, very open-minded.'

'Thank you.' Charlie gave her a small, relieved smile. 'Thank you.'

Olive returned his smile but swallowed a sigh. It was good news, no doubt, that Charlie wouldn't be going to prison. But she nevertheless felt as if, despite all the detective work over the past few days - of which she'd been very proud – she was now back to square one. She'd pursued so many avenues, only to have them all lead to dead ends.

'Look,' she said. 'If you didn't kill Dr Hopkins, and your father didn't and your mother didn't – do you have any idea who did?'

Charlie said nothing, only glanced out of the window in the direction of Pembroke College, a blush rising up his neck.

'Wait.' Olive eyed him. 'You *do*.'

'No,' Charlie said, suddenly looking scared again. 'No, I don't.'

'Look.' Olive leant forward, fixing him with her most serious gaze. 'The police know about your father's relationship with Dr Hopkins and right now, he's their most viable suspect. So–'

'But he's innocent,' Charlie protested. 'You'll tell them that, won't you?'

'I will,' Olive said. 'But it might not matter. Plenty of innocent people go to prison, plenty of are convicted for crimes they didn't commit.' She thought of the tarot card again: Justice, reversed. 'The world is rife with injustice, Charlie. You must know that.'

Charlie shook his head with a groan. 'No, no.'

'If you know who did it,' Olive persisted. 'You need to say so. Or I don't know what'll happen. And, honestly, I'm already very fond of your family and would hate for them to suffer any more than they already have.'

Charlie met her gaze.

'I think you know,' Olive repeated. 'I think you know who killed him.'

'I don't,' Charlie said. 'At least, I don't know who. But I do know why.'

Chapter Twenty-Four

Olive stared at him, almost unable to believe that her interrogation technique had actually borne fruit. Indeed, she was so astonished and so delighted, that for a few moments she forgot to speak. It was Biscuit's yap under the table that brought her back.

'Why?' Olive echoed. 'If you know, tell me.' She waited on tenterhooks for Charlie to answer. But the poor boy – his left knee now jiggling so vigorously that Biscuit soon removed herself to a safe distance – remained silent.

'Please,' Olive persisted. 'Think of your father, of yourself. The police want to interview you; they're coming here, in a few hours, to take you to the station. Is that really something you want everyone to witness?'

At this, Charlie let out a whimper, sounding so forlorn that, for a moment, Olive thought it was Biscuit, unhappy that her mistress was hoarding all the Chelsea buns for herself.

'Are you protecting someone?' Olive asked. 'If you are, you need to understand that it might come down to making a choice between them and your family. The police won't stop till they've caught someone and, as I said, it doesn't necessarily matter to them whether it's the right person or not.'

She felt another twinge of guilt at this statement, since it reflected so poorly on Hugo, but still, even though she knew he'd never personally arrested and charged an innocent man, Olive knew of other officers who had. And she really didn't want the same thing to happen to Charlie or his father.

Olive watched Charlie take a deep breath. 'Not someone,' he said. 'But everyone.' His bottom lip trembled and, once more, Olive felt the urge to reach out and hug him. 'Every friend I have here, every...'

'Oh, Charlie,' Olive said. 'I'm so sorry that you're going through this and I understand that you feel – so it sounds – as if you're going to lose everything you care about by telling me the truth. But, I can promise you, you won't. And you *will* recover. Life is long. And it contains many paths you can travel down and many people you can meet. This place, these people, are only a small part of that. And if they've done something–'

'Have you heard of Fairy Dust?' Charlie mumbled.

Olive frowned. 'As in... magic?'

She thought of her tarot cards and, despite her speech on the many various paths of life, the unexpected twists and turns, she certainly hadn't expected a diversion towards the supernatural.

In spite of his obvious misery, Charlie gave a small smile. 'As in drugs.'

'Drugs?' Olive echoed. And, while this new twist was slightly less surprising than the other, it still threw her. She'd been so focused on the affair, on the expectation of a crime of passion, that she'd never properly considered other avenues. Certainly not this one. It was a lesson, she reminded herself now, not to be so fixated on one particular path that you ignore all others. 'What do you mean?'

'This place is hard,' Charlie explained. 'I suppose every top institution is, and Cambridge University is... intense. We have to work very hard to keep up with the reading lists, the weekly essays – thirty books and five thousand words – and we're studying among the cleverest people in the country, the sense of competition pervades everything along with the perpetual feeling that – in comparison to everyone else – you're miserably inadequate, not good enough to be here, a fraud and a failure.'

Olive nodded sympathetically. She had no experience of what he was describing, a relief in itself, but she could imagine how hard it must be, especially for someone from his background, being so desperate to prove himself and fit in.

'So,' Charlie dropped his voice, even though the café was still empty, none of the counter customers having yet filtered through to sit on the tables. 'Some of us started taking drugs to stay awake longer, to be able to finish the reading lists and complete the essays. And soon everyone in the cohort of Classics students – at least in our year – were taking them. It didn't matter, we weren't hurting anyone, except maybe ourselves, except that we were less worried, less scared because now we had the edge to achieve the results that kept us on top.'

'Who gave you these drugs?' Olive asked, though she already knew the answer. Now, at last, everything was starting to fall into place. 'Dr Hopkins?'

She expected Charlie to nod in agreement, to tell her she was right but instead he looked horrified.

'No!' He exclaimed. 'Of course not. Whatever gave you that idea?'

'Well, I...' Olive began, a little taken aback. 'I don't know, it just seemed to make sense.'

'No,' Charlie said again. 'He wasn't the one giving us the drugs, he was the one who stopped us. At least, he tried, but no one wanted to listen. We were doing too well, none of us wanted to go back to life being so challenging, so effortful again. It was like… we'd been crawling through quicksand and then suddenly we were flying. No one would give that up. Dr Hopkins was worried, he told us about the risks, that we might overdose or become addicts. But we didn't listen.'

Olive sighed. 'Let me guess. He threatened to tell your parents?'

'Worse,' Charlie said. 'The Dean. We would've all been sent down. Expelled. We would've lost everything. Everything we'd worked so hard for, risked our lives for. A–'

'And so one of you killed him,' Olive whispered. 'To shut him up.'

Charlie nodded.

'But you don't know who?'

Charlie shook his head. 'We haven't spoken about it, not since it happened. But we all know it was one of us.'

'And which one of you was supplying the drugs?' Olive asked. 'Wait, let me guess. It was Josh?'

'Yes.' Charlie looked surprised. 'How did you know?'

'I had my own encounter with your fellows,' Olive said. 'And he seemed to be the leader. My money is on him being the one who killed Dr Hopkins.'

'I thought so too,' Charlie agreed. 'But I can't be certain. We were all terrified of being sent down. I went to Dr Hopkins' house, to beg him not to say anything. I even' – he dropped his gaze to the table, ashamed – 'I even threatened to expose him if he wouldn't keep our secret.'

'What did he say?'

'He begged me not to, of course. But he wouldn't back down. He said he was doing it for our own good – if we wouldn't stop on our own then he'd have to make us – he said he was doing it to save our lives.' Charlie's voice caught, snagged by emotion. His next sentence was heavy with guilt. 'And it cost him his.'

Chapter Twenty-Five

OLIVE CAUGHT HUGO JUST as he was driving out of the police carpark, on his way to Pembroke College. He parked the car on the pavement and listened intently as she told him everything, then let out a miserable sigh.

'And you believe him?' he asked, when Olive had finished. 'You're certain he wasn't the one who did it?'

'Yes,' Olive nodded. 'Pretty certain. Ninety percent.' She reassessed. 'Ninety-five. I'd put my money on Josh.'

'Alright,' Hugo agreed. 'Then let's go and track down this Josh. Along with the rest of his gang. We'll bring them all into the station and find out who did it.'

'Okay,' Olive said, suddenly feeling a little sad now that it was (almost) all over. 'And when you find out, will you come and tell me? I really-'

'Come and tell you?'

'Yes,' Olive persisted. 'I mean, I know I had no business interfering and–'

'Olive!' Hugo stopped her with a laugh. 'What on earth are you talking about? I know I had a bit of a moan about you going off book and all that. But I was wrong. Without you we wouldn't now be within spitting distance of catching the culprit. We'd still be rambling in the bushes following procedure and failing to make any progress. You might not be on the force but, honestly, I think that's a bonus. It's part of why you've managed to do what you've done – you can do what we can't.' He smiled. 'Also, you're utterly brilliant. Which, I hope, goes without saying.'

Olive blushed, then grinned. 'Well, perhaps it does, but I give you full permission to say it as often as you like anyway. Every day might be nice for starters.'

'Every day?' Hugo met her smile. 'That sounds fair enough to me. Although, you know, it would mean then that we would have to see each other every day.'

'Oh yes,' Olive said. 'I hadn't thought of that...'

Hugo's smile widened. 'You're still forgetting that I can always tell when you're lying.'

'How remiss of me,' Olive murmured. 'Well, I suppose it wouldn't be so very awful seeing your face every day. I think I could cope.'

'You could?' Hugo's blue eyes glittered with amusement. 'That's good to know.'

'And how about you? Do you think you could cope with seeing me every day? Or would my mischievous ways drive you crazy with vexation?'

'Yes.' He took a step towards her. 'I'm sure it would. But then vexation is one of my favourite feelings – didn't I mention that before?'

'No.' Olive shook her head. 'You didn't.'

Now he was within inches of her again, their noses almost touching, and Olive held her breath. *Surely, surely he was about to kiss her.* She almost closed her eyes, but found it impossible to draw her gaze away from his. She could, she thought, stare into those blue eyes forever. It was a dangerous thought.

'So...' Hugo whispered.

'So...?'

And then, before she knew it, his lips were on hers and they were kissing. Every thought left Olive's head, every sensation too as she felt nothing else but the kiss. He brought his hand to her face and cupped her cheek, stroking her skin with such tender affection that it made her sigh. And then, he stopped.

'I stand corrected,' Hugo said. '*This* is my favourite feeling.'

'What?'

'The feeling of you.'

For a moment Olive was so touched by his words that she couldn't speak. Instead, she stood on tip-toes and kissed him again. And when she finally took a breath, she smiled.

'I've had a few kisses in my time,' she said. 'But none that tasted as good as apple pie, and *almost* as good as Bakewell tart.'

'Almost?' Hugo asked, feigning disappointment. 'Only almost?'

'Well,' Olive shrugged. 'You'd have to be super-human for your kisses to taste as delicious as my Bakewell tart.'

'Yes,' Hugo laughed. 'I suppose that'd be a tall order. But, perhaps with a little more practice...'

He leaned towards her again, but Olive stepped back.

'I think you're forgetting something,' she said. 'You've got a killer to catch.'

'Dammit, you're right.' Hugo stepped back towards his car and opened the driver's door. 'I suppose the kisses will have to wait.'

'Fraid so,' Olive said, feeling a little disappointed and not simply for that but because, after having solved all the mysteries, she'd now have to stay behind and miss out on all the excitement of actually catching the culprit. 'I'll see you later.'

But Hugo was still standing beside the car. 'Come on then,' he said, nodding at the passenger's door. 'What are you waiting for?'

Olive grinned. 'Really?'

'Of course,' Hugo said. 'You think I'd let you do all the work without getting any of the glory?'

Chapter Twenty-Six

'He kissed you? He really *kissed* you?'

Blythe was gazing at Olive as if she'd just revealed the secret to eternal life.

'Yes,' Olive said, a little impatiently. 'He kissed me. But didn't you hear what else I said? *I* caught the chap who killed Dr Hopkins.'

'Yes, yes, of course,' Blythe said quickly. 'The Pembroke student who he was selling drugs to. That's amazing. But let's get back to that kiss before you forget all the—'

'No,' Millie laughed. 'The *killer* was selling the drugs, Dr Hopkins was trying to stop him. And we're very proud of you, Olive.' She raised her teacup in a toast. 'Cheers.'

'Thank you.' Olive chinked her cup with her friend's. 'At least someone is.'

'Truly,' Millie said. 'You should set up your own detective agency.'

'Shush.' Olive held her finger to her lips, glancing back at the kitchen. 'I like the sound of that, but they won't. And I'm not in the mood to sweep up any more smashed crockery. Anyway, it's lovely to see you a little happier today.'

'It's a diet of your cakes that does it,' Millie said. 'Sometimes I think your recipes contain spells.'

Olive laughed. 'Speaking of recipes, I've decided to do a home delivery service for a few special customers. Today I'm taking a lemon chiffon cake to number thirteen Arthur Street and, since George is now back at work, a batch of almond croissants to the Porters' Lodge of King's College. Perhaps you'd like to come with me?'

'Well...' Millie said. 'Yes, I'd like that, thank you. But I notice that you didn't answer the question.'

Olive gave her friend an enigmatic smile. 'You didn't ask a question.'

'Yes, I did.'

'You did not.'
'I implied one.'
'You did n–'
'Oh, for goodness sake!' Blythe exclaimed. 'Will you two stop talking nonsense and get back to the bloody kiss!'

THE END

Chocolate Flapjack Recipe

If I had to choose only one chocolate-related recipe to last the rest of my life, this would be it. I can never stop after one, and I defy you to do so. For a truly heavenly experience, eat on an chilly autumn evening with a cup of milky tea while snuggled on the sofa in front of an open fire. This recipe is taken from my novella, Men, Money & Chocolate.

Makes 16, but how many it serves depends on how generous you're feeling...

Ingredients
250g salted butter
1 vanilla pod
85g dark brown sugar
3 tablespoons golden syrup
Several pinches of salt
60g best quality cocoa powder
300g organic oats (a mix of rolled and porridge if possible)

Method
Melt the butter in a saucepan, then take off the heat and scrape the vanilla seeds into the pan along with the salt. Return the pan onto a low heat then add

the sugar, syrup and cocoa. Simmer and stir for five minutes. Add the oats and mix together thoroughly. (Try not to eat TOO much of the raw mixture, though it is delicious!) Pour the flapjack mixture into a baking tin and pat it down to a thickness of a few centimetres.

Bake for 16 minutes at 160oc.

Remove from the oven and cool for half an hour before cutting into squares and cooling on a wire rack before indulging in as many as you can eat in one sitting...

The Biscuit Tin Murders # 3

"Death of a Businessman"

Chapter One

Cambridge. 1st December, 1970

'I'M NOT GOING TO fall in love,' Olive protested, for perhaps the hundredth time. 'I'm not like you, my dear, always falling in love at the drop of a hat.'

'Humph,' Blythe snorted. 'That's ridiculous.'

'Really?' Millie laughed. 'It seems a pretty accurate assessment from where I'm sitting.'

The three friends were sitting at their favourite table - beside the window overlooking Bene't Street, enjoying their daily afternoon tea. It always took place later than the traditional time, since they had to wait till the café closed at five o'clock, but just as soon as the last customer had left[1] and her friends arrived, Olive flipped over the sign and locked the door then, while Millie made the tea and Blythe plated up all the leftovers, Olive cleared the dirty crockery to wash later and set the table for their daily, delicious tête á tête. Olive's spaniel, Biscuit, sat in her usual place at her mistress's feet eating her very own afternoon tea which today consisted of buttered blueberry scones.

'Just because I've courted a few men in my time, doesn't mean I'm not discerning,' Blythe objected. 'I've not fallen in love with *all* of them. What about Alfie? Or Percy? Or...' Realising she'd run out of examples of men she hadn't loved, she trailed off and took a large bite of peach flapjack in order to try and hide the fact.

'Alfie, the new postman?' Millie clarified. 'Didn't you get up at five o'clock every day for weeks so you could answer the door in full make-up, wearing your posh silk dressing gown that you "accidentally" let slip open to reveal your posh silk nightie?'

'Not weeks!' Blythe exclaimed, spraying flapjack crumbs across the table. 'Days at most. Well, maybe one week. Perhaps two. But that's it.'

'And for Percy, that overly handsome porter at St Cath's,' Olive set down her teacup to chime in. 'You mysteriously flew into the café thirty seconds after he did every day for an entire month, until you discovered he was engaged. Almost,' she added with a smile, 'as if you'd been watching from the bookshop to monitor his arrival.'

'I did not!' Blythe protested. 'That was entirely coincidental.'

'Coincidental?' Olive echoed. 'Once or twice, I'll give you. But not thirty-one days in a row.'

'Twenty-seven days,' Blythe corrected. 'You're closed on Mondays.'

'Oh, right, of course,' Olive said, lifting the cup to her lips again. 'I stand corrected. That makes all the difference. You definitely weren't stalking him then. However could I have thought such a thing?' She winked at Millie, who giggled.

'Hey, you can't talk,' Blythe turned to Millie. 'I might have been in love with a few men over the past few years, but now I don't have eyes for anyone else but Elliot Harrington.'

'Harrington?' Millie echoed. 'I thought he was old news. You said–'

'Yes, well, he *was*,' Blythe said quickly. 'But now he's new news again.' She sighed happily. 'And anyway, *you've* been in love with the same man all your life. So that's even worse.'

Olive held her breath, bracing herself for the row. At her feet, Biscuit, sensing the tension, momentarily paused in licking butter off a scone and laid her head on Olive's feet. But Millie only sighed.

'True enough,' she said. 'True enough. You might be a ridiculous romantic, B. But I'm even more pathetic; in love with a married man for thirty-five years. It doesn't get any more pathetic than that.'

'Widower,' Blythe said, looking regretful and clearly trying to make amends. 'So your patience might be about to pay off.'

'Unlikely,' Millie sighed. 'I've never seen a man so deep in mourning. I don't think there is, or will ever be, any space in his heart for someone new.'

Blythe, about to take another bite of her flapjack, set it down again to pat Millie's hand. 'Don't fret, my friend. Men don't fare well alone, especially not once they've tasted married life. Widowers always re-marry, given half the chance, you mark my words.'

'Really?' Millie sipped her tea. 'You really think so?'

'Absolutely.' Blythe munched decisively on her flapjack. 'If he's not courting you by the New Year, I'll eat my hat.'

'Don't be silly,' Millie said, though the hope in her voice was undeniable. 'I can't–'

But her words were lost as the door swung open and Grace tumbled into the café, wrapped up in a woollen scarf, coat, dress and tights, complete with suede boots. And everything all in various shades of green: her favourite colour.

'Sorry I'm late,' she gasped, her breath like puffs of smoke. 'I thought I'd cycle but it's too icy so I had to walk. I-I...'

'Sit, sit.' Olive immediately stood, startling Biscuit who whined, and pulled over another chair. 'Sorry Bics,' she apologised, before addressing her friend. 'You need a stiff cup of Earl Grey and several slices of lemon curd cake, perhaps a few hot crumpets too. With lashings of butter. That'll see you right soon enough.'

Grace smiled as she unwrapped herself, hanging all her winter woollens on the hat rack beside the front door. 'I don't think I'll ever get used to that door opening without me pushing on it,' she said as Olive poured her tea and Millie plated up a slice of cake. Biscuit, from her vantage point hoovering up crumbs under the table, barked her greetings and Blythe even set down her tea and flapjack to give Grace a wave.

Grace, who'd been serving at The Biscuit Tin for several months now, had finally been entrusted with the secrets of the strangely supernatural ways of the café only a few weeks before and was still coming to terms with the quirks of the resident spirits. The door opening to greet her upon arrival, no matter if it'd been locked or not, being the thing that so far never failed to surprise her.

'Sit, drink, eat,' Olive ushered Grace into the waiting chair. 'Thank goodness we managed to plump you up a little before the cold set in – you were thin as a pin six months ago and now we're making progress, though we've still got a little way to go.'

'I think you want to heal all the world's ills with cake,' Grace said as she sat, reaching under the table to give Biscuit's ears a quick scratch. 'And I daresay, for me at least, it's working.'

'Glad to hear it,' Olive smiled. 'And yes, if I could cure everyone's sadness with cake, and make them happy again, I certainly would.'

'I think it's a combination of the cake and the café,' Grace said, dipping her finger in the lemon curd. 'Stepping inside here is like...' she mused on it as she sucked her finger, searching for the right words. 'A warm hug. And not just for the body, but also the soul.'

At this, the three other women sighed contented sighs and the café walls seemed to join them as a gentle breath swelled the air.

'Yes,' Blythe said. 'I do believe you're right.'

They all sat in silence for a while, quietly chewing cake and sipping tea, appreciating their good fortune that, although fate had thrown them some curve balls, they'd been brought to this place. *If only everyone had the opportunity to visit The Biscuit Tin,* Olive thought as Biscuit – now full to the brim with buttered scones – slipped her head onto her mistress's lap, *what a wonderful thing that'd be.*

'Anything in the news?' she asked, nodding at the evening paper Grace had placed on the table. 'Seems like nothing of note has happened since Mr Hopkins was killed.'

'You say that as if it's not a good thing,' Blythe laughed. 'You know most people don't actually want their towns to be rife with murders and the like. A low crime rate is supposed to be a *good* thing.'

'Yes, of course it's a *good* thing,' Olive said, absently scratching Biscuit's ears before reaching for the paper. 'It's just also, I don't know, a bit dull too.'

'Dull is also what most people favour when it comes to illegality,' Millie added, as Olive unfolded the paper and started to read. 'No murders, burglaries and general breaches of the peace: nice and dull.'

'That's easy for you to say,' – Olive didn't look up from the paper as she flicked through it – 'but you don't enjoy solving mysteries like I do.'

'I enjoy mysteries and murders in books,' Millie clarified. 'But not in real life. The fictional ones are pleasantly free of blood.' She gave a little shudder. 'I've never been a fan of–'

'Oh!' Olive exclaimed. 'Look!'

'What?' Millie, Blythe and Grace exclaimed in unison.

Olive brandished the newspaper. 'There's been a murder!'

༺༻

---

1. Usually, the customers needed a little "encouragement" to leave - given that no one ever wanted to relinquish the comfort of the café once they'd settled into it - and this was a service the resident ghosts took pride in fulfilling. Sometimes they wobbled the tables or tipped over cups or even, when a customer proved particularly stubborn, upended them out of their chairs.

Chapter Two

'Who?' Blythe asked.

'Where?' Millie asked.

'When?' Grace asked.

Biscuit, feeling the waterfall of excitement pouring over her like honey on hot cakes, barked with delight.

'You see,' Olive exclaimed, triumphant. 'You're all as excited as I am!'

'I wouldn't quite say that,' Millie clarified. 'I'd say it's rather more: shocked, unsettled, agitated...'

'Dismayed, distressed, dumbfounded,' Grace added. She was taking a Masters in English Literature and loved a little alliteration.

'Everything they just said,' Blythe confirmed, as Olive turned to her for support. 'Sorry.'

'Well, fine,' Olive huffed. 'It's just me then. But look, it should at least please you to see who it is.' She flipped over the paper and held up the page for them all to see.

'Millionaire property developer and philanthropist, Phillip Mayhew, bludgeoned to death in his four storey mansion on Millington Road in the early hours of Saturday morning,' Grace read, before looking up again. 'Why are we pleased about that?'

'Oh!' Millie clapped. 'Oh yes, we *are* pleased about that.'

'Why?' Grace repeated. 'I don't-'

'He's – was – Millie's landlord,' Olive explained. 'And he increases her rent above market rate every time the lease comes up for renewal. Along with trying to add unlawful clauses and generally making untenable demands. In short, we hate him.'

Millie nodded vigorously. 'We do. We did. No, hang on...' she hesitated, contemplating the correct grammatical expression. 'We can still hate dead people in the present tense, right?' She looked to Blythe who, as the bookshop owner, was their resident grammarian.

'Well, technically it's past tense,' Blythe said. 'I "hated" him etc. But I reckon with someone like Philip Mayhew we can make an exception, given that we hate him with as much passion dead as alive.'

Grace laughed. 'If you're bending the rules of the English language for this man then he must have been pretty despicable. I'm glad I never met him.'

'You should be,' Olive said. 'Everyone he encountered always ended the experience worse off than they had been. He spread misery and discontent wherever he went.'

Biscuit barked, adding her voice to the mix of malcontents.

'He once purposefully stood on Bics' tail,' Olive added. 'Just to make her squeal. She's loathed him ever since.'

'Well.' Millie smiled. 'What goes around comes around, so they say. Which, sadly, I find to be mostly untrue. But it looks like the chickens came home to roost today.'

'Chickens?' Grace frowned. 'What chickens? Did he keep chickens?'

'No.' Millie frowned. 'Isn't that the saying? I thought it was.'

'I'm sure I don't know what you're talking about, Millicent Burrows,' Olive laughed. 'And nor, do I think, do you. Anyway...' She set aside the paper to pick up a lavender biscuit. 'What bothers me is that Hugo didn't mention this when I saw him yesterday. Keeping secrets like that this early on doesn't bode well for things to come, does it?'

Now Blythe laughed. 'Secrets? I don't think most people would class not mentioning a murder as keeping secrets.'

'Yes, well, our Olive isn't most people, is she?' Millie said, while Olive crunched gloomily on her biscuit.

'You make me sound unhinged.'

'No, not that,' Millie said. 'Never that. Just special. Unique. I mean... if you were a pie, for example then–'

'What sort of pie?' Olive interjected.

Millie frowned, taken aback. 'I don't know; what sort of pie do you want to be? Apple?'

Olive swallowed slowly as she considered this. 'Not just apple though, that's too plain. How about blackberry and apple? Or gooseberry? Or rhubarb and ginger?'

Millie laughed. 'I might have known you wouldn't be something simple. Alright, if you were a ten slice gooseberry pie, then you'd be one part butter, two parts sugar, three parts fruit and four parts Miss Marple.'

'Yes.' Olive couldn't help but smile. 'Yes, I suppose that sums me up perfectly. But I'll tell you something else: when Hugo Dixon comes to the café for his breakfast tomorrow morning, he won't be getting his usual slice of Bakewell tart. He'll be getting a piece of my mind.'

Chapter Three

'Why didn't you tell me?' Olive stood behind the counter, arms folded, brow furrowed. Biscuit sat beside her, cocking her head to fix Hugo with her hardest of hard stares.[1]

'Tell you what?' Hugo, who'd come to visit Olive at the café, looked confused.

'What?' Olive echoed, as her frown deepened and the annoyance in her voice rose. 'About the murder, of course.'

'The murder?' Hugo sounded incredulous. 'Really? That's what you're upset about? Thank goodness for that,' he laughed. 'I thought it was something serious.'

'Serious?' Olive parroted him again. 'Serious? You don't think that's *serious*?'

Now Hugo frowned, confused. 'Why are you shrieking?'

'I'm not shrieking,' Olive said, fully aware that she was.

'You are so.'

'Yes, well, if I am that's because, because you're not understanding what I'm saying.'

'You're right,' Hugo said. 'I'm not. I'm sorry, but you're reacting as if I... hadn't told you I was already married or something.'

Olive narrowed her eyes. '*Are* you already married?'

Biscuit barked.

'No!' Hugo exclaimed. 'Of course not!'

'Alright then,' Olive sniffed. 'Well, that's good. But still, you should've told me about the dead millionaire. You know how I like to keep abreast of the crimes around Cambridge, especially the ones I might, um, investigate.'

'Yes,' Hugo gave a wry smile. 'How could I forget? So now you're saying you want me to inform you of every crime the second the police are involved?'

'Well...' Olive, now feeling a little embarrassed, gazed down at her display of cakes and picked a fallen crumb from the Victoria sponge and popped it into her mouth. 'Not the *very* second, no. But the same day isn't too much to ask, is it? I mean, at least before the newspapers get hold of it, so I'll know before every other Tom, Dick and Harry.' She glanced up, giving him what she hoped was a winning smile. 'There must be some perks to courting a detective, after all...'

'Oh?' Hugo returned her smile. 'Is that what we're doing then?' She could hear the hope in his voice and it touched her. 'Only I'm never quite certain how you feel...' He eyed her. 'I'm usually an expert at reading people but you, Miss Crisp, are quite the enigma.'

Olive picked up another crumb of cake and nibbled it. Biscuit, sensing an opportunity, nudged her mistress's leg and was rewarded with a piece of Victoria sponge.

'So I've been told,' Olive said, studiously avoiding the question of her feelings. She was certainly very fond of him, especially when she wasn't annoyed, but that didn't mean she'd risk her heart by falling in love. She'd made a promise to herself, to her ancestors, and she wasn't about to break it. Not if she could possibly help it. Not for Hugo Dixon nor anyone else.

'Alright,' Hugo conceded. 'I'm sorry I didn't tell you about the murder. I should've known. I won't do it again, I promise.'

'Thank you.' Olive smiled, aware that her heart became dangerously buoyant whenever Hugo fixed her with those beautiful blue eyes of his. 'And, in return, you can have whatever you want, whenever you want.' She gestured at the counter, but Hugo didn't take his eyes off her.

'*Whatever* I want?' He repeated. 'Really? Well, in that case–'

'Hold it right there, cheeky,' Olive interrupted. 'You know what I mean: any *cake* you want. Or pastry, biscuit, tart...'

'Oh, well,' Hugo winked. 'It was worth a try. And that's certainly not a bad second choice.' He nodded at the sliced Bakewell tart on the display counter. 'But I'm going to be boring and have my usual.'

'Well,' Olive said as she picked the biggest slice and slid it onto a plate. 'I suppose if you know what you like then there's no need to try something new.'

Hugo smiled. 'My thoughts exactly.'

'Why do I get the feeling that all your thoughts are heading in the same direction,' Olive said, rolling her eyes though her voice was laced with affection. 'Now, sit down, eat your tart and tell me everything you know about this dead businessman.'

'And that's everything.' Hugo licked his fork. 'He was slumped over his desk in his Grantchester office, having been slammed in the back of his head with a shovel. No prints and, strangely, no blood, but the force of the blow must've been enough to cause internal bleeding and kill him that way. Not a nice way to go, I'm afraid. Probably very slow and painful.' He gave a slight shudder. 'The door was unlocked, no forced entry, so we're acting under the assumption that he knew his killer. Unfortunately, that doesn't significantly narrow down the suspects since Mr Mayhew knew *a lot* of people and–'

'And most of them hated him,' Olive added.

'Yes,' Hugo sighed. 'It certainly seems that way. We've interviewed over a dozen potential suspects so far and all of them had some sort of motive to kill him.' He topped up his coffee from the cafetière. 'And while no one actually confessed to murder, none of them even bothered – with the possible exception of his family – to hide the fact that they were glad he was dead.'

'Well, I'm not surprised.' Olive added another dollop of marmalade to her breakfast crumpet before taking a bite and chewing thoughtfully. 'He was a cad of the first water and that's putting it politely. You could add Millie to that list of those who wanted him dead not' – she added quickly – 'that you *should*. I'm absolutely certain she didn't kill him, I'd stake everything I own, the café, my–'

'Don't worry,' Hugo laughed. 'I know Millie's not a murderer. Anyway, she'd have to be pretty silly to kill someone under *your* nose now, wouldn't she?'

Olive took another bite of crumpet, then bent down to slip the remainder under the table for Biscuit, staying a moment longer than needed to conceal her smile. Despite accidentally almost implicating her best friend in a murder, she felt undeniably proud to be given recognition for her detective skills from a real detective.

'Have you ever thought about training to be a police officer?' Hugo asked, not for the first time. And, not for the first time, Olive pretended that it'd never crossed her mind.

'I'm a baker,' she said, polishing off the last bite of the crumpet. 'Not a policewoman. Besides, I've never even *seen* a policewoman. I'm not sure they exist.'

'There aren't many on the force,' Hugo admitted. 'But I did meet one in London. I believe the Met has, um, several.'

'Humph,' Olive sniffed. 'Several, eh? That's a lot. Sounds like I'd fit right in.'

'You could be the example.' Hugo stirred another spoonful of sugar into his already over-sweet coffee. 'The example that inspires women all over the country to join you.'

'*Me?*' Now Olive laughed. 'The poster child for female police officers? If only my mother could hear you now, she'd have another heart attack.' As she said this, Olive glanced towards the kitchen in anticipation of Myrtle's noisy objections and, sure enough, the subsequent rattling of cutlery in the drawers – along with her signature scent of baked marzipan – was a cacophony of discontent.

'What was that?' Hugo asked, startled.

'Oh, nothing,' Olive said quickly. 'Just Grace cooking up something delicious in the kitchen.' She regretted the lie, and hoped to heck that he wouldn't discover it by calling out his greetings to Grace, but it was necessary. Olive couldn't risk telling Hugo the truth about her ghostly ancestors, both because he'd likely think she'd lost her grip on reality and, even if he believed her she wasn't ready to share such a significant secret with him just yet.

'I'll be visiting the crime scene again this evening,' Hugo said, oblivious to Olive's thoughts. 'Would you like to accompany me, once you've closed up the café?'

Olive looked at him as if he'd just invited her to dine at Buckingham Palace. 'Really?'

'Well,' he said with a smile. 'There's no point in trying to extract false promises from you not to visit when we both know that you'll be heading over there anyway, first chance you get, so you might as well come with me.'

'I would not...' Olive began, before trailing off. There was little point in objecting when they both knew the truth. Instead, she gave him a wry smile. 'What time will you pick me up?'

---

1. Biscuit had, naturally, been inspired by Paddington in this regard. Olive had read all the books to her as a puppy.

Chapter Four

A FEW HOURS LATER, Olive was alone in the café with only Biscuit for company. Grace had left an hour earlier for the university library to continue her studies of the literary intricacies of something highly academic and clever, a feminist reassessment of Agatha Christie's late novels or some such, Olive wasn't entirely sure, and there was a momentary lull in customers. So Olive chatted freely to the ancestors while applying herself clearing remnants of teas and cakes from the table beside the counter.

'I know what you're thinking...' Olive said, as she wiped up lemon cake crumbs. 'But it's far too early yet to talk about babies or anything like that. We've only been seeing each other a few months and we've only kissed. We're taking things very slowly, and I've a feeling anyway that he's not the casual type. He doesn't seem like the sort for one-night stands to me, more like a marriage and kids man – the whole nine yards – but I don't know for certain yet.'

Bustling into the kitchen with the dirty crockery, Olive saw – as she knew she would – the six regency tea cups rattling on the shelf, displaying the annoyance of her ancestor Charlotte Krisp who daily expressed her frustration – via the medium of rattling antique tea cups – that Olive hadn't yet provided an heir for The Biscuit Tin. *We must keep the café safe, and the only way to do that is to keep it in the family.* While it might have seemed a stretch that Olive could extract an entire sentence from a bit of abstract jingling and jangling, she was an expert in interpreting the cacophony of clattering and clinking which constituted her ancestors' conversations, just as all family members can interpret the slightest whisper of each other's sighs or the multiple subtextual meanings beneath a single "hello", be they alive or dead. *Time is ticking, you're nearly forty-two, in my day most women were dead by forty-five* – the cups clattered – *So get a bloody move on!*

'I'm not a piece of cattle,' Olive muttered. 'And peoples' feelings are involved. I like Hugo – a lot – I'm not going to use him. At least, not without his consent.'

Now the oven door swung open and a whiff of almonds and marzipan filled the air.

'Hello, Mother.' Olive smiled. 'Let me guess, you want to remind me – for the thousandth time – to be careful and not risk getting my heart broken by a man. Is that right?'

The almond scent intensified. Myrtle Crisp, Olive's mother, had only passed to the other side a few years ago but her communications were just as strong, if not stronger, than Olive's ancient relatives who'd had centuries to practise their powers of contact.

The oven door rattled and Olive sighed.

'I know you want me to put Battenburg[1] back on the menu, Mother.' Olive snuck a chocolate biscuit out of the tin beside the toaster. 'But whenever I do it never sells and then I'm the one who has to eat the leftovers and I hate Battenburg.'

There was no point in lying to her mother, but Olive did it anyway. They both knew that slices of Battenberg sold like the proverbial hot cakes they were, but Olive hated marzipan and hated making that cake, with its fiddly little squares and layers of jam, and since Myrtle was no longer in charge (though she tried her best to be, even from beyond the grave) Olive could do as she wished. It just meant enduring a litany of maternal complaints. But if it meant avoiding the perils of marzipan, then it was worth it.

'Hello! Hello? Hello!'

The voice – a child's by the sound of the pitch – was coming from the café. Olive, happily abandoning the dirty dishes along with her ancestors, hurried from the kitchen back to the café. There she found a brown-haired boy, bespectacled and freckled, standing behind the counter, barely tall enough to peer over the top.

'Hello.' Olive smiled down at him. 'How may I help you?'

The boy pushed his glasses, which were slipping, higher up his nose. 'Are you Mrs Crisp?'

'*Ms* Crisp,' Olive corrected him. 'Yes, I am.'

'And is this The Biscuit Tin Detective Agency?'

'No!' Olive laughed. 'No! Whatever gave you that idea? This is The Biscuit Tin, yes. But it's a café, not a detective agency.'

The boy's face fell. 'Oh.'

Then, much to Olive's dismay, his eyes filled with tears. She watched as one spilled over and rolled slowly down his cheek.

'What's wrong? Do you – would you like a biscuit?'

At the sound of her name, Biscuit, who was taking a mid-afternoon, post-prandial nap under a table, perked up. Anticipating a potential walk, she cocked a hopeful ear.

The boy brightened slightly and sniffed. 'I 'suppose,' he said. 'What sorta biscuits you got?'

Accurately assessing that her diminutive customer wouldn't hold much truck with lavender biscuits, Olive glanced about for what else might be on offer.

'How about a fresh custard cream?'

The boy wiped his nose on his sleeve and nodded.

'Okay, perfect.' Olive turned back to the biscuit tin standing beside the shelf of assorted teapots and extracted three custard creams. Placing them on a plate she slipped them across the counter towards the boy. 'Here you go. Dig in.'

'Thank you.' The boy sniffed again, then polished off the biscuits so fast that Olive wondered if he'd just performed a magic trick and was hiding them up his snotty sleeve.

'So,' Olive ventured, now that the danger of more tears seemed to have passed. 'Why did you think this was a detective agency?'

The boy shrugged. 'Billy Jenkins told me you found his missing dog,' he mumbled. 'So I want you to find my lizard.'

'Lizard?' Olive echoed, thinking she must have misheard. 'Your *lizard*?'

The boy frowned, as if he didn't understand the question and was quickly deciding that the person asking it must be far too stupid to be a real detective.

'Yes,' he said. 'So, can you?'

'Can I what?' It was Olive's turn to frown.

'Can you find my lizard? O'course.'

'Well...' Olive hesitated, anxious lest her reply evoke more tears. 'I'm not sure. I mean, I can't promise but – what's your name?'

'Jimmy,' he said. 'Jimmy Mayhew.'

Olive grip on the counter tightened.

Surely not. It was a common enough name, wasn't it? She couldn't *possibly* be this lucky. Could she?

'Mayhew, eh?' Olive repeated. 'That's, um, a nice name. Is it...? Are you...? Was, um, Phillip Mayhew your father?'

It was a very risky question, especially in terms of provoking tears, but she had to ask. *Not* asking would be tantamount to not eating a large slice of chocolate fudge cake when offered one. Biscuit, who'd given up waiting to be summoned for a walk, emerged from under the table and approached the boy, tail wagging. Boys, in her experience, were typically excellent targets for delightful things such as walks and treats.

'Yeah.' The boy sniffed again. 'Yeah he was. But he died.'

Biscuit nuzzled Jimmy's leg. The boy looked down, instantly brightening. He patted Biscuit's head, then scratched her ears and buried his face in her neck, his own hair now almost indistinguishable from the spaniel's soft curly fur.

'I'm so sorry,' Olive said, giving silent thanks for Biscuit's timely arrival. 'That's very sad.' With Jimmy momentarily distracted, Olive turned to grab the tin of custard creams, whipped off the lid and set it down in front of young Jimmy Mayhew who, having sensed the arrival of more sweets, had lifted his face from Biscuit's neck and now regarded the unexpected offering with wide-eyed delight.

'It is,' he said matter-of-factly while expertly cramming several custard creams into his mouth at once. 'But now he can't lock me in my room anymore, or hit me with a belt or make me wash my mouth out with soap.' He shrugged again. 'So I suppose that's good...'

Olive regarded the small boy with astonishment. It was hard to resist the urge to run around the counter and pull him into a maternal hug, but Olive forced herself to stay put. Instead, she reached for an entire plate of vanilla sugar doughnuts and pushed them across the counter towards him. Without pause, little Jimmy Mayhew snatched up one in each hand and began wolfing them down as if he hadn't just consumed half a dozen custard creams. Olive gave silent thanks that the boy was still young enough for a doughnut to provide (albeit momentary) relief to all ills.

'So,' he said, revealing a mouth full of masticated dough. 'Can you find my lizard or not?'

'Well, I can't promise I *will*,' Olive admitted, desperately wishing she could. 'But I can promise that I'll do my very best.'

∽

---

1. A light sponge made up of pink and yellow chequered squares held together with jam and encased with marzipan. First bakes in 1884 to celebrate the marriage of Princess Victoria (Queen Victoria's granddaughter) to Prince Louis of Battenberg. A firm favourite of the British public ever since, till it fell out of favour in the twenty-first century. The 1970s was perhaps the height of its popularity and Olive was certainly in the minority in her dislike of the sickly sweet cake. A dislike the author shares. But give her a Black Forest Gateaux any day and she's happy.

Chapter Five

'It's rather fun being inside a police car, isn't it?' Olive said, as Hugo drove at a snail's pace along Silver Street towards Newnham. It was a shame she'd had to leave Biscuit behind, on account of her potentially contaminating the crime scene, since the spaniel would've certainly enjoyed the adventure. 'Do you often break the speed limit and put the lights on just for fun?'

'Of course not, is the official answer to that question,' Hugo said. 'That'd be illegal, if done intentionally. Though, once in a while, one might just make a mistake…'

'Oo, can we make one now?' Olive asked, sitting forward. 'Can we go at ninety?'

Hugo laughed. 'Not in rush hour traffic. And these streets are too narrow for anyone to pull over without risking the lives of all the pedestrians.'

Olive glanced out of the window to see a woman pushing a pram along the pavement and a little old lady pulling a shopping trolly. 'I suppose so,' she conceded, sinking back into the seat with disappointment.

'Don't worry,' Hugo said. 'It's not far to go. We'll be there in ten minutes. Fifteen at the most.'

'Alright.' Olive reached into the bag on her lap and extracted a bag of doughnuts, the few remaining that hadn't disappeared down the gannet-like gullet of young Jimmy Mayhew. She started munching one, before offering the bag to Hugo. 'Doughnut?'

'Not right now. Save me one?'

'I can't make any promises,' Olive said. 'They're very good and I've not had dinner. Well, I've had a pork and apple pie, followed by a few chocolate flapjacks and perhaps a biscuit or two. But other than that…'

'Have you read *The Hobbit?*' Hugo asked, glancing from the road to Olive. 'If not, you really should.'

'Why?'

'Because I think Bilbo Baggins is your kindred spirit.'

Olive licked the vanilla sugar from her lips. 'Who on earth is Bilbo Baggins?'

'The hobbit in the book,' Hugo explained. 'He's mostly human but very small and quite plump with big hairy feet and-'

'Ah, let me stop you there,' Olive cut him off. 'Because, as flattering comparisons go, you're already way off the mark. Women-'

'Wait,' Hugo protested. 'You didn't let me-'

'Women,' Olive persisted. 'Do not, as a rule, tend to enjoy such parallels being drawn, especially when wildly inaccurate. Now-'

'But,' Hugo protested. 'You're not-'

'Now, short and plump I'll give you,' Olive spoke over him. 'But I certainly do *not* have big hairy feet!'

'I didn't suggest you did!' Hugo laughed again. 'I was only explaining to you what hobbits were, though I can see that, in retrospect I perhaps didn't make the introduction in the right way. However, if you'd just let me finish, I'll explain-'

'Go on then.' Olive popped the last of the doughnut in her mouth and folded her arms across her chest. 'Explain.'

'Alright then.' Hugo turned the police car slowly onto Queen's Road. 'So, what I was trying to say – what I *meant* – was that hobbits have something like two breakfasts, three lunches and supper, but – and this is why I say you're kindred spirits – this Bilbo always, if I recall rightly, then later had two seed-cakes for his after-supper "morsel." Not one, mind you, but two.'

'Well,' Olive conceded, 'then I suppose these hobbits *do* sound like kindred spirits and, all in all, very sensible sorts of fellows. And seed-cakes,' she mused, 'now I've not had a seed cake in quite some time. What sort of seeds? Poppy? Caraway?[1] Or something different? And with other flavours or without?'

'I'm not sure,' Hugo admitted. 'I don't think Tolkien was very specific about that.'

'Well, I know caraway is more traditional,' Olive continued. 'But personally I prefer poppy, which is very nice with lemon. My mother had a rather delicious recipe for that, actually; perhaps I should add it to the menu...'

'More cake? Sounds good to me,' Hugo said, offering her his most winning smile. 'So, am I forgiven?'

'We'll see,' Olive said sniffily. 'Maybe you can make it up to me at the crime scene.'

'There's a line never before heard in a romantic conversation,' Hugo said, pulling to a stop outside a large white building. 'But here's hoping it's grisly enough to persuade you to forgive me.'

'Perhaps,' Olive snorted. 'But you've lost your chance at the last doughnut, that's for sure.'

⁓

'And this is where he was found?' Olive asked, pointing at the spot on the floor outlined in chalk. It was a large outline as befitting the hefty man Phillip Mayhew had been and the substantial corpse he had left upon his demise.

'Yes, and the murder weapon was right beside him.'

'Prints?'

'Wiped.'

'Of course,' Olive said, as if she spent her days analysing crime scenes rather than baking Bakewell tarts. She walked slowly, making a circuit of the large office, relishing every step, absorbing every detail, imagining herself a real detective – the one in charge of every investigation – and Hugo, her assistant. 'But a shame.' She focused on memorising it all so she could recall it later and continue her investigations later in her mind, when she was alone and not sleeping for excitement. Fortunately, Olive was blessed with something of a photographic memory so she'd be able to see it all again, just as it was, whenever she wished. Which really was lucky, since this room was a chaotic mess; every wall flanked by filing cabinets and the multiple desks stacked high with trays which were, in turn, filled to the brim with papers.

'We've got a number of leads to follow though,' Hugo said. 'Even without the prints.'

'Oh, yes?' Olive's spirits lifted, reigniting the delightful fantasy of her alternative career. 'What?'

'Well, there was a man's footprint in the mud outside the back window - size nine. And a piece of torn fabric at the site of the broken window.' Hugo pointed at a small window alongside the door. The glass had been smashed and the hole had been taped up with a plastic sheet.'

'Is that large enough to squeeze through?' Olive asked.

'You wouldn't have thought so,' Hugo agreed. 'But I suppose if he was small enough it's possible.'

'Small enough to fit through,' Olive mused. 'But strong enough to overpower Mr Mayhew.' She paused to gaze at a framed document hanging on the wall. 'This is…' She read it once, then twice. 'He framed a hate letter.'

Hugo laughed. 'I know. He certainly was a strange one, that's for sure.'

'I don't believe it,' Olive said, incredulous. 'Why would anyone do that?' And, as if to convince herself she wasn't hallucinating, she read it aloud. '"Dear Mayhew, As a prison officer it has been my unfortunate duty to spend my days among the greater criminal elements of society, the most nefarious, cunning, despicable specimens mankind has to offer. Yet, in all my twenty-seven years working at Whitemoor, I have yet to meet a man quite so contemptible, vile, reprobate, loathsome, detestable, wretched, abominable, devious, dishonest, underhand and treacherous as you. We all know that this life is unfair and justice rarely done. But I have reason to believe that Justice is coming for you. And it'll come when you least expect it. Faithfully yours, Mr Gary Watson." Well, whoever Mr Watson is, he certainly has – or had – a way with words.'

'Perhaps that's why he framed it,' Hugo said, still laughing. 'He admired the eloquence.'

'Or he relished the hatred, which makes him even stranger. I mean, I've heard of people not caring what other people think,' Olive said, longingly. 'I've always wanted to be one of them. But I've never heard of someone who actually *enjoys* being hated.'

'It takes all sorts.' Hugo shrugged. 'And when you've been a police officer you, sadly, stop being surprised by all the bizarre whimsies of human nature.'

'I've never seen so much paperwork,' Olive said as, moving over to the main desk – twice as large as the other two and centred at the back of the room – and she started surreptitiously rifling through a few piles. 'He's got an in-tray labelled "hate mail" and it's full to the brim.'

'I know,' Hugo chuckled. 'I had a look, it makes for interesting reading. We've got someone coming to pick up all this later, then it'll be my happy job to read through every single page. Although,' he considered, 'on second thoughts, I might put Constable Cooper on that task in the first instance, get him to weed through all the irrelevant stuff. Mind you, the man is something of a moron, so that might not be the best idea. I suppose I'd better–'

'I could read it for you,' Olive volunteered. 'I'm very diligent and not remotely–'

'Oh, Olive,' Hugo said as he crossed the room. 'I wish I could – believe me, I really do – but this is a police investigation and you are, although brilliant and lovely – with perfectly human-sized, non-hairy feet – still technically very much a civilian. So, much as I'd love to let you and, much as I know you'd do a *far* better job than Cooper, I'm afraid my hands are tied.'

Olive's spirits, buoyant since stepping into the victim's office, now sank. 'Of course,' Olive said. 'How silly of me.'

'But... since they won't be taken away for another few hours yet,' Hugo offered. 'There's nothing to stop you taking a little peek now.'

'Really?' Olive brightened. 'Are you sure?'

'Why not?' Hugo said. 'Especially if it might make you change your mind about that last doughnut.'

1. It's likely that Bilbo made his seed-cakes with caraway since those, as Olive mentioned, were the more traditional choice in the earlier part of the 1900s. They went out of fashion after WW2 being replaced by poppy seeds which are still very popular today, especially with lemon. See recipe at the back of the book. Hugo was quoting from The Hobbit, p8: "Bilbo found himself ... scuttling off ... to a pantry to fetch two beautiful round seed-cakes which he had baked that afternoon for his after-supper morsel."

Chapter Six

Olive had, regretfully, declined Hugo's offer of a lift back to the café for, much as she wanted to spend more time with him and take another trip in a police car, there was something else she needed to do.

Jimmy Mayhew had given Olive his address, begging her to come and check the "crime scene" for clues that might determine the whereabouts of his missing lizard. Convinced that the creature had been kidnapped and sensing that Olive wasn't taking this particular theory seriously, Jimmy promised that he'd prove it if only she'd come and take a look.

Deciding not to mention this little matter of lizard-napping to Hugo – it was surely nonsense after all – Olive set off for the Mayhew's family residence which was happily situated only a few streets from Mr Mayhew's office. It was a shame, Olive thought as she walked, that she'd had to leave Biscuit behind since the adorable, friendly dog, who always knew when someone was in need of a cuddle, would have offered the perfect emotional balm to a household deep in mourning. Olive felt entirely unsure that she was fully equipped to face the situation alone but she'd promised Jimmy she'd visit as soon as possible and so must keep to her word.

When she reached the front door of 29a Millington Road, having walked quite a considerable way up an elaborately tiled path to reach it, Olive took a deep breath. The house loomed above her, splendid and intimidating. Its splendour encompassed ten latticed windows, three chimney stacks and tall olive trees flanking a rather magnificent stained-glass door. Every inch of every brick oozed wealth and sophistication. And Olive, having been raised in a tiny flat above a café, felt extremely out of her depth.

Still, a promise was a promise. So she lifted her hand and knocked.

Having half-expected a butler or maid to answer the door, Olive was slightly taken aback by the appearance of young Jimmy himself on the doorstep. He, on the other hand, was delighted.

'Detective!' He exclaimed. 'You came!'

'I, um, well…' Olive tried to correct him but the delight of being addressed as a detective, even by a ten-year-old boy, was too great. 'Yes, but you may call me Ms Crisp.'

Jimmy's face fell. Clearly he enjoyed the idea of Olive being a detective almost as much as she did. Deciding not to break the spell by using her real name, Jimmy said nothing. He stepped back to allow her inside.

'Thank you,' Olive said as she walked into the marble-floored hallway. Doing her best to remain professional – a detective, after all, would not gawp at the grandeur of a client's house – and focus on the matter at hand. 'Is your mother home?'

'She's in her bedroom,' the boy said. 'She's been there since Father died.'

'Oh yes,' Olive said. 'Yes, of course. She must – it must've been an awful shock for you all.'

Jimmy shrugged. 'So, are you coming to see the crime scene now?'

'Y-yes,' Olive was hesitant. 'Where is it?'

'In my bedroom.'

'Okay.' Olive glanced up at the glittering chandelier hanging from the ceiling. 'But I really think I ought to speak to your mother first.'

The boy shrugged again. 'You can, but she won't talk to you. She's not talked, not since…'

'Oh dear,' Olive said quickly, so the poor boy didn't have to spell it out and wishing once again that she had Biscuit with her. One look at the spaniel's big dark eyes, one touch of her soft brown ears, and Mrs Mayhew's spirits would've been lifted just a little. 'Yes, of course, I understand. Why don't you just show me where your lizard was taken and then we'll go from there.'

As she followed Jimmy Mayhew up the long, winding staircase, carpeted with a red-velvet runner, Olive replayed those words in her head, almost unable to believe that she'd just said them. What on earth was she doing? A lost *lizard*? Her life had sunk to new lows. Still, she had, by this bizarrely circuitous route, gained access to the victim's home and that was no small thing. Whether or not she'd be able to execute any significant snooping while under the watchful eye of the Mayhew boy was another matter.

Olive followed him down a long corridor, passing half a dozen closed doors, each of which she longed to open and take a peek inside. Did the dreadful Mr Mayhew have a home office? And might it contain further evidence that could incriminate his killer? Although, Olive had to admit, the more she learnt about Mr Mayhew the less effort she wanted to put into actually catching his murderer. It was wrong, of course, to take a life, but certain lives were, arguably, less wrong to take than others.

This conclusion was challenged, however, when Olive shuffled silently past the third door on the left and heard the unmistakable sounds of feminine weeping from inside. Olive hesitated, feeling a sudden compulsion to knock but knowing, at the same time, that it would be a mistake and that Mrs Mayhew - for it was surely she who lay within - would not appreciate the intrusion.

'Your mother?' Olive whispered.

Jimmy glanced over his shoulder saying nothing, but the look was enough. So there was at least one person devastated by the death of Mr Mayhew. And, for this reason alone, Olive thought she ought to apply herself to solving the mystery of his murder.

'This is my room.' Jimmy, finally stopping at the end of the seemingly endless corridor, now stood before a bright yellow door. Upon it was sellotaped a paper note that stated:

PRIVET. KEEP OUT.

'It's very messy.'

He didn't say this by way of apology, simply as a statement of fact.

'Are you sure your lizard's not hiding then?' Olive suggested. 'He might've escaped and got lost under your bed or something.'

Jimmy gave Olive what she recognised by now as his own brand of withering look and, without deigning to answer such an absurd suggestion, opened his door.

To say that the room was messy was an understatement of epic proportions. Olive's mother, Myrtle, had always been rather slovenly so Olive had grown up with a certain amount of disarray, but she had never seen the like of this before. She noted innumerable wooden sticks – enough to populate a small forest – fashioned into various things with pieces of string, and dirty clothes lay in discarded piles like molehills across the floor and scattered among them: upended books, empty biscuit packets, soft toys – some dismembered, others intact – and clusters of tin soldiers enacting epic battles amid the apocalyptic chaos.

It wouldn't have surprised Olive in the slightest to have found ten lizards lost among the grubby disorder, let alone one. Along with a couple of chickens, a handful of kittens and several rats. At this thought, Olive gave an inadvertent shudder. She hated rats.

'So, um, you've had a good look for him' – she took a guess at the lizard's gender – 'in here, have you? Just to be sure.'

Jimmy gave Olive another withering look. 'Come on and take a look at his terrarium.'

Terrarium? This was a new word on Olive, but she could guess what it meant. And so, stepping gingerly between the molehills, she followed the boy across the room.

'Sorry.' She winced as she heard the crack of something breaking beneath her shoe. 'Sorry. Sorry.'

But Jimmy, seemingly caring for nothing but his poor lost lizard, ignored all apologies and continued onwards towards the back of the room and his bedside table. When she reached it a moment, and several shattered toys later, Olive saw – placed upon the only clear space in the room – a glass box. It was lined with an inch-thick layer of sand which was, in turn, sprinkled with rocks, plants and the corpses of several dead cockroaches. Olive shuddered again.

It was, even to the untrained eye, definitely and decidedly missing a lizard.

'You see,' Jimmy said. 'I told you so.'

Olive nodded, thoughtfully. 'Yes,' she said. 'I see.' Though she certainly didn't see everything she felt she *ought* to be seeing, especially the reason for the empty glass box being treated as suspicious.

'Look.' Jimmy pointed. 'There.'

And then Olive saw. For the boy was pointing to a sizeable padlock that had clearly been forced open. It was curious, but still confusing.

'Why do you keep it locked?' Olive had to ask.

The withering look returned to the boy's freckled countenance. ''Cos he's valuable, 'course,' he said. 'And I knows plenty of folks keen to nick him. So I have to keep it locked and nailed down.'

He nodded down at the base of the terrarium which, Olive now saw, was nailed – at each of its four corners – down to the desk.

'So,' Olive said, now stating the obvious. 'He definitely *was* stolen.'

'Like I said.' Jimmy rolled his eyes. 'So, can you see any clues to tell you which of my nasty thieving classmates took him?'

'Well, not off hand,' Olive admitted. 'Unless they, um, left a note?'

She looked at him hopefully. He looked back at her with great annoyance.

'No, 'course not.'

'No ransom demand?' Olive made another grab for hope, already rapidly diminishing before her eyes. 'Or–'

'No.'

'Oh,' Olive said. 'Shame. Then I'm afraid…'

But she trailed off, having at last spotted something.

A large fingerprint on the glass. A print left not by the hand of a child but an adult, most probably a man.

'Did your father ever come into your room?' Olive asked. 'To feed your lizard, perhaps?'

'No.' Jimmy frowned. 'Course not. He hated Franklin. That's why I had to keep him in here. Father said if he ever set eyes on him anywhere else in the house, he'd stamp on him without thinking twice.'

'Ah,' Olive said. That certainly sounded in character. 'Right. And, erm, how about your mother?'

Jimmy shook his head. 'She was scared of Franklin. She wouldn't come anywhere near him.'

'I see,' Olive said. 'Then that *is* baffling. And curious.'

Which again raised the question she'd been asking herself all along: why on earth would someone steal a lizard? And, more importantly, did this strange theft have anything to do with Mr Mayhew's murder?

Chapter Seven

OLIVE LAY IN BED that night gazing up at the ceiling and thinking back on the bizarre events of the day. Lizards and letters. One lizard and hundreds of letters. That was the crux of it. Whether or not those two things were linked, Olive had yet to discover, but for now she passed the midnight hours re-visiting the letters. Blessed with something of a photographic memory, Olive was able to recall word-for-word documents that she'd only scanned briefly. It was a shame, really, that she wasn't permitted to read them all for Hugo since she'd make both short and excellent work of it. Scratching the sweet spot behind Biscuit's left ear, Olive mused on the exceptionally large quantity of murderous correspondence received by the deceased.

> *Dear Mr Mayhew,*
> *You've just evicted my widowed aunt from her one-room flat on 22b Cavendish Road after she could no longer afford to pay the rent. You'd recently increased it by 250% in the course of 2 years. You are a heartless, mercenary scoundrel and I hope you die a painful and untimely death. Now that I will no longer be able to sleep at night, I will spend those hours planning on how I might bring that about, sooner rather than later.*
> *Sincerely,*
> *Mr Frank Jackson*

> *Dear Mr Mayhew,*
> *I've repeatedly begged you not to put up the rent on our property which is already far above market value and now my family and I will be forced to live in an over-priced hostel while we search for alternative accommodation*

> *lest we end up on the streets. You are a cruel and unfeeling human being and you deserve to suffer as much as you've made others suffer. I loathe you and wish you dead.*
> *Regards,*
> *Mr H. Snow*

> *Mr Mayhew,*
> *You are a cad and a bounder. May you burn in hell.*
> *David Skinner*

And so they went on. And on and on...

Every letter a variation on the theme of Philip Mayhew's evil-doings and the multitudinous ways (all painful, most fatal and many rather imaginative) he might be duly punished. It was just as Hugo had said, never had so many suspects presented themselves in a murder case so readily.

'What do you think, Bics?' Olive mused as she continued to scroll through them in her mind's eye. 'Who did it?'

Biscuit, who was dreaming about chasing four-legged blueberry scones, half-cocked an ear in Olive's direction but was otherwise unresponsive.

'It's actually a far harder job,' Olive continued. 'With *so* many suspects. Like trying to find a poisonous needle in a poisonous haystack. It's a real shame I didn't manage to escape the boy's watchful eye and sneak into his dad's office or anywhere else. I wonder if the police have searched his house...'

Olive thought of Hugo, of how much she'd like to talk all this through with him right now. Although that, of course, would mean that he'd be lying next to her in bed – in Biscuit's place. Olive had slept with men before, but never actually *slept* with them and never in her own bed. This was her sacred space, reserved for her alone. And Biscuit too, of course. And that was always how she'd wanted it. Olive didn't feel lonely; her imagination was far too rich for that. She loved her own company, indeed preferring it to being with most other people – excepting her best friends – but Hugo was different. He was the first person – the first man – who she enjoyed being with as much as she enjoyed being alone.

∽

The following morning, a still-sleepy Olive shuffled into the kitchen to begin baking. Fortunately, it was Tuesday, a typically quiet day in the café, so she didn't have to bake too much. A lemon curd cake, a few batches of lavender biscuits – she still had plenty of still-fresh caramel-chocolate flapjacks left from

Sunday (the café was closed on Mondays) – and a few dozen blueberry scones. If Grace were here to help, Olive would've liked to add a couple of Bakewell tarts and two dozen almond croissants to the menu, but she'd have to give those a miss today: too much trouble to do alone, especially when exhausted.

'I think it's time to bring Grace into the kitchen.' Olive addressed her ancestors as she stirred vanilla seeds into the flour and caster sugar flecked with lavender flowers. 'I know you want to keep everything in the family, but since I don't yet have a daughter to help out, I could really use an extra hand.'

This statement elicited a cacophony of responses: rattling tea cups, clattering spoons, the scent of marzipan, along with burnt toast – the signature scent of her great-great-great aunt Philomena – creaking hinges, swishing curtains and banging cupboards.

'Alright, alright.' Olive held up her wooden spoon. 'Calm down. Anyone would think I'd just suggested selling up and moving to Blackpool.'

At this her ancestors, not known for their sense of humour, increased their objections so vociferously that a cupboard door almost came off its hinges.

'Oh my goodness, I'm joking!' Olive exclaimed. 'And do be careful, please. You'll wake the neighbours or, worse still, destroy our beloved café yourselves.'

A reluctant silence fell. But Olive still felt their disgruntlement, as palpable as a sulky child sitting in the corner of a room. A few dozen invisible eyes glowering at her.

'You know, I don't actually *have* to get your permission,' Olive said. 'I'm only asking as a courtesy. I'd like to get your agreement, I'd like to have your support. But, at the end of the day the café is mine now and those decisions are up to me.'

The precariously hinged cupboard door banged twice again, punctuating Olive's statement with annoyance, and the smell of burnt toast intensified.

'Yes,' Olive conceded. 'Yes, I know, you probably *could* scare her off with all your ridiculous shenanigans, but you'd only be shooting yourselves in the foot. If you want the café to thrive, you have to accept that we – that *I* – need help. I can't keep up with the demand by myself. Cambridge gets busier every year. The students, the tourists. We used to be like a sleepy little village but not any more…'

The teacups rattled like maracas.

'No.' Olive cut up a pat of butter and added it to her bowl. 'No, it's *not* because I'm spending too much time on investigations – and they're *not* pointless – they're actually very helpful. Without me they wouldn't have caught the killers of Jack Witstable and Gerald Hopkins, and a good deal of missing pets and errant husbands would've remained lost too. To say nothing of–'

But Olive's further accomplishments were lost amid the outraged bangs, creaks and clattering.

'Enough!' Olive slammed her spoon on the table, simultaneously splattering butter across the counter and up her apron. She brushed a fleck of buttery dough from her cheek. 'That's enough.' Her voice was steady but her hand was shaking. 'I'm forty-one years old, for goodness sake. You have to let me live my life. You have to let me make my own decisions.'

The silence now was a little contrite – but only a little – and mostly sulky. Still, save from causing chaos by haunting the café, which they knew would be an act of self-sabotage as much as anything else, Olive's dead relatives had to concede that there was not much they could do to stop her.

Chapter Eight

GRACE ONLY CAME TO the café as often as her academic schedule would allow, which meant that Olive was left to meet the steady stream of customers by herself. Biscuit provided company and entertainment – she was much beloved by the regulars – but was neither permitted nor able to serve tea and cakes. The customers might adore the spaniel, but they wouldn't have adored dog hairs in their blueberry scones. And so, during opening hours, Biscuit had to remain in her bed by the door unless she was touring the tables, which she did every hour or so (any more often and Olive would throw her a hard stare) to lick up crumbs from the floor and gobble any offerings from generous patrons willing to part with a more sizable portion of their treats.

To see Biscuit scoffing cakes, anyone would be forgiven for thinking that she was malnourished, but nothing could be further from the truth. She was quite as well fed as her mistress, which was to say very well indeed. And this morning, as every morning, they sat down at the table by the window to breakfast on buttered crumpets – today with honey brought by a beekeeper who'd exchanged five jars of his finest for three batches of lavender biscuits – and Earl Grey. Biscuit wasn't a fan of tea, she preferred milk, but she'd happily eat as many crumpets as she was allowed.

'We need to visit some of those letter writers,' Olive said, looking out onto the street which, at just past seven o'clock, was still quite dark and only just getting light. 'I recognised some of the names as our regulars, and I bet they'll be more willing to talk to us than the police.'

Biscuit barked her agreement, before wolfing down another crumpet. And in the silence – punctuated only by the sounds of doggy munching – Olive considered again the fact that *not* being a police officer was actually one of her super powers and that *if* she was an official detective she'd probably solve far fewer cases than she did now.

'I suppose I have the best of both worlds here,' she mused. 'I can go incognito among the potential criminals and because they underestimate me, in the same way everyone did Miss Marple, I can catch them unawares. Also' – she took a bite of crumpet and licked a dollop of honey from her lips – 'it means I avoid all the tedious paperwork Hugo complains of so much and continue to live among the deliciousness of The Biscuit Tin. What more could a person want?'

Sitting back in her chair to sip her tea, Olive felt a sudden flush of absolute contentment and gratitude for her life. It was an unexpected feeling and she wondered if the realisation had come as a consequence of finally standing up to her ancestors. While Myrtle Crisp had been alive, Olive had rather lived in the shadow of her mother – a most formidable woman – and allowed her to dictate the terms of their existence. And not much had changed since her death. But this moment, Olive thought, might mark a turning point: the day she finally took hold of the reins of her own life.

Olive was still musing on this when the café door opened and Grace walked in. Given that she hadn't been expecting to see Grace until Wednesday, Olive was rather surprised. Biscuit, on the other hand, who hadn't *not* been expecting Grace, was only delighted. Abandoning her plate of crumpets, she scampered across the floor, tail wagging.

'Morning, Biccie.' Grace knelt down to stroke the spaniel, who nuzzled the girl's neck and whimpered affectionately. 'Enjoying breakfast?'

'Grace, what a lovely surprise,' Olive said. 'Have you come to join us?'

'No, no,' Grace said. 'That's to say, I mean, I came to see you. Not to spoil your breakfast – I'm sorry – I just wanted to catch you before opening time. I wondered if we might have a quick chat?'

'Of course.' Olive nudged out a chair. 'And don't be silly; your appearance could only improve our breakfast, never spoil it. Now, sit and help yourself to a crumpet. This honey is awfully good.'

'Thank you.' Grace smiled and took a seat.

'So, what did you want to talk about?' Olive asked as she spooned a generous helping of honey onto an extra crumpet and Biscuit made herself comfortable at Grace's feet.

'Well...' Grace began. Then promptly burst into tears.

༺༻

It took a good deal of shushing and back patting before Grace finally caught her breath enough to stop sobbing and form coherent words.

'What is it?' Olive asked, for perhaps the hundredth time. 'What's wrong?'

'I-I had an argument with my father,' Grace sniffed, wiping her eyes on one of the many napkins Olive had given her. 'And he's so angry with me and I don't know what to do.'

'Tell me,' Olive said. 'Tell me everything and let's see what we can do. There's always something to be done.' Still emboldened from standing up to her relatives, Olive now felt able to make such positive pronouncements. A few years ago, while still living under the matriarchal thumb, she would not.

'H-he wants me to be an academic,' Grace sniffed. 'It's what he's always wanted for me. When I was admitted to Cambridge it was the proudest moment of his life – he always wanted a son, but I was all my mother gave him. Only one child, and a girl to boot. So he invested all his hopes and dreams with me. I alone inherited the whole of his expectations and it's – it's a heavy burden to carry.' She took a deep breath. 'You know what fathers are like.'

'Not really,' Olive admitted. 'I never knew my father. But I do know' – she dropped her voice, even though she knew it'd do no good, and gave a wry smile – 'what mothers are like.'

'I'm sorry to hear that,' Grace said. 'Did he – did you–?'

'Don't worry,' Olive said. 'It's not a tragic story. He didn't die or anything like that. I just...' She hesitated, not wanting to scandalise the girl, then decided that she was old enough and anyway that she deserved a reciprocal offering of intimate information in light of what Grace had just told her. 'I never knew him; my mother refused ever to even tell me his name. And, eventually, I gave up asking.'

'Goodness,' Grace said, not looking remotely shocked, only sympathetic. 'I'm so... sorry. I just said that, didn't I? Still, I mean it doubly. I do.'

'Thank you,' Olive said, touched. 'But don't worry, I gave up on all that a thousand years ago. I've hardly thought about it since I was a child.' This wasn't strictly true, or even slightly, but it was hardly the time to get into all that now. 'So, tell me more about your father.'

'Well...' Grace reached for a crumpet. 'He thinks that I'll do a PhD, that I'll become a fellow of Newnham, that one day I'll be Principle. But, but I can't...'

'Oh, Grace.' Olive put her arm around her protégée's shoulder, while Biscuit put a gentle paw on Grace's foot. 'Of course you can. You're brilliant and talented and amazing – I've never known anyone who has such a way with words – I've no doubt you could be the Principle of Newnham College if you put your mind to it.'

'That's very kind of you to say,' Grace said. 'And perhaps I could. But that's not what's making me miserable. Maybe I *could* be an academic and spend my life reading, researching and teaching literature but I-I don't think I *want* to.'

'Oh.' Olive sat back. 'Well, then that presents a different kind of problem.'

Grace sighed again. 'Exactly. And I tried to tell my father, gently, how I felt but he got so upset, so angry, that he wouldn't even listen to reason. I couldn't say anything, I couldn't explain...' She nibbled the edge of her crumpet, licking off the marmalade.

'And what about your mother?' Olive asked gently. 'What does she say?'

Grace shrugged. 'She's even worse. She only wants me to get married and have half a dozen children.' She shuddered. 'I'd rather be an academic than that – I'd rather do anything than that.'

'So...' Olive formed the question in her mind, even though she had a feeling she already knew the answer. 'What *is* it you want to do?'

Grace wiped her eyes and dabbed her nose on a napkin, then she turned to look at Olive. 'To work here,' she said. 'That's my dream now.' She glanced back at the counter, now laden with lemon curd cakes, lavender biscuits and caramel-chocolate flapjacks, then looked to the floor. 'Ever since I stepped into the café, I've loved it. Being here makes me feel happier, more content, than I've ever felt before. I used to love the library like that and I still love it, but not quite like this. Books are wonderful, being surrounded by them is like being among the dearest of friends but they only truly come to life when I open their pages. Here, I feel that aliveness, along with the comfort and contentment it brings, the moment I step through the door.' Grace gulped, as if what she was about to say might cause her great embarrassment. 'This place healed me, it gave me back my joy again. And now I find that I want to be here every day, for the rest of my life.' She laughed. 'I suppose, I've fallen in love.'

Olive laughed too. 'That's a beautiful way of putting it,' she said. 'And yes, having been here every day of my life, I quite understand your feelings.'

'So,' Grace said. 'You see my problem.' She took another bite of crumpet and chewed slowly, postponing the inevitable. 'My double problem. I can't work here full-time because you don't need me and yet I can't bear the thought of doing anything else, certainly not being an academic anymore. Sometimes' – she sniffed – 'I think it might have been better that I never met you, that I never discovered The Biscuit Tin and then I might have just continued to live my life in ignorance that I could've been any happier than I was.'

'Oh, Grace.' Olive placed her hand on the girl's arm. 'Don't say that. Don't you *ever* say that. Finding you was one of the best things that ever happened to me, and the café too, and I'm delighted to hear that it's the same for you.' She glanced towards the kitchen. 'And in fact, we might just be able to make this work out perfectly for everyone.' Olive paused. 'With the possible exception of your father.'

Grace's face lit up, her expression radiant with hope. 'Really?'

'I think so,' Olive said, as she sniffed the smell of burnt toast and marzipan wafting in from the kitchen. 'Leave it with me.'

Chapter Nine

Hugo didn't arrive at the café until closing time. Darkness had fallen outside and he brought with him a rush of winter wind as he stepped through the door. Olive, who was scrubbing down the counter, looked up and grinned with delight at the sight of him.

'I like that,' Hugo said as he walked towards her.

'Like what?' Olive asked, wiping her wet hands on her apron.

'That you seem as happy to see me as I always am to see you.'

Olive frowned. 'You say that as if I'm *not* always happy to see you.'

'Well...' He gave a slight shrug. 'Not always. That's to say,' he reconsidered. 'I don't always know how you're feeling, deeper down. Sometimes I think you really like me, other times that you just want some fun.'

'Can't it be both?' Olive asked when Hugo reached her. 'Can't I like you a lot and also want to have fun?'

Hugo opened his mouth, then closed it again. In the silence, she took his hand and kissed it. He closed his eyes and sighed.

'You really are unlike anyone I've ever met,' he mumbled. 'Most women your – most women want to settle down when they–'

'Most women *my* age,' Olive interrupted. 'That's what you were going to say, isn't it? You cheeky bugger.'

Hugo opened his eyes and gave her a guilty smile. 'No, of course not.'

'Liar.' Olive let go of his hand. 'And you're probably also thinking that women of my - what was it you said? – Hobbitian bodily proportions are even keener to "grab their man" – especially one as gorgeous as you – and settle down as fast as they can. Isn't that–'

'Wait, wait!' Hugo interrupted. 'First of all, I thought we already cleared all that up yesterday? I *never* said that about your figure. I adore the way you look, you know that. How could you ever doubt it? Surely you can tell how very keen I am on you. *You're* the one who doesn't seem so keen on me.'

The look of hurt in his blue eyes that accompanied this statement triggered in Olive a pang of guilt. She reached out for his hand and, a little reluctantly, he let her take it.

'I *am* keen on you,' she said. 'It's just ... it's complicated. I–'

'What's complicated?' Hugo interrupted. 'Either you like me or you don't. It's simple.'

'No,' Olive persisted. 'It's not. I do like you, very much. I just don't want to like you *too* much.'

Hugo frowned, his handsome face wrinkling in such a way that only seemed to make him even handsomer. 'Too much? What's *too* much? Surely, if I feel the same way for you there's no harm in liking me just as much as you want?'

With all this talk of liking, in its varying degrees, all Olive could hear was the word they were stepping so carefully around: "love". He wanted to say it, she knew. Because he *felt* it, she knew that too. Or, at least, she did now. She'd suspected it before but this fresh quarrel – and that pained look in his eye – confirmed it.

But the word "love" scared Olive, and the feeling it described scared her even more. 'Have you ever been in love?' she asked, speaking the unspeakable before she'd even realised, then immediately blushing and wishing she could open her mouth, take a bite of air and swallow the word down again – like a bite of genoise sponge – before it'd been heard.

But it was too late, Hugo had already heard it.

'Yes,' he said softly. 'Once.'

Olive let his hand go and fixed her gaze to the floor.

'And how did it end?' she asked. 'Not happily, I'm guessing. Or you wouldn't be here with me.' Olive could feel him looking at her, but still she didn't look up to meet his eye.

'No,' Hugo admitted. 'Not happily. It ended ... painfully. Very painfully.'

'Yes,' Olive said, feeling a twinge of jealousy, despite herself. 'That's what I thought. And, I'll bet that the amount of pain you suffered was in direct proportion to the amount of love you felt. Am I right? Tell me I'm not.'

'Of course you're right,' Hugo conceded. 'But you can't - you can't go through your life avoiding love just so you can avoid pain. Well, you can, of course, that's absolutely your choice. But it'd be an awful shame.'

Still, Olive avoided his gaze. *Can't I?* She thought. *That's exactly what I've been doing these past forty-one years, I'm sure I can manage to keep it up till I die.*

'Well...'

'Oh,' Hugo said as realisation dawned. 'You've never been in love before.'

Olive shook her head.

'Then I'm sorry.' He took her hand again and she let him. He kissed her fingers, slowly, one by one. 'I know you disagree, but I believe that not allowing yourself to love is a great waste of your heart. Just as not speaking would be a great waste of your voice, not singing even more so, and not dancing a great waste of your beautiful legs. You've been blessed with a body, a spirit, a soul. And to leave any limb unused, or any emotion unfelt, would be to die leaving so much of your life unlived.' He paused, casting his eye to the remaining cakes on the counter. 'Or, to put it another way, leaving half the cake uneaten. And you, my dear, strike me as a woman – and do *not* take this the wrong way – who devours the entire cake and relishes every crumb. Those who relish food relish life and you, incredibly brilliant and wonderful as you are, are one of life's relishers.'

Now, at last, Olive looked up. And when, at last, she met his eye, she couldn't help but smile. It seemed so ridiculous, all of a sudden, how she'd been trying to live her life. For he was right, she *was* a woman who devoured and relished every cake, pastry, biscuit, tart and pie she ate and yes, she really ought to live her life in the same way. It was a great shame to avoid some of the most delicious flavours simply because she was scared of the more unpalatable ones.

Sorry, Mum, Olive thought. *But I don't think I'll be taking your advice anymore.*

'Yes,' she smiled at Hugo. 'You're right, I am that woman. And yes, I *do* want to live as I eat.' She laughed. 'Relishing every crumb.'

And then, as if to prove her point, she kissed him.

It wasn't fully a declaration of love. But it was a step in that direction.

※

'So, I've been thinking...' Hugo said, when they'd finally stopped kissing. Or, more to the point, when Biscuit had decided that they really *ought* to stop kissing and so had gripped Olive's apron between her teeth and given it a sharp tug, nearly toppling them both over.

'Sounds ominous,' Olive said. 'I'm not sure I'm ready for more of your thoughts. You've just provided me with enough thinking to last me a lifetime.'

'Don't worry,' Hugo laughed. 'It's not advice, it's an offer.'

For a split second, Olive thought he was about to propose - too much, too soon - and yet, to her surprise, it didn't feel nearly so terrifying as it would have been only a moment ago. *Astonishing how quickly everything can change, what possibilities can unfold if only you allow them to...* But she could see by his expression that it wasn't marriage he had on his mind. *Thank goodness.* And yet, amid the wave of relief she felt a pinprick of disappointment.

'An offer?' she echoed. 'What offer?'

'Well...' He prolonged the moment, a little teasing to lighten the mood. 'I've been thinking about how brilliant you are at this detective work, and how much you enjoy it too. And, given that you'll go ahead and investigate everything anyway, behind my back, I thought you might as well do it in front of my front, as it were.'

Olive frowned. 'In front of your front?'

'That didn't come out quite right,' Hugo said. 'What I meant was, would you like to join me on investigations from time to time? When you're not at the café, of course.'

'Join you?'

'Yes,' Hugo said. 'You can be my consultant. It'd be in an unofficial capacity, so unpaid I'm afraid. I wish I could hire you on an official basis, but then you'd need to be fully qualified and-'

'Wait,' Olive interrupted. 'Are you saying that I can work with you? That we can work together solving cases?' Her voice pitched as her excitement rose, till she was barely squeaking out the words. 'Is that true? Really? You're not pulling my leg?'

'No.' Hugo's smile widened. 'I'm not pulling your leg. So, what do you say?'

'What do I say?' Olive squealed. This was better than any proposal, be it of marriage or anything else. Better even than winning the lottery. 'Yes! Of course! Yes, yes, yes!'

Throwing herself into his arms, she scattered kisses over every inch of his face. Laughing, he lifted her off the ground while Biscuit, enjoying the excitement, scampered round them in circles yapping.

'Right,' she said, when there was not an inch of him un-kissed. 'So, where do we start?'

Hugo laughed. 'You don't waste any time, do you?'

'Well...' Olive grinned. 'The case won't solve itself now, will it?'

Chapter Ten

At Olive's suggestion they didn't drive to the house but walked, following the meandering path through the side streets. This was partly because, despite the chill of the dark winter air, Olive needed to give Biscuit some exercise. The unexpected appearance of Grace that morning had meant she'd missed out on her morning perambulations and had thus been restless all day. But it was also because Olive knew that the panic-inducing sight of a police car outside one's home only caused people to clam up rather than spill secrets. That it also meant she had a good reason to walk arm in arm with Hugo as he guided her protectively along the frosty pavements was simply a bonus.

'When people are scared they lie,' Olive said as they walked. 'It's only when they feel safe that they'll take you into their confidence.'

'I'm sure you're right,' Hugo said. 'But that's a handicap I can't really do anything about. The appearance of a police officer doesn't generally put anyone at their ease. So I generally have to rely on them getting flustered and so letting something slip by accident. Or snapping under pressure.'

'It's a shame though, isn't it?' Olive mused, as Biscuit stopped to sniff a lamppost and they stood, still and shivering slightly, in the pool of its soft light. 'That everyone's scared of you. I mean, it must…' She hesitated, still formulating her thoughts. 'It must be horrible, that every time you turn up on someone's doorstep, they're never pleased to see you. Even if they're innocent. Whereas when people turn up on *my* doorstep – of The Biscuit Tin – they're always pleased to see me. Well…' Olive paused as Biscuit, finally tiring of that scent, tugged at the lead. 'Almost always. And, if they're a little out of sorts when they arrive, they're always happy when they leave. I suppose… I never really realised how lucky I am in that regard.'

'You are,' Hugo agreed as they walked on. 'And yes, I suppose it does get a little dispiriting at times. I certainly don't make any friends in my line of work.' He gave a wry smile. 'And the regulars are the worst.'

'Yes,' Olive giggled. 'I guess they are. My regulars are lovely, and I'm always the happiest to see them. But yours, I bet they can't stand the sight of you nor you them.'

'True enough,' Hugo said with a sigh. 'True enough.'

'Still…' She squeezed his arm. 'The excitement of solving crimes must make up for all that, right?'

'Mostly. But, and I hate to break your bubble, police work is as much about filling out forms as it is solving intriguing cases. Honestly, you've got the best of both worlds being a consultant detective rather than a fully-fledged copper. Believe me.'

'Consultant detective,' Olive echoed, rolling the words around her tongue. 'Gosh, I *do* like the sound of that.'

∽

They arrived at the potential suspect's house on Portugal Place ten minutes later. By this time Olive's toes were numb, despite her wool-lined boots, and she was sincerely hoping that this particular suspect was a) innocent and b) friendly and c) thus inclined to invite them all in for a cup of tea.

Hugo knocked. Twice. And then again.

After what seemed the length of a second freezing Ice Age, the door finally opened and an older man, balding and rotund, squinted out at them in the dark. His gaze was not friendly, as Olive had hoped, but suspicious.

'Yes?' He barked. 'What do you want?'

'I'm Detective Dixon,' Hugo said. 'With the Cambridgeshire Constabulary. And this is my Consultant Detective, Miss Crisp. We'd like to ask you a few questions, if you wouldn't mind.'

The man snorted. 'If I wouldn't mind?' He mimicked. 'Do I have a choice?'

'Of course you do, Mr Watson,' Hugo said. 'You're always welcome to come to the station and we can ask our questions there. The choice is entirely yours.'

Mr Watson's scowl intensified. 'Don't sound like much of a choice.' He yanked the door open. 'Come in then, and be quick about it. You're letting in all the cold air.'

'Lovely home you have,' Olive said as she sat on the sofa, while Biscuit waited patiently in the hallway. 'Very … plush.'

This was a reference to the prolific use of velvet throughout the living room: the curtains, the sofa, the chairs, the rugs… And all of it orange.

'Thank you.' Mr Watson gave a begrudging sniff. 'But I'll tell you right now, I know how you police do this "good cop, bad cop" routine and I won't be falling for it.'

'Um, I'm not a cop,' Olive said. 'I'm only a–'

'Course you're not,' Mr Watson cut her off as he sank into the chair opposite, beside the fireplace, itself clad in matching orange tiles. 'I get it.'

'No, really,' Olive tried again, but Mr Watson wasn't listening.

'So.' He turned to Hugo. 'I'm guessing this is about the letter I wrote to that bloke who was murdered last week, right?'

'The letter in which you threatened his life,' Hugo confirmed. 'Yes, indeed.'

'I don't recollect that,' Mr Watson demurred. 'And I don't think I'd forget such a thing.'

'Oh, no?' Hugo reached into his jacket pocket and extracted a sheet of paper wrapped in plastic. 'Because I have it right here, in black and white. "I have reason to believe that Justice is coming for you. And it'll come when you least expect it." Did you, or did you not, write that, Mr Watson?'

The suspect took a moment to consider. 'Yes,' he said. 'Now that you jog my memory, I'd say yes that sounds about right.'

Hugo nodded. 'I thought so. And why? Why did you say such a thing?'

'Because he had it coming to him,' Mr Watson said. 'He was a frightful so-and-so, causing hurt to an awful lot of people. He was bound to get what was owing to him in the end.'

'And were you the one who intended to give him what was owing to him?' Hugo asked. 'Was that your intention?'

Mr Watson shrugged. 'I'm not a violent man, Detective. I simply said it how I saw it.'

'You work at Whitemoor?' Olive piped up. 'Surrounded, I imagine, by some of the most violent men in the country. Have you never had to use anything stronger than words against them before?'

'I used to work there,' Mr Watson corrected. 'I'm retired now. I wrote that letter half a dozen years ago, maybe more. And no, I never did. I am a pacifist, Miss Crisp.'

Olive nodded, feeling deeply uncomfortable. She wasn't used to the cold, calculating nature of this situation. She wanted what she knew, she wanted tea and cake, she wanted everything to be pleasant and convivial so they could have a cheery, civilised conversation and resolve matters that way. Being a consultant detective, Olive could see, would take some getting used to.

'So, now you refer to Mr Mayhew as "a frightful so-and-so",' Olive began, slightly hesitant. 'But you wrote in your letter that he was the most "contemptible, vile, reprobate, loathsome, detestable, wretched, abominable..." – she paused momentarily – '...devious, dishonest, underhand and treacherous" man you'd ever known. Those are very strong feelings for a stranger. Can you tell us what prompted such a wellspring of hostility?'

Olive didn't take her eyes off Mr Watson but she could feel Hugo's gaze on her and she knew it was a gaze of admiration and, probably, surprise given that she hadn't yet told him about her photographic memory. Olive felt a flush of pride, a glow of contentment in her belly, just as she'd always done whenever she'd been praised for getting good marks at school.

'He stole from my son,' Mr Watson muttered. 'He ruined him, simply for the fun of it and because he was so damn greedy. He couldn't bear other businesses to thrive in the city, no matter how small. He outbid Joe on everything and then used nefarious means to take his shop out from under him. Soon after that, Joe's wife left him and' – Mr Watson's voice quivered – 'a month later he drowned himself in the River Cam.'

'Oh, no,' Olive exclaimed. 'How awful. I'm so sorry.'

Entirely forgetting she was there in the capacity of consultant detective, Olive rose from the sofa and hurried over to Mr Watson to place a consoling hand on his shoulder.

'No parent should ever have to live through the death of a child,' she whispered. 'It's not fair, it's not how life should be.'

For a few long, painful moments, the room filled with silence. Then Mr Watson reached up and patted her hand. 'Thank you dear,' he said, softly.

Then, all at once, he wasn't a possible killer but a sad, old man who'd tragically lost his son. And now Olive was convinced that Mr Watson hadn't been the one to murder Mr Mayhew. Having inherited the sixth sense from her matriarchal lineage, she'd have bet her life on it. She glanced over at Hugo, who nodded.

'Mr Watson,' Olive said gently. 'Do you have any idea who might have committed this crime? That's to say–'

'Why do you care?' Mr Watson interrupted with a snap. 'Why waste police resources trying to capture someone who killed an evil, heartless excuse for a human being? I've not the first idea who did it but I tell you what, if I did, I'd walk right up to him and shake his hand.'

༄

'Six suspects,' Olive said as they walked slowly back towards The Biscuit Tin, Great St Mary's Church chiming the hour of ten o'clock. 'And they all deny killing him, while at the same time saying they'd have gladly done it if given half the chance. And, I get the distinct feeling that, no matter how many of those letter writers we interview, they're all going to say a variation on the same.'

'Yes,' Hugo agreed. 'I fear you're right.'

'Also...' Olive slowed to a shuffle as they passed alongside King's College, both because her feet were freezing by now and she could hardly put one foot in front of the other, but also because the moon was full and the glow it cast across the white stone of the turrets and towers was magical and Olive never tired of gazing up at it. 'I can't help but think they have a point. I mean, don't you ever want to drop an investigation because you think the victim deserved it?'

Slightly worried that she'd just said something scandalous, Olive was rather relieved when Hugo only laughed.

'More often than I'd like to admit,' he confessed. 'But unfortunately, my position often entails things I'd rather not do. Still' – he shrugged – 'it's my job. I don't have a choice.'

'Have you ever' – Olive dropped her voice, though the streets were empty – 'broken the rules and let someone go free, even though you knew they were guilty, just because it was the right thing to do?'

Hugo considered this a moment. 'Yeah,' he said. 'Once or twice. But never for something as serious as murder.'

'But would you?' Olive pressed, as they turned the corner onto Bene't Street. 'If you had the chance?'

'I don't know,' Hugo said, then laughed again. 'But something tells me that *you* would and that you don't quite have the uncompromising moral outlook to be a police officer.'

'No,' Olive agreed with a smile. 'I don't think I do.'

At the sight of The Biscuit Tin, the spaniel tugged at her lead and they hurried towards the café. 'So...' Olive hesitated at the door. 'Do you want to come in?'

Chapter Eleven

WHEN OLIVE STEPPED INTO the café, she almost missed the note. It was folded several times into a tiny square and stuck itself to the bottom of her boot, hidden from view until Biscuit started barking.

'What is it, Bics?' Olive frowned. 'What's wrong?'

Biscuit placed her paw on Olive's boot and Olive, gripping Hugo's arm for support, lifted her foot with her other hand and turned her boot upside down.

'Oh!' she exclaimed in surprise as she peeled it off. 'What's that?'

Slowly unfolding the paper, the square revealed itself to be a note:

> *Detective Krisp,*
> *Have you found my lizard yet? Please ~~tell~~ inform me straightway if you discover any clues. Also, I have another crime ~~you must~~ for you to please investigate <u>urgintly</u>. One hour ago my monkey was kidnaped. Please find him.*
> *Sinceerly,*
> *Jimmy Mayhew*

'Monkey?!' Olive exclaimed, surprise eclipsing her secret delight that the boy still considered her a detective. 'His *monkey*? What the...?'

'Monkey?' Hugo echoed, as he hung his coat and scarf on the hatstand beside the door. 'What monkey?'

'My point exactly,' Olive said. 'I didn't even know he had a monkey.'

'Who has a monkey?' Hugo persisted. 'I'm confused.'

'You're confused? How do you think I feel?' Olive marched towards the counter, still holding the note, discarding her winter clothes as she went. Biscuit scurried behind her, picking up the discarded items and returning them to where they belonged.[1] 'I need a cup of tea and several slices of cake.'

'Alright,' Hugo said. 'And after that, I hope you'll tell me what on earth's going on.'

'I would, if I knew,' Olive said, as she hurried into the kitchen. At the doorway, she stopped and turned back to him. 'Aren't you coming?'

'I'd love to.' Hugo hurried forward. 'I didn't know mere mortals were permitted entry onto such hallowed grounds.'

'Only by special invitation,' Olive said with a smile.

'Then it's my lucky day.' Hugo smiled back.

It was only when he stepped over the threshold that Olive realised the danger of what she'd just done. Inviting Hugo into the kitchen, the domain of her ancestors, was simply asking for trouble. *How foolish*! Ordinarily, conscious of all the secrets she was keeping, Olive was cautious, always wary of making a mistake. But the sudden and entirely unexpected entrance of a mysterious monkey onto the scene had thrown her into a muddle.

'Are you okay?' Hugo asked, noting the change in her expression. 'Is everything alright?'

'What? Yes, fine,' Olive said, still flustered. How could she explain throwing him out now, having just invited him in? 'Of course. Why wouldn't it be alright? So, what do you fancy? Biscuits or cake?' Flicking on the light, she cast a stern glance about the kitchen, a warning to her ancestors to behave. A warning she knew, from experience, that they would likely ignore. As strong women who'd survived and thrived under three hundred years of the patriarchy since The Biscuit Tin was founded; they were not the sort who did what they were told. Even when it was Olive doing the telling.

'I don't mind,' Hugo said. 'Whatever it is, if you made it I know it'll be delicious.'

'Blythe's right,' Olive smiled as she opened the tea caddy, momentarily forgetting the problem of her dead relatives. 'You really are a charmer.'

'Am I?' Hugo sidled closer, squeezing between the kitchen island and the oven. 'That suggests insincerity, but I mean every word.'

'Oh, I don't doubt that.' Olive inched towards him. 'And I don't think she was referring to your words so much as that irresistible twinkle in your eye.'

'Twinkle?' Hugo's breath was warm on her cheek as he leaned in to kiss her neck. 'I don't have a twinkle.'

'Oh yes you do,' Olive said, shivering at the soft touch of his lips. 'You've got the twinkliest twinkle I've ever seen…'

'And you've got the softest skin of anyone I've ever kissed.'

'Oh? And how many is that then? Just out of interest...' Olive whispered. 'Am I top of ten? Five? Or a hundred?'

'A hundred?' Hugo laughed, the tickle of his breath making Olive giggle. 'What do you take me for? I wouldn't solve a single case if I spent that much time kissing.'

'Oh, I don't know about that... Mind you, men are notoriously bad at multitasking, so you could be right.'

'Wait, what's that smell?' Hugo wrinkled his nose. 'Smells like .... burnt toast.'

With a huff, Olive pulled back, folding her arms. 'Well, you just went from being the most charming man I ever met to the most indelicate. Don't you know it's awfully rude to tell a woman she smells?'

Of course, Olive smelt it too – her great-great-great aunt Philomena's signature scent – but she hoped a show of being affronted might momentarily distract him.

'What?! I never did anything of the sort!' Hugo exclaimed. 'Don't you smell that?'

Olive regarded him innocently. 'Smell what?'

'Like burning toast. But nothing's toasting.'

'Then it can't be burning,' Olive said, opening a biscuit tin on the counter and holding it out to him. 'Stands to reason. Anyway, forget about that and let me tell you about the monkey.'

'Oh, yes, the monkey!' Hugo slapped his forehead with one hand and seized up a proffered cherry flapjack with the other. 'How could that've slipped my mind? You're clearly right about men and multitasking. I kissed you and every thought left my head. So, tell me about the monkey.'

'And the lizard.' Olive reached for a flapjack for herself and took a big bite. 'We must remember the lizard.'

'Lizard?' Hugo frowned. 'What lizard?'

Now the scent of almonds perfumed the air. Olive studiously ignored it while Hugo, attention suddenly drawn to his flapjack, merely gave an appreciative sniff. 'These things smell as delicious as they taste.'

'Yes.' Olive scowled in the direction of the oven, then hurriedly changed the subject. 'So, back to the lizard and the monkey. And I know this is all going to sound utterly ridiculous, but bear with me.' Olive took another fortifying bite. 'The son of the victim – Jimmy Mayhew – has hired me to find his lizard, which he's convinced has been kidnapped or killed or some such, which I've agreed to do though I've no idea how to do it. Unless we can utilise police resources to analyse a rogue fingerprint found at the scene. Anyway, this lizard was taken last week and now, so it seems, was his monkey.'

Hugo stared at Olive, utterly perplexed. A few moments passed before he found speech. 'A lizard *and* a monkey?'

Olive nodded.

'I thought boys generally had dogs or cats as pets? Budgies, perhaps,' Hugo said. 'Maybe the odd tortoise. But this boy sounds like he's Noah, collecting species for The Ark.'

Olive laughed. 'Yes, I suppose it does rather. Well, I've no idea why he favours such exotic creatures, but there you have it.'

'And you think these ... pet-nappings are somehow related to his father's murder?' Hugo swallowed the last of his cherry flapjack and reached for a second. 'May I?'

'Of course,' Olive said. 'And I've no idea. Right now I don't really see how they can be, which is why I didn't mention the lizard at the time - I've only just found out about the monkey - because it all sounded so ludicrous. And, anyway, at first I naturally just assumed he'd lost it.'

'But now you don't?'

'Not after I found the fingerprint. And anyway, it all seems a little too coincidental, don't you think? His father is killed the same week his lizard is stolen, and then his pet monkey too. What are the odds?'

Hugo chewed thoughtfully on his flapjack. 'I agree. Either that or he's one *very* unlucky kid.'

The six antique teacups on the shelf across the opposite wall rattled – Charlotte Krisp joining the conversation. Hugo glanced up. The cupboard door beside Olive swung open then banged shut.

Hugo frowned. 'What was that?'

'What?' Olive knocked her knee against the cupboard. 'The door? I'm only messing around. Fidgeting helps me think.'

'And the cups?' His frown deepened. 'What's–'

He was interrupted by the blender in the corner whizzing up – though it was empty and unplugged (fortunately Hugo wasn't able to see that from where he stood) – and two (stale and forgotten) crumpets popping out of the toaster.

'It's a very old kitchen,' Olive said, before he could say anything else. 'Faulty wiring and all sorts everywhere. An absolute nightmare, really.' She shrugged. 'But what can you do? Anyway, why don't you go and sit down in the café? Make yourself comfortable and I'll bring the tea – coffee for you – and assorted cakes.'

'But–'

'No buts.' Olive shoved him in the direction of the doorway. 'You've been on your feet all day, you need to sit down.'

'Me?' Hugo protested. 'You're the one–'

'Nonsense,' Olive interrupted. 'You sit, I'll bring. Now, be off with you.'

1. Biscuit had been inspired to this behaviour after watching *Peter Pan* with Olive a few weeks before. Seeing how well Nanny took care of her charges, Wendy, John and Michael Darling, Biscuit had decided that Olive was in need of the same care.

Chapter Twelve

OLIVE AND HUGO HAD stayed up talking, eating – occasionally kissing and constantly touching, in that way that new couples always do – into the small hours. Olive felt, though she was too shy to voice those feelings, that it was the perfect ending to the most perfect day of her life. And Hugo, though he couldn't help but entertain a longing, every now and then, that they were upstairs rather than downstairs, had also never been happier. He'd only finally left because Olive fell asleep on the table with Biscuit curled up at her feet, snoring gently. After waiting till Olive was sleeping fully and wouldn't easily wake, Hugo carried her upstairs to bed, followed by a sleepy Biscuit. Navigating his way in the dark, having never been upstairs before, he finally found the bedroom after first finding the bathroom and almost settling Olive down in the bath. Tucking her in, he kissed her cheek then gazed at her a moment or two, before pulling himself away.

Taping a handwritten note to the café door, Hugo locked up and left.

> *Due to unforeseen circumstances*
> *The Biscuit Tin will be opening late today.*
> *Apologies for any inconvenience.*
> *I promise it will be worth the wait.*

It was Millie who finally woke Olive late that morning. Olive had been sleeping like a baby; the sort of baby all parents hope for but are very rarely favoured with, the sort of baby that *if* you are blessed with such a miracle you ought to shut up about it because every other new parent will (quite rightly) hate you. In short, she slept for eight hours straight, a deep and peaceful sleep filled with delightful dreams, the sort of sleep Olive hadn't known since childhood.

Despite being locked, the café door swung open even before Millie had put her hand to the glass. Which meant that, due to her poor eyesight, she didn't see the note. The café always opened its door to its favourite customers, and frequently caused the door to stick against the less favoured ones. The ancestors, who held strong and decisive opinions on everything, were especially particular about manners and should anyone be found to be lacking in that regard they'd likely find themselves barred from The Biscuit Tin for life. Similarly, men who cheated on their wives could be certain of a frosty reception. But Millie and Blythe were, as Olive's oldest friends, always welcome. Today, Millie was rather astonished to find Olive still in bed at ten o'clock. And, thinking something might be terribly wrong, gently shook her friend awake. Biscuit, delighted at the sight of Millie but troubled by her demeanour, started barking frantically.

'W-what?' Olive squinted up at Millie. 'W-what's happening?'

'What's wrong?' Millie demanded. 'I thought – I thought perhaps...'

'What?' Olive, still groggy, pulled herself up onto the pillows. 'What? You thought I was dead?'

'No, no, of course not,' Millie lied. 'I thought maybe you were... drunk. And–'

'Drunk?' Olive frowned as she rubbed her eyes. 'Since when have I been drunk on anything but caffeine and sugar?'

'I know.' Millie sighed and sat on the bed beside her. 'I'm sorry, I just... I only popped in to pick up almond croissants for George's elevenses' – she swallowed a smile – 'he invited me to join him. Anyway, it's not for that that I hounded you, only that I couldn't recall a Friday when the café's been closed without notice and you've not been at the counter. So I, I panicked.'

'Oh, Millie,' Olive laughed, touched by her friend's concern. 'Bless you.' Then she glanced at her alarm clock. 'Oh my goodness!' Olive sat up so fast she accidentally kicked Biscuit off the bed and almost sent Millie to the floor along with her.

'Heeey!' Millie squealed and Biscuit whined, all twisted up in Olive's blankets, wrapping herself tighter while she tried to get free.

'I'm late, I'm so, so, so late!' Olive scrambled out of bed, toppling head first onto the carpet and bringing Millie with her. 'I've got to get up, get ready, get the café open.'

'Calm down, calm down.' Millie pulled herself back up by the bed frame. 'You sound like the White Rabbit in Wonderland. But there's no Red Queen who'll behead you. You own the café, remember, it doesn't matter if you open late once in a blue moon.'

'It matters to the customers!'

Still on all-fours, Olive started to stand just as Biscuit clawed free from the pretzel of blankets and lurched forward into Olive's path, bringing her mistress thumping to the ground again.

'Bics!' Olive scolded. 'What on earth are you doing? This isn't the time for messing about! We've got to get ready!'

Biscuit whined, upset at being blamed unfairly, but Olive was too frantic to notice.

'Calm down,' Millie said. 'Stop panicking, it'll be fine.'

'You know,' Olive snapped back, 'the very worst thing you can say to someone who's panicking is "stop panicking" – it's utterly useless! And who ever calmed down after someone told them to calm down?! If it was that easy to be calm, I'd already be calm now, wouldn't I?!'

Swallowing a smile, Millie regarded her friend. 'Alright,' she said. 'You keep panicking and while you're doing that and getting yourself ready, I'll be in the kitchen to crack on with the baking, alright?'

'Alright,' Olive sniffed. 'That'd be – thank you.' Dashing off in the direction of the bathroom, she did a u-turn at the doorway. 'But wait, what about the haberdashery? Should you be there? You can't afford to–'

'My sister's in town,' Millie said. 'She's been taking charge of the shop all morning, so the best thing I can do is not–'

'Say no more,' Olive said. 'I'll see you downstairs in five minutes.'

'Take a few more,' Millie advised. 'Unless you want to scare the customers away as soon as they come in.' She bent to pick up Biscuit, who was still downcast. 'Come on, let's get you some breakfast, shall we. Then I'll get to work before your mistress gives herself a heart attack.'

∽

With Biscuit settled in her favourite spot by the window, munching on two small chicken and tarragon pies Millie had found in the fridge, she set to baking. Given that it was almost midday, there wasn't any point in making two-tiered cakes or croissants since they'd take too long, so Millie stuck to biscuits, flapjacks and fairy cakes. This way they'd have something to serve within the hour and keep the treat-loving denizens of Cambridge happy.

Millie was spooning golden syrup into a hot saucepan of melting butter and brown sugar when she heard Olive hurtling down the stairs before careening into the kitchen.

'Well, you weren't wrong about my advice backfiring,' Millie said with a wink. 'If anything you seem twice as panicked as you were–'

'Enough of that,' Olive interrupted. 'I'm in no mood to be teased today. Just make me two more batches of those biscuits, along with three dozen fairy cakes and I'll be forever in your debt.'

'Consider it done.' Millie saluted. 'Also, I used your telephone to call the porters at Newnham, they're tracking down Grace as we speak. So, fingers crossed and we should have a third pair of hands before too long.'

At the mention of Grace's name, the oven door swung open then banged shut as the scent of frangipane filled the air.

'Enough of that, Mother,' Olive admonished as she lifted her apron from the hook on the wall and tied it around her waist. 'We need her now more than ever and I for one hope they locate her fast.'

'Your relatives still holding out against sharing the café's secret recipes?' Millie asked as she tipped flour into the bowl. 'Speaking of which, I'm using my grandmother's recipe for these flapjacks, so I'll need you to add your own clandestine ingredients before I add the oats.'

'Give me a moment.' Olive darted over to the fridge. 'I think I've got a few things I saved from yesterday that we could use.' She yanked open the door and pulled out a stack of Tupperware tubs fit to bursting with all manner of baked goods: hazelnut brownies, custard tarts, mini lemon meringue pies…

'A few?' Millie laughed. 'That's enough to feed all the residents of Newnham.'

'Nonsense.' Olive set them on the counter. 'You, Blythe and I could gobble up all this in a single sitting of Afternoon Tea. Now, enough chattering, we've got work to do.'

⁂

Half an hour later, with Olive up to her elbows in cake batter and Millie pulling two trays of lavender-sugar-honey biscuits out of the grumpy oven, the bell above the front door tinkled and both women looked up, eager for the appearance of Grace.

'That was quick,' Olive called out. 'I've said it before and I'll say it again, you're an absolute marvel and–'

But her words evaporated on her lips as not Grace but Hugo strode into the kitchen.

'Oh,' she said. 'It's not – it's you.'

'Who were you expecting?' Hugo smiled. 'Whoever it is, consider me jealous. I don't think I've ever felt so unwelcome.'

'Sorry,' Olive hurried over to him. 'I didn't mean… it's just, we're having a minor crisis here and, although you're a top class detective and all-round delightful human, I'm guessing you're not much of a baker.'

Hugo held up his hands. 'Guilty, I'm afraid. I doubt I could even identify sugar from flour at a push. But,' he added, before he rendered himself too redundant, 'I *do* have something else to offer you. First thing this morning, I visited Mr Mayhew's personal residence and took a copy of the fingerprint you mentioned. Young master Mayhew wouldn't let me in the house till I showed him my badge and told him that I worked for you.'

'For *me*?!' Olive laughed. 'Whatever did you do that for?'

'Oh, just maintaining your street cred.' Hugo grinned. 'He was awfully impressed, I must say. Anyway, I've set Constable Numpty Cooper on the case, comparing it with every print we've got on file. It'll take a while, but even he shouldn't be able to mess that up. I hope.'

'Really?' Olive felt a flush of excitement, momentarily quelling her panic. The notion of comparing files of fingerprints was a thrilling one, even if Hugo regarded it as a job beneath him. It was far more exciting than beating eggs into butter and the result, if successful, might taste even sweeter. 'When will you get the results?'

'Two weeks, if his usual speed is anything to go by,' Hugo said. 'I'm joking,' he added, at the sight of poor Olive's horrified expression. 'I impressed upon him the urgency and importance of the case - without mentioning the matter of a missing lizard, of course – and, given that our database isn't huge, especially if we're just focusing on the last twenty years or so, it shouldn't take longer than a day at most.'

'Okay,' Olive exhaled. The idea of waiting more than a few hours for the chance of exciting news was painful, the idea of waiting more than twenty-four hours was unbearable. 'And what do you think the odds are that you'll find a match?'

'Hard to say,' Hugo admitted. 'Depends if the thief has any priors - if we've caught him doing anything illegal before,' he added, in case they didn't understand him. 'And since criminals tend to re-offend, then I'd say the odds are quite good. Although, that's more likely for crimes like stealing bikes, shoplifting, drug dealing, assault or murder. I'll admit we don't tend to see much in the way of lizard abduction, I'm afraid. So, unless we've got ourselves a perp who's diversifying, then...'

'Hum,' Olive mused. 'Then here's hoping.'

The bell above the door chimed again and Olive looked up, full of expectation.

Hugo looked from her to the café. 'I think this is my cue to leave,' he said. 'Since I'm guessing this is who you wanted when I arrived instead.'

'Oh no,' Olive protested. 'Well, yes, but only because we needed – Grace!' she exclaimed as her protégé hurried into the kitchen. 'You're here!'

'So sorry I'm late,' Grace blurted out as she dropped her bag to the floor. Then, realising she was still wearing her winter coat and scarf, she hurried back into the café to hang them on the hat rack by the door. 'There's a protest march along Silver Street,' she called out. 'So many people blocking the pavements and road, I couldn't run.'

'I do hope it's not getting out of hand,' Hugo said, suddenly looking startled. 'That's the last thing we need. Any civilian casualties and I'll have the Commissioner breathing down my neck. And those hippies might seem mild-mannered, but when they get fired up about injustice they can get quite ... impassioned. Understandably so, of course. But, I'd anyway better go and keep an eye on things.' He stepped over to Olive, giving her a quick but heartfelt kiss on the cheek. 'I'll call you as soon as I can if we get any results, or I'll pop by.'

'Yes, please,' Olive said. 'Come by later anyway, after closing time. If you can.'

'Of course.' Hugo nodded then, saying his goodbyes to Millie and Grace, hurried off.

'Right, grab an apron,' Olive said to Grace. 'Then get started on a batch of fairy cakes.'

'Absolutely,' Grace said, sounding thrilled. 'What flavour?'

'Cardamom and coriander, I think.' Olive turned to the sink to wash her hands. 'And a little allspice. The customers can't get enough of Christmas flavours this time of year. We'll have to start making gingerbread soon.' She strode across the kitchen to delicately lift a heavy leather book from the shelf beside the antique teacups then brought it back to Grace. 'I have the recipe in here, this one courtesy of my great-great-great-great grandmother, Maud.'

Setting the book with great care on the counter in front of Grace, Millie looked on, open-mouthed.

'This book contains all the recipes collected by my ancestors over the past three hundred years,' Olive said solemnly. 'All of them are to be treated with the utmost secrecy and respect. Understood?'

Grace nodded, very slowly, very surely. Her eyes wide with exhilaration and awe, as if she was being handed the Holy Grail.

Olive smiled, slipping her arm over Grace's shoulder and giving her a tight squeeze. 'Welcome to The Biscuit Tin, my dear. And don't worry, I've dealt with my mother – more on that later – and we'll deal with your father when the time's right. But for now, let's get baking!'

'Yes, boss.' Grace rolled up her sleeves and began studying the book's open page, unable to stop grinning. Then she glanced up. 'I think something's burning.' She frowned, confused. 'Smells like toast.'

Chapter Thirteen

HUGO DIDN'T RETURN TO The Biscuit Tin till the following morning, when Olive and Grace were in full swing with the breakfast takeaway rush. Weaving around the line, he reached the counter where Grace was brewing and pouring cups of tea and Olive was boxing up buttered crumpets.

'Long time no see,' Olive said with a wink; an impressive attempt at composure. In truth, she'd been on tenterhooks waiting for him to return with a report on the fingerprint analysis since yesterday and had hardly slept for excitement and anticipation. But she didn't want him to know that. No, if one was to garner any respect in relationships, Olive believed that nonchalance was always the order of the day.

'What can I get you?' She handed over the box of crumpets to the happy customer. 'We've got everything today.' She nodded at Grace. 'Thanks to my lovely protégé now being a fully-fledged, full-time member of staff.'

'Wonderful.' Hugo cast a delighted eye over the café counter heavy with Bakewell tarts, chocolate flapjacks, cherry scones, almond croissants, lemon curd cakes, lavender-sugar biscuits, currant buns... 'I'll have one of everything, please.'

Olive laughed. 'Alright then' – she nodded at the line stretching through the shop – 'get to the back and I'll prepare you a feast,' she added, then, in response to his disappointment, 'Well, I can't be seen to have favourites now, can I? And you'd be accused of corruption.'

'Jumping queues for free croissants?' Hugo laughed. 'I'm pretty sure the Commissioner himself does worse than that a dozen times a day.'

'I hate to think,' Olive said, then caught the eye of the next person in line. 'Good Morning, Miss Westmacott.' She smiled brightly. 'Here for your usual? Custard creams today, or lavender-sugar biscuits? Darjeeling or Earl Grey?'

'That's fine, I can wait,' Hugo said, taking a seat at the nearest table. 'It's not as if I have to be back at the station for anything important, like – I don't know – interviewing a suspect we've got in custody, a suspect whose thumbprint just happens to match the one found on the lizard's tank.'

'What?' Olive dropped the crumpet. 'You *found* him?!'

'We did.' Hugo smiled, thrilled to have made Olive so happy and wishing that he could do the same every day. 'But it wasn't from someone already on our database–'

'Then how?' Olive interrupted. 'How did–?'

'The protest yesterday,' Hugo stood again, stepped over to the counter and dropped his voice to a whisper. 'It was against animal testing – specifically the university's Department of Medicine. The hippies got a little out of control, no doubt provoked by some of my officers who, I'll admit, can be rather ... provocative. It's an ongoing issue and a general nightmare. But, back to the point; seven protesters were arrested, fingerprinted and kept overnight. And one of them, a Mr Roger Kimber, was in possession of that infamous right thumb. Miraculously, it was Constable Cooper who spotted it, so I might have to reassess my judgement of his character as a total incompetent half-wit. At least until the next time he does something utterly idiotic so, probably for about a day. Anyway–'

'Can I come?' Olive interrupted again. 'Can I come to the interrogation? Please.'

'I'm sorry,' Hugo said, genuinely regretful. 'If it was in the field, it'd be no problem. At least, we can get around it. But at the station, I'm afraid I can't allow a civilian into an interrogation room. That'd be flouting far too many protocols.'

'Yes, of course,' Olive said, her bubble of excitement deflating. 'I forgot... It's fine. But will you come back and tell me everything, soon as you can?'

'No question,' Hugo said. 'Even before I've filled out the paperwork.' He dropped his voice even lower. 'I wish we didn't have such an audience and then I could kiss you.'

'If only.' Olive smiled as she bagged up a miniature Bakewell tart and slipped it to him. 'Here's something to keep you satisfied until then.'

'If only,' Hugo echoed. 'Everything is a poor substitute for you. Still, as substitutes go it's the best of them.'

'See, what did I say? Charming to the core.' Olive grinned. 'But off with you now, you've got work to do!'

True to his word, Hugo returned later that day, arriving at The Biscuit Tin while a slightly preoccupied Olive was enjoying her daily after-hours Afternoon Tea with Millie and Blythe and, now that she'd been officially adopted into the café's family, Grace. Along, naturally, with Biscuit who sat under the table gratefully and gleefully gobbling up everything she was offered.

'Don't get me wrong,' Blythe was saying when the door opened, letting in a draft of winter wind. 'I'm very fond of Mr Harrington, but he's taking his time. I honestly thought he'd have proposed by now but there's really no sign-'

'Hugo!' Olive, who'd been distractedly munching on a cream bun, jumped up from her chair at the sight of him and dashed across the café to the door.

'Why do I get the feeling that this wonderful welcome isn't simply because you're so pleased to see me?' Hugo said as she barrelled into his arms. 'Why do I-?'

'What happened?' Olive cut him off. 'What did he say? What's the news?'

'Well, hello to you too,' Hugo laughed. 'How about a cup of tea? And perhaps some leftovers. Interrogation is hungry work, I'm starving.'

'Okay, okay,' Olive squealed. 'You can have whatever you like' – she gestured at the kitchen – 'right after you tell me everything.'

'I'm not sure I can,' Hugo teased. 'I think I'm too weak from missing lunch, it's affecting my memory. Perhaps, if you take me into the kitchen and feed me then I'll be able to recall all the salient details.'

'You cheeky monkey,' Olive gave him a playful . 'Stop teasing and tell me.'

'Well, I'd love to,' Hugo dropped his voice. 'But I can't really, not exactly, not in front of...' He nodded at the circle of friends gathered around the table laden with tea and treats, all now staring at them, hanging on their every word.

'Don't worry about them,' Olive said. 'They're all discreet as the day is long, I promise.' She thought of her ancestors, and their recipes, of the other secrets her friends knew about her but to which Hugo was still oblivious.

'I've no doubt,' Hugo agreed. 'But it's not me, it's the police – it's the trouble I'd get into – you understand? Now, if you choose to tell them everything I tell you after the fact, then that's up to you. But if I tell them myself, it's a different story. You see?'

'Yes, yes, of course,' Olive said, though she didn't see much in it. 'Come into the kitchen.' Then, quickly re-thinking as she remembered her ancestors' cheeky behaviour last time he'd encroached on their space, she added, 'Actually, let's go outside. It's, um, an absolute mess in the kitchen.'

'But it's freezing outside,' Hugo protested. 'And anyway I don't mind a little mess. You should see the station, it's a pig-sty.'

'Yes, well, it's not so much a mess as a health-hazard,' Olive said, already reaching for her coat. 'And I'm sure it's not *so* bad out there. Just a little nippy is all.'

At the sight of her mistress pulling on her coat and the promise of a walk, Biscuit scrambled out from under the table.

'If you say so,' Hugo said. 'But afterwards I'll need twice as much coffee and cake.'

'Deal.' Olive laughed, feeling like a kid at Christmas on the brink of opening a sackful of presents. 'Alright, Bics, I know you're desperate for a little air. And probably a piddle too' – she unhooked the dog's lead – 'so let's go.'

༄

'Oh!' Olive squealed again as they stepped outside. 'You're right, it's blinking freezing!'

'I told you so.' Hugo's sigh puffed out like smoke. 'Shall we walk?'

Taking this as permission, Biscuit scurried off (without her lead) in the direction of the graveyard, leaving Olive and Hugo to dash after her.

'So, tell me everything!' Olive gasped as she hurried along. She couldn't run, she never ran, but for the opportunity to hear Hugo's news she gave it a blooming good try.

'Long story short,' Hugo called back over his shoulder, 'he confessed!'

'What?' Olive cried. 'I can't hear you! What?!'

Catching up to Biscuit at the corner, Hugo picked up the spaniel and held her close, nuzzling her neck. Several minutes later, Olive, gasping for breath, reached them both.

'W-w-w...' She grabbed Hugo's arm and hung on. 'I-I...'

'Are you alright?' Hugo laughed. 'You look like you're having a heart attack.'

'I-I'm fine,' Olive huffed, still clinging on as she refilled her lungs with freezing air. 'Utterly fine. Now, tell me, what did–'

'He confessed.' Hugo grinned, every inch of him quivering with excitement to be bringing her this news, rather like Biscuit when she brought her mistress a dead rabbit. If Hugo had been a spaniel, right now he'd be wagging his tail. 'Mr Roger Kimber confessed. He murdered Mr Mayhew.'

Olive stared at him, speechless. But Olive Crisp was never speechless for long.

'He confessed?' She echoed. 'Just like that?'

'Well, yes,' Hugo said. 'I mean, it took a little interrogation on my part, but not as much as I thought it might. He was quite easy to crack, clearly not much of a hotshot criminal. And something of a surprise to peg him as a killer, I confess. I've not seen many murderers so clueless, so naive. But it takes all sorts, I suppose.'

'So, why did he do it?' Olive asked, clipping on Biscuit's lead as they set off along the street again. It was too cold to remain still. 'And why on earth did he steal the lizard? And, I imagine, the monkey too.'

'Well, he said he stole them to prove a point about the illegal trafficking of exotic animals,' Hugo explained. 'And he killed Mr Mayhew because, although he claimed to be a philanthropist, bestowing substantial donations upon all sorts of good causes, the protection of animals among them, apparently he wasn't doing anything of the sort. Quite the opposite, in fact. Kimber claims that Mayhew was investing his riches in immoral and corrupt ventures that "exploited humans and animals alike" and, since no one was stopping him, Kimber took it upon himself to serve up justice, as he saw it.'

'Really?' Olive said, taking a moment to digest all this. 'But – so he did what? Followed him or waited outside his office and then went in with the shovel and whacked him over the head?'

'After having a row first,' Hugo added. 'But yes, that's the long and the short of it. Kimber says he tried to convince Mayhew to mend his ways, to become a better man... But you can guess how well that went.' He paused. 'Mr Kimber claims it wasn't premeditated, that the shovel was leaning against the back wall of the office and he grabbed it in a fit of rage...'

'A shovel, in an office?' Olive frowned.

'Yes, I know,' Hugo agreed. 'It doesn't sound likely, does it? I doubt it'll hold up in court, so unfortunately he'll likely go down for murder rather than manslaughter.'

'Oh,' Olive sighed. 'That's not good.' She hesitated. 'But then, why did he steal the monkey *after* Mr Mayhew was dead?'

Hugo shrugged. 'I think that was simply for its own sake. He planned to release the animals back into the wild, I believe.'

Olive frowned. 'I don't think they'd survive long in Grantchester Meadows. Cows don't make the best bedfellows with monkeys, or lizards, I'm guessing.'

'True enough,' Hugo laughed. 'He was planning a trip abroad – has contacts in Heathrow security apparently. He had it all set up to smuggle them back to their homelands, quite impressive actually. And commendable. The motive, I mean, not the murder. Although...'

'Given what an absolute devil Mayhew seems to have been, perhaps his death wasn't the greatest loss to humanity,' Olive said, eyeballing Biscuit who was busy sniffing a postbox. 'Come on Bics, take your piddle now will you? Before we all turn into ice sculptures.'

'Yes, well I'll admit it's fairly rare that the victim is so much less sympathetic than the killer,' Hugo agreed. 'But it happens. Mostly in cases of domestic abuse, that sort of thing. Like I said, there have been a few times I wanted to turn a blind eye to a murder but once someone's been caught there's sadly nothing much to be done.'

'So he'll go to prison for the rest of his life?' Olive rubbed her hands together, desperately regretting not having brought any gloves.

'Well, probably "only" twenty-five years considering his character and the fact that it's his first offence,' Hugo said. 'Although I'm afraid a man like that won't last long in prison, not with such a delicate constitution.'

'Oh dear,' Olive sighed, her teeth now chattering. 'Oh dear.'

At last, Biscuit lifted her leg. And Olive gazed on, feeling that mixture of elation and disappointment that always came with the solving of a case. This time, the regret outweighed the joy for two reasons. Firstly, since she hadn't been the one to solve it. Secondly, for the sake of poor Mr Kimber, she rather wished they hadn't solved it at all. And she still couldn't believe that someone who cared so deeply about animals could kill a human. Even a human a horrible as Mr Mayhew.

∞

Later that evening when she was alone again – Hugo leaving, regretfully, to fill in reams of paperwork; Millie leaving, regretfully, to rejoin her sister; Grace leaving, regretfully, to return to Newnham College and Blythe leaving to woo Mr Harrington with one of her spectacular roast dinners (beef, roasties, Yorkshire puds and all the trimmings[1]) in the hopes that he might finally propose – Olive snuggled up on the living room sofa with Biscuit, a plate of currant buns and a big mug of hot chocolate.

Olive only drank hot chocolate in the winter, and only then when she was feeling particularly melancholic. Generally, she favoured tea with cake, or any assorted pastry or biscuit since its subtle flavour generally complimented everything she baked and anything stronger tended to be overpowering. But, sometimes, only overpowering would do. Olive could only hope, after all, that it would end up overpowering the melancholy.

Biscuit, sensing her mistress' downcast mood, settled her chin on Olive's knee.

'I know I shouldn't be feeling this way.' She stroked the spaniel's silky ears, rubbing the soft fur between finger and thumb while sipping the smooth, sweet chocolate. 'I should be happy.' She sighed. 'After all, the mystery is solved and *I* helped to solve it. And little Jimmy will be reunited with his beloved pets, which will thrill him, if not them, poor little things.'

Sighing again, Olive gazed out of the bay window and down onto the street below.

It had started to snow.

Olive thought of when she was a little girl in the wintertime. Whenever it snowed (perhaps only three or four times) she would run onto the street, wrapped in all her woollens, and throw snowballs and make snowmen and snow angels, she'd stand under the light of the lampposts and open her mouth, dip back her head and catch the flakes on her tongue. She'd stay out in the freezing cold until she couldn't feel her fingers or toes anymore and was dizzy with joy. But now she was middle aged, joy was watching the snow from the warmth of her sofa.

'It's funny, isn't it?' Olive scratched Biscuit's chin. 'How humans, mostly, lose their sense of adventure and delight so soon in life but dogs don't really change, they're always jumping headfirst into joy, they never get bored or blasé... If only I was like you, Bics, I wouldn't need mysteries to solve, would I? I'd just be content to go for long walks, chase squirrels, sniff lampposts and gobble crumpets.'

Biscuit yapped.

'Oh, yes,' Olive added. 'And have my ears stroked on a regular basis.'

She took another biscuit from the plate on her lap. These were custard creams but on Saturday she'd start baking gingerbread before the customers started demanding it.

'I hope Mr Harrington is being suitably kind to Blythe,' Olive mused aloud. 'And generally behaving in a way that she deserves to be treated. Do you think he'll propose tonight? Certainly the prospect of those roast dinners for the rest of his life will be a good incentive.' She smiled. 'Along with the fact that Blythe is one of the loveliest people in the world. I hope he'll be a good husband, though he'll have to be a saint to be good enough for her.'

Biscuit yapped again in agreement.

'And I wonder if good old Mr Bennett will end up with Millie after all? At least we know that *he* is deserving of her. I've rarely met a better man than him.' She smiled to herself. 'With one exception, of course.'

She took another gulp of hot chocolate, the warmth slipping down into her belly and she opened her mouth again, imagining the snowflakes settling on her tongue. At last, the melancholy slowly began to release its grip and her mood started to lift.

'Hey, Bics,' Olive said. 'Fancy another walk in the snow?'

---

1. In the 1970s this meant the addition of Bisto gravy. Those venerable enough to recall the 1970s will recall the iconic advertisement on TV - remember the days when there were only three channels? - "aah! Bisto". It came in granules and powder and tasted as one might imagine such a concoction would: yucky.

Chapter Fourteen

The following morning, while Olive served assorted baked delights to a long queue of customers who'd come for their elevenses, and Grace was brewing them cups of tea and coffee, she glanced out of the window to see Blythe waving madly from her own window across the street.

Olive waved back and, in response, Blythe beckoned her over.

'I can't,' Olive mouthed. 'Not yet. I'll pop over as soon as the queue has died down.'

Blythe, who'd been sporting a look of utter joy, was suddenly disappointed. And now Olive didn't need to possess psychic tendencies to know what was going on. Mr Harrington had come to his senses and recognised on which side his bread was buttered. Olive grinned.

'I won't be long!' She called and her friend's smile returned.

Twenty minutes later, when the customers' appetites had been sated and the café had emptied, Olive left Grace in charge to oversee things until the lunch rush descended and hurried across the road to One More Chapter Books to congratulate her friend. As soon as she stepped into the shop, Blythe let out a squeal of excitement so shrill that Biscuit could have heard it across the road.

'I'm getting married!' Blythe cried. 'I'm getting married!'

The diminutive old lady standing beside Blythe in the Russian Literature section perusing Tolstoy, dropped her copy of *Anna Karenina* with a start.

'You are!' Olive cried. 'You are!'

'I am! I am!'

And the startled customers watched as Blythe and Olive danced around the bookshop, laughing like lunatics till tears ran down their faces and they flopped, exhausted, into the comfy chairs in the Children's Literature section.

'Isn't it beautiful?' Blythe flashed Olive the ring for perhaps the hundredth time. A huge, sparkling diamond that flashed and glittered under the lights. Mr Harrington was clearly a rich and generous man. 'Isn't it just about the prettiest thing you've ever seen?'

'It is.' Olive grinned. 'Very ... twinkly and shiny.'

In truth, Olive found Bakewell tarts and Black Forest gateau a far prettier sight than a diamond ring and would take a slice of either over an engagement ring any day; she also found solving crimes far more exciting than planning weddings, but the last thing she'd ever do was rain on her friend's parade.

'You'll be next,' Blythe grinned back. 'The way Hugo looks at you... you won't have long to wait.'

'Perhaps,' Olive said, hedging her bets. She didn't want to say anything to dampen Blythe's spirits but she couldn't lie; her friend always knew when she was lying. And so there was only one thing for it: distraction. 'So, how did he ask? Did he get down on one knee?' Olive fixed all her attention on Blythe. 'Tell me everything.'

'Wait,' Blythe said, already suspicious. 'Don't tell me that you're *still* convinced that you don't want to get married? Not even to Detective Dixon!'

'I didn't say that.' Olive glanced up at the bookshelves. 'Oh, look. I love *The Secret Garden*. Mum used to read it to me over and over again. I couldn't get enough of-'

'Nice try,' Blythe stopped her. 'But you don't get away that easily. I won't let you push aside happiness all your life simply because you're scared of being hurt. And it's not even your own fear, it's your mother that drummed it into you and her mother before that and-'

'Stop it,' Olive interrupted in turn. 'I'm not doing that. At least, not as much as I *was*. That's to say, I'm no longer stopping myself from falling in love. Which doesn't mean' – she added at the sight of her friend's delighted expression – 'that I ever want to marry. I'm happy for you, B., truly I am. I couldn't be happier if I tried. Because *you* are happy and I want for you whatever makes you happy. But that doesn't mean that what makes you happy would make me happy too.'

Blythe frowned, as if she didn't believe Olive for a moment. But she knew when to pick a fight and when to let it go. And anyway the last thing Blythe wanted was an argument with her best friend on the happiest day of her life. That is, it would be, until her wedding day.

'Alright then,' Blythe said. 'Then let me tell you absolutely everything from the beginning. So, Elliot arrived half an hour early, as usual, but this time I could tell that something was different because he kept patting his breast pocket, so naturally I hoped...'

That afternoon happened to be a slow one at the café, with the lunchtime flood quickly dwindling to a trickle, leaving Olive and Grace twiddling their thumbs behind the counter. Naturally, there was much to do if they'd felt so inclined to do it. Much to say too – Olive still needed to sit down and explain the exact nature of the café's ghostly inhabitants (thus far she'd been putting the strange noises, smells and other strange things down to the idiosyncrasies of an ancient building) – but she didn't feel in the mood to face that particular challenge just yet. Olive tended to put off difficult conversations, along with any sort of confrontation, especially with those she loved. It was a trait she didn't like in herself and had been trying to change for years but to no avail. Thus, she did what she usually did when faced with such circumstances: avoidance.

'I'm a little tired,' Olive said to Grace. 'Do you mind if I pop upstairs for a nap?'

'Why are you asking me?' Grace smiled. 'You're the boss, you can do what you like.'

'Well, yes...' Olive considered this. 'I suppose so. But that's not... disregarding other peoples' needs and feelings isn't okay, no matter whether you're the boss or not.'

Grace sighed. 'Try telling that to my parents.'

'Yes,' Olive muttered, since this was another conversation she wasn't relishing the thought of. Still, she'd finally stood up to her own mother and, so she reasoned, standing up to someone else's parents should be far easier. Shouldn't it? 'Yes, we'll definitely need to do that soon. Before you go home for Christmas is probably best. Although, maybe you don't want to ruin all that ... It might make for some very awkward family dinners... Perhaps we should wait till the New Year?'

'Yes.' Grace nodded. 'Yes, good point. I think waiting till after the holidays would be much better. You know, I wish...' She laughed, as if it was an entirely fanciful notion, one that'd just occurred to her rather than one she'd been fantasising about for weeks. 'I wish I didn't have to go home for the holidays at all, I wish I could stay here with you.'

'Me?' Olive asked, slightly disconcerted. 'Oh...' But the more she mused on the idea the more she thought it a delightful one. 'It's usually just Millie, B and me. And Bics too, of course. Perhaps Hugo might be there this year too, I don't know, we've not talked about it yet. But you'd be most welcome to join us. If – if it wouldn't upset your parents too much.'

'They'd probably have a fit.' Grace sighed again. 'Still, why let reality get in the way of a little wishful thinking, right?'

Olive thought for a moment of her own wish for another juicy mystery to solve. 'Exactly.' She patted Grace's arm. 'Life's dreamers might not make the world go round, but we do help make it a happier place. So, I'll see you in about half an hour.'

'Take as long as you like,' Grace said. 'I'll be washing up the teapots.'

'That sounds most industrious. Alternatively, you could just sit behind the counter drinking tea and eating crumpets,' Olive suggested. 'That's what I usually do when it's quiet.'

Grace laughed. 'Maybe when I've finished the teapots.'

'I've got a feeling,' Olive said, as she picked up Biscuit. 'That we're going to make an excellent team.'

Upstairs, Olive couldn't nap. She tried for a few minutes but then gave up. In truth, she hadn't really had much intention of napping, even though she was pretty exhausted, she'd just wanted a distraction, a little excitement to brighten the post-crime-solving-lull. So, as she often did, Olive left Biscuit (who could happily nap at the drop of a hat) on the bed while she went to her desk and took out her Tarot cards.

While Olive sat and shuffled, she thought about which question to ask. A specific question wasn't essential, the cards would tell the stories and reveal their signs even without her guidance. But still, it was easier to understand their messages if one had pinpointed the subject first. Or it could all get a little unwieldy and misinterpretation became more likely. In the past, Olive had made a few major mistakes that way, once believing a boyfriend to be having an affair when he was actually wanting to move in with her, another time suspecting a customer of stealing when they were in fact having an affair with her mother.

Being vague, Olive had learnt, was a risky strategy.

'What about Mr Harrington?' She mused. 'We ought to know more about him, don't you think? Especially given what a hopeless romantic B. is, she won't have delved into his past at all.' Olive began shuffling more purposefully. 'Alright, so my question is this: tell me about Mr H. Is he worthy of Blythe? Should she marry him? Will she be happy with him?'

As Olive dealt out the cards, it occurred to her that if the cards weren't positive in this regard then it'd put her in a bit of a sticky situation with her friend who, being so attached to her fiancé (and invested in their romantic fantasy), was unlikely to believe anything Olive said against him. But there was no going back now; it was bad luck to put the cards back when one was in the middle of dealing them. At least, that's what her mother had always said. And so, Olive mentally crossed her fingers and hoped for the best.

What she got was: The Lovers, The Fool and The Tower. Which, by anyone's reckoning, was anything but the best. Olive gazed down at the cards, wishing that by staring hard enough she could change them into a happy ending for her friend. Yet, alas, Olive Crisp was no witch.

She traced her finger around the image of The Lovers: a man and woman arm in arm strolling through a meadow of wildflowers. Olive sighed. This was the only promising element of the reading; at least it meant that Mr Harrington, whatever his faults, did in fact love Blythe. Which was something. And yet, Blythe was also The Fool. In this image a man dressed as a clown was walking blindly towards the edge of a cliff. Olive sighed. She already knew that her dear friend was a naive innocent – it was one of the many things that made her so loveable – but this was different, this meant that she was setting out on a journey that would likely not end well. And, the fact that The Fool was followed by The Tower, turned "not well" into "an unmitigated disaster of monumentally catastrophic proportions". The Tower, showing a crumbing stone tower with flames at its windows, was always a harbinger of doom; but in a romantic context it promised total heartbreak and utter emotional annihilation.

Olive rubbed her eyes. How was she going to tell Blythe? How could she bring such misery to her friend's doorstep? Blythe, who'd wanted to marry a man, settle down and sprout babies – if that was the term Olive wanted – ever since hitting puberty. It would be devastating. And that was in the unlikely event that Blythe actually accepted Olive's diagnosis. Having finally (almost) achieved her dream, her friend wouldn't be willing to let it go easily. Indeed, it was extremely likely that Blythe would simply decide to ignore her. Which meant that Olive needed proof. Evidence. Something to back up the cards.

Suddenly, she smiled. She'd just had a thought that lifted her mood immeasurably.

It was time to turn detective again.

Chapter Fifteen

OLIVE ALREADY KNEW WHERE Mr Harrington lived. She knew that fact, along with a good many others she'd rather not, after Blythe's exceedingly detailed recounting of his marriage proposal. Fortunately, a little boring though the whole story had been, Olive had been paying attention. As she always did.

And so, despite the winter weather, after closing up the café that evening, and shortening the usual dinner of leftovers by saying she had a date with Hugo, Olive set out with Biscuit across town in the direction of number 37 Lensfield Road. Fortunately, Cambridge was so small that no place was ever that far away from any other, and in this case it was only a matter of a fifteen minute walk. However, in the current icy conditions, even that was fourteen minutes and thirty seconds too long.

'Come on Bics.' Olive's teeth were chattering even before they'd passed Fitzbillies. 'Not much further now...'

Biscuit replied with a miserable bark. She knew when her mistress was lying.

'Alright,' Olive said. 'When we get home it's tea and buttered crumpets all round, I promise.'

Biscuit barked again.

'Okay, okay,' Olive added. 'Buttered crumpets *and* blueberry scones.'

This bargain made, they continued along Trumpington Street in silence, both rapidly becoming too cold to risk opening their mouths and letting in more gusts of freezing air, hurrying along to reach their destination faster but not too fast that they'd slip on the icy pavements.

Finally turning the corner onto Lensfield Road, after what felt like an eternity trekking across the frozen wastelands of Siberia, Olive sped up slightly, slowing whenever she reached a puddle of light beneath a lamppost, using it to peer at the house numbers until, at last, they reached the house of Mr Harrington.

Olive gazed up at the imposing three-storey building with its bay windows, high ceilings, elegant awnings and beautiful red brick. In the driveway sat a rather splendid pea green Aston Martin which, even as someone who cared nothing for cars, Olive could see was an impressive ride. She knew her friend was far from being shallow, but it was unlikely that she didn't appreciate his wealth as a nice bonus among his other personal assets. What was his profession? Oh yes, a doctor. No, not simply a doctor but a consultant cardiologist. With a love of Dickens. And a collector of rare books. It was hard not to be impressed. Yet, she knew that the Tarot cards were never wrong and so, unfortunately, his credentials didn't matter. He might have seemed to be a virtual saint, but if the cards told a different story then theirs was the one to be believed.

'What are we going to do now?' Olive mumbled, realising that she hadn't really thought this through. She couldn't simply knock on the door, as she usually did when investigating suspects or witnesses, and there was little to be gained by peering through the windows – unless she might catch him having an affair. But the Tarot reading hadn't suggested that particular brand of betrayal.

The upper two bay windows were illuminated and Olive shuffled her feet in a vain attempt to stave off the freezing chill that was rapidly threatening to numb her toes and was already creeping up to her ankles. Even with a dog, she couldn't afford to stay in this spot for much longer without drawing suspicion. The net curtains would soon start twitching.

'Take a pee,' Olive hissed. 'And take your time. Go on!'

Fixing her mistress with a hard stare which seemed to convey the sentiment: *Why should I, crazy lady? If you want to be a detective in sub-zero temperatures when we could be at home napping on the sofa and dreaming about chasing rabbits with buttered crumpets, take your own blooming pee!* Or something to that effect.

'Please,' Olive begged. 'Please, please, please...'

And so, with the canine equivalent of a sigh and eye roll, Biscuit relented and cocked her leg against the nearest lamppost while Olive surveyed the landscape, now with rapidly freezing knees, desperately wishing she'd properly thought this through. Why was she always so impulsive? Professional detectives were methodical planners and strategic thinkers. They didn't find themselves utterly unprepared in arctic conditions with no idea what to do next.

If only I had a car, Olive thought as she glanced about. That's what I need for this sort of situation. If I had a car I could be sitting in it right now, all nice and warm, parked on the other side of the street and watching Mr Harrington's house from there. But, with the exception of Hugo, no one she knew had a car. And why would they? You didn't need one in Cambridge, a bike was all one needed to get around. And everything she needed for The Biscuit Tin – industrial sized bags of flour, sugar, butter, milk etc – was delivered by nice men in white vans who brought everything on time and undamaged because Olive always gave them builder's tea and bacon butties.[1]

Just then, as Olive was ferreting about with her gaze, the light on the ground floor came on, casting Olive in a spot light as if she was on centre stage at the National Theatre, and she just caught sight of Mr Harrington striding into his living room before she darted behind his bins. Yanked towards Olive's hiding place, Biscuit gave an indignant yelp followed, though Olive couldn't see it by the shadows of the bin, by an extremely indignant hard stare.

'I'm sorry,' Olive whispered. 'I didn't know he was going to do that.'

And then, just as quickly as it'd come on, the light went out.

Olive waited a few moments before pulling herself up to gingerly step back onto the open pavement again. Her cold, aching knees sent pricks of pain up her legs as she stood. Olive groaned, quietly. And then, gripping the bin lid to steady herself, she had an idea. Evidence. Proof. What did people with secrets to hide do with things they didn't want anyone else to find? Buried, burned or simply threw them away.

'Oh, well,' Olive muttered. 'It's worth a shot.'

And so, with Biscuit watching on in bemused annoyance, Olive began rooting through Mr Harrington's bins as silently as possible. Fortunately, the glacial weather meant that the streets were empty and the curtain twitchers too busy huddling around their gas fires to be monitoring their neighbours' activities. Unable to carry much – why hadn't she even brought a decent sized bag? – and too close to freezing-point to spend very long on the task, Olive took every piece of paper she could find on the grounds that paper was most likely to contain incriminating evidence, and was convenient to carry.

'Right,' Olive said as soon as her arms were full. 'Let's go.'

Then she, and a grateful but grumpy Biscuit, scurried off back home.

༄

An hour later, Olive was sitting on the living room floor surrounded by a wide spread of scattered papers. She'd intentionally taken only the relatively clean and untainted pieces but even then the whiff of rubbish permeated the air, undamped by the scent of burning logs in the grate or fresh brewed tea in the pot or the remaining buttered crumpets on their plates. Having drunk half a gallon of piping hot Earl Grey to thaw out her limbs and eaten half a dozen hot crumpets to warm her belly, Olive now began sifting through Mr Harrington's correspondence.

As she picked up and discarded each paper in turn, Olive felt a twinge of guilt – not for violating the privacy of their owner (as perhaps she should) but for betraying, by association, Blythe, who would be utterly horrified at the sight of

Olive reading her fiancé's stolen post and searching it for reasons to discredit him as her future husband.

'She'd have an absolute fit,' Olive muttered to Biscuit, who was now happily sleeping off her own feast of tea and crumpets on the sofa. 'An absolute fit. But we must plough on, for her own good and all that.'

Not entirely sure what she was searching for – romantic entanglements, financial fraud? – Olive hoped she would know when and if she found it. And so she continued to read on.

Most of it, disappointingly, was fairly boring. Bank statements. Council tax invoices. Letters from his mother. He wrote to his mother a lot. Which perhaps didn't bode well so far as Blythe's potential mother-in-law went (one didn't want a husband overly attached to his mother) but wasn't in itself a deal-breaker. Letters from the City Council regarding an ongoing problem with a pothole about which Mr Harrington was clearly incensed. So he was pedantic and petty, as well as being a Mummy's Boy. But still, it wasn't nearly enough to qualify as evidence against him in the potential husband stakes.

'You can learn a lot from a person by going through their bins,' Olive mused. 'Perhaps I should go through Hugo's; see if he's hiding any secrets…'

And then, Olive picked up a piece of paper – a pink carbon copy from a typewritten letter – that she didn't put down. Instead, she read it twice, then a third time. It read:

> *Dear Mr Mayhew,*
> *I am writing to you on behalf of my mother, Mrs Edith Harrington. She informs me that you've written threatening to evict her as the tenant of 48 Park Place. My mother has lived at this address for forty-seven years. Multiple times over the years she has made offers to purchase the property for a price well above market value. Every time you have refused her. I'm writing to you now to offer you £100,000 for this property. This is, I'm sure I don't have to tell you, over five times what it's currently worth. I do this for peace of mind for my mother and, as a businessman, I'm sure you'll see the sense in it. I look forward to hearing from you at your earliest convenience.*
> *Sincerely yours,*
> *Mr Arthur Harrington*

Olive sat up a little straighter, all her senses tingling. At last, she had discovered something. And there was more. Among all the white papers were several pink papers, all carbon copies from typewriters, copies of the letters he had sent to Mr Mayhew. They'd been engaged in quite a correspondence, it seemed.

Olive's heart started to race as she scanned the other copies. Sentences jumped out at her while she anxiously speed-read each in turn:

> *It's my understanding that you own over one hundred and fifty properties in Cambridgeshire and the surrounding areas. You are a very wealthy man who has no particular nor personal interest in any single property and thus there's no reason why you should not let go of this particular one.*
>
> *I fail to understand why you can't see sense in this situation. Surely, you are a sensible, rational man. I confess I am becoming incensed that you will not see reason.*
>
> *I have increased my offer to £125,000. For this amount I could purchase the entire street. However, since you continue to refuse, I have no choice but to hire a solicitor and take this argument into the courts. No judge will permit you to evict an eighty-one year old woman from a house that has this past forty-seven years been her family home.*

After reading each copy several times, Olive put them down to better consider the evidence she had uncovered. It was all very curious, certainly. But not damning. Blythe's fiancé had been fervently fighting with the murder victim over his mother's house – perhaps further demonstration that he was under her thumb, although it was certainly a good sign that he hadn't invited her to move in with him as an alternative – but there was no evidence of anything else. And the tone, while clearly angry, never tipped into rage and no threats of any kind had been made. The letters Mr Mayhew had preserved among his "hate mail" souvenirs had all, from what Olive had read, been far worse than anything here. And yet, still they niggled.

Shifting her position to stretch her legs, which were in danger of cramping, Olive surveyed the rest of the papers. Perhaps a dozen more remained unread but no more pink carbon copies. She sighed, wondering what remained hidden in Harrington's bin and what had already been taken away by the refuse collectors and destroyed. What day was it? Olive took a moment to recall: Thursday. *Dammit.* The next collection was tomorrow and then whatever remained would be removed and she'd be thwarted. Glancing out of her window, Olive saw that the snow, which had started falling shortly after she'd returned home, was coming down hard now, collecting in drifts on the roofs of the church on the opposite side of the street. The wind howled and Olive shuddered. And yet she couldn't possibly return to his house again tonight.

With another sigh, she returned to the papers and began shuffling through them, her speed now slowed by the rising feeling of despondence. If she didn't find anything more damning than what she'd found so far then it'd been a wasted trip. And what else could she do to try and find evidence against Harrington's character? Short of stalking him – a venture for which she sadly couldn't spare the time – or breaking into his home – she didn't think Hugo would approve, especially not if she was caught and hauled into the station – Olive was at a bit of a loss.

'Oh, Bics,' she lamented. 'What sort of useless detective am I, eh?'

But Biscuit's only comment was a contented doggy snore.

'Fat lot of use you are,' Olive snorted, picking up yet another paper. She'd just rejected three letters from the City Council about the blasted pothole, a telephone bill from BT and an invoice from British Gas. And, giving this next page a cursory glance, she was about to toss it to the floor again when she stopped. For this one wasn't nothing, it was most definitely *something*.

As Olive read, her heart started to quicken again.

Mayhew,

I've never wished anyone ill before. But then I've never so fully hated another person as I have you. Indeed, I am so consumed with hatred that I cannot think of anything but how I want you dead, and all the varied ways - if only I had the chance - that I might dispatch you from this earth. My hatred possesses me so completely now that I cannot sleep for wishing you fatally harmed, for imagining you thusly, and when at last I sleep I only dream of your death and how I might hasten your descent into hell.

Olive shuddered again. Now this letter was different, *this* letter was more than fitting for the "hate mail" pile. For pure bitter loathing, this one topped them all. *This* one was fit to be framed.

It was unsigned, but that was of no matter. Even a cursory study of the letter showed that it was written on the same typewriter, in the same font, with the same ink. Except that it wasn't a carbon copy but on paper. And it had been found, along with all the others, in the possession of Mr Harrington. Written, but never sent. Which, if anything, was even more damning. Clearly, he had motive and intent. And yet, he couldn't have been the killer since Mr Kimber had already confessed to that very same crime. Still, Olive could not put the letter down; it seemed almost to palpate with murderous intent, as if the words themselves could kill.

Was it possible that Kimber was in fact innocent? That, for some reason, he'd claimed to have committed a crime which he had not. And, if so, why? Had Mr Harrington blackmailed him, or bribed him to take the fall? Or had Harrington paid Kimber to do it? Or, perhaps they had been in it together. Olive wasn't certain. But she *was* certain of one thing: Blythe's fiancé had blood on his hands. And it was up to her to prove it.

---

1. A nod to my Yorkshire heritage (on my father's side) where the favoured tea of tradesman was PG Tips, Yorkshire Tea or English Breakfast, universally referred to as "Builder's Tea" for the fact that, traditionally, builders drank it by the bucketload. Bacon butties were the perfect accompaniment and consisted of buttered white bread rolls with rashers of fried streaky bacon and the addition of ketchup or brown sauce.

Chapter Sixteen

'What do you think?'

'I think, if Kimber hadn't already confessed then I'd be bringing this Harrington in for an interrogation.' Hugo took another gulp of hot coffee. 'But since we already have our murderer, I'm afraid I don't think there's much to be done about it.'

They sat in The Biscuit Tin together, at Olive's favourite table by the window. Technically, she was working but it was a slow day – the icy conditions keeping customers at home – and Grace was in the kitchen baking batches of gingerbread from the book's 1698 recipe, with Olive's tweaks. On her third tray, the café was filled with the deliciously comforting scent of dark syrup and spices.

'Hum...' Olive sipped her own tea then set down her cup and leaned over the table to take a bite of their (third) shared slice of pecan pie. She chewed slowly, considering his point. 'But what if they were in it together? Or what if Harrington was the brains behind the operation? I mean, you said yourself that Kimber didn't seem the type to kill, so what if Harrington forced him, or threatened him or bribed him... To keep his hands clean. Powerful people do that all the time, don't they?'

'Well...' Hugo said with a wink. 'Not *all* the time. But yes, it's certainly not unknown.' He dipped his fork into the pie. 'By the way, this is the best nutty tart thing I've ever eaten – what are they, peanuts? You've outdone yourself here.'

'Not mine.' Olive smiled. 'That's Grace's handiwork. And just wait till you try her gingerbread. She'd been making tweaks to my tweaks, mixing the molasses with muscovado sugar and a few other things... Anyway, it's delicious.' She picked up her tea cup. 'Anyway, what do you think of my theory?'

'It's good,' Hugo said. 'But unprovable, unless we search this bloke's house, or his office, and uncover something. So–'

'So, then let's do that,' Olive interrupted. 'What's stopping us?'

'Well... quite a few things, actually. Remember how I mentioned that awkward stuff about following police protocols and procedures, all of that?'

'Yes.' Olive sighed, already anticipating the depressing dead end this conversation was heading towards. 'I vaguely recall all that – utterly boring – stuff.'

'Then you'll remember about not being able to search people's private spaces without warrants and not being able to get warrants without cause and–'

'Without cause?' Olive interrupted again, this time with a shriek that startled Biscuit, who was napping in her basket by the door. She fixed her mistress with an affronted look, before settling back to sleep again. 'What about the hate letter? Surely that's more than enough cause? It shows he was obsessing about murdering Mr Mayhew.'

'It might have been,' Hugo said. 'If we didn't have a hundred just like it. And anyway, it's not signed. So we don't even know if Harrington wrote it.'

'We could prove he did if we went into his house and found his typewriter.'

'Well, yes,' Hugo conceded. 'But you see the problem, don't you? It's a bit of a catch twenty-two. We're already on thin ice with the fact that you acquired those letters by plundering his bins, which – any decent barrister would argue – is tantamount to theft. So–'

'But they weren't in his house,' Olive protested. 'He'd thrown them away. That's like public property then, isn't it?'

'No, because they weren't in a public bin. And the bins weren't even on the pavement, were they?'

Regretfully, Olive shook her head.

'Right, so since they were still on his property, that's trespassing in addition to theft. Which makes it much worse.' Hugo gulped down the last of his coffee. 'The reason we have all these tedious protocols is so evidence doesn't get thrown out before it even reaches court. We want convictions, not simply prosecutions. Guilt doesn't mean much unless it comes with a prison sentence.'

Olive wrinkled her nose in frustration but said nothing.

'And, before you say it,' Hugo added. 'Don't even *think* about sneaking into his house all by yourself. That's breaking and entering and, if you actually find and take his typewriter, that's stealing too. And, hard as I'll try, I can't guarantee I can protect you from prosecution. Not if he's adamant about pressing charges, not if he knows people in high places...'

Olive frowned. 'I thought you *were* people in high places.'

'Not high, exactly.' Hugo shrugged. 'Middling at most. I'm halfway up the steps to the ladder, maybe, I can pull a fair few strings. But I'm still being watched; I'm far from free to do as I wish. I'll have to wait till I'm Chief

Constable here, or Commissioner if I ever make it to the Met, though that's unlikely.' He gave her a shy smile. 'I rather like it here.'

Olive sipped her tea, smiling at him over the rim of the cup. 'So what you're saying is, if I want to get away with trespassing and stealing and generally breaking all the laws, I should be shacking up with Cambridgeshire's Chief Constable, not you.'

'Okay' – Hugo's fork hovered above the pecan pie – 'now you've got me worried. I know, at least I hope I do, that you like me. But I get the feeling you like breaking laws even more.'

'That's not true,' Olive laughed. 'I like you just as much as I like breaking the law.'

෴

'Right, I'd better be off,' Hugo said, when they'd almost polished off the entire pie. 'I've got a monkey and lizard in my car that need returning to their rightful owner.'

'I'm not sure "rightful" is quite the right word,' Olive returned. 'I rather think wild animals should own themselves, rather than be considered property, but anyway...'[1]

'I'm sure you're right,' Hugo agreed. 'And I'm sure Mr Kimber would be pleased to hear you say it. But I'm afraid my hands are tied. Anyway, setting morals aside in the practicality of the moment, would you like to come with me?'

'Really?' Olive perked up. Despite her distaste for keeping animals in captivity, the chance to ride in a police car again was just too good to pass up. Besides, visiting the victim's house in the company of an official police officer might actually afford her the chance for a little unofficial snooping this time. 'Can I?'

'Of course, come on.'

෴

They arrived outside number 29a Millington Road less than ten minutes later, due to a little official speeding and some (perfectly safe) skipping of red lights. As a result, Olive was feeling rather giddy as she stepped out of the car, as if she was a kid again and had just been on her first roller coaster ride. Being a real detective might mean you had to do things by the book, but it certainly had its perks.

'Why don't you knock?' Hugo suggested, as he opened the back door.

'Are you sure?' Olive asked. 'Shouldn't you–?'

'Go ahead,' Hugo said, unstrapping the monkey's cage. 'I'll be your second in command.'

Olive smiled, touched by how generously, how graciously he indulged her fantasies. 'Alright then, thank you.'

And so, she knocked.

Expecting young Jimmy Mayhew to answer, Olive found herself staring at the woman's midriff before bringing her eyes up to meet the woman's face.

'Oh,' Olive said. 'Sorry, I thought – is Jimmy at home?'

'It's Friday afternoon.' The woman frowned. 'He's at school.' Then she seemed to get lost in thought. 'At least, he was off after his father died. But then...' She trailed off, gazing out into a spot above Olive's head.

This, Olive realised, must be Mrs Mayhew. Intrigued, Olive took this opportunity, during the woman's moment of distraction to study her. Judging by her complexion and composure she couldn't have been much older than thirty but she looked at least a decade older, even two. Unsurprisingly, her eyes were puffy and red from crying, and she looked utterly exhausted. But it was more than that; she looked hollowed out and haggard, and so thin – unnaturally so – as if someone had taken a chisel and whittled her down to the bone. And, Olive noticed, she also sported a rather nasty yellowing bruise just above her left eye.

'You hurt yourself,' Olive said. 'Are you alright?'

'What?' Mrs Mayhew returned from her thoughts. 'Oh, yes, I'm fine. It was caused by a monkey which sounds absurd, I know, but we used to have one. It was the bane of my life. Thankfully, it escaped.'

'Ah, yes.' Olive gulped. 'Well, speaking of monkeys...'

'Are we standing outside for a reason?' Hugo came up the path behind her. 'Because this monkey is one chubby little ball of fur.' He set the cage down on the doorstep.

'It's a monkey.' Mrs Mayhew looked down at it, horrified.

'Yes.' Hugo frowned. 'It's *your* monkey. Rather, it's your son's monkey.'

Mrs Mayhew brought her eye up from the monkey and up to Hugo. 'And who are you?'

Hugo reached out his hand. 'Detective Dixon,' he said. 'A pleasure to meet you; Mrs Mayhew, I presume.'

She nodded, still looking appalled.

'I'm here to return your son's pets,' Hugo explained. 'They were kidnapped, that's to say, pet-napped. And you'll be glad to hear, we recently apprehended the perpetrator and we're here to return them. A monkey' – he nodded down at the monkey, in case it wasn't self-evident – 'and a lizard, still in the car.'

'The lizard too?' Mrs Mayhew echoed. 'Please tell me you're joking.'

'No, Ma'am,' Hugo said. 'I'm quite serious.'

'Well then,' she sighed. It was a sigh full of regret. 'I suppose you should come in.'

∞

---

1. She might have gone on to discourse about the days when humans were considered property - slaves and wives - and in many ways still were. But she didn't think it was the time and anyway her brain cells had been blunted by a belly full of pecan pie.

Chapter Seventeen

TEN MINUTES LATER, OLIVE and Hugo returned the unfortunate animals to the chaos of Jimmy's room, and bid them good luck. Then they trudged back downstairs to the kitchen where Mrs Mayhew had insisted, albeit reluctantly (her manners only just trumping her desires), on giving them tea.

'Thank you, Mrs Mayhew. This is very kind of you,' Olive said. 'And, I should have said this before, but I'm very sorry for your loss.'

When Mrs Mayhew said nothing, Olive sipped her drink and winced. It was, without a doubt, the foulest cup of Earl Grey she'd ever tasted. As if she'd stirred in vinegar instead of milk which, perhaps, she had. Either on purpose – as revenge for returning the loathed animals – or because she was so distracted that she mistook the bottle of vinegar for the bottle of milk.

Still mute, Mrs Mayhew sipped her own cup of tea and continued to look decidedly annoyed.

'Yes,' Hugo agreed, filling the slightly awkward (at least for himself and Olive) silence. 'Very kind. And I'm very sorry too.'

'Yes,' Mrs Mayhew said. 'Everyone keeps saying that. But most of them don't understand.'

The next awkward silence was, mercifully, soon interrupted by the ringing of a telephone from the hallway. It rang once, then twice, then a third time before Hugo gave a meaningful cough.

'Mrs Mayhew,' he ventured. 'I believe that's your telephone. Would you, um, shall I answer it for you?'

'Telephone?' she repeated, setting down her cup of tea. 'Why ever would you answer my telephone?' And then she stood and shuffled off in the direction of the hallway, leaving Olive and Hugo staring at each other in slightly dazed befuddlement, as if their host's fogged state was infectious.

They heard her muttering from the hallway but, despite leaning in, neither could make out a word. Until she called out.

'Detective Dixon, it's for you!'

Hugo and Olive exchanged another look of confusion.

'You?' Olive mouthed.

Hugo shrugged, then stood and hurried out into the hallway.

When Mrs Mayhew returned Olive, unable to simply sit in silence – some people are able to tolerate, even enjoy, a shared moment of silence, but she was not one of them – attempted to generate friendly chatter with her hostess, while simultaneously eavesdropping on Hugo's phone conversation.

'So, um...' Olive's gaze darted about the kitchen, frantically searching for a benign yet captivating topic upon which to discourse. She settled on the rows of jars and bottles lining the shelves above the stove. 'Do you enjoy cooking then? I see, um, I see you like herbs and spices. Not many people do, not in this country at least. I'm impressed.' She paused, giving Mrs Mayhew her opportunity to speak while also cocking her ear to try and catch whatever Hugo was saying. Frustratingly, she could only hear the odd "yes" and "no" and "are you certain?" but nothing of consequence. And when Mrs Mayhew did not heed her cue, Olive continued.

'I love cooking, baking most of all. I have a café, you know? The Biscuit Tin on Bene't Street in town.' She paused again, waiting for a look of interest, curiosity, delight or, at the very least, a flicker of recognition. But Mrs Mayhew's expression was blank. 'So, um, I thought you might have been, given that your son found me there and–' Olive stopped mid-sentence for at the mention of her son, Mrs Mayhew's face lit up as if alight had suddenly been switched on in a previously empty room.

'My son?'

'Yes, he came to me, to the café, when–'

But Olive was cut off by the reappearance of Hugo, who barrelled into the kitchen as if he was being chased by wolves. He looked to Olive first. 'We've got to go.' Then, collecting himself somewhat, he turned to their hostess. 'Thank you so much for your hospitality, Mrs Mayhew, but I'm afraid we must leave. Urgent police business.'

Olive frowned up at him from her seat but, when she saw the rather wild look – of shock and excitement – in his eye, she quickly stood.

'Thank you so much for the tea, Mrs Mayhew. Apologies for dashing out like this. I-I promise to return another – at a more convenient time and bring you some treats from the café. Your son enjoyed, well, everything so...' Hugo grabbed Olive's hand and started pulling her towards the door. 'A-a selection, I'll bring a selection.'

Mrs Mayhew said nothing, just stared at them both vacantly.

'Please, don't get up. Don't trouble yourself,' Hugo said, though his host clearly had little intention of doing so. 'We'll see ourselves out.'

∽

'What is it?' Olive called out as they dashed along the path towards the car. 'What's going on?'

'You were right,' Hugo called back, as he reached the car and started fumbling with his keys. 'Kimber didn't kill Mayhew.'

'What?' Olive scrambled round to the passenger side. 'What do you mean?' For, while she'd certainly been hoping for this outcome, she hadn't expected it to come in this form, to be so clear-cut. 'But I thought, I mean, he still hit him over the head with a shovel, right? So he must have had *something* to do with his death.'

'Well, yes and no,' Hugo said as they both got into the car. 'Kimber *did* hit Mayhew with a shovel but that wasn't what killed him.'

'It wasn't?' Olive regarded Hugo with some incredulity. 'He must've had a pretty hard head then – to survive that.'

'Yep,' Hugo agreed. 'Hard head, hard heart. Nothing about that man was soft or kind. But, anyway, that was the reason for there being no blood at the scene. We thought it was internal haemorrhaging but it wasn't. He was already dead when Kimber hit him.'

∽

Chapter Eighteen

'ALREADY DEAD?' OLIVE ECHOED. 'But how? How is that possible?'

'Well, Kimber claimed that Mayhew was slumped at his desk, ostensibly having a nap, while he proceeded to have a one-sided argument with him and, becoming increasingly infuriated that Mayhew was ignoring him, refusing to concede any of his points – so he thought – then, in a fit of rage, he bonked him over the head with a shovel and, naturally, once he heard of Mayhew's death he assumed that he was the one who killed him.'

'Yes, I suppose you would,' Olive agreed as Hugo pulled out of Millington Road and turned left onto Barton Road in the direction of the police station. 'Makes sense. But then, what *did* kill him?'

Hugo turned to her, unable to conceal his excitement. 'Ten milligrams of arsenic. He was–'

'–poisoned.' Olive was incredulous. 'I can't... I really didn't expect that.'

'No,' Hugo admitted. 'Neither did I.'

'So then, who...?' And then, realisation dawned. 'Mr Harrington!' Olive exclaimed. 'He's a doctor, a consultant. Top brass at the hospital. Surely he could get hold of anything he liked.'

Hugo nodded. 'Yes, and arsenic is used in small doses in cancer treatments[1] so it'd certainly be possible for a doctor to get hold of it. We convicted a pharmacist a few years back for doing just that. Murdered his mother-in-law.' Hugo shook his head, tutting. 'The old bird was sitting on a huge inheritance and just wouldn't die, so he helped her along.'

'Is this enough cause to search his house?' Olive asked. 'Now we know he had the motive along with the means, can you get a warrant based on that?'

'Yes.' Hugo turned the car onto Trumpington Road. 'That's what I'm planning on doing as soon as we get back to the station.' He gave her a wink. 'It's quiet on the roads, do you fancy going a little bit faster?'

'Absolutely.' Olive beamed, gripping her seat with both hands. 'Let's go!'

༄

They sped into the police station parking lot a few minutes later, tyres screeching, lights flashing, siren wailing and Olive grinning from ear to ear, heart pounding, still holding on for dear life.

'T-thank you,' she gasped. 'That was ... spectacular.'

Hugo laughed. 'You're very easy to please. A cake, a fast car and a cup of tea.'

'The simple things in life.'

'Right.'

Olive reached for his hand. 'And you.'

'And me?' Hugo asked, looking both surprised and elated in equal measure.

Olive nodded. 'Of course.'

She'd said it to make him feel good, she'd said it because it seemed only right. But now that she'd said it, she realised it was true.

Hugo leaned over to kiss her. The kiss lingered and sent delightful little shivers down Olive's spine and warmed her belly like drinking a cup of hot cocoa. When at last he pulled away, she kept her eyes closed. Until a banging on the car window caused them to spring apart with a start.

A police officer stood outside at Hugo's door, leaning down to peer into the car. Hugo rolled down his window, while Olive pushed herself back into her seat, gaze fixed to the floor, trying to make herself as small and insignificant as possible.

'The Chief's saying we've got to let Kimber loose, sir,' he said. 'But I didn't want to till you got back, sir, just in case you-'

'That's very thoughtful of you, Constable Cooper,' Hugo said. 'But the Chief's right, we can't continue to hold him if he didn't actually kill anyone. The law's the law, I'm afraid.'

'But he broke a window at the protest, sir, and hit an officer and-'

'Just let him go, Constable.' Hugo sighed. 'We've got bigger fish to fry. I need you to submit an application for a warrant.'

'A warrant?' Constable Cooper's brow furrowed.

'Yes. Do you know how to do that?'

'Er, well, no,' Cooper admitted. 'Not exactly, sir.'

'You don't...' Hugo trailed off with an exasperated sigh. 'Alright, fine. I'll show you – again – how to do it and this time try to pay attention, alright?'

'Yes, sir.'

'I should've kept that monkey,' Hugo leaned over to whisper to Olive. 'He'd have made a better officer than Constable Numpty here.'

Olive giggled, relieved it wasn't the Chief who'd surprised them and she wasn't about to get in any trouble.

'I wish I could come with you to search his office,' Olive whispered back. 'Promise to call me as soon as you've done it, especially if you find anything.'

'You'll be the first to know,' Hugo promised. 'Well, not the first exactly, but the first civilian at any rate. That okay?'

'That's okay.' Olive smiled. 'That's more than okay.'

---

1. Arsenicals have been used in ancient Greek and Roman civilisations and in traditional Chinese medicines. In the West, they were employed for ailments and malignancies in the early 20th century, then arsenic trioxide was reintroduced as an anticancer agent in the 1970s after reports emerged from China of the success of an arsenic trioxide-containing herbal mixture for the treatment of acute promyelocytic leukaemia. *Thomas X, Troncy J. Arsenic: a beneficial therapeutic poison - a historical overview. Adler Mus Bull. 2009 Jun;35(1):3-13. PMID: 20052806.*

Chapter Nineteen

Hugo arrived late that evening when Olive had already retired upstairs to the sofa with Biscuit, a cup of cocoa and a plate of lavender-lemon biscuits. At the sound of the bell, Olive nearly toppled head-first to the floor in her keenness to get to the door. Biscuit, who was snoozing beside her, slid to the floor and woke with a bump.

'Sorry Bics,' Olive called as she dashed out of the living room, along the corridor and down the stairs. 'I'll make it up to you!'

Slipping twice on the stairs in her slippers and once on the tiled kitchen floor – crashing into the island in the process – Olive reached the door with rather more bumps and (pending) bruises than she'd left the sofa with, but the sight of Hugo alleviated any pains.

'You came,' she said. 'I thought perhaps–'

'Of course I did,' he said. 'When I call, I can't see your face.'

Olive smiled and stepped back so he could come in. 'Coffee?' she asked. 'Cake?'

'Both, if you'd be so kind. It's been a frightful day.'

'Sit, sit.' Olive ushered him towards the table by the counter (best to avoid prying eyes while he was here on police business). 'And talk.'

'What? Even before I'm allowed a drink?' Hugo joked. 'What kind of service is this?'

'Tell me everything,' Olive demanded. 'Or there'll be nothing for you. I've been on tenterhooks for twenty-four hours now–'

'Twenty-four?' Hugo laughed. 'I only saw you this morning.'

'Alright,' Olive shrugged as she filled the cafetière with ground coffee. 'Twelve then, if you're nit-picking.'

'Twelve?' Hugo smiled. 'Closer to six, I'd say. Anyway, I know you're the most impatient person in Cambridgeshire, so I'll put you out of your misery.' He took a deep breath. 'But I'm afraid it's not what you want to hear.'

'Oh?' Olive's spirits sank. She reached for a biscuit to comfort herself. 'You didn't find anything.'

'I'm sorry, but we lucked out on all accounts.' Hugo shook his head, sadly. 'We searched his home, had forensics examine the typewriter but not only did it not match the letters, but it wasn't even in working order. An antique, just for show.'

'Maybe he had another one, hidden somewhere else.' She finished the biscuit and reached for another. 'I mean, if he *is* the murderer it makes sense that he'd cover his tracks.'

'Absolutely,' Hugo agreed. 'But the officers did a meticulous sweep of the property and found nothing.'

'Are you *sure*?' Olive interrupted, as panic started to set in. She couldn't believe he hadn't written the letters himself. It made no sense. Why had they been in his bin? 'Were *you* there? Did you check–?'

'Not personally,' Hugo said. 'Because I was with the team searching his offices at Addenbrooke's, but I can assure you my men know what they're doing. They've done it hundreds of times; they could find a poisonous needle in the proverbial haystack, I promise you.'

'Alright,' Olive conceded, finishing her second biscuit and taking a third. 'But you didn't find anything at the hospital either?'

'No.' Regretfully, Hugo shook his head. 'And we investigated the pharmacy too, checking all the records which log the arrival and departure of every millilitre and gram of medication. And, before you say it, even if Dr Harrington stole the arsenic the discrepancy couldn't have gone without notice. Every day checks are made by the hospital's pharmacists and meticulous records are kept; they necessarily take the tracking of their medicines very seriously indeed.'

'But what if he bribed the pharmacist?' Olive objected as she nibbled the biscuit. 'What if he replaced it with a substitute? What if–?'

'We interviewed everyone,' Hugo cut in. 'No stone left unturned and all that, but still we found nothing. I'm sorry, Oli, but there's absolutely no evidence that he got his hands on any arsenic at all.'

'I can't believe it.' Olive sighed. 'I thought... I was so convinced it was him. It would've been the perfect solution.'

'I know.' Hugo took Olive's hand and pulled her gently into his lap. 'But I'm afraid that when there's no evidence to fit the theory it usually means that the theory isn't right and we have to go back to the drawing board.'

'Yeah,' Olive muttered. 'Unless it *is* right and we've just not found the proof or it's been destroyed. Just because I can't prove it doesn't mean he's not guilty.'

'True,' Hugo conceded. 'But remember what I said about that, I'm afraid the prosecution services don't much care about guilt without proof. In court, guilt without proof is innocence.'

'But–'

'And intuition doesn't count as proof.'

Olive sighed.

'I'm sorry.' Hugo put a consoling hand to Olive's back and rubbed her shoulders. 'I'm sorry. But don't worry, we won't give up. We'll keep looking. We'll follow the evidence and, sooner or later, it'll lead us to the culprit.'

Olive nodded, feigning agreement. But she didn't agree. Not at all. No matter what Hugo thought, she *knew* Harrington had killed Mayhew and was determined to prove it.

Chapter Twenty

Frustratingly, Olive was forced to wait till the following morning before she could carry out her plan. After Hugo left, she passed a fitful night in anticipation of the crime she planned to commit: breaking and entering, with the possible addition of theft. It wasn't the breaking of laws she minded, indeed that was something Olive rather relished since it was so thrilling. She could understand why criminals found it so hard to give up the lifestyle. But she did fear being caught.

As soon as Grace arrived, Olive dashed out of the café, calling her goodbyes over her shoulder, and apologies to a grumpy Biscuit who sat abandoned in her basket. Outside, as she scurried past the bookshop, she waved guiltily at a bemused Blythe through the window. *She's already thinking me crazy,* Olive thought, *but if she had any idea what I'm about to do she'd have an absolute fit.* And she prayed there would be no reason for her friend ever to find out what she'd done.

This time, when she arrived at Lensfield Road, Olive made her way to Mr Harrington's house but instead lingered behind a tree on the opposite side of the road. It was nearly eight o'clock and the morning now light enough for the murderer (as she'd now, in an act of defiance, labelled him) to spot her, which mustn't happen given that they'd met enough times for him to recognise her and (quite rightly) question why on earth she was lingering on his street in the freezing cold watching his house. However, she hoped it was almost time for him to leave for work - he seemed the fastidious, punctual type, traits suited to meticulously planned murders involving poison rather than the spontaneous whacking of someone over the head with a shovel - and so she wouldn't have to wait long.

Sure enough, at eight o'clock precisely, the front door opened and Mr Harrington stepped out. He was suited in tweed and booted in suede, the whole outfit topped with a fedora (fashioned with a small, bright feather) to complete the pretentious, self-important air he carried with him along with a highly polished briefcase.

Olive held her breath as he opened the car door and slipped inside. She waited several minutes (allowing herself to exhale) while he let the engine warm up and the windows defrost, stamping her feet on the frozen ground to stop them from going numb. *He's a pretentious idiot,* Olive thought, *he doesn't deserve someone as beautiful as Blythe, she'll be grateful once I've exposed him.* This second thought was probably – definitely – a bit of a stretch, but Olive could only hope that, in time, she'd understand. And meanwhile Olive would dedicate herself to finding Blythe a new man. She had plenty of customers; it shouldn't be too hard to find a decent one or one who, at the very least, wasn't a murderer.

She'd just finished this thought when Harrington pulled out of the driveway.

'About time,' Olive sighed, expelling another breath that whitened the air. 'Right, Olive Crisp' – she rubbed her mittens together, stomping her feet again as the car sped off down the street – 'let's go do some breaking and entering.'

She'd been hoping that Harrington, like most Cambridge residents, kept a key somewhere on the premises outside – *probably for his maid,* she thought – and she wasn't disappointed, for there it was, hidden under a flowerpot (containing a miniature fern) only a few feet from the front door. In fact, she *was* a little disappointed, since she'd rather relished the prospect of pretending to be a real burglar and actually breaking into the house. For, while opening a stranger's front door without their permission offered the thrill of trespassing, it wasn't quite so delightfully illegal as, say, smashing a window with a rock. Still, using a key afforded less chance of getting caught and, subsequently, a lighter punishment (she presumed) if one was.

Stepping inside his house, Olive was gratified to see that everything looked exactly as she expected: expensive fabrics, sophisticated colours, antique furniture... For a moment, standing on the intricately woven rug, Olive felt the impulse to remove her shoes.

'Don't be daft,' she muttered to herself. 'You're a burglar, not a dinner guest.'

With that in mind, Olive removed her mittens and slipped on the plastic washing-up gloves she'd brought for the purposes of thieving without leaving fingerprints. Feeling another thrill of excitement as she snapped on the gloves, Olive had the fleeting thought that perhaps she'd missed her calling and wondered if being a thief would be even more fun than being a detective. Quite possibly. But then, rather like the legal and political professions, it was a trade fraught with moral thorns. At least as a detective she was staying (mostly) on the right side of the law. Also, she doubted Hugo would take kindly to his girlfriend (as she supposed she was, though it sounded strange to say) making a career shift from café owner to criminal.

Mindful that she shouldn't linger too long – a first-rate thief would be in and out faster than it took butter to melt on a hot crumpet – Olive hurried into the drawing room to search for... Well, she didn't know exactly *what* she was searching for, but nevertheless she felt confident that she'd find *something*. Something Hugo's officers had missed, something that would provide evidence to incriminate Harrington. It was highly unlikely that she'd find something as obvious as a half-empty bottle of arsenic but that wasn't going to deter her.

As she stepped into the living room, she saw the antique black and gold typewriter sitting in prime position in front of the beautiful bay window atop an antique oak desk.

Olive glowered at it. 'Alright, so you're not what will prove he did it,' she muttered darkly. 'But I'll find the thing that will, I promise you that.'

As she slowly scanned the room her gaze settled on the mantelpiece above the marble fireplace. At first glance, she didn't notice anything remarkable, only a cluster of silver framed photographs and tiny porcelain figurines of ballet dancers and shepherdesses. But, driven by an intuitive nudge, Olive looked again. Then she turned from the typewriter and hurried to the mantelpiece for a better look.

'What on earth...?' Olive lifted the largest photograph to peer at it more closely, wanting to be certain that she was seeing what she thought she was seeing. And, sure enough, two faces she knew beamed back at her: Mr Harrington and Mrs Mayhew.

It was definitely him and (almost) definitely her, although she looked very different. Not only much younger, but that was the least of it; she was plumper and fuller in every way: eyes clearer, face brighter, gaze confident and buoyant. In a word, she looked *happy*. She looked to be in her late teens, perhaps, and he, probably, in his mid-twenties. He had his arm around her in a protective, loving gesture and she leaned into him. Olive's first (shocked) thought was that they were married – could she be a bigamist? – or, at the very least, long-term lovers who were still having an affair. Olive's second (miserable) thought was for Blythe, who'd then been doubly betrayed. And yet... as she studied the picture more closely, that theory didn't stand up. Because the gesture didn't seem romantic but friendly, possibly familial.

Carefully setting down the picture exactly where it'd been, Olive scanned the others for clues as to the nature of their relationship: friends, cousins, siblings? But the other pictures were only a collection of Mr Harrington's proudest (and smuggest) moments: one of him graduating outside the Senate House, another in his surgeon's scrubs – his superior grin still evident even beneath his mask – standing beside his Aston Martin, outside his house beside a SOLD sign.

Olive sighed. Murderer or not, she liked this man less and less the longer she spent in his house. *Insufferable,* was the word that came to mind. Swiftly followed by, *Smug prat.* She shook her head at her dear friend's questionable taste in men. In search of more photos, Olive moved onto the walls, but they were only adorned with expensively framed oil paintings of arable scenes. Fortunately, the bookshelves proved more fruitful. There, in front of the rows of leather spines with their gold lettering, sat several more photographs, sepia and soft focused, of a much younger Mr Harrington, along with a much younger Mrs Mayhew. One showed them on a beach together, building a sand castle. In another they stood holding ice creams with Blackpool Tower behind. In a third they wore fancy school uniforms and were joined by two adults, a man and a woman standing shoulder to shoulder. The picture-perfect family unit.

Siblings, Olive thought. *He's her brother.*

Just as she was about to slip a selection of the photographs into her bag, before returning to the typewriter, Olive heard a noise above her sounding like a scratching on a windowpane. For a second, she thought that perhaps Mr Harrington was being targeted by another burglar, until she glanced out of the window and saw the ladder and, behind that, a white van in the driveway emblazoned with the words:

HARRYS WINDOW CLEANING: NO WINDOW TOO BIG OR TOO DIRTY.

Her first thought: if Blythe was here she'd be infuriated at Harry for his lack of possessive apostrophe. Her second thought: though perhaps not as furious as she'd be at Olive for breaking into her fiancé's house. Her third thought: who the heck cleaned windows in the dangerous depths of winter?

Cursing the over-zealous work ethic of this window cleaner who so casually flouted the rules of grammar, Olive reluctantly abandoned the photos and crept out of the living room, down the hallway and out of the front door. Closing it very softly behind her, she slipped the key back under the plant pot and tip-toed out of the driveway. Mercifully, Harry was too focused on his work to notice.

It doesn't matter, she told herself. *It's only a momentary interruption, a slight delay.* She might have hidden in the house, of course, but it would've been a risky move especially considering that the window cleaner probably had access to the key in order to clean the windows from the inside and, when he discovered that it'd been taken she wasn't sure what he'd do next. No, hot-footing it out of the house was the most sensible decision and Olive, a deeply impractical person, felt proud of herself for making it. She could return for more breaking and entering at a later, safer time.

Now, she had something else to do.

⁓

Chapter Twenty-One

Olive returned to Millington Road via Bene't Street. Reluctantly, she left Biscuit behind with Grace again – a decision she knew the sulky spaniel would make her pay for later – knowing that Mrs Mayhew definitely wasn't an animal lover. Though perhaps she simply took a dim view of lizards and monkeys in particular, not animals in general. Still, Olive's agenda was a delicate one and she didn't want to get off on the wrong foot to begin with.

Olive hoped, as she hurried in stops and starts (on account of the icy pavements), that Mrs Mayhew's reception, given that Olive came unencumbered by exotic creatures, would be a little less frosty this time. Fortuitously, on her previous visit she'd promised to bring a box of baked goods for little Jimmy next time she was passing. And now, so far as Mrs Mayhew was concerned, she'd simply come to make good on that promise.

Olive knocked twice, then once more. Tapping her feet on the path, she wondered if Mrs Mayhew had gone out. Yet, she didn't seem like the type that went out. At least, not anymore. Not since marrying a man who had stripped her of all her spirit and joy.

And, sure enough, on the fourth knock, the door opened.

'Hello?' Mrs Mayhew peered at her, clearly having entirely forgotten their previous encounter. Or, at least, Olive's part in it.

'Good afternoon,' Olive said, trying (and failing) not to feel bothered at being so unmemorable. 'I'm Olive Crisp. We met a few days ago. I was with the detective who brought your son's, um, pets home.'

'Oh.' It took a few moments for recognition to dawn and, when it did, it was still behind the fog of dazed disinterest. Olive wondered if anything could permeate the anaesthetized mists that enveloped Mrs Mayhew and if they'd been triggered by the grief of losing her miserable husband or if that miserable husband had caused them to descend himself while alive. She suspected the latter.

'I brought you and Jimmy some assorted treats.' Olive produced the box from her bag. 'You mentioned you'd never been to The Biscuit Tin, so I thought I'd bring The Biscuit Tin to you.'

'The Biscuit Tin?' Mrs Mayhew pronounced the words slowly and deliberately, as if speaking a foreign language.

'My café,' Olive offered. 'In town. On Bene't Street.'

She expected another question to follow this clarification, but instead Mrs Mayhew surprised her by stepping aside and inviting her inside. Hesitating only a second, lest Mrs Mayhew change her mind, Olive stepped back into 29a Millington Road.

༄

Ten minutes later, Olive nursed another cup of vinegary tea. Every now and then she took tentative, polite micro-sips and tried resist reaching for the box of baked treats which, after all, was supposed to be a gift. The pinnacle of impoliteness, so Olive's mother had always taught her, was arriving at someone's house without an offering or, if one had, to subsequently nibble upon that offering without the host sharing. But, knowing the delights that lay within (lemon curd biscuits, cherry tarts, gingerbread, spiced apple flapjacks) they were proving hard to resist, especially in the absence of conversation. *If only*, Olive thought, *there was a subtle way to encourage the opening of the box...*

'Do you like biscuits with your tea?' Olive prompted. 'We've got gingerbread on the menu now, for the Christmas season. It's, um, very good with tea.'

'Gingerbread?' Mrs Mayhew regarded Olive through her fog and frowned. 'I don't think I've ever tried it.'

Olive stared at her, incredulous.

'Oh. Well, alright. How about, um, cherry tarts?'

Mrs Mayhew shook her head.

'Um, flapjacks?'

Mrs Mayhew shrugged.

Now, Olive was speechless. *Who born and bred in this country hadn't tried flapjacks? It was virtually a national dish. This was tantamount to saying you'd never had baked beans on toast, or marmalade or fish and chips.* She didn't dare ask.

But the topic of food as a way either into the box of treats or her host's confidence wasn't working so then, if the subtle approach wasn't working she'd have to be direct. *In for a penny*, as her mother used to say, *in for a pound.*

'So,' Olive ventured. 'Might I ask your name? I thought perhaps we could move onto a first name basis.' She didn't want to admit that she hated using the moniker "Mrs" signalling as it did patriarchal possession over the female and the identification of woman as wife rather than individual. But, more than that, Olive wanted to know her name, wanted to separate her from a man she hated. 'I'm Olive.' She said again, sure that her host would have already forgotten, placing a hand to her chest. 'Olive Crisp.'

She waited.

'Olive,' she said again, in case she hadn't been heard. 'And...'

Then, at last her host responded. 'Esther.' She stared down into her teacup. 'I'm Esther.'

'It's lovely to meet you, Esther,' Olive said. 'And, um, it's good because we'll know each other better soon. Given that your brother is marrying my best friend. That's to say, of course you know your brother is marrying Blythe, but you didn't know that she's my best friend and...'

Olive trailed off because now her host was staring at her strangely.

'My brother? No, no, I don't have a brother.'

'Yes, you do.' Olive frowned. 'Mr Harrington. He lives on Lensfield Road, works as a fancy surgeon at Addenbrooke's and...' She just stopped short of adding "poisoned your husband with arsenic, you know the one."

'N-no,' Esther stammered. 'What do you mean? He's not – I just told you, I don't have a brother.'

Olive's frown deepened. 'I thought – is he your cousin then?'

'My cousin?' Esther echoed, still not lifting her eyes from her tea. 'Mr Harrington? No, no. I-I've never heard of him.'

Wondering why she was lying, Olive took another micro-sip of the foul tasting tea then set her cup on the table. 'Then why does he have pictures of you all over his house?'

Esther looked stricken, then horrified, then promptly burst into tears.

Olive stared at her, once more struck dumb. She opened her mouth, then closed it again. And then, when Esther didn't stop crying, Olive pushed back her chair, stood, walked over to her host and gave her a hug.

In response, Esther only sobbed louder.

'I'm sorry,' Olive whispered. 'I'm so sorry, I didn't mean to upset you. You've lost your husband, you're probably still in shock...'

But Esther just shook her head and continued sobbing.

'That's it,' Olive whispered, rubbing Esther's shoulders. 'Just let it out. You just cry it all out...'

Then, still weeping, Esther started muttering inaudibly.

At first, Olive couldn't make out a single word and then they began drifting up.

'... hurt ... hated ... helped ...'

'It's alright,' Olive murmured. 'It's alright, I'm here.'

Recalling how long Esther had cried the first time she'd ever visited the house, Olive started to wonder how long she might be standing there and if it might be wise to call someone. What would she do when Jimmy came home from school? What would she do when she needed to pee? This thought had the unfortunate effect of immediately making Olive need to pee.

'I hated him. I hated him so, so very much...'

Olive stopped thinking about needing the toilet and focused on the words.

'He hurt me. He never stopped hurting me. Every day. From the first day, he never let up...' Now that Esther had started speaking, she seemed unable to stop. Like a flood gate finally opened, her prolonged reticence had now triggered a verbal explosion. 'He hurt me. He hurt my boy. My darling boy. He hurt us, every day. Until Eli helped us and at last, at last we were free...'

Eli? Olive caught the name, turning it over in her mind, trying to find a place for it in what she knew. But she didn't know anyone of that name. Unless... And, all at once, the penny dropped and the puzzle piece slotted into place.

Elliot Harrington.

'Your brother,' Olive whispered. 'He helped you.'

It wasn't a question, for this was that special piece that, once put into position, enabled so many others to fit around it, finally revealing the complete picture in all its shocking glory. But still, Esther nodded.

'My husband, he... He hurt...'

'He hurt you,' Olive thought of the yellowing bruise. The one the monkey had been blamed for. 'He hit you. Very often?'

A fresh sob sprung from the poor woman.

'Every day,' Olive guessed. 'He hit you every day. Until your brother saved you.'

At this, Esther dropped her head to the table and dissolved into tears.

Chapter Twenty-Two

NEARLY A FULL HOUR passed before Olive could coax Esther away from the table and up to her bedroom where she tucked her into bed amid the safety and comfort of thick blankets and quilts. She found extra pillows in the airing cupboard and laid them beside and around her so she'd feel cocooned by their warmth and solidity. On her bedside table Olive set a fresh pot of tea and a plate of biscuits. From the corner of her eye, she'd spotted a typewriter half-hidden behind a mirror on Esther's dressing table and had the distinct feeling that, if she were to investigate, this would prove to be the one from which the letters found in Harrington's bin had been written. Whether by Esther or Elliot, she didn't know. Olive had the sudden thought that perhaps Esther had written *all* the letters herself; Olive hoped so. It would've been a small but sweet reprisal. She turned back to Esther, pretending not to have seen it.

'Just in case you wake hungry,' Olive whispered. 'You'll be able to eat again now, now that you've expelled that awful secret. It was blocking your throat. It was eating you up.'

Esther blinked up at her, eyes wide in her hollow face. 'He must take Jimmy.' She spoke so softly that Olive had to lean down to catch the words. 'Go to Eli and tell him, please. Before you go to the police.'

'The police?' Olive frowned. 'But–'

Esther extracted a bony hand from beneath the swathes of blankets to find Olive's hand and grip it tight as she could, which, given how weak she was, wasn't very tight at all.

'I poisoned him,' she mumbled. 'Eli got it for me, but I did it myself. He never...'

This new information rather surprised Olive but, as she processed it, she realised it didn't matter. Except in the sense that it helped to know that Harrington hadn't been the one to kill him, meaning that Blythe wasn't engaged to a certified murderer, just a very devoted brother. Which, Olive had to admit, was making her reconsider his character. Yes, she still thought him a smug git, but perhaps he wasn't quite so insufferable as all that. And, in fact, rather than judging Esther, it pleased Olive to know that she'd got her full revenge against her tyrannical husband.

'Shush.' Olive lifted a finger to her lips. 'It doesn't matter. You did what you did. And he deserved it, a thousand times over. I don't judge you for it, and nor will anyone else. You've given me your secret and I will keep it for you.'

Esther opened her mouth but didn't speak. Tears slipped silently down her cheeks.

'You've suffered enough for a dozen lifetimes,' Olive said. 'It's time to start living again, a new life. A safe, happy life. But, for now, just sleep.'

Chapter Twenty-Three

ON THE WAY HOME, Olive promised herself that she wouldn't tell Hugo. She wouldn't say *anything*. She would take Esther's secret to her grave. Olive muttered this mantra to herself over and over again as she trudged back along the icy streets towards the café. *I won't say anything, I won't, I won't, I won't...*

Olive's resolve was tested as soon as she reached the café because when she arrived she found Hugo standing at the counter chatting to Grace.

'It's so cold out there!' She stamped her feet on the mat in hopes of dispersing the dirt and ice from her boots and the chill from her toes. But, most importantly, in hopes of keeping the subject as far from murder as possible.

'Sit,' Grace said. 'I'll put on a pot of tea.'

'Here,' Hugo stepped towards her. 'I'll take your coat.'

'Thanks,' Olive said, fumbling with her mittens. *I won't*, she thought. *I won't, I won't...*

'Where did you go?' Hugo asked, as he helped her off with her coat. 'I could've given you a lift, spared you the frostbite.'

'Oh, um, I... just a walk, you know, to stretch my legs...'

Hugo frowned. 'A walk? In this weather. Without Biscuit?'

Olive glanced at Biscuit who lay in her basket by the door, pretending to sleep but really sulking. *Traitor.* Olive wracked her brain for a believable lie. Unfortunately, as well as being highly impatient, Olive was also terrible at keeping secrets.

'Yes, well, um, I went for a walk to see a friend who needed a chat and...' Olive trailed off. Ordinarily, she wasn't such a bad low-level liar but lying about something of great significance to her boyfriend, as she supposed she should call him now, who also happened to be a professional lie detector was something altogether different.

'Alright, come here.' Olive stepped over to the window, gesturing for Hugo to follow. 'So,' she whispered once they were out of earshot of Grace. 'What would you say if I told you that Mrs Mayhew poisoned her husband? And that he absolutely deserved it.'

Hugo frowned. '*Are* you telling me that?'

'No,' Olive clarified. 'I'm simply asking what would you do, if I did?'

Hugo's frown lifted and he raised an eyebrow. 'What would you *want* me to do?'

'Nothing,' Olive said, quickly. 'I'd want you to do absolutely nothing.'

Hugo was silent for a moment. He glanced out of the window as he considered, then looked back to Olive. 'Well, as hypothetical questions go, that's a big one.'

'I know.' Olive held her breath. From the look in his eye, she couldn't tell which way he might lean. 'I know it's a lot to ask and it puts you in a frightfully awkward position. And I wouldn't ask, not if I didn't wholeheartedly believe it was the right thing to do.'

Hugo was silent a moment. 'I'll need to think about it.'

'Of course,' Olive said. 'No problem.' Naturally, this was a lie, since if Olive hated waiting for anything then waiting for the answer to a very important question was the worst of all. She wanted to ask just how long this particular wait might be, so she could at least attempt to brace herself. But then she was already being pushy, she didn't want to push it *too* far.

Hugo gave her a tentative smile. 'You can't stand it, can you?'

'No,' Olive laughed, despite her inner tension. 'How can you tell?'

'Usually you're hard to read,' he said. 'But right now you're transparent as glass.'

'Am I?' she asked, secretly touched that he could see her so clearly. 'Well... perhaps I promised her – Esther Mayhew – that I wouldn't tell you.' She took a deep breath. 'That I'd let her go free.'

A flicker of frustration passed across Hugo's face, like a storm on the horizon. 'You made a promise you didn't know you could keep, a promise you didn't have the authority to make.'

'I know,' Olive sighed. 'And I'm sorry. But if you'd been there, if you'd seen her confess, if you'd heard what she'd suffered. I think you'd have done the same.'

Hugo echoed her sigh. 'I've no doubt,' he said. 'And, as I told you before, I've sometimes had to prosecute people I wish I could simply turn a blind eye to and let go.'

'Then why don't you?' Olive implored.

'Because,' Hugo gave her a regretful look. 'Because it's not that simple. It's the law, it's–'

'But can't it be? Sometimes?' Olive persisted. 'I mean, life can be so frightful, so unfair. And if we have a small chance to tip the scales in the other direction, shouldn't we take it?'

Hugo hesitated. He tipped his head back and turned his eyes to the ceiling. The moment stretched out between them. Olive waited on tenterhooks, feeling as if *she* were the in the dock while the judge prepared his sentence. It'd been eight years since the last hanging in Britain, but Esther would still face a lifetime in prison and little Jimmy would be raised in a children's home without his mother. And then, Hugo spoke.

'Well, since this is only a hypothetical matter,' he pronounced. 'Then I'll say this: *if* you tell me she did such a thing, then I would have to charge her. However, if you did *not* tell me such a thing then I would do exactly that: nothing.' He reached for her hand. 'And, into the bargain, I think I'll decide that enough police resources have been expended on the Mayhew case and we should focus them elsewhere. After all, there are plenty of unsolved crimes in the world. I don't think one more, especially the death of someone so dreadful, will make much of a difference.'

'Really?' A smile broke slowly across Olive's face as she looked at him, feeling a sudden rush of deep and abiding affection such as she'd never felt before. At least, not for a man. She felt as if her heart was swelling with it, her chest expanding like her lungs had become balloons and she was being lifted from the floor. All at once, she wanted to grab Hugo and hold him, and kiss him, and never let him go. 'I-I...' Olive fumbled with the unfamiliar, alarming words. 'I-I... love you.'

Hugo gazed back at her, big blue eyes widening. 'You do?'

Olive nodded. 'But please, don't make me say it again.'

Hugo's eyes softened into a smile and he laughed. 'Don't worry, I know how much that pained you. And, I tell you what, how about if I say it every day for the both of us so you never have to say it again?'

Olive grinned, thinking this was just about the kindest thing he could have said.

'So long,' Hugo added. 'As you promise to always look at me exactly the way you're looking at me right now.'

'Deal.' Olive nodded, and kissed him. This time, she didn't stop.

☙

There was only one thing left for Olive to do today. She needed to have an awkward conversation with her best friend's fiancé. It wasn't right, she thought, to go behind his back and tell Blythe directly, but it wasn't right not to tell her anything either. The knowledge that he'd assisted his sister in killing her husband was another secret too epic to keep to herself. Besides, she never lied to her friends. Not about important things, anyway. However, telling Harrington that *he* needed to tell Blythe the truth was just the sort of confrontation Olive always sought to avoid. Yet this was one she couldn't postpone for long.

First, she needed to fortify herself with another cup of tea and a slice of cake. Or two.

Chapter Twenty-Four

A WEEK OR SO later, Olive was standing behind the counter arranging a plate of gingerbread biscuits to their best effect when the bell above the door chimed and she looked up to see little Jimmy Mayhew tumble in. He was glad in all his winter woollens and the effect was to render him almost rotund. *Like Tweedledum or Tweedledee,* Olive thought with a smile.

'Good morning, Master Mayhew,' Olive said, offering him the plate. 'What brings you here? Has your pet elephant been stolen?'

Jimmy, taking a biscuit with one hand and tugging at his knitted hat with the other, fixed her with a perplexed frown. 'Elephant? I don't have a pet elephant!'

'I know.' Olive smiled. 'I was just making a little joke.'

Jimmy raised an incredulous eyebrow, as if Olive were the worst joke-teller he'd ever encountered. And an absolute idiot into the bargain. He shook his head, as if to say, "adults: what can you do?"

'Mum sent me to invite you over for afternoon tea on Christmas Eve.' He paused. 'Could you bring the cakes 'n' stuff? Cause she's a stinking bad cook.'

Olive laughed. 'Yes, of course. It'd be my pleasure. Here.' She reached for a small cardboard box under the counter and tipped the plate of gingerbread biscuits inside. 'Why don't you take her these? A gift.'

Jimmy's eyes widened as he took the box and Olive deeply suspected that the box would be emptied before it reached his mother. She made a mental note to pop round to Millington Road later with some leftovers.

'So, how can I help you?' Olive asked as she watched Jimmy hopping from foot to foot.

'No me,' he said. 'My friend William. He's been expulsioned for stealing from the tuck shop. But he didn't do it, I know it. He needs you to prove him innocent.'

'Expelled?' Olive clarified. 'I'd like to help, but I don't know – I've never done anything like that before.'

Jimmy frowned again, as if she was speaking in tongues. 'Of course you can,' he said. 'You're a detective.'

'Well, not officially,' Olive said. 'But–'

She was cut off by Jimmy fishing something out of his pocket and handing it over to her, across the counter. A folded piece of paper. Olive opened it to read:

> THE BISCIT TIN DITECTIVE AGENCY.
> No crime (or custermer) too small. Please com in.

Olive laughed then, at the sight of Jimmy's serious look, quickly stopped. 'Thank you,' she said. 'I love it.'

Jimmy nodded, as if this was the correct response. 'Good,' he said. 'Now you can put it in the window.'

'The window?' Olive echoed. The distinct smell of burnt toast, and her mother's disapproval, drifted in from the kitchen. She swallowed and stood taller, fortifying herself. 'Give me one of those.'

With great reluctance, Jimmy offered her the box. Olive took a biscuit, satisfied by the gingerbread snap and the soft chew as she bit into it. The sugary spice settled on her tongue and she smiled again.

'Alright then, Master Mayhew,' Olive said. 'Let's do it.'

She took a deep breath, along with another bite of gingerbread, stepped around the counter and walked over to the window. Placing Jimmy's card in the corner, she turned back to him.

'There you go. The Biscuit Tin Detective Agency is open for business.'

THE END

Jack's Cinnamon Biscuit Recipe

ONE OF MY FAVOURITE *places to visit in Cambridge is Jack's Gelato. I'm extremely fortunate, and honoured, that the visionary founder and gelato genius, Jack van Praag, happens to be my dearest brother. The Observer Food Monthly voted his the best ice cream in the UK. His thousands of fans – myself included – would say the world. Needless to say, I eat a lot of gelato. His cinnamon biscuit gelato is one of my favourites and Jack generously permitted me to share it...*

Ingredients
- 450g plain flour
- 250g salted butter (or vegan butter – all it takes to make this recipe vegan!)
- 295g granulated/caster sugar
- 150g dark soft brown sugar
- 9g cinnamon
- 45g water
- 13g bicarbonate

Method

Cream everything but the water and flour for ten minutes. Halfway through, slowly add the water while creaming. Add flour all at once.

Chill overnight before baking, or it won't have that snap.

Roll out to 2mm thick. Heat oven to 170c for 12 mins. Cool on baking tray before decorating or just eat as is. Perfect accompanied by any flavour of Jack's Gelato, especially (in my humble opinion) Vanilla or Baked Vanilla or Vanilla Brown Sugar, Mascarpone or Vanilla Mascarpone, Cinnamon or Cinnamon Waffle/Biscuit, Roasted Hazelnut, Baked Milk, Grilled White Chocolate, Clotted Cream Fudge... Or anything else you fancy!

Preview of The Biscuit Tin Murders #4

Chapter One. Cambridge. March 1st, 1971.

'What do you think?'

'I think...' Olive paused, cocking her head to one side and smiling. 'I think that pictures of food always make me hungry. And that cheese looks delicious.'

'I think' - Hugo lifted her hand and brought it to his lips - 'that *everything* makes you hungry, no matter what it is.'

Olive laughed. 'Yes,' she admitted. 'I can't argue with that.'

As if to prove the point she used her other hand - as yet unkissed - to ferret about in her shoulder bag and extract a blueberry scone wrapped in clingfilm. She never left the café without supplies. One never knew, after all, when one might be caught in a long queue or at a bus stop, for example, without adequate access to (delicious) sustenance.

Olive and Hugo were standing, hand in hand, in the main gallery of the Fitzwilliam Museum, gazing up at an assortment of classical oil paintings of food and flowers. The Museum, being perfectly located between The Biscuit Tin and the police station, had become a favourite place over the past few months for Olive and Hugo to meet when they wanted to get away and just enjoy each other's company, along with the beautiful art and a few snacks, surreptitiously consumed whenever possible.

'Do you think I'll get away with eating this here?' Olive whispered. 'Or should I wait till we get to the Egyptian exhibit with that guard, the one who's always falling asleep?'

Olive glanced behind her to survey the room: long and windowless, with several dozen priceless oil paintings hung on the walls and a few priceless sculptures encased under glass. Admiring these assorted Renaissance masterpieces were a handful of visitors displaying varying degrees of interest. With her detective's eye, Olive could instantly spot the tourists, even the ones without the guide maps and backpacks, ticking the Fitzwilliam Museum off their lists of Important Cultural Places To Visit, but those genuine art-lovers who'd taken a day-trip to soak up all the aesthetic delights Cambridge had to offer. She recognised a few Biscuit Tin regulars, along with, sitting on a leather bench gazing rapturously at *The Bridesmaid* by John Everett Millais, a particular favourite: Miss Westmacott who, at ninety-three-years-old, had been visiting the café since her infancy in the 1870s. Rarely deviating from her favoured diet of lavender-sugar biscuits and custard creams, she'd sometimes indulge in a jam tart or an iced bun if it was her birthday or some similarly special occasion, always coming in at precisely eleven o'clock and sitting alone at the table by the window for half an hour before saying her goodbyes. On the rare days that she was kept away by another pressing engagement or illness, especially in recent years, Olive spent the day worrying that her beloved customer was dead.

At the room's entrance sat the young guard overseeing all these priceless public treasures, a chap Olive also knew by name - Christopher Pride - not because he'd ever frequented the café (clearly not being a person of discerning taste) but because he wore it printed onto a badge on his lapel. He lived up to this moniker, taking great pride in his job, being ever alert to even minor infractions of museum policy. Woe betide anyone who stepped too close to an exhibit or dared to extract a bottle of water from their bags. Children in particular were barely tolerated by the young man as being, to his mind, ticking time bombs with their sticky fingers, their invariable flouting of authority and their lamentably cavalier attitude towards priceless objects.

'I think you can risk it,' Hugo whispered back. 'While he's distracted.'

Sure enough, the guard was currently focusing the beam of his suspicious gaze on a group of teenagers and their teacher standing before a Gainsborough landscape. Judging by their expensive uniforms and their impeccable behaviour, these particular students hailed from one of the many private schools dotted around the city, and though they were doing nothing wrong - with the exception of looking exceptionally bored - still the guard sat on the edge of his seat in anticipation that they might be on the verge of rule breaking.

'Right,' Olive said. 'I'm going for it.'

Hugo stifled his laughter as Olive took a furtive bite. He always took delight in Olive's refusal to be bound by regulations, either of propriety or law, as if he lived vicariously through her being unable, as a police detective, to do the same. At least, not when anyone was watching or with the risk of being caught, it being his duty to present himself as an upstanding member of the community, an example of decency and decorum for all to emulate. As most duties went, it was a frustrating and tedious burden that made life dreary and dull. Thus, although Hugo felt it his duty to warn Olive against particularly serious infractions (warnings she invariably ignored) he nevertheless enjoyed the retellings of her adventures after the fact. So long as he had plausible deniability of whatever illegal or illicit naughtiness she'd got herself into in the first place.

'Does it taste all the better for being forbidden?' Hugo asked.

Taking another bite, Olive shook her head. 'Nope,' she said. 'My scones taste equally delicious no matter where or how they're consumed.'

This time, Hugo couldn't suppress his laughter. 'No false modesty for you, eh?' He grinned. 'I love it. There's nothing more attractive than a woman who knows her own worth.'

Olive nudged him, giggling. 'In that case, I think my biscuits are pretty spectacular too.'

'Oh, I know they are,' Hugo smiled. 'And your Bakewell tart even more so. Which is saying something.'

'Go on,' Olive said, breaking off a piece of the scone and offering it to him. 'Just a little bite.'

'I can't!' Hugo feigned horror. 'It's alright if young Pride over there chucks you out on your ear for unauthorised scoffing, but if *I'm* caught-'

'Then frogs will fall from the sky and the rivers will run red,' Olive teased. 'And the Chief Commissioner will confiscate your badge.'

'Not quite, but the *Cambridge Evening News* will have a field day,' he said. 'I can see the headlines now: Disgraced Detective Pigs Out in Public Places.'

'High-Ranking Officer Proves Himself a Greedy Pig,' Olive adds with a derisive snort. 'Copper Thrown Out on His Ear When He Can't Keep His Hands Off His Scones...'

She leans against him, giggles erupting into laughter. Hugo, attempting to shush her, is unable to resist dissolving into chuckles himself. They collapse against each other like silly school children until Hugo feels a finger tapping his shoulder with a stern staccato rhythm. A second later, Olive felt the very same finger on her own shoulder.

Instantly, they both fell silent. Slowly, they pulled apart to stand straight as soldiers and turn, rather sheepishly, to face the owner of the authoritarian fingers.

'This is a museum,' the guard admonished them. 'Not a playground. And, frankly, I'd expect better from you both, especially you Detective Dixon.'

Hugo hung his head. 'Of course,' he said. 'I'm sorry. It won't-'

'Miss Crisp!' Pride exclaimed, as he suddenly caught sight of the contraband she'd forgotten she was still holding. 'Is that a *cake*?'

'Well, um, no,' Olive muttered, avoiding his appalled gaze while trying not to burst into giggles again at the absurdity of it all. 'It's a scone.'

'A scone!' Pride scoffed. 'A scone?!'

Her own gaze fixed on the floor, Olive caught sight of the scattering of crumbs at her feet and gulped, praying their accuser wouldn't notice them too. But, when he'd been trained in the ways of museum guards, Pride must have excelled at the sniffing out of all such infractions, for in the next moment his eye fell upon them as if he'd just spotted a ten pound note.

'Crumbs!' He cried. 'You've been dropping crumbs!'

He issued this declaration with the same level of scandalised outrage as if he'd just discovered that Olive had been drowning puppies and was offering up their corpses to the museum as a distasteful art display.

'Well, I, um…'

'It's entirely my fault,' Hugo interjected gallantly. 'My scone, my fault, my crumbs.'

'Then why is *she* holding the scone?' Mr Pride protested.

'I asked her to hold it. I-'

'No he didn't,' Olive objected. 'It's my scone and my fault. I'm-'

'No,' Hugo interrupted. 'It's mine.'

'No, it's mine.'

'It's mine.'

'It's mine.'

'Stop it!' Pride, who was quickly turning a dangerous shade of puce, silenced them. In this moment, he reminded Olive of a younger version of her secondary school headmaster, in whose office she'd spent far too much time being admonished for the multitudinous inventive and elaborate ways she found to break his *many* draconian rules.

'I don't care *whose* scone it is,' he continued. 'Only that it's dropping crumbs on my-'

'STOP! THIEF!'

This (merciful) interruption to the ridiculous and humiliating interrogation to which they were being subjected, caused Pride (after momentarily freezing in shock) to run from the room as if someone had just tied a firecracker to his tail. A split-second later, Hugo dashed off, quickly followed by Olive, who stuffed the reminder of the offending scone in her mouth as she scurried after them.

If there was a juicy crime in progress, she certainly wasn't going to miss it.

Acknowledgments

As ever, deepest thanks to all my family and friends, especially those who kindly indulge my endless wittering about all things literary and culinary... ☺ And particular thanks this time around to the following: Emily, for all your brilliant (and bountiful) insights and crime knowledge; invaluable for my first foray into the genre. Al, for your unsurpassed eagle eye – always catching what everyone else misses – and deep generosity in everything you do. Naz, for your beautiful map – you're so incredibly gifted. Ova, for your unwavering encouragement and invaluable support. Special and delicious thanks to Alison and Jenny for generously sharing your recipe and Jack, for the same.

To my students, readers and friends: whenever you buy/borrow/review my books I'm always deeply touched for your support: thank you. And huge thanks to the marvellous Laurie Robertson, agent extraordinaire – I'm grateful every day for everything you do!

About the Author

MENNA VAN PRAAG WAS born in Cambridge, England and attended Balliol College, Oxford. Her first novella – an autobiographical fable about a waitress who aspires to be a writer – *Men, Money & Chocolate* has been translated into 26 languages. Her novels are set among the colleges, cafés and bookshops of Cambridge.

Men, Money & Chocolate
The House at the End of Hope Street
The Dress Shop of Dreams
The Witches of Cambridge
The Lost Art of Letter Writing
The Patron Saint of Lost Souls
The Sisters Grimm
Night of Demons & Saints
Child of Earth & Sky

Printed in Great Britain
by Amazon